HAAKON

NOVELS BY C. F. Griffin

Nobody's Brother

The Impermanence of Heroes

Not Without Love

Instead of Ashes

Haakon

A NOVEL BY C. F. Griffin

Thomas Y. Crowell Company

ESTABLISHED 1834   NEW YORK

Grateful acknowledgment is made for permission to reprint lines from "Sailing to Byzantium" from *Collected Poems of William Butler Yeats* by William Butler Yeats. Copyright 1928 by Macmillan Publishing Co., Inc.; renewed 1956 by Georgie Yeats and Miss Ann Yeats, and Macmillan Company of London and Bassingstoke.

FIRST EDITION

Designed by Sidney Feinberg

Library of Congress Cataloging in Publication Data

Griffin, C. F.
  Haakon.
  I. Title.
PZ4.G8496Hac 1978   [PS3557.R4887]   813'.5'4   77–26043
ISBN 0–690–01703–0

78 79 80 81 82 10 9 8 7 6 5 4 3 2 1

*I am most grateful to Marjorie Peters and
the North Shore Writers for their help with this book.*

"The desires of the heart are crooked as corkscrews."
                                    W. H. AUDEN

HAAKON

I

August 15, 1945

England had long since disappeared below the horizon. Gulls, dyed salmon-pink by the setting sun, called to one another, circled and headed back toward Land's End. A British subchaser, wings of water peeling back from its bow, dashed toward the old freighter that lagged behind the convoy. A blinker flashed irritably from its bridge.

Soldiers: an artillery company and an outfit of engineers, indistinguishable from each other in faded green fatigues, lounged on the freighter's decks, leaning on the tarpaulin-shrouded guns, sitting on the splintery wooden crates that smelled of oil, fresh pine and tar. An artilleryman said, "Damn Limey tin can showing off."

Bells rang and the beat of the engines intensified.

Smoking a last cigarette in the open before dark, Private Haakon Hvitfelt, Ph.D., addressed a letter and set it down on the crate beside him. It said, in suitably formal language, that he would be happy to return to the university as a full professor, and that he expected to be out of the Army by the beginning of the fall term.

He imagined what it would be like to be standing in front of a class again and found himself looking at his heavily callused palms, his nails still stained with black grease. Strange how these last three years seemed more real than his entire life before that. He threw his cigarette butt over the stern rail. The wake boiled behind the ship in ever-changing patterns, a brief mark on the sea, soon healed.

Who was he now? Not the withdrawn professor he had once been. He was still a teacher. He had taught his way through the war—grammar, spelling, math, beginning German. But the man who had spent hours squatting in the dirt with friends writing the truth of six-times-seven on a bulldozer blade with a hunk of plaster was not much like the man who had spent most of his life standing on a lecture platform pontificating, handing out judgment and conjecture as fact.

He was not even the same physically. Stronger than he had ever been before, hard and fit. His body knew the rhythm of driving a spike with a sledgehammer, the satisfaction of putting in a day's work laying train track or grading an airstrip. The pull of the shrapnel scar on his shoulder blade was a reminder that he could endure pain as well as any other man, that he was less afraid than most under fire. And he had dug too many graves and buried too many bodies to ever be the same again.

As they had gone deeper into Germany, the German dead had stopped being the enemy. They had not been fit to fight: boys not full-grown, old men with dentures, veterans with artificial legs, wearing ill-fitting uniforms and civilian shoes, armed with obsolete weapons and the wrong ammunition. Had those boys known how to use the guns they carried?

Then Schwartzgarten. Their outfit was the first in. The village by the small river was quiet, undamaged, peaceful with spring green. Pleasant to the eye, but pervaded by a faint stench. They drove on down a winding road between tall pines, serene in the sun, toward black smoke, the smell becoming worse and finally identifiable as a combination of carrion, burned flesh and kerosene.

Buildings burned dark-orange in the sun. The dead were in heaps in rectangular open pits, naked, skeletal, a tangle of arms and legs. Barbed wire. Empty, abandoned machine guns. He had touched the barrel of one. It was still warm.

A hundred newly dead, and those on top had had their throats cut. If only they had gotten there sooner, even by an hour, those people might have lived. A movement, a twitch of a hand, and he had extricated a child from the heap. Small, perhaps six or seven. She looked at him, eyes wide with fear. He made a sound intended to comfort and the fear faded. Her mouth was bloody, her smile sweet and utterly ghastly. Then she died. He hugged her, feeling the warmth of her blood soaking into his uniform.

Lieutenant Travis, neat and clean in his jeep, above it all, had ordered them to begin work on the other side of the camp. Haakon walked over to him, laid the dead naked child across the lieutenant's lap and said quietly, controlling his rage, "You asshole. If one was alive, there may be others."

He turned away immediately, not waiting for any response, and must have motioned to the other men, because they ignored the officer and came to help him. At first they were careful, tried to be respectful, but as they worked they began to hate those bleeding corpses for being dead. They became frantic to get it over with, casting the bodies aside like cordwood.

The search had been futile, and afterwards he had felt as if he would never be clean again.

Weeks had passed before he had been able to smile. He forced himself to make the effort when he realized that the other men in the unit were treating him as though he was an invalid.

Just days ago, when a joyful voice had announced how many thousands had died in less than a minute when the atom bomb was dropped on Hiroshima, he had felt nausea. A new dimension of horror. Dresden was a cinder from standard incendiaries. What difference whether the people in the city died in a minute or over the course of a night? They were all dead in the morning.

"Hey, Professor!"

Gratefully he turned toward the voice. Roger, an energetic, powerfully built man, bushy black eyebrows drawn together now in a fierce, worried scowl. "Hi."

"You seen Polecat?"

"Not for quite a while."

"He owes me a twenty. If you see him, will ya remind him?"

"Of course."

Someone was playing "When the Lights Go On Again All Over the World" on a harmonica. Not Finkelstein—the phrasing was unfamiliar—but someone equally expert. An artilleryman most likely.

Roger was back. "Sure you ain't seen him?"

"Not for at least an hour. Any way I can help?"

"There's a crap game in the head." Looking even more worried than before, mouth tight and tense. So that was it. Roger had been talking about the down payment he was going to make on a house with the money he had saved, showed pictures his wife had sent of the one they wanted. He must have gambled away the pay he had not sent home. But if he won now, he might be able to hang on to it.

Haakon took a twenty out of his pocket. "Here, I'll get it from Polecat when I see him. Good luck."

He found himself rubbing his eye and made himself stop. Must have gotten some grit in it. Blinking did not help. He gathered

3

up his letters and put them in his pocket, then made his way forward. The sky ahead was gaudy with rose-reds, purples and yellows. The sea was the color of brass in the fading light. Like a second-rate Turner. He wished Simon had not made that remark. Or that he had not remembered it.

He caught himself reaching to rub his eye again and went below to the head to look in a mirror. As he leaned closer, dark blue iris swam at him. It took an effort for him to refocus. Was he becoming farsighted? At forty-five he could well be. He caught the speck on the corner of an envelope and straightened.

There were two deep worry lines between his eyebrows. He tried to relax his face. No appreciable difference. His face looked unfamiliar. Not a bad face. The bones were good, strong. Head too narrow, mouth too sensual. Nothing different about that, but somehow not the same face he had had before the war.

Little squint lines at the corners of his eyes now, deeper lines around his mouth. And, odd that he had not noticed before, his blond hair had gone almost white. Who was he anyway? He turned away.

Dice rattled across the tiles. Roger was standing to one side scowling fiercely, making side bets. As the dice came to rest, Roger smiled. Good, he was doing well.

The loudspeaker crackled. "Now hear this. Now hear this. The smoking lamp is out. The smoking lamp is out." If he could not smoke on deck he might as well go below. He used the urinal, chasing a cigarette butt down the drain.

As he started down the long metal ladder to the bowels of the ship below the waterline, he heard voices above. Strangers. "Life jackets? Shit! This tub go down, we'll drown like rats in a barrel. We're ex*pend*able."

A muttered reply.

"Shut up, will ya? There's no fuckin' U-boats, the fuckin' war's over for Chrissake. Even the fuckin' Japs gave up. It's just the fuckin' Navy likes ta play war."

Rows of bunks stacked seven high, fat olive drab duffel bags hanging from the ends. Barely room for two men to pass in the aisles. After less than twenty-four hours the place stank of vomit, dirty socks and too many sweaty, unwashed men. A whiff of cigar smoke. A fart.

A drop of sweat ran down his nose. Hot. He stepped onto the deck and glanced back up the long ladder. The only way out. "Rats in a barrel" was too accurate for comfort.

All around him the buzz of voices, the deep hum of exhaust

4

fans, the beat of the engines. Overhead bare bulbs on long wires swung gently to the slight roll of the ship. Halfway up the vast square darkness of the hold were spotlights fastened under a catwalk. Too bright to look at comfortably. There were no definite shadows, only areas of greater obscurity. The lights were too many and too far away, diffused by the bluish dust and cigarette smoke that filled the air.

At his bunk he stripped off his fatigues and cleared the pockets, laying his letters beside his pillow. He got a flashlight from the duffel bag and stuffed in the fatigues. Wearing skivvy shorts and socks, he shelved himself on his bunk, second from the top, then tried to get comfortable. When he lay on his back with his legs drawn up, his knees pressed against the bottom of the bunk above. When he straightened out, his feet hung over and the edge of the frame cut his ankles. The Army made few allowances for men over six feet tall.

Settling on his side, he picked up the flashlight and sorted through his mail again. Higgins, his editor at Meadows Press, wanted him to update his history text. How could he? He had no perspective on this war. No need to answer that yet though. He set it aside.

Simon's dark, square, distinctive handwriting. Highly legible, masculine, familiar. It began, "Darling," and he wished again that Simon would be more circumspect in letters that could have been censored.

I've been at the catacombs photographing what the Nazis did to some Italian civilians. The British are sorting the bodies and trying to identify them. Not easy at this stage of decomposition. Did you know that notes written in pencil stand up to soaking in body fluids better than anything else?

As one of the doctors keeps repeating like a dripping tap, "Bloody bad show." There's no earthly way to get a good camera angle in a small dark cave stuffed with corpses. Furthermore, the concentration camp pictures have glutted the market.

He had reread the passage often enough so the shock had worn off. Fastidious Simon taking pictures of corpses? Perhaps they were less real when they were clothed and had been dead a long time. Simon was covering his distress with a façade of heartlessness, but even so, how could he write about the dead this lightly? Simon knew how he had felt after Schwartzgarten. No, not quite. He had never told him about the child. He skipped the rest of the page.

5

. . . all that travertine. Every time I come to Rome I'm surprised anew by the goldenness. I must locate some color film. I'm sitting in a sidewalk cafe now, drinking vermouth con ghiaccio *and thinking of you. Do you remember that summer here? The Baths of Caracalla, the Capitoline, the garden outside our window?*

He had known Simon for only three weeks when they arrived in Rome, and it was not for a summer; it was less than a month. Their room had a floor of cool polished square tiles. Slatted wooden blinds kept out the hot Italian sun. The garden outside was thickly planted with vegetables, fruit trees and grapevines. The back wall was part of a fortification built in the reign of Tiberius.

They had made love in the warm afternoons. Afterwards, drowsing, he watched Simon sleep, his long eyelashes dark on his tanned cheeks, his clear classic profile etched against the paleness of the wall. Too beautiful to be quite real. Serene as a Renaissance angel.

Listening to the birds rustling and singing in the vines outside the window, he would drift off to sleep, to be awakened at seven by the geese that served as watchdogs, honking for their supper—and the voice of the landlord, who had long animated conversations with them while he fed them.

That whole summer was magical. He had walked in the sun and felt free in foreign lands. Unobserved, unrecognized, happy. Simon laughed easily, his eyes sparkling, full of mischief. He would tip his head and look up with a kind of joking disapproval when a remark of Haakon's seemed to him bookish, dull or timid.

The world had seemed safe then, even though Hitler had already defied the Versailles Treaty and was training troops. Only a few had seen the implications. He certainly had not. Not until that September when the Nuremberg laws deprived Jews of citizenship had he begun to see the pattern of oppression.

"I'll be leaving here within a fortnight," Simon's letter finished. "I'll see to your apartment, air it and clean it. You'll be discharged soon. I've missed you, my beautiful Dane. Love, S."

Sweating in the heat, his fingers stuck to the paper as he put the letter away. He remembered Simon's brownstone house. The space in the huge studio that took up most of the ground floor, the coolness. He imagined going up the curved metal stairway that led to the living quarters on the second floor, crossing the conventionally masculine living room with its waxed wood, cases of books and leather chairs, and entering the bedroom.

The walls were covered with tawny damask. There were too many mirrors. The mirrored ceiling reflected the entire room and repeated it upside down. Satins and velvets, softness. All the quiet

6

colors blending into gold-tan, like a lion in a desert. A perfect back-drop for Simon's dark beauty. He had never become accustomed to it, had never felt entirely easy there. It was too much like a bordello, or a sensual daydream. But now he longed for the pleasant textures and subtle lighting, yearned to stretch out full length on that enormous comfortable bed, to feel the softness of Simon's curly hair against his throat. His hands remembered the shape and texture of Simon's shoulders.

He felt cramped in the hard bunk, and all around him was the buzz of conversation, an occasional phrase loud in a voice raised for emphasis.

"Full house! Ya bastid!"

". . . on a hoor . . . give it away in this fuckin' game."

". . . and Sylvia wrote . . ."

". . . that kid of mine . . . a baseball and . . ."

". . . those broads at Big Mama's? Let me tell *you*. Real eatin' stuff. Yummmmm." A tense burst of hard horny laughter.

What would the others think of his homecoming plans? They would probably refuse to believe them.

Dan pushed his way past the duffel bags and came into the aisle. White stripe bright against the dark chestnut of his hair, source of his nickname, Polecat. Strong-boned, pleasantly homely face. No longer ugly since the Army had repaired his badly broken nose. He had a hunk of bread in one hand, cheese in the other.

Through a mouthful, he said rhetorically, "Whatcha doing, Professor?"

"Do you ever stop eating?"

"Not if I can help it. Hey, Roge said you gave him that twenty. I don't have it any more, you know. Dropped it trying to fill an inside straight."

"Again?" He got a whiff of the warm yeasty scent of the fresh bread. "Never mind, there's no hurry. How is Roger doing?"

"Fine, last I saw, but that was half an hour ago." He crammed the last of the bread into his mouth, took off his fatigue jacket, wadded it up and threw it onto his bunk across the walkway. "Hotter than hell down here." He carried so much tension that the muscle masses were distinct, more sharply delineated than most men's. He smelled clean and slightly musky.

"Have you decided what you're going to do when you get back?"

"I think I'll go to Frisco with Roge and work on the docks. He has an uncle. How about you?"

"Teach at the university, as I did before." Why was he sounding formal?

"That's all? You get letters."

"From friends. I've no family. You know that." Dan had now begun to gnaw on a K-ration fruit bar. The only man in the outfit who actually enjoyed the things, he always had a supply. Dan rested his forearm on the edge of the bunk, leaning comfortably. Close enough to touch by just lifting a hand. The skin of his cheek was smooth and beardless, his mustache a faint beginning of a shadow on his upper lip.

"If you ever come to New York," Haakon said, "I hope you'll look me up," trying to sound casual.

Dan gestured with the fruit bar, indicating the dusty air above. "Ever stop to think we're breathing that shit?"

"I try not to think about it."

"Hey, Professor, you smile a lot. How come you never laugh?"

"I don't know."

"I thought about re-enlisting, but I don't think the peacetime Army's for me. Maybe later if I don't like being a civilian. Roge says you can make a fortune on the docks."

"There are docks in New York."

"Yeah, but Roge don't have no uncle in New York."

"Doesn't have any," he corrected automatically.

"Yeah, all right," Dan agreed, straightening and moving away. "See ya," and he went off toward the card games by the exit ladder.

Dan had reverted to his former ungrammatical speech to put distance between them, to force him back into his teacher's role. Dan did not do it deliberately, did not think it out, but it always happened when he felt crowded.

A stevedore—what a waste! Dan had learned enough these past three years to almost certainly pass a high school equivalency exam and get into college. Haakon had hoped—but what right did he have to make plans for him? Dan was not his son.

He had first noticed Polecat sometime early in basic training. He was not sure exactly when. Those first weeks were such a nightmare of exhaustion and physical pain from the unaccustomed exercise that they tended to blur together.

Showers had been an ordeal. Never in his life had he been subjected to such total lack of privacy. He hated having to wash in front of others. His nakedness embarrassed him, and he was always afraid of becoming aroused in the presence of all those nude men. He never knew where to turn his eyes and tried not to look at anyone.

Once, as he stepped out from under the water, Coston blocked him. Big loose-lipped grin contradicted by a malicious sparkle in small close-set hazel eyes. Coston reached out and picked up one of his dog tags, held it up to read it, balancing it on a forefinger. "Hake-on Horseshit. What kinda Polack name is that?"

*"Hawk*on H*vit*felt," he corrected, trying to sound indifferent. Angry and afraid, aware he was showing his discomfort, fumbling with his towel.

"Hake the fake." Coston flipped the tags so they flew up and slapped his cheek. Someone laughed.

He could not think of anything to say. Why couldn't he deal with this Neanderthal clown?

Just then Polecat had shouldered between them, shoving Coston so that he reeled against the wall. Paying attention to Polecat now, Coston yelled, "You little bastard, it's my turn."

Polecat turned his back, soaping himself. "Fuck off!"

Coston could do nothing but swear. He obviously did not want to take Polecat on. Not only was Polecat strong for his size, but there was an aura of dangerousness about him, as if he might run amok if sufficiently provoked.

At the time it had not occurred to Haakon that the intervention might have been deliberate. He had not been grateful.

Then on his first twenty-mile march under full pack he became convinced that the doctors who had passed him as fit had erred, that he was too old, too soft, and would inevitably collapse and die. He could hardly lift his feet. Each branch or stone in the path was a major obstacle, but he kept staggering on in a fog of exhaustion.

He bumped into someone. The man he had jostled, tired too, grunted and stuck out an elbow. He fell face down, breath knocked out of him. Paralyzed. Sure he was dying.

Then someone took the heavy pack off him. At last able to breathe, he looked at the hand holding it. Broad, muscular, tanned. The knuckles were scabbed and swollen from a recent fight. Polecat, that violent, ignorant little beast! Struggling to stand, he protested, "No, I'm all right."

Polecat snarled, "Shaddup," and helped him to his feet, then walked off with the pack dangling beside him. After a short time, others noticed that Polecat was carrying double and began passing the pack around among them.

Just short of camp, Dan returned it, his hands gentle as he tried to arrange the straps so they would not rub on the raw areas. On being thanked, he muttered, "Fuck that shit," and walked away.

After that neither he nor Polecat was an outsider. Part of it was Dan's leadership in seeing that something needed to be done and doing it. And his covert kindness made his verbal nastiness forgivable. In Haakon's case, his refusal to give up or complain had earned him respect.

After basic training most of the unit was assigned to the engineers. Sure that the Army had made a mistake and that he was being wasted, since he was fluent in six languages, he put in for a transfer.

In the meantime he had to learn to drive a bulldozer, though he had never even driven an automobile. But neither had Polecat, and when his turn came he gleefully clashed gears and drove in circles.

Haakon could not match the headlong commitment that Dan seemed to bring to any new challenge, but he was able to stop worrying about making a fool of himself and did far better than he had expected to.

The pleasure in learning something new was familiar, but the joy he discovered in using his hands to take engines apart and put them back together was new. He had hardened up and felt more confident than he ever had in his life before. He was surprised to discover that he had a knack with engines, could understand and interpret their knocks, pings and grumbles.

Realizing that he hoped the transfer would not go through, he went to Lieutenant Travis to ask about it. He and Travis had developed a mutual dislike on sight. The lieutenant, a college graduate, was offended by his Ph.D., and he on his side was annoyed by the lieutenant's arrogance.

He waited at attention while Travis shuffled papers. The sun glinted off the lieutenant's spiky blond crew-cut, and there were scabs on his face where he had popped pimples. Haakon recalled someone saying, "He's the clean-cut all-American prick," and remembered to keep his face blank.

Travis asked, *"What* transfer?"

Obviously his request had been filed in the wastebasket. Travis looked surprised. Haakon realized he was grinning.

Shortly before the outfit was due to go overseas, everyone had a Saturday night pass into town. He accepted the good-natured kidding that he must really be over the hill if he did not want to go too, and he settled down to enjoy the unusual luxury of having the place to himself.

He wrote Simon a long, hungry letter. He wrote friends at the university, the Van Zandts, the Enfields. He wrote Lucy. She had been a surprise. As his secretary she had always been shy, so unassuming he had hardly noticed her. But her letters showed a cool wry wit, a kindly clear-sightedness that was thoroughly enjoyable.

Polecat passed his bunk on the way to his own. He looked up from his pad of stationery. "Back early?"

"Mind your own fuckin' business, you old prick!"

He should not be hurt. That was only typical Polecat. He finished his letter.

He became aware somewhat later, having finished his correspondence and having begun to read Charles Ardant du Picq's *Battle Studies*, that Polecat was standing at the foot of his bed. He closed the book on his finger. "What is it?"

With a kind of childlike directness, looking into his face, Dan said, "Look, I'm sorry. You din't mean nothing. You was being nice."

Dan looked puzzled, young and lonely. That streak of white hair and those overly strong bones, the smashed nose, made him appear older than he apparently was. For the first time he saw that Dan's expression was not angry so much as haunted.

Several days earlier Coston had been tormenting Little Billy. He had gotten hold of a letter from Billy's fiancée and was reading passages from it in a mocking voice.

Haakon had been wondering how he could intervene when Polecat had gone over, grabbed Coston by the shirtfront, and demanded, "You prick, I just wanna see that pack of cards you was usin' last night." Coston had dropped the letter and forgotten Billy—exactly the way he had forgotten about him that day in the showers.

Now Haakon said, "It's all right." Then asked, "Polecat, why do you always act so angry?"

"Dunno . . ." A pause. "Well, that way nobody asks me dumb questions. I mean, they leave me be, you know?"

"I suppose so."

"Well, I din't mean to take up your time."

"You're not taking up my time."

"I can talk to you? It's OK?"

"Of course." He put aside the book and wondered what to say.

"You're some kinda teacher, huh?"

"Yes, I teach history." Then amended, "Taught."

"Yeah. You know what I useta do? Worked on a fuckin' ice truck lugging fifty-pound hunks of ice up miles of fuckin' stairs. Not much class." He smiled.

He had never seen Dan smile before and was startled by the way it changed his face, rearranging the harsh plane, wiping away the tenseness, showing the warmth and kindness that prompted him to help others.

11

He knew Polecat had decided to trust him and, aware that he might regret taking the responsibility, nevertheless felt he had no choice. "Please, sit down."

Dan sat on the neighboring bunk. "I wish to Christ I wasn't so goddamned dumb."

"You're not dumb at all," he said more sharply than he intended. Several days earlier, having decided that the instructor's explanation was too garbled to make sense of, he had been trying to figure out a gear linkage for himself. Polecat had been watching. Then he had said, "See, this gizmo fits there," and sketched a quick diagram in the dust that had explained the whole thing.

Polecat certainly was not stupid. He was not only quick to learn, he could also think for himself. He asked him, "How much schooling have you had?"

"Began high school, but I hadda work, you know."

"What chance have you had to learn?"

Polecat thought about this for some time. He took a pack of Camels from his shirt pocket and tapped a cigarette on his thumbnail, then looking at him, said happily, "How about that? Hey, Professor. I think maybe you're right. I don't know nothing, but it doesn't hafta be like that. Look, I don't wanna be a stupid Kraut kid all my life."

"Yes." He had spent half his life assessing the quality of students. He was sure of himself here. He wondered why he had not seen past the execrable English sooner. "Would you like me to teach you?"

"Naw, you don't wanna."

"Yes, I do."

"You do?" Dan inspected him, apparently trying to assess his sincerity. "Yeah, you do. OK, Professor, it's a deal." He smiled.

"Where do you want to start?"

"Teach me to talk right."

"Yes. May I ask you a question?"

"What?" Green eyes suddenly wary.

"What did you mean about being a Kraut?"

"Yeah—well—Albany ain't my name. Look, I was born here, but my folks—all the people in the neighborhood—came from the Old Country. You know? Look, don't tell nobody."

"Of course not."

And Dan had soaked up learning. He was particularly good at math, and the only reason he had not progressed past quadratic equations was that there was no one to teach him. He could now speak acceptable English if he chose.

The beat of the engines increased as if they had picked up more speed. The ship had begun to pitch in the North Atlantic swells, and somewhere nearby someone began to retch. The buzz of conversation was less, making the hum of the fans seem louder.

All right. To some extent Dan was like a son. He would never have one of his own. He genuinely wanted to see him get an education, become somebody. He could be satisfied, even happy, to settle for that.

True as that might be, his altruism would be a damned sight more impressive if he didn't also *want* him so goddamned much.

But what a waste for Dan to become a stevedore. And he would inevitably be bored by physical labor. Would that motivate him to enroll in school in California, or just make him angry? With his propensity for fighting when drunk—and without the others in the outfit to stop him, protect him, drag him out the back door—he might hurt someone seriously, end up in jail.

And if Haakon loved Simon, how was it possible for him to be in love with Dan too? He had never believed that one could be in love with two people at the same time. But further speculation was a waste of time. It made no difference anyway. He would never have Dan.

Dan was straight, and even if he did come to New York, he would still be untouchable. Whenever Haakon's interest reached a certain level, Dan reacted almost instinctively to put distance between them, as had happened not half an hour ago. If he ever made any overt move to seduce him, Dan would run like hell.

He hoped Dan would at least go to school on the West Coast. No matter what happened, he would have to content himself with knowing he had done what he could for him.

August 29, 1945

He unlocked the door to his apartment and walked in, dropping his duffel bag in the entry. He could smell Turkish tobacco smoke, furniture polish and coffee. Obviously Simon had gotten here ahead of him. He called, "Simon?"

No answer. He went a few steps into the living room and paused to look around. The colors of the oriental rug that covered most of the floor were brighter than he had remembered. Open drapes allowed the early afternoon sun to stream into the big room. The curtains were badly faded. He would have to replace them. The books filling the floor-to-ceiling bookcases along two walls were solid, comfortable, welcoming. Light glinted off the gold on the bindings. He ran his hand along the spines of a set of the Encyclopaedia Britannica.

Simon had laid a fire of birch logs, and more logs filled the copper woodbasket on the brick hearth. On the mantel the bronze lioness he had bought in France before the war lay licking her paw while two cubs scuffled beside her and a third peered over her back as if about to pounce. He let his hand linger over the cool smoothness of the metal, appreciating the curves. He stuck the tip of his forefinger into the mouth of the cub that was hissing and felt the tiny pointed teeth. Gold replicas of a pair of Mycenaean bull cups were on the other end of the mantel. He picked them up and looked at the reliefs before setting them down again. Over the mantel was a seascape he had bought years ago when still an instructor. He wondered again why the painter had apparently never gone on to do anything with his talent. Perhaps he was dead.

He crossed to the open bedroom door, thinking that possibly Simon was asleep. The bed was made, the room empty. He turned away and went to his desk between the windows. Hardly glancing at it, he picked up the red soapstone paperweight from the blotter and stood hefting and fingering it while he looked out at Riverside Park and the Hudson River. The view was one he had remembered nostalgically in the Army. Like everything else he'd seen since his return, the park seemed smaller. Why was his memory playing him tricks?

He set down the paperweight and went back to the coffee table in front of the couch, sat down in his leather armchair and lit a Lucky Strike.

On the table was a half-empty bright yellow pack of Africa cigarettes, probably purchased in Rome, and a copy of a national magazine open to a full-page photograph of a single standing wall, four stories high, somewhat ornate, stark and empty-windowed against fluffy clouds. A row of stalls huddled against its base. The credit line, "Photo by Simon Foster," was circled in black ink, but he had recognized the wall before reading the caption.

Why had Simon left this for him to find? The occasion when Simon had taken the picture had not been pleasant. He lifted the magazine to look for a note. None. What message had Simon intended to convey? Perhaps that now that he could see what Simon had seen, he could understand why Simon had had to stop.

No doubt about it, this was a sample of Simon's genius. It was not, as he had thought then, one wall among hundreds. Simon had captured the sense of the bombed city, of all bombed cities. Not only the scale of the destruction, but the individual efforts to pick up the pieces, to keep living.

That had been a strange meeting. All during the long bone-jolting ride in the Army truck to Munich, he thought of Simon. It rained most of the trip, and someone's radio was blaring "You Are My Sunshine," and later a hard German contralto was belting out "Lili Marlene."

He and Simon had not met since London, prior to the invasion. He hoped Simon had not changed too much. When he saw him and realized that he had not changed at all, he felt oddly estranged. Simon was elegant in British tweeds, very much the civilian, bubbling over at his own ingenuity in getting to Munich to meet him.

Simon made no secret of the fact that he had gotten there in the company of an aging colonel with whom he had been sleeping. He saw nothing wrong with this, and was particularly delighted with his cleverness in getting the colonel out of the city so they could use his flat.

Haakon had not wanted to go to a place Simon had shared with another man, but there was no choice. His need was so great that he set aside his distaste. Once he had decided he could do it, however, he was in a hurry. And Simon refused to be rushed, kept stopping to take photographs.

This wall had intrigued Simon. He walked back and forth, climbed on a heap of rubble, squatted in the middle of the street, changed cameras and tried different filters.

Haakon asked, "Couldn't you do that another time?"

Simon replied impatiently, "Another time those clouds won't be there, the light won't be right," and continued working.

He fidgeted, and Simon said almost scornfully, "What's the matter with you? You never used to be so horny. We have a full week, for heaven's sake!"

At the time he had not been able to reply. Now he could look back and better understand his state of mind. He had needed to hold and be held, he had been desperate for comforting. Sex entered into it, but it was not the most important part.

He had watched. Simon was slender, graceful, darkly handsome, untouched by war or death. A faun, Dionysus, Pan. Mythological. Uncontaminated. He had to hold him to make himself whole again. Desperate and angry, he said, "Simon, please! Let's go."

"In a minute," Simon said, going down on one knee, still looking through his camera at the wall.

15

"Simon, listen to me."

"Yes, in a minute."

"Do you know what I've been doing while you were drinking champagne with the brass? I've been burying corpses, Simon. For weeks. First it was German soldiers—old men, boys not old enough to shave. With worms in their mouths. Arms, legs, entrails. Pieces. Digging mass graves with a bulldozer and shoving them in with the blade. And then Schwartzgarten. More mass graves. Women and children, Simon. Thin and nameless as dead leaves. The stink so bad that afterwards I wanted to take my skin off. I can't get rid of it; it's still with me. Simon, I need you now."

Simon stood, letting his cameras hang from the straps around his neck. "I wish you'd told me sooner. Let's go then."

"You don't understand. I dream about it."

At the flat, Simon had been gentle and patient, almost motherly. He had not insisted on talking. Simon had done his best, and had been helpful, but Haakon doubted that he really understood.

He told himself now that it was not Simon's fault. Simon had not been where he had, he not seen and smelled it. He had not had to do the same things.

Later Simon had tried to amuse him, had cooked him a gourmet dinner using ingredients that could only have been obtained with great difficulty and expense on the black market. He tried to respond to Simon's efforts to cheer him up but could not. He could not set aside his despair, his feeling of having somehow been responsible, irrational though that was.

He had felt guilty simply for belonging to the human race. For not seeing the evil behind the clean-swept cities, the trains that ran on time. For laughing at Hitler's mustache. For not asking more questions, for not investigating, for not speaking out. For not having been more than he could be.

Haakon put aside the magazine and stood up, took off his Eisenhower jacket and dropped it on the back of the chair. He must stop thinking about it now. He crossed to the bookcase opposite the windows and took down his world history textbook, automatically blowing across the top. No dust. Simon had outdone himself dusting his library. This book had gone to press in November of 1938. The last sentence read, "We will not have 'peace in our time.' Appeasement will not work. This is the beginning of the next war." Higgins had wanted him to delete this judgment, complaining that he was a historian, not a prophet. He had seen it but he hadn't—had not guessed the depth of the evil.

Higgins had been certain Haakon was wrong. Now he wished

he had been, but when war had been declared he had seen it almost as a personal justification. Thank god he had not given in to his impulse to phone Higgins. Petty? Yes, but he had not known anything about war then.

The book had opened to a neat diagram of the Battle of Agincourt, drawn to scale, squares and rectangles labeled archers, cavalry, foot. At the top of the page he read, ". . . the second line again became cramped in the center and could not advance beyond the barrier of dead and wounded in front of the English line." The longbowmen had been more important to the outcome of the battle than the knights. But he had not mentioned that the reason the English had longbowmen and the French did not was that a man needed constant practice in order to use that weapon effectively, and France did not permit commoners to possess weapons of their own. A point he ought to have made.

The text needed rewriting from beginning to end. A shift of emphasis from dates and tactics to reasons and underlying causes was needed, not a couple of tacked-on chapters covering this war. He snapped the book shut and shoved it back into its space.

Two o'clock and still no sign of Simon. He had an appointment with Dean Grimes at four. He wandered into the bedroom and looked into the closet. Simon had arranged all his old civilian clothes for him.

He took down the suit that had fitted him best after basic training. It smelled of the cedar chest in which it had been stored. He found the trousers so big in the waist he could not wear them, the jacket so tight he got stuck in it and ripped it struggling out. His shirts were a neck-size too small. Even his shoes were too tight. He would need a whole new wardrobe.

He got back into his uniform, and as he turned to leave the room he caught sight of himself in the dresser mirror. After a moment's shock (What is that soldier doing in my room?) he recognized himself. How white his hair had gotten. Odd that it did not make him look older. And he seemed taller. Had he stooped that much? Apparently.

He straightened his tie and rubbed his fingertips up his cheek. No, he did not need a shave.

Where in hell was Simon? He had made half a dozen restless tours of the apartment before asking himself why he was irritable.

Was he afraid of Dean Grimes? Certainly he was far too nervous about the interview. He picked up his Eisenhower jacket, put it on and left the building. He would walk the few blocks to the university, look around and try to relax.

The Dean's last letter had certainly been correct enough, offering him a full professorship on his return. But the tone was chilly—as if the Dean was making the offer under pressure and without enthusiasm.

Grimes didn't like him. He could hardly blame him for that. Before the war he had not much liked himself.

The sun was hot across his shoulders, the wind off the Hudson was chill and smelled of autumn. A few leaves were falling and the gusts of wind blew them rustling across the octagonal paving stones of the sidewalk above Riverside Park.

A red-and-white-striped ball bounced off his foot. He stooped to catch it, then looked back to see where it had come from. On a bench was a young dark-haired woman with a toddler. The boy was staring intently and doubtfully at the ball with wide gray eyes. He walked back and handed it to the child.

The woman was looking at him with interest. "I'm not his mother," she said, smiling. "I'm the babysitter."

She was enough like Simon to be his sister. Dark curly hair, cut short, smooth olive complexion, large dark eyes. Her smile was pretty, but he was put off by her dark lipstick. His fleeting interest in her was gone. He smiled briefly in return and walked on.

She looked Italian, as did Simon, though Simon claimed he was not. Simon had said he was a descendant of English landed gentry with a pedigree that predated the Norman Conquest. But Simon had told him so many mutually contradictory stories that he had long ago stopped trying to sort them out.

He turned east at the university and went slowly up the broad steps of the library, looking up at the facade, at the seated statue in front that, according to undergraduate legend, would stand and salute if a virgin ever walked in front of it.

Suddenly aware of a movement, he reached out to steady a man just as they ran into each other. Books flew through the air and clapped down on the steps below.

"Sorry, sir, I wasn't looking where I was going." He bent to pick up the books.

"That's all right, son, neither was I."

He recognized the voice immediately and straightened, holding out the books. "George! How are you? And Mary? And the kids?" So delighted to see him, he would have hugged him if the books had not been in the way.

George had changed in three years. He was almost bald now, a tonsured rim of gray around the back of his skull. He had gained weight too, probably as much as twenty pounds. He seemed shorter than before.

"I'll be damned! Haakon!" George stood looking up at him, mouth slightly ajar, then smiled broadly. "You're back! Why didn't you let me know? Are you back for good?"

"I asked first." It was an old joke dating back to their undergraduate days.

"What was the question?" George said, then following the rules of the game, which were that he not only· should reply to all the questions, but do it in sequence, said, "I'm fine. Mary's the same, busy as always. George Junior is due home from the Pacific theater in a month. Sally's engaged—to that young man just out of the Marines. The one she met at the party. I wrote you about that. Now it's your turn."

"I wasn't sure of a pass until last night. I tried to call, but there was no answer. I'll be discharged within the month."

"You've got to have dinner with us tonight. Mary'll never forgive me if I let you get away."

He hesitated. He would have liked to spend his first evening home with his oldest and dearest friends, but not only did he know that Simon had made plans, he would also rather be with Simon. "I can't. Could I take a rain check?"

"Of course. How about making it definite for Saturday? In a way that's better, gives us time to kill the fatted calf."

"I'd love to. What time?"

"Oh, early. Come in time so we can get in a game of chess first. I haven't had a worthy opponent since you left. Around four?"

"Yes. You'll find me rusty, though. I've played very little chess these past years, and rarely with anyone who was a challenge."

"How did it go in the Army? Was it very difficult for you?"

"Difficult?" He thought he detected an edge of concern behind the question that should not have been there and told himself not to be oversensitive.

"Well, after talking to Sally's young man, I know your letters reflected very little of what basic training must have been like. I wonder that you survived it."

"I almost didn't. You can't spend your entire life sitting around on your dead ass and not expect to suffer when you're required to exercise. But once I got through the first part, I actually enjoyed it in some ways. I liked being physically fit, and I wasn't exaggerating when I wrote I liked learning about engines."

"Yes, I see," George said slowly. "You know, I can't help envying you. I feel as if I'd been left behind. Oh, I know I was needed here, but— There are always 'buts,' aren't there?"

"Yes."

"You look great. You've dropped ten years. I can't believe it." He looked away, then, across the broad street toward the Business Building. "Mary and I were particularly worried about you after Schwartzgarten. You were so shaken, and then you never referred to it again."

"There are times when I think I never will get over it. But then I tell myself I'm dramatizing. One gets over anything, given time." To change the subject, he said, "I picked up some Dürer etchings for you in Germany. I think they're authentic, but as you know, I'm no expert. You can check them out. There's one of a madonna with a monkey that I've seen somewhere before, the others are unfamiliar, but the style seems right. I suppose they could be forgeries, but if so, they're handsome ones on very old paper. I'll bring them over Saturday."

"You must let me pay you for them."

"All right, but no more than I paid—three cartons of American cigarettes." Then, in response to George's astonishment, "That's right. Plus a couple of fruit bars, but those were GI and I didn't want them anyway."

"Do you still smoke Luckies?"

"Yes, when I can get them. I guess from now on I'll be able to, won't I?"

"Yes, the war's over."

After leaving George he still had over half an hour before it would be time for the appointment. On the lawn by Schermerhorn Hall students were feeding peanuts and potato chips to the pigeons and squirrels. One squirrel would sit on a hand to take nuts in its paws. Was this the same one that had done that three years ago? How long did squirrels live?

He made his way to the History Building and walked down the empty corridors. He stopped by the open door of a classroom, and after a moment's hesitation went in, over to the platform in front of the blackboard. His footsteps echoed in the emptiness. Row after row of desk-chairs, dust motes dancing in the bars of sunlight. A smell of chalk dust and floor-cleaning compound.

Soon he would be here, where he felt as if he belonged. Teaching again. The first class was always the most difficult. Assessments and judgments, the students looking at him blankly, hidden behind their faces.

He would wonder which of them were dull, which bright, who

would be genuinely interested, who there only for the three points of credit and dedicated to sliding through with a minimum of effort. They would wonder what he was going to expect of them, whether he graded hard or easy or "on the curve." How many tests would he give, how hard would they be? They would wonder if he had anything to teach them, if they would be bored.

He had been considered a good teacher before the war. He would be better now, he had more to offer. The ex-GIs should be an interesting and rewarding bunch. Odd to consider that he was, in a sense, their contemporary. He had been through the same war.

He felt a deep, quiet excitement, an eagerness to begin classes. He looked forward to the challenge of finding new ways to bring students out of themselves, help them understand, think and grow.

He glanced at his watch. Time for his appointment. He was considerably less nervous now. The anteroom was empty, the inner door open. He knocked on the frame.

Grimes looked up, adjusting bifocals. He had not had bifocals three years ago. "Yes? What can I do for you?" Then recognizing him, "Dr. Hvitfelt!"

He smiled carefully. "Hello, sir. I hope I'm not too early." The room smelled very much like burned marshmallows. Bill Grimes was still smoking the same brand of honey-cured pipe tobacco.

"I didn't recognize you for a moment there. Must be the uniform." Grimes stood and bumbled around the big mahogany desk toward him. He was ten pounds heavier than before and looked more like a rhinoceros than ever. A big, blocky, coarse-featured man with a pointed mobile upper lip, a curve of mouth that had bothered Haakon for months until he had seen a rhino in the zoo and recognized it. Lumpy forehead, as if he were on the verge of sprouting a horn. Grimes pumped his hand, held on to it and patted him, going on at too much length about how glad he was to have him back. "And decorations"—with too much enthusiasm—"fruit salad, I believe you boys call them."

"Yes, sir."

"But do sit down, have a cigarette." Back behind his desk, proffering a pack. "How was it? Tell me about it. Making the world safe for democracy."

Apparently an attempt at a joke. Why was Grimes so nervous? He must be uncomfortable to find him changed, did not quite know how to react to him. To put the Dean at ease, deliberately trying to sound stuffy, he said, "The last war was the one that made the world safe for democracy. I wouldn't care to guess what this one accomplished."

Grimes relaxed. "Ah-ha, now that sounds like you, always the historian. You must have learned a great deal."

"No, just that if you're warm, dry, fed and not being shot at, you're relatively happy. No broad perspectives for dogfaces."

"Ah, yes, I suppose not. Now. Down to business. I do hope you're coming back. We need you. You'll be a full professor, of course." Pleased about it now.

"Yes, sir, I'd planned on coming back."

"Please stop calling me 'sir.' You make me feel like Methuselah."

"Sorry, sir," he said automatically, smiled apologetically while Grimes chuckled. "That's a habit it will take me a while to break, I'm afraid." He was struck by the warmth and approval in Grimes's manner.

"Is that the Purple Heart?" Grimes asked abruptly, pointing.

"Yes, sir." He did not want to explain, but the Dean was waiting. He obviously was going to have to say something. "D-Day. Omaha Beach," he said, "I was grazed by shrapnel, nothing much. I wasn't even out of action."

He had left out so much it amounted to a lie. The only reason he had not been hospitalized was that he had walked out on the doctors and gotten away before they could stop him. But he certainly was not going to explain that.

"D-Day," Grimes repeated.

Suddenly it all came back to him. Armored bulldozers, the scream of the barrage overhead, shells exploding, the rattle of machine-gun and rifle fire. Hurrying to drag the crippled tanks out of the way to clear a path for the next wave of armor. The first LST's in the new wave were already butting their way through the surf. Sand sliding under his boots, the smoking tank smelling of hot metal, burned wool and cordite. The magazine had blown. Gripping the heavy hook, dragging cable behind him.

Then a whiff of roasted meat, and he realized that the blackened thing hanging out of the turret was the remains of a man. He stood there stupidly staring at it. Behind him Dan gunned the motor of the bulldozer and yelled, "Get your thumb out of your ass, you stupid cocksucker!"

Jarred, he bent quickly to attach the hook and suddenly felt as if he had been kicked in the back. He fell, getting sand in his eyes and mouth. If Dan had not yelled, the fragment would have hit him squarely in the chest and killed him.

Where was Dan now? Before they had gone on leave, Dan had said he might go home to Albany to see his sister. But the Dean was talking about the courses he would be teaching in the coming semester and he had to pay attention.

September 12, 1945

The sun was low. Each pebble in the vast graveled expanses between the rows of barracks cast its own shadow. As he walked away from the main gate onto the base, his shadow stretched diagonally away from him, ungainly and elongated as a praying mantis.

A jeep crossed the emptiness of the parade ground trailing a long tail of dust. Small twittering birds, black against the sky, flew across and disappeared behind a building. A fitful breeze brought smells of gasoline and fresh paint.

Gray two-story barracks were lined up in neat rows. The way the Army always wanted everything. The spaces between them were probably the same down to the quarter inch. Wars cannot be fought with undisciplined rabble, but the Army always seemed to him to go too far in its passion for uniformity.

The shrapnel scar on his shoulder blade had begun to pull. He stood straighter and it stopped. Apparently he was doomed to good posture for the rest of his life, like it or not.

Back again. The two-week furlough had passed like hours, yet he felt undone by it. He was no longer sure of his own reactions. He was not afraid of getting into trouble officially. What worried him was that he might expose himself enough to lose the respect of the other men, and he cared deeply what they thought of him. He had liked being straight for three years, even though it had been difficult and in some ways had made him less sure of who he was. A moratorium on himself, a respite that had become important to him. He did not want to foul it up with some last-minute foolishness that would cast a shadow over all of it. And there was a part of him that was totally impatient with these last days he was being forced to spend here, that wanted to get back to Simon, pick up his old life.

Simon had driven him back to Fort Dix, stopping the car down the road from the main gate. They had sat a moment looking at each other, then slowly had shaken hands. A busload of soldiers passed. Defiantly they held on to each other's hands, then found themselves clinging, not wanting to break the contact. Simon looked oddly forlorn. It had been a wrench to have to let go.

"Soon," Simon said.

He nodded, then quickly got out of the car and sketched a salute of thanks before walking off without looking back. Behind him he heard the car make a U-turn and drive away.

He wanted to be with Simon now and wished he could at least dare to carry his picture in his wallet.

The furlough had not started out very well. Odd how they usually grated on each other when they first met after a separation.

He had come back from the university that first afternoon and Simon had been there, had come over to hug him as soon as he stepped into the living room, apologizing for not having been there earlier.

Then, a moment after the apology, Simon held him away and looked at him, "God, you're handsome in that uniform!"

"For Christ's sake, Simon. Don't give me that shit. I'm not one of your goddamned bird colonels."

"Yes, sir. Sorry, sir." Mockingly.

"Come off it!"

Simon laughed. "All right, Haakon. But you really are beautiful. And honestly, uniforms do something to me."

The hurt had been familiar, the anger less so. "I suppose that's why you spent the war shacking up with half the Allied brass in the European theater."

"Oh, don't be so *jealous*." Sounding faggish.

"Simon, please stop playing games with me."

"You shouldn't be jealous, you know. A lot of it was work."

"Isn't it nice you enjoy your work." He had felt bitter then, and still did now.

"Look! You *know* I couldn't have got where I wanted without them. I never could have met you in Munich if I hadn't had that fat pig of a colonel. Do you think I *enjoyed* him? Let me tell you— he had halitosis, was a lousy lay, and had a prick the size of a peanut. He was an *utter* bore out of bed too. Knew the price of everything and the value of nothing. Really!" Then, in a persuasive tone, "Please, Haakon, let's not fight. I do things my way and you do things yours. Let's just leave it at that." Then waspishly, "Furthermore, what have *you* been doing for three years? I can't imagine keeping *my* hands off all those beautiful young bodies for so long."

"If you don't know I did, you really don't understand me."

Simon had become serious and said, "Not really, I guess. But I do love you, insofar as I can love anyone. Yes, I believe you kept hands off, though I can't imagine how."

"It's easy," he had replied. "All it takes is inhuman self-control." Meant as a joke, and Simon had laughed. But true in a sense. Not easy though.

And after that initial unpleasantness—the almost obligatory squabble that marked their meeting—almost everything else about his leave had been good.

Simon was slender, strongly muscled, his body hard and wiry. Haakon's hands remembered Simon's contours, the softness of the dark curly hair that furred his chest and belly, the wonderful vital solidity of him. Bourbon-flavored kisses. The warmth of Simon's body against his, the taste and shape of him in his mouth. Simon's mouth on him, licking, loving. Completeness, repleteness. Simon's sigh, and the soft tenderness in his voice. That strange endearment that was the only one Simon used that seemed to mean anything: "I love you, my beautiful Danish cocksucker." Almost funny, he could smile thinking of it. But meaningful . . . perhaps because it implied acceptance of him as he was.

He almost shuddered. Here he was on his way back to his barracks. He must not think of that. His heart was beating too fast. He had to get back into the frame of mind that had made the past three years possible, not daydream about his lover. He slowed his pace to give himself time to collect himself.

He had to stop thinking about Simon. But why couldn't he satisfy Simon with his mouth? Why did Simon always want to be screwed, claiming he needed it? So this time he had tried again. And failed again. He always failed. Could his defeatist attitude in itself be influencing the outcome?

He found it difficult to imagine what enjoyment there was in being the passive partner in sodomy. Once, that first summer they had met, Simon had persuaded him to try that, and he had not been able to go through with it. Far too painful. And the idea was frightening enough to him so he knew he would never be able to relax sufficiently.

Yet oddly enough, in spite of repeated failures, the thought of having Simon that way was always exciting. There were never any problems at the outset, though he always worried that Simon might be hurt. But Simon knew what he was doing, was expert.

Would Simon find it easier to be faithful to him if he could give him what he wanted? No way to know, since he never had. What was the matter with him? He remembered this last attempt vividly. He had been lying on his back, Simon kneeling astride him, easing himself down. Simon so beautiful, olive skin contrasting sharply with his own paleness. Sensual warmth and softness. More than just pleasant. And wanting desperately to please. Lying still while Simon impaled himself on him.

Impale was not an accurate metaphor. The executioner at an impalement cut a slit in the perineum, passed the dull stake through it, and had the victim drawn slowly down onto it so as to avoid puncturing the intestines, major blood vessels or vital organs. The victim was intended to suffer as long as possible, die of thirst after several days, not within fifteen minutes of shock and blood loss.

25

Crucifixion was only a variation, introduced because the executioner needed no special skill. God, what an image! Why had he thought of that?

Was Simon's preference that distressing? No . . . yes. At first he had been all right. At first. Then something went wrong. Why did everything quit on him just as he began to think that this time he would not fail?

This last time Simon had only said, "Go wash up. We'll finish your way." No trace of annoyance in his tone. Resignation, perhaps some disappointment.

Even in ancient Rome, where so many of the emperors had been homosexual or bisexual, Julius Caesar (wife of all men, husband of all women) slept his way to early success in the bed of Nicomedes, King of Bithynia. Vitellius worked his way toward the throne as one of Tiberius's catamites—one of the *spintrae* at Capri, screaming queens, Simon would have called them. Augustus, Nero, Trajan . . . Simon's preference had always been the acceptable one, not his. A man known to indulge in oral sex was not offered the common cup at a banquet, and if he drank from it, it was afterwards broken.

Worth noting, however, that he was invited to the banquet.

He stepped up onto the small porch of the barracks and went into the building. Rows of double bunks, each with olive-drab blanket, white cuff of sheet and pillow. Square posts held up the second floor, two rows of them all the way down the long room. Yellowish overhead lights, bare bulbs. He dropped his duffel bag, ducked and sat on his bed. Aside from the inside of his head, the only privacy available. He could see a pinochle game, three poker games. Doubtless the usual crap game was in session in the latrine. Back again. Everything as before.

Morrie was making his way down the room, stopping to talk to friends. The only man in the outfit taller than Haakon, and far more massive, he had even worse problems finding clothes that fit and getting used to sleeping in too-short beds.

Morrie had worked for a veterinarian before he enlisted. Haakon had asked him, "Why didn't you try to get into the Medical Corps?"

"I guess I was too goddamned discouraged," Morrie said. "After flunking German and Latin, I figured there was no way I could get into med school with grades like that.".

He talked him into studying again, and helped him with the grammar. Morrie had been the one who remembered enough math to take Polecat past simple arithmetic.

Strange how that agreement with Polecat had developed into a kind of informal class. To a large extent, no doubt, the men saw it as a way to kill time during the endless waits. But some of the men had been genuinely interested, had learned a great deal. He could become angry thinking of how many good minds were wasted because a teacher called a child stupid or lazy, would not take an extra five minutes to explain, or to discover what the problem was.

He still remembered the day he had come around a bulldozer blade he had used earlier for a blackboard and seen "The Professor was here" written at the top. He had felt as if he had been awarded an honorary degree.

Morrie saw him now and was coming toward him with that farmer's walk of his, as if he were trudging down a plowed field, lifting mud on his boots, holding his feet a little apart to keep his pants clean. When Coston had tried to tease him about it, he had grinned and agreed, putting on a Swedish accent: "I'm just a simple farmboy from Iowa."

The bunk next to him groaned under Morrie's weight as he sat. "Guess what?" His pale blue eyes were bright. "It turns out I'm the local hero. They can't do enough for me. I took a test in Latin and another in German, and passed with A's, and they're going to call those bad grades incompletes, so they won't be on my record. With the GI Bill, I'm home free."

"That's great."

"Thanks, Professor."

"No, I didn't do much of anything," he contradicted. "You put in the work. But you're welcome."

Morrie talked about his family, his girl friend, then said, "I think I'm going to go into pediatrics. Of course, I know I may change my mind, but you know how silly I get over any kind of baby."

Morrie cupped his hands, as if to cradle an infant, and he remembered the procession of abandoned puppies, kittens and, on one occasion, a lamb that Morrie had rescued and nursed back to health.

"You have a gift," he told him.

"Yes," Morrie agreed thoughtfully, "I've thought perhaps I do. I was always good with the animals, and they can't tell you where it hurts any more than a baby can."

After Morrie left, he remembered how Morrie had noticed he had a fever after he had been wounded. Had treated the wound and removed a quarter inch of discolored metal. Morrie had been quick and deft. He almost winced, recalling the feel and sound of metal against his shoulder blade. But he had kept quiet. He must have had his teeth clenched; his molars had ached for three days afterwards.

Over the next few hours he talked to almost everyone. Men

kept straggling in by ones, twos and threes. There was still no sign of Polecat.

Haakon said he had his old job back and diverted questions from himself by asking questions that got the men talking about what they had done on leave.

He had worried that his time with Simon would leave him vulnerable the way it had that time in London, and he was relieved to find that he was no more interested in the other men than he was in his students. He was leaning against the end of his bunk smoking a cigarette and congratulating himself when Dan came in.

Dan was walking carefully and precisely, as he did when he was trying not to show how drunk he was. In the harsh overhead light his face was hard and haunted, his eyesockets shadowed, the hollows under his cheekbones accentuated. His jaw was clenched, mounds of muscle showing at the corners.

As he watched him approach, he could not help thinking of the body under the uniform, the ridges of muscle over the hipbones, the powerful torso. He imagined flattening his hand on Dan's naked shoulder, feeling the hard shape of the muscles under that fine-grained skin. What would it be like to make love to a circumcised man?

His heart was racing and he was breathing too fast. He glanced hastily around, afraid his face might have betrayed him, but no one was looking at him. He forced his breathing back to normal, was immediately short of breath, and put out the cigarette. His hands had begun to shake. He put them in his pockets and gripped the outsides of his thighs with his fingertips. No good. In a moment he would be shaking all over.

He went to his footlocker and pulled out the first book he touched. Shakespeare. He made sure it was right side up and opened it, sat on his bunk and stared at it. "And all our yesterdays . . ." He had not done anything very wrong with his yesterdays, but nothing very good either.

How could he tell himself he loved Dan when just now he had been slavering over his body rather than wondering why Dan looked hag-ridden?

Dan was obviously upset, and there was something extremely odd about his appearance. It took him a while to figure out what it was.

Dan was as drunk as Haakon had ever seen him, but he did not have a hair out of place. He was as neat and clean as if he had just finished getting ready for inspection. Every other time Dan had gotten drunk he had been a mess long before he reached the stage where he was now.

28

"Just got back," Dan said, speaking slowly in an attempt not to slur his words, "Din't think I'd make it."

"What happened?"

Dan stared at him, eyes unfocused, the pupils dilated. "In Albany. I found out . . . She's been dead a year. My mother's dead. I've been celebrating."

"Celebrating?"

"Celebrating! You're fuckin' right!" Then he asked himself softly, puzzled, "Why in God's name am I still afraid?" He turned and began to wander off as if he had not been aware he was talking to anyone. Coming up against one of the square posts, he stopped, holding on to it, standing very quietly. He rested his forehead against the wood. At first glance he seemed relaxed, but the muscles across his shoulders were bunched and tense.

"What did she want of me?" Dan asked, "I can't help it if I look like my father, can I? Why wouldn't she believe me when I said I didn't know where he'd gone? She could have made a good guess, better than me. Out whoring, is what. Or getting drunk, poor bastard." He sighed. "Poor dumb bastard, lying there in the charity ward brushing off maggots that weren't there. Din't even know *me*."

"Who?" he asked, confused.

"My father." Dan turned his head toward him, but did not look at him. "She did it to him—chopped him up in little pieces. No matter what he did, it wasn't good enough. It wasn't his fault the factory closed, was it?"

Dan was waiting for a reply. "Of course not."

"And then she'd go after me, when he wasn't around. Not when I was little, but later, after I started to look like him."

"What did she do?" He had always wondered about Dan's background, but the few times he had asked, Dan had sworn at him, kept away from him for days afterwards.

"Yelled, mostly. Beat me too sometimes," Dan said with no feeling in his voice. Then he rubbed his eyes and, turning a little more, focused them on him with an obvious effort. In a more conversational tone he said, "I saw my sister. Jeanie's big now, and she's got a white stripe and green eyes just like me—only she's pretty. Real pretty. I couldn't talk to her though. She's staying with Aunt Freda now, and well . . . shit! That old bitch is as bad as her sister."

"But—"

Dan was not listening. He said, "So now she's dead. Dead and buried." He was talking to himself again, apparently unaware of his surroundings. "I went to the cemetery and looked at her grave. It's there, all right. Name, birth date, death date. Everything all official, cut nice and neat into the stone. Shiny gray stone you can see your face in. Expensive. Wonder who bought it. Aunt Freda most likely. Dirt's not sunk in yet, there's still a mound.

"The leaves have begun to turn up there in the hills. Gold and red maple leaves, falling. Like sunshine, burning. They were burning leaves, you could smell the smoke, but the grass is still green as summer there in the cemetery. Excuse me, Professor, I think I'm gonna puke." He said the last with no transition or shift in tone. He pushed himself away from the post, wheeled wide, then headed for the latrine, walking carefully, as though he were on a tightrope.

A moment later there were cries of outrage from the latrine. He followed Dan in. Dan had tried to take a shortcut to the toilets through the middle of a poker game and had vomited all over the cards and the players. He was standing sheepishly in the middle of the uproar, blinking.

"Feel better?" Haakon asked quietly, steering him away from the others.

Dan smiled, "Yeah, sure do."

Holding his shoulders, he guided him to his bunk. "Lie down."

"Yessir," Dan agreed blurrily, did as he was told and passed out. Neat and clean, not a speck on him. Bill Prideaux had gotten most of it. He was still bellowing and stamping around.

Haakon took off Dan's shoes and stayed to watch him for a few minutes, sprawled out with his mouth open, snoring.

His desire was gone, and for that he was grateful. Now the next few weeks before his separation from the service would be possible. He loosened Dan's belt and tie, undid his top shirt button and left him alone to sleep it off.

The following day Dan told him he had seen his sister, but made no mention of his mother's death. After a few minutes' conversation, it became apparent that Dan remembered nothing of the night before. When told what had happened in the latrine, he was surprised and apologetic.

He wanted to ask Dan about his mother's death, but somehow the time never seemed right, and Dan seemed to be avoiding him.

The night before they were formally discharged, Dan was unusually cheerful. He seemed to be all over the barracks, eating, laughing, joking as he normally did not. He got out all the souvenirs he had brought back with him—SS daggers, a Luger, a Leica with a bagful of lenses, a handful of Nazi medals—and proceeded to auction them off.

Then Dan came over to him with an antique chess set he had bought in the free city of Rothenburg. "Do you want this?"

30

Thinking he was being given first refusal, he asked, "How much?"

"No, I wanna give it to you."

"Why?" Hearing himself, he knew he sounded cold, but he was tired of worrying, wanting and feeling helpless. Dan was definitely going to San Francisco with Roger. He had lost him, would probably never see him again.

Dan looked puzzled, then explained: "Because you've been good to me, and I never know how to say thank you." He set the box down on the olive-drab blanket. "I thought . . ." Then angrily, "Throw 'em away if you wanna. I don't give a shit."

"Polecat, please."

Dan turned. "What?"

"Thank you. But in case you want them back someday, I'll keep them for you." He had to hope, he needed a thread to Dan, even so absurd and frail a one as this.

Dan shrugged. "I don't give a shit."

He watched him walk off and almost felt like crying.

December 13, 1945

The smell of chalk dust and damp wool. "In review," he lectured, "there was a long period of Roman rule lasting from approximately 146 until . . ." He surveyed the class. He should call on a student he had not picked recently. Steam knocked and banged in the radiators and pipes. It must be getting colder. Outside the window a few flakes of snow were falling. "Mr. Marsden."

He had to hunt for the name. The boy was so relentlessly average he had difficulty remembering it. Marsden duly disgorged a chunk of undigested text. He could not object. The information was accurate. But he suspected that it would only be retained until after exams.

A hand was raised in the back of the room. Steve Miller, shaggy brown hair, a chunky young man sprawling in his chair, head pillowed on the sheep's-wool collar of his Air Force flight jacket, looking bored. "Yes, Mr. Miller?"

"Greece wasn't a country then, it was a bunch of city states. So what happened in one place didn't necessarily happen in the next county."

"True, but this is supposed to be a survey course. There isn't time to go into much detail. Greece does get short shrift post-classically. Once a country is no longer powerful, its influence on the future diminishes."

Bart Oliver stopped staring out the window and scowled at him. "What was going on in China?" A clear challenge. Bart needed a haircut and a shave, looked piratical with his blue jaw, heavy eyebrows and hostile expression, but his hazel eyes were puzzled and searching. He seemed to have intimidated Randall, who had him in his American History class. Randall was constantly complaining about the ex-GIs' lack of respect anyway. He could not get it through his head that with these men you had to prove yourself, you could not expect your position alone to impress them. Easy enough to field Bart's question.

He said, "The end of the Han Dynasty, and the breakup of the country into three kingdoms. There was a period of almost constant war, internal discord and invasions from the borders. You can do your next paper on it if you like."

Looking vaguely interested, Bart grumbled, "Maybe I will."

"You do call the course World History," Patsy Frankle said, trying to apologize for Bart. She was one of the bright ones, intense dark eyes, straight silky black hair. Not too smart about Bart though. She could not keep her eyes off him, and he didn't know she existed. He was involved with a flashy big-breasted blonde called Chichi.

"Yes," he agreed. "It probably ought to be called European History with perfunctory notice taken that the rest of the world existed."

A bark of laughter from Bart. Steve smiled. A titter of nervous laughter rippled across the room; several students looked disapproving. Some students got upset if a professor openly admitted a shortcoming. Should get back on the subject.

But there was less than a minute left of class time. "In a sense," he said, "there's no way to tell the truth about history. If you take a broad view you have to leave out all the details, yet if you take a narrow view you become lost in them. What you have to work with is a loose mass of facts, guesses, documents that may or may not be truthful, and you have to organize it somehow. The organization is necessarily somewhat arbitrary—at least I know of no other way to do it. What I have tried to do is look for patterns, attempt to create a picture that makes sense and approximates the truth in hopes that it can be learned from. To quote Santayana, 'Those who do not learn from their mistakes are doomed to repeat them.'" His time was up; he gave the next week's assignment.

When he came out of the classroom he found Steve waiting for him in the hall. "Professor Hvitfelt?"

"Yes."

"How can there be a broad view? It's all such a mess, one god-damned thing after another. And you say, because this happened, then that happened, but you don't know that. You're only guessing."

"Not always, but yes, I see your point."

"None of it makes sense," Steve said moodily. "I was a bombardier, and I just looked at the crosshairs and dumped the load when I was supposed to. Afterwards I saw the cities we'd bombed. Have you any idea what Königsberg looked like after the war?"

"Yes. It was a flat horizon-to-horizon desert, white with plaster dust. A train track running down the middle. My outfit laid the track."

"I might've known you were in the service. You make some sense," Steve grumbled, then glanced at him and, seeing him as a person instead of only a professor, said, "When you drop those things you don't think, This one's going to land on a mother and her week-old baby. You know perfectly fucking well that when you do saturation bombing a hell of a lot of civilians are going to die, but you don't think about it. You worry about cloud cover and ack-ack. Then you look down, and there're no people. Just little toy houses and railyards and stuff. You don't remember the people till later, and by then it's all over and it's tomorrow."

"There's no answer to that problem in history or anywhere else," he said bleakly. "And I believe the Nazis had to be stopped."

"Babies aren't Nazis."

"No, but neither were the mothers and children my outfit shoved into mass graves at Schwartzgarten."

"No matter who kills them, no matter what the reason, that doesn't make any of them any less dead. And babies aren't guilty of anything." Then, appealing to him, "Don't you see? I feel responsible."

"Yes, so do I." An existential problem. How to help? Steve was a senior, and in general the quality of his thinking was good. "There's an informal discussion group that meets at my place Fridays around eight. No credit, but perhaps you'd be interested in dropping over."

"I thought only grad students were invited."

Amazing how fast word got around. "Mostly, but there are a few seniors."

"Hey, thanks!"

Later, walking home through the early December dusk, he found himself looking forward to the following evening when the group would meet. He could bring up the problem of guilt and responsibility. Many of the ex-servicemen were struggling with it, and just knowing he was not alone should help Steve feel better.

He would have liked to include more students in these discussions, but he did not have enough time to devote two evenings a week to it, and he could not allow the group to get too big. One year he had had twenty-five, and that had not worked out at all. He had to keep it somewhere around a dozen.

He could relax and enjoy the students more tomorrow with Simon out of town. Simon resented anything that curtailed his freedom to come and go as he pleased, and Friday evenings Simon had to stay away from the apartment. He could not risk questions.

Simon was in London now, taking pictures for advertising brochures. From there he would be going to Los Angeles. Portraits of celebrities. The kind of work Simon liked best, in big cities where the night life was exciting.

Large snowflakes fell slowly, melting as they touched the ground. The reflections of the traffic lights were red and green daggers on the wet asphalt streets. Cars passed infrequently. A bus roared and groaned its way uptown, leaving behind a stench of exhaust. Water dripped from the trees in the park.

At the corner of his street he hesitated, then walked on downtown to Gino's for dinner. His briefcase was not heavy and the restaurant had excellent food. He was always greeted warmly, as an old and valued patron, and given a table with good light.

While he waited for his veal scallopine he took a sheaf of term papers from his briefcase and began reading his way through them, penciling notes in the margins and grading them.

Most were better than passable, a few excellent. Then one that was not only incredibly dull and badly organized but so poorly written that he could not, even with effort, puzzle out which antecedents were intended to go with which pronouns. The name at the top was Walt Neumeyer. Sandy hair, football sweater, a copious taker of notes. Talked better than he wrote. Obviously in need of help. Give him an F with an explanation? No, better to give him a scare. If the boy did not come to him to ask about the grade he would schedule a conference.

After he had eaten he looked around the restaurant. It was not so busy that his table was needed, so he ordered a pot of coffee and spent the next half-hour finishing the papers.

Outside it was snowing more heavily, and the flakes were beginning to stick to the ground. He felt content.

He had another cup of coffee. He did not want to be alone, but he also enjoyed the freedom of not having to accommodate to the fact that Simon might be waiting. He did not need Simon as he once had. There had been a time when he had always rushed

home to him eagerly, had felt lost when he was out of town. Infatu-
ated, entranced by Simon's aliveness, bewitched, beguiled—all those
words. What was love anyway?

Simon threw the word around so freely it meant nothing coming
from him. He had used it the day they had met, and certainly had
not been telling the truth then.

Ten years ago, a decade. In Greece on sabbatical leave, he had
gone to see the Acropolis. Once there, he felt beset by the noisy
tourists and yammering guides, so he pretended to speak only Danish and went off by himself with his Baedeker.

He was walking slowly through the pale dust, referring to the
guidebook, half blinded by the whiteness of the pages, squinting
against the sun, wishing he had brought sunglasses. Sweating. He
came around a heap of marble blocks and saw Simon leaning negligently against a section of fallen Doric column—without sunglasses,
not squinting, hatless in the blazing light. He looked cool in pressed
shantung, impeccably British-tailored. Like a faun, not quite real.
Struck by his beauty, Haakon paused to look at him as if at a piece
of art. Dark, ageless, exotic. As if Pan, who belonged in green se-
cluded woodland glades, had irrationally decided to dress in a suit
and come to stand on this barren hill among the ruins. He became
instantly and thoroughly aware of his own grubbiness, of his crumpled suit, of the fact that he was disheveled, hot and all too human.

Realizing that he was staring, he started on. Simon came over
to him then, holding up a camera. "Would you mind terribly if I
used you in a picture? I've been waiting for ages for someone to
happen along. I need a figure, right over there, for the composition."
British-American accent. He had assumed he was Greek and was
surprised to discover he was not.

Taking acquiescence for granted, Simon guided him to the indi-
cated spot and arranged him. At that time he had disliked being
touched, especially by strangers, but he had liked Simon's hands
on him. Knowing him as he did now, he knew that Simon had been
seducing him automatically, almost by reflex, but at the time he
had been enormously flattered.

It was Simon's touch that had kept him from turning into stone,
given him life. Simon had taught him to laugh, to enjoy himself,
not simply endure one day after another. From the time Jim had
died he had lived ascetically, becoming drier by the year, as if the
quiet dustiness of library stacks had desiccated and mummified him.

Where had Simon learned to read ancient Greek and Latin?
So well that he could give a running translation of Pausanias. When
he had asked, he had been told airily, "Classic British education,

35

you know." No explanation at all. Simon was not British. He had an American passport: place of birth, Providence, Rhode Island. What an unlikely place for a faun to be born! At first he had asked questions, but had finally given up. Simon never refused to answer, but he made no effort to keep his stories consistent. He made up interesting, plausible-sounding tales to fit the occasion, laughed when reminded that this story did not fit the last and, if pressed, told another one equally fictional. Like quicksilver. Impossible to grasp.

He finished his coffee, paid the check and paused to button his topcoat before stepping out into the snowy dark. He owed Simon a lot. He had almost stopped living after Jim's death, had allowed none but the most superficial relationships. The pain of loneliness had become so familiar he had almost ceased to notice it.

The snow was falling more thickly and was beginning to pile up on the tree branches, to collect on the sidewalk. He glanced back at the dark imprints of his shoes. It had been snowing like this the day Jim died.

His mind automatically supplied him with the date: December 16, 1932. He had stood the deathwatch with Jim's wife and sons, his presence not questioned. Even though Martha Harrison had known for years that Jim was homosexual, she had never suspected that Haakon, the son of her best friend, was his lover.

He was five years younger than Jim's younger son. Since it provided a legitimate opportunity to be together, he and Jim had frequently gone horseback riding in Central Park, attended sports events together. "Jim was like a father to me" was sufficient explanation coming from a man who had never known his own father. And true as far as it went.

At the end Jim had asked for him and he had gone into the green hospital room. He looked at the gray wasted face and hardly recognized the man he had loved for almost half his life. The room smelled of strange medications, alcohol and harsh soap. Jim wanted him to kiss him goodbye, and he did, feeling only pity and horror, for he did not want to touch him. Jim's lips were dry and lifeless as ancient leather. White sediment crusted the corners. He could still almost shudder at the memory.

He turned quickly into his building, crossed the lobby and stepped into the elevator. He could not stop thinking.

He had known Jim all his life as a distant, benign figure. Whenever there was a household crisis, his mother had said, "Jim Harrison will know what to do."

But he had—in a sense—met Jim one October day two weeks

after his nineteenth birthday. After his mother's stroke Martha came several times a week to read aloud or chat while she did petitpoint.

That October day she brought Jim with her. One of those minor legal or monetary crises that required the family lawyer. When the doorbell rang he was sent to let the Harrisons in. He escorted them up to his mother's room and waited to be dismissed. After the round of greetings was over and the business attended to, his mother sent him downstairs with Jim with instructions to "entertain" him and give him a glass of sherry.

He followed him down the thickly carpeted narrow stairs. Jim was as tall as he, much broader and heavier, a man who had been physically powerful but was getting soft with age. His hair was thick and iron-gray, his eyebrows black. He had a closed-in lawyer's face, unresponsive, almost forbidding.

The sitting room was dark and gloomy. Thick velvet drapes closed out the afternoon sun. He went around turning on lamps. The room, as always, smelled faintly of potpourri and his mother's cologne. It was a high, narrow, claustrophobic room with dark wallpaper. He could not remember ever having felt comfortable in it. He got down the heavy cut-glass decanter of sherry and poured a glass, handed the glass to Jim. Their hands touched and they both stood unmoving, looking into each other's eyes. Jim's face changed. The stiff everyday mask disappeared and he looked almost like another person. Sensual, needy and open. Vulnerable. Suddenly handsome, as he ordinarily was not. There was no doubt in either's mind of the instant recognition.

Jim's acknowledgment of him and his own response had set the seal on his opinion of himself. He had been reading up on homosexuality for months, wondering if that was what was wrong with him, because he was not attracted to women and he dreamed of men. A relief, yet at the same time terrifying, because he did not want to be a "pervert."

Yet he had accepted the truth that day, and it had been less frightening because of Jim's respectability and because he was no longer utterly alone.

Jim took the glass of sherry and went to sit on the black horsehair loveseat. The lamp at his elbow cast ruby lights into the amber wine, and behind him his mother's Dresden figurines minced and simpered on the ornately carved mantel. Jim casually began talking about how he spent his days, his weeks. To anyone overhearing, it would have sounded like a banal recounting of schedules. Haakon responded by giving a similar account of his time, trying to match Jim's casual tone, gripping his hands together to keep them from shaking. By the time Jim had to leave they had worked out a time and place to meet, and no one listening could have guessed.

He unlocked the door to his apartment and went in. The oriental rug he had in the living room was the same one. In spite of his memories of his mother's house, he liked the rug—its looks as well as its practicality—for it did not show spots. Anyway, it didn't look the same here; the colors glowed richly in the light.

Jim had always been so unbelievably, neurotically careful, or so he had thought then. Now he could appreciate Jim's fear of losing everything. At the time, when he was young and had little to lose, he found caution an exciting game. They had met two days later in a delicatessen. He had hardly slept in between. A hundred times he resolved firmly not to go. In the end he went, torn between panic and desire. Not willingly, but not unwillingly either. He had to find out if he wanted Jim as much as he thought he did. He had to know who and what he was.

Jim took him to a small furnished apartment. He had been shocked that Jim kept such a place, yet he had gone to bed with him. After their first kiss he felt there was no turning back, for he had to recognize his response. Jim was gentle and careful, and did nothing to startle him. He made love slowly and skillfully, leading him to such a pitch of desire that when Jim finally put his mouth on him it seemed right, felt right. Was what he wanted. Afterwards, partly because the experience had been so shatteringly intense, he wept. Jim held him and comforted him, talked to him and told him he loved him.

Had he become set in his preference because that was Jim's, the only thing Jim wanted? Would he be different if Jim had been different, or had Jim simply happened to fit his needs? Before he had gone to Jim that first time he had not asked any questions. He was so naïve he hardly knew what the questions might be. He was afraid to think past a kiss.

And he had fallen in love with wholehearted adolescent passion. He would have done anything at all for Jim. Anything? he wondered now. Yes, perhaps. Difficult to say now. Could he have learned to like Simon's preference? Perhaps. He had been miserable for weeks because he could not keep himself from gagging. Ashamed to be letting Jim down, and simultaneously disgusted with himself because he was somewhat repelled by the whole thing. Jim had been patient, he had not hurried him. By a slow progression of stages he learned first how not to gag and then, finally, to want, even need, the texture and flavor of semen in his throat and on the back of his tongue. Over a year passed before he was excited by that part of it. It had not been easy, had not come naturally.

38

Not a built-in preference then, but something learned. But that being true, why couldn't he change? He did not know.

A strange sort of life he had led. All those years tied to his mother's sickbed. Jim, then Simon. And all during that time teaching, thinking and writing. Yet the only genuinely creative, definitive book he had written was locked away in his desk. He dared not publish it, assuming that he even could. It was titled, with bitter amusement, *Fairystory: A Study of Persecution.*

Jim had helped him with the beginnings of it, had helped him research anti-homosexual laws across the country and in other countries. He could still be shocked at how many places still had castration as a penalty, and how often it was enforced. He had begun the book in 1929 after Denmark passed a castration law.

He had never gone out to do research on the book the way he did on an article or a text, but he had collected information over the years and had kept it up to date. A sobering thought that in roughly half the states in the union he could be castrated or sent to prison for the rest of his life for being a practicing homosexual.

Jim had said once, "What a strange world we live in. It's beyond me how society can impose the same penalties on two consenting adults that it does on a child rapist. But to quote Mr. Bumble, 'The law is a ass.'"

What had begun as infatuation had grown into a mature love. There were still times when he missed having Jim to talk to.

He hung his wet overcoat on the corner of the closet door to dry and went to the windows to close the curtains. Instead of pulling the cords, he stood staring out into the night.

Automatically he picked up the stone paperweight from his desk. His fingers remembered all its contours. Jim had given it to him the first Christmas they were lovers. He held it cupped in his hand and looked at it, thinking how strange it was that he held it so frequently and looked at it so seldom. Red Manchurian soapstone. Rare and precious because it was not streaked with black. Old, very old, carved in China, where red and dragons were both considered lucky. Almost the size of a fist, a good, heavy handful. Only after close inspection could it be seen that the entire egg-shaped stone was carved into the design of a curled-up dragon.

"Like you," Jim had said, "ready to be born."

Half joking, half cynical, he replied, "Yes, and already petrified."

"Don't say things like that," Jim said, gripping his shoulders and shaking him. A rare flash of anger. "You're too young."

Not long after that Jim wanted to break off the relationship. He said, "Haakon, you're younger than my sons. I can't do this to you."

"You're not doing anything to me. I made my own decision."

That had been a week after Christmas. He wept, argued, pleaded and threatened, but Jim was adamant. On the way home he began to have trouble breathing. By the next afternoon he collapsed and had to be hospitalized. The worst asthma attack he had ever had. The more distressing because he had almost entirely outgrown his asthma years before.

He lay in the hospital fighting to breathe, worrying about his mother. Who would take care of her if he died? His fingernails were blue. Cyanotic. A doctor said, "Think he'll make it?" and he opened his eyes in time to see the other doctor shake his head. Every time he thought of that his chest constricted further with fear. He felt as if his lungs were stuffed tight with cotton.

Jim came to visit him and when they were alone said, "All right, Haakon. You win. I know you're telling me you can't live without me, and I believe you. Stubborn as you are, you just might do it."

He had felt outraged then, but when his breathing eased not ten minutes later he had to admit that Jim was probably right.

Love? What was it anyway? At that time he would have said that he and Jim were in love. Certainly they needed each other and cared deeply about each other.

After his mother's second stroke, when taking care of her became even more difficult and repellent, Jim had comforted him, always been there for him to turn to.

But Simon was different. Simon leaned on him, tormented him, beguiled him and only seemed to need him sometimes. That was not love—though perhaps it was for Simon. He did not understand him and never had. That was part of the fascination. Did he love him? A meaningless question in a way.

December 28, 1945

The early afternoon sun was beginning to shine into the room when he came back from lunch and sat down to reread the longhand chapters dealing with World War I. Yellow paper with blue lines, legal-sized.

He made a few minor changes, then put the sheaf of paper into a folder and took a subway down to his typing service. He paid for the work in advance—knowing the job would be errorless, for he had used the same service before—and asked them to send the completed typescript directly to Higgins at Meadows Press, the carbon to him.

He was tired of it, now that he was finished, and did not want to look at it again until he had to correct the galleys. He had begun to miss Simon. Simon had not written, but he had not expected him to. Simon sometimes did not write for months at a time when he was gone. He expected him back within the week, however, for Simon invariably showed up around New Year's—and just as invariably was gone over Christmas.

He got home at dusk to find a fire going in the fireplace and Simon singing in the shower. Liturgical music as always, plainsong this time. The cadences were strange, reminiscent of Arabic or Hebrew music. Simon's baritone was so clear and true he felt the hair on the back of his neck prickle. The sound of the water stopped and Simon finished his song.

He put his coat away and went over to the coffee table. He picked up the odd-sized cardboard box on it, sniffed it, looked inside. This week, apparently, Simon was smoking an exotic brand of scented Russian cigarettes with built-in holders. Violet-colored paper. God!

Even if he knew nothing else about Simon's lovers, he knew what brand of cigarettes the last had smoked. When these things were used up, Simon would start smoking his Luckies again. An odd quirk that Simon never bought his own cigarettes if he could possibly avoid it. Simon liked to give expensive presents and never concerned himself with the cost of anything, so why did he always mooch cigarettes?

Simon came out of the bathroom with his head enveloped in a towel, drying his hair. He had a deep tan, with no bathing-suit marks. To get a tan that dark Simon would have had to spend quite a while in the sun, but he had been in California, after all. Los Angeles.

Simon took his head out of the towel and saw him standing by the coffee table. "Darling, hello." He crossed to him, dropped the towel and put his hands under his jacket, deftly pulled out his shirttails and began stroking his back. "I've missed you," he said, looking up at him, smiling.

Simon was still wet. Water beaded the hair on his chest. Simon hugged him close, rubbed up against him, getting his shirt damp.

He stood with his hands hanging awkwardly at his sides, unable to respond and equally unable to push Simon away. Now that Simon was back he could admit to himself how much he had missed him, but he also knew that he was in for an exceedingly unpleasant half-hour. Simon was never able to refrain from telling him far more

41

than he wanted to hear about what he had been doing. Simon was moving in on him too fast. He felt overwhelmed.

Simon asked, "What's the matter?" And when he did not reply, stood on tiptoe, pulled his head down and kissed him.

After brief resistance he could not keep from responding as hungrily as ever. He did not remember putting his arms around Simon, but he was holding him tightly. Resignedly he thought, Here we go again.

Was there any way to keep Simon from telling him what he had been doing? If he so much as asked him how he had been, Simon would use that as a lead-in. He tried to brace himself for what was sure to come and said noncommittally, "Hello, Simon." Brandy would help him through it. He held Simon away, said, "Excuse me," and went into the kitchen, where he poured himself half a glass straight.

Simon had gone to stand in front of the fireplace, leaning on the mantel, smoking one of the long violet cigarettes. It smelled vile. Firelight flickered across his body.

He sat down in his leather armchair and lit a Lucky, hoping to blank out some of the odor. He drank some brandy and watched Simon. Waiting, trying to turn off all his feelings.

"Aren't you going to ask me about my trip?" Simon complained.

"No. I don't want to know about your lovers."

"Oh, Haakon! You're such a drag sometimes. I keep telling you that none of them mean anything to me."

"I don't want to hear about them."

"But listen! Take Norm, for instance. How could you be jealous of *him?* Granted he was a lovely piece of beef. Body beautiful and all that—ate all sorts of strange things like wheat germ and soybeans. Lifted weights. But at twenty all he could do was look in mirrors and alternate between admiring his muscles and worrying about wrinkles. It didn't take me long to get tired of listening to his head echo. I'd have left him in a day or so even if he hadn't blown it. We were in Frisco and came around a corner right into a bunch of fairyhawks. Do you know what Norm did? All 218 pounds of him? Shoved me into their arms and ran."

Concerned, he asked, "Did you get hurt?" And realized he had been suckered again.

"Not much. Got one of my better nosebleeds and ruined a new suit though. I bit one, kicked another in the basket and got away. Norm apologized, of course, but I told him that if he ever *spoke* to me again, I'd stick a pin in his muscles and let the air out."

Simon was trying to be comical and his timing was superb. He could not keep from smiling, though even as he did he knew he was only encouraging Simon to go still further.

"I almost came home then, but I was in the middle of a series of portraits of an over-the-hill actress who's trying to make a comeback as Queen of the Purple West or some such nonsense in a sagebrush epic. She wanted everything soft-focus, of course, but I have some superb shots she doesn't know about. She'll sue me if she ever sees them. She talked me into staying with her as a houseguest. Of course I had to grease up her ego and screw her a couple of times. God, what a bore! But she had a marvelous heated pool and an extraordinarily talented protégé—in bed, that is. As an actor he was a disaster. He'd been an acrobat, had muscles all over, but flexible. Could he give a shrimp job!"

"Simon, stop it." He was angry with Simon for telling him so much and even angrier with himself for listening. "No more. Nothing at all. Why in hell do you always insist on giving me the gory details?"

"It's your own fault," Simon said sulkily. "I'd have come home *ages* ago if you'd just give me sex the way I want it."

"I've tried to," he told him wearily. Then, angry, "You damn well know I've tried. If I can't keep it hard, what in hell am I supposed to do? Tie it to a stick?" He drained the last of his brandy and went to the kitchen for more. But anger was not going to solve anything. Perhaps if he explained reasonably, Simon could be convinced that he really did not want to know about his affairs. Not even that he had had them, and certainly not the details.

He brought his drink back into the living room and reseated himself. "Simon," he said slowly and carefully, "I can't imagine what you like about being buggered, but all right, I'll believe you when you say you want it and need it. Since I can't oblige you, maybe you do have to go elsewhere for it, if it's that important to you. But for Christ's sake, stop coming home and talking about it. There's no need for you to torment me."

"I don't mean to torment you. I won't do it any more." Simon sounded sincere, but he always did.

He had the nightmarish feeling of being caught in a movie, of doing the same scene over and over. There seemed no way out, short of breaking up with Simon, and he could not do that.

Simon was posing. He did it automatically, but he was also counting on Haakon's reaction to him. He looked very much like the Cellini Perseus, most of his weight on one foot, his head bent, face pensive.

He could not keep from admiring him. He was beautiful, and with the dark tan looked almost like a bronze in a museum.

43

Simon was watching him calmly, waiting out his upset. Simon knew the script as well as he did, knew that all he had to do now was keep quiet and be patient.

Did Simon hurt him purposely? Or was it possible that Simon really could not comprehend that he hated hearing about his liaisons? Simon certainly took them lightly, ascribed little meaning to them. Was it possible to stop caring so damn much?

Almost at the moment that his anger was replaced by sadness, Simon threw his cigarette into the fire and crossed to him. Simon knelt in front of him and took off his shoes and socks, then began to unbutton his shirt. Kissing his neck and chest, his breath warm against his skin, whispering, "My love, my beautiful Dane."

Still hurt, even though no longer angry, he wished to resist, but unable to deny his love, he heard himself say, "Oh, hell, let's go to bed."

"Yes, much more comfortable," Simon agreed, kissing him. Then taking his hand, he pulled him to his feet and started toward the bedroom saying, "God, you're a slob! You hadn't changed the sheets since I left, had you? They were absolutely *black!*"

"Perhaps I need you to take care of me," he said, trying to make it sound like a joke.

He was awakened later by Simon shaking him. Simon sat up in bed and switched on the light, demanding, "Who in hell is Dan?"

"Huh?" He sat up, shading his eyes against the sudden glare. "Huh?" He could not collect his thoughts.

"Dan. Who's Dan? What have you been up to? One of your students? People who talk in their sleep shouldn't cheat."

"I don't understand."

"You woke me just now feeling me up and calling me Dan. Now who is he?"

"Did I do that?" he asked, appalled. He could not remember having dreamed.

"You sure as hell did. And I want an explanation."

"Oh." He felt stupid and confused. Hoping to wake himself up more, he got out of bed, went into the living room in his pajamas, sat down in his chair and lit a cigarette.

Simon followed him out, turned on a lamp and went into the kitchen. He came back with a bourbon and water and flopped down on the couch. The ice in the glass clinked. Simon's face and hands were dark against the white of his pajamas. Why did Simon always wear white pajamas? Irrelevant.

"Well?" Simon demanded imperiously.

"Dan is not a student, and I haven't been up to anything. And

44

even if I had been I don't see where you get off objecting. Considering how you behave."

"That's different."

"One set of rules for you? Another for me?"

"No, but you know I don't love any of them. And just this evening you said you understood that I really have to go elsewhere sometimes."

"I suppose I did."

"Now, who's Dan?"

It was none of Simon's business. There was no reason why he had to tell him anything at all. But he had never spoken of Dan to anyone, and he wanted to talk about him. Perhaps talking would ease the sadness of having lost him, enable him to deal with it better.

"Dan is Polecat Albany. You met him in London when we were there before D-Day."

"I remember him," Simon said immediately. "That obnoxious little beast you had trailing after you for half a night. Ugly face, smashed nose, stripe of white hair. And yes, a truly magnificent body—a body worth dreaming about, I'll grant you *that*." Then reproachfully, "You told me you never did anything like that in the Army."

"I didn't. I never touched him. All I did was teach him—and not what you're thinking—how to speak good English, some history and geography. That's all."

"No, that's not all," Simon contradicted. "You're still dreaming about him after all this time. It can't be all. You're in love with him, aren't you? Good God, Haakon! How can you be? You of all people in love with a sadist?"

"He's no sadist."

"If he's not, I don't know what else to call him. I was there, remember? The night he got in that fight. I watched him break that sailor's arm over his knee. He did it deliberately."

"He's not like that at all when he's sober. That streak of savagery only comes out when he's both drunk and angry."

"Not savagery, sadism. And you love him."

"I didn't say that."

"You don't have to. And I remember how you talked about him in London. About his quick mind, his eagerness to learn, how you enjoyed teaching him. And I said, 'Watch out, Haakon, don't play Pygmalion. You could be in over your head before you know it.' And you laughed at me and said there was no danger of that. I believed you because I couldn't imagine you getting involved with a sadist."

"Stop calling Dan a sadist! You're completely wrong about that.

He's certainly hostile and seems angry a good deal of the time, but under that he's kinder than most people. He was the one who helped me out during basic training, carried my pack. He helps people, but he always does it in such a way that I think he doesn't want to get caught at it. He's worth a great deal, Simon. And he's never had a chance. I had hoped—"

"So you want to save his soul."

"Don't make fun of me, Simon." As soon as he spoke he knew Simon was not making fun of him. Simon was being completely serious for once, and his face looked different. There was a sadness and regret in his expression that made him look more mature. A facet of Simon he had never seen before.

"I wasn't," Simon said quietly.

"Yes, I spoke too hastily. I'm sorry."

"No, it's all right. I don't blame you, considering how I usually treat you."

Yes, for now Simon had stopped all his playacting. He could trust him, talk to him. He said, "Save his soul . . . yes. You could put it that way. It's as good a way as any. I wanted to see him make something out of his life, Simon. Not just piss it away whoring, drinking and fighting. I wanted to see him get an education, become somebody. But he's not my creation, it's not a Pygmalion thing. I love him like a son too. . . . I'll never have a son of my own, Simon."

"I know."

Yes, Simon knew. He found himself remembering the last time he had seen Dan—the threadbare hope that he might come back for the chess set—and he said despairingly, "But I'll never see him again unless he contacts me, and why should he do that? He's straight, as far as I know."

"Then why are you hoping he'll come to you?"

"Hope? Not any more. I've run out of hope. It's been too long now."

"But you have hoped," Simon said gently. "You must have had a reason."

"It seemed . . . for a while . . . perhaps self-delusion, but I thought he might be a latent homosexual. He chased women as if his life depended on it, joylessly, grimly, with single-minded determination. As if he were seeking something and was trying one woman after another hoping to find it. But he never did, because he was always hungry, always desperate. He never came back from town satisfied or happy."

"Yes, I see. Yes, when I was in university I did that for a while. Finally gave it up as a bad job. It was worse than a bore, it was a chore. You could be right about him."

46

"Even if I am, what's the difference? If he hasn't come to me yet, he won't."

"Oh, Haakon."

The compassion in Simon's tone made him look up. Simon stubbed out his cigarette and came over to him, sat on the arm of the chair and put his arm around him, holding him comfortingly, without a hint of seductiveness.

Despondently he said, "Simon, what can I do?"

"I don't know. I suppose eventually you'll get over him. One always does, you know. You'll have to stop hoping first, though."

"I guess I am still hoping. You see, even if he's straight, even if I can't have him, I still don't want him to go to waste. And he's so damn self-destructive, so angry. I worry about him. He could kill someone in a drunken rage, end up in jail, or get himself killed. And maybe there's still an off-chance that he'll come to New York, that I can at least see he gets educated. I'd settle for that."

Simon had pulled his head against his side and was stroking his hair. He rested against him, needing him, knowing that at least for now Simon would be kind.

After a few minutes Simon said thoughtfully, "I hope he comes to you, Haakon. I hope he doesn't, but I hope he does."

"Why?"

"Because you want to save his soul, I suppose. I guess it isn't all gone. There's more left in me than I'd thought."

"What?" The remark made no sense at all.

"Never mind."

Or did it make sense? Simon could sing his way through an entire High Church Anglican mass, including the consecration. Simon never went near a church except to take pictures, he avoided religious holidays and was bitingly anti-clerical, yet every time they had been in England together, Simon had been recognized and greeted by Anglican clergymen. They were usually not very warm, but they were obviously curious and always asked what he had been doing. Simon could have learned Latin and Greek in divinity school. He asked, "Simon, were you a priest?"

"Not quite." And before he could ask anything more, he went on: "Haakon, please don't push me. I know you're hurting, and I don't want to make it worse for you, but if you ask me any more questions, I'll just have to make up a story for you, and you don't need that. So don't, please."

"Yes, all right." He had to respect Simon's request. Simon had never before been so honest and open with him. He did not want to do anything to drive him back into his usual pose.

After some time Simon said, "Perhaps—just perhaps—someday

I'll tell you. But there are some things none of us want to remember. And, even if I wanted to, I'm too old to change now."

"You're not old, you're only thirty-four."

"I was born old. And to get back to Dan. He worries me. If he shows up and he's not gay, that's all right. You could send him to school and that's safe enough. But if he's gay—and from what you said, he could well be—then I'd worry."

"Why?"

"You deny he's sadistic, but I've seen him in action, and I must disagree. I'm afraid that if you get sexually involved with him, he'll hurt you. I mean physically. I've had a few go-arounds with men like him, and they're dangerous."

"No, Simon. I knew him for three years. Ate with him, worked beside him, spent hours teaching him. He's not like that."

Simon shook his head. "You don't know that, all you know is the face he shows and what you want to see. Can you imagine what he could do to you if he became disappointed in you? Got jealous? Was drunk?" Then he answered himself. "No, you can't. You're so naïve it's a sin. Listen, I spent six months with a man like that. Before we met. People like that fascinate me, I'll admit it, and I always think I can manage them. Generally can too. I like to play with fire. There's enormous excitement in danger, you know. But that time I came close to dying very unpleasantly. Please, Haakon, if he comes to you, and turns out to be gay, be careful."

"He wouldn't hurt me."

"Perhaps not. I've never seen him sober. Perhaps not. But I think— If he shows up I'll get out of the way. I don't want to be responsible for making him jealous and getting you hurt. And more important, I'll never really have you back until he's out of your system one way or another."

"Simon—"

"Shhh." Simon kissed the top of his head. "Come on now, it's late. Let's go to bed and get some sleep."

January 23, 1946

Just before dawn the phone rang. He came awake instantly and hurried to the living room, picked it up on the second ring. Last time it had been a wrong number, an apologetic drunk.

"Hvitfelt here."

"Professor?"

His chest constricted. "Yes, is that you, Polecat?"

"Far as I know." Dan's voice sounded strange and he began coughing almost before he finished speaking.

"Where are you?"

"Dunno. In a phone booth someplace. Wait a sec." Coughing again. It sounded as if he had dropped the receiver. There was a long pause, then, "At 103rd and Second Avenue. How the fuck did I get *here?*" His cough interrupted him. *"Ich bin . . ."* Dan's voice trailed off. "I mean, I'm kinda sick. Everything keeps getting wavy alla time."

"Polecat, wait for me? Let me come and get you."

"Wait?"

"Yes, please, Polecat? Just stay where you are. I'll come and get you."

"Got no place else to go, Professor. Sure, why not?" Coughing again, it seemed for minutes, then before he could double-check to be sure Dan had given the correct location, Dan repeated, "Sure, why not?" and hung up.

In the thin predawn light from the window, he wrote, "103 & 2d," on the pad by the phone. Sleet tapped on the glass, driven by a steady wind. Cold out. He looked around. Simon was standing in the bedroom doorway watching him. "So he came to you," he said, showing no emotion at all, in either his face or voice.

"Simon, he's ill. Seriously from the sound of his cough. And he says things look wavy to him. I have to go and get him. He's waiting for me."

"I'll be gone when you get back."

"No, Simon, don't do that."

"You mean you want to take us both on?"

"Nothing of the sort, and you know it. He's sick. I have to see that he's taken care of." He went into the bedroom, stripped off his pajamas and began to dress.

Simon lay down on top of the covers and watched him, hands behind his head. "Actually," he said, "this solves a little problem I had. Narcisio—perhaps I mentioned him? No? He's a manufacturer I met in Rome. He's been in the city for a week, and he's been *begging* me to fly to Brazil with him on his private plane. I've kept the poor fellow dangling for days now, trying to make up my mind. I've never been to São Paulo, and I hear it's an interesting city." He grinned like a lascivious angel. "All those passionate Latins. Including Narcisio too, of course. He's nearly as well-hung as you are—"

"Simon, please?"

"Oh, yes, I forgot you don't want to know about that."

"Don't go."

"Don't be a dog in the manger. And anyway, I've no intention of staying here in the city eating my heart out and wondering what you're doing."

"But he's probably straight. There's no need for you to leave. I'll only keep him here until he's back on his feet, that's all."

"No, that's not all."

"How can you know?"

"Because he came to you. And, as I told you, I'm going to give you a clear field. I think the farther away I get the better, because I'd rather like to behave decently for once. And if I'm around, I'm sure to meddle. I always do."

He finished tying his shoes and went to the living room closet for his topcoat. Simon followed him and helped him into it. He embraced him. "Simon, really, you don't have to run away."

"I'm not running away," Simon said indignantly. "I'm taking a plush vacation with Narcisio. Now you just run along to Wolf Boy."

"Simon . . ."

Simon prevented him from saying more by putting his hand over his mouth. "I'll keep in touch," he said. "If Wolf Boy isn't gay, or if you get tired of him or whatever, you can write and I'll come home. And if he's gay, for God's sake be careful." Simon kissed him gently and thoroughly. "You poor love-struck idiot." He pushed him toward the door. "Goodbye, darling." Simon kissed him once more, then bundled him out into the hall and closed the door.

The cab he had finally managed to hail seemed to be hardly moving as it proceeded crosstown. The sleet was mixed with rain, the tires swished through puddles, the windshield wipers clicked like a mechanical heart. The city was a black-and-white photograph, all color washed out. What if Dan did not wait? Perhaps he had given the wrong location and was waiting for him somewhere else where he could not find him. Perhaps he had wandered off. He had sounded delirious. It was not like him to lapse into German. "Couldn't you hurry?"

The driver grunted and the cab continued at the same slow pace. Sleet spattered on the windows, raindrops ran down the glass like tears.

Simon should not be leaving, should not have taken Dan so seriously. He could not be sorry Dan had called, but it seemed ironic that he had done so now, just as he was finally getting over him, just when Simon was showing a side of himself that was more lovable.

As soon as they turned into 103rd Street he saw Dan standing in the middle of the sidewalk, head tilted up so the rain fell on his face, making no effort to protect himself from the cold. Dan slowly turned his head and looked at the headlights of the taxi, but otherwise did not move. His clothes were black with water, and neither his shirt nor his thin denim work jacket was buttoned.

Dan seemed not to recognize him. He did not respond when he spoke to him, just stood with a kind of animal patience, rain running down his face and chest. When he took hold of him to steer him into the cab he could feel the heat of fever through the chill of the sodden clothes.

"What in God's name were you doing out there?"

"Nice, cool, felt good." Dan sounded sleepy. The sound of his breathing filled the cab. Dan was thin and dirty. His stripe of white hair was gray as the city sidewalks, and he reeked. A nauseating stench compounded of cheap whiskey, vomit, old stale sweat and an incongruous blend of salted fish and the tannery smell of raw hides. Where had he been? Perhaps sleeping on the cargo in a warehouse or the hold of a docked ship.

Haakon struggled out of his overcoat and tried to put it around him to get him warm. Dan pushed him away. "No, I'm hot."

When they reached the apartment, he took him directly to the bathroom and undressed him while he ran a tub of warm water. Dan was quiet and passive, allowed himself to be undressed, but was of very little help.

He got him into the tub and began to wash him. Strange, he had dreamed about him, daydreamed, imagined what it would be like to touch him. Yet now that he had his hands on him, washing him all over, soaping and rinsing him, he felt only tenderness. What he imagined a mother might feel toward a sick child. Dan's cough and difficulty in breathing were becoming frightening. He washed his hair, considered cleaning his ears more thoroughly than he could with the washcloth and decided that could wait. He had to get him to bed and call a doctor.

Getting Dan out of the tub was far more difficult than getting him in had been. Dan was wet, slippery, and less rational than before. As the dirt had come off he had seen that Dan was covered with scrapes and had a severe, badly swollen bruise across his ribs. The probability of broken ribs made handling him even more of a problem.

Finally he talked him out of the tub, dried him and steered him into the bedroom. He covered him to the chin. He noticed that Simon had changed the sheets.

He had to get a doctor and did not know where to start. He had no personal physician, and he certainly could not call any of the doctors who were connected with the university.

He went to his desk in the living room to look in the phone

book. On the blotter near the phone, weighted by the soapstone egg, was a note.

Darling,

Sometimes I'm so noble it sickens me, but if Wolf Boy is as ill as you seem to think, you'll need a doctor. Ben Solomon is one of the best, lives in the building. He's not gay, but he won't give you a hard time.

Love, S.

There was a phone number under the signature. He dialed it, grateful to Simon. Simon had been kind when he had told him about Dan, had seemed to understand. If only Simon could show such consideration more often.

Dr. Solomon agreed to come and was at the door within minutes, still yawning, hair uncombed. The doctor was not at all what he had expected. He was young, a little chubby, and walked with a pronounced limp. As soon as he saw Dan's face, he came wide awake. "What happened to him?"

"I've no idea. I picked him up in a cab a little while ago and just finished getting him to bed. He starts coughing if he tries to talk, and he isn't making sense anyway, so I haven't tried to ask him any questions." He had seen Dan often enough after he had been fighting so that the state of his face had not disturbed him. He had hand-checked it for broken bones, found none and dismissed the black eye and bruises as unimportant. It took the doctor's questions now to make him realize how bad Dan's face really looked. He noticed that two of Dan's front teeth were broken diagonally.

Solomon looked up from his examination. "He has pneumonia. He belongs in a hospital."

At this Dan opened his eyes. "No! I won't go to no fucking hospital. No, god damn it, no!" He tried to sit, could not, began coughing and reaching out appealingly, said, "Don't let him, Professor."

He took Dan's hand. "Calm down." Dan pulled him closer and gripped his wrist. He said to the doctor, "Let him stay here."

"Have you any idea what that involves? Round-the-clock nursing care, glucose, oxygen, shots every four hours—in short, a hospital. I couldn't allow it."

"I'm competent to care for him," he said, feeling distant and cold, reminded of the years of caring for his mother. He had lived in an emotional vacuum, pity nullified by disgust, tenderness nullified by despair, chained by duty, guilt, love and his own timidity. He said, "For years my mother was almost totally paralyzed. She

52

didn't like the nurses to handle her, so I had to do everything. Bed pans, enemas, catheters, Levine tubes, injections, all the massaging and cleaning necessary to prevent decubitus ulcers. He won't need half of that. I've not administered oxygen, but you could show me how."

"IV?"

"Yes, in the Army."

"Please, Professor." His arm ached in the tightness of Dan's grip. Dan looked frightened, helpless. "No hospital, they hurt you there. They tied me up and hurt me, and . . ." He lapsed into German, delirious again.

He listened intently, trying to make sense of what Dan was saying, trying to put the fragments into some kind of order.

"Do you understand him?"

"Yes." He motioned the doctor to be quiet. But Dan stopped muttering. "As far as I can make out, he was in a hospital as a child. Nobody there spoke German, and he didn't speak English. He thought they were going to kill him, saw the ether as an attempt to smother him. Odd, the Army hospital didn't seem to bother him."

"No, he wasn't toxic then. He'd been wounded. Different situation. Yes, I thought so, he's had his tonsils out. Probably around age seven—that's when it's usually done. What was that about his mother?" Then, at his inquiring look, shook his head, "No, I don't understand him, but I do know a little Yiddish."

"That was most unclear, but I think he thought she wanted to get rid of him. I would guess that some sort of family crisis coincided with his tonsillectomy."

The doctor nodded. "He seems to have been beaten up."

"He gets in fights when he's drunk."

"Hmmm . . . wonder what the other guy looks like."

"Will you let him stay?"

Solomon got out adhesive tape and began applying it to Dan's ribs. "Sure, why not? He's strong. He probably hasn't eaten in over a week, but he was in top condition before that. And I've been watching him. He reacts well to the sound of your voice, becomes less restless. He could be a real handful in a hospital, strong as he is, delirious and frightened. Might have to be put in restraints." He shook his head. "Have you some extra pillows we can use to prop him up?"

When the doctor went to phone for oxygen Haakon stayed behind with Dan, who had surfaced and stopped muttering in German. Dan looked at him anxiously.

He smoothed the hair back out of his eyes, shocked again by

the heat of his fever. "It's all right, Polecat, you can stay here. Do you understand?"

Dan nodded, closed his eyes and relaxed.

It was not until he got into the living room that he remembered that he had left Simon's note beside the phone. Solomon had hung up. He said curtly, "Sorry, I saw my name and recognized Simon's handwriting." He held out the note to him and Haakon took it.

The change in the doctor's attitude was too striking to be overlooked. Simon had said this man would not make things difficult. Simon must have found him tolerant. "What's the matter?"

"On second thought, I think I'd better cancel the oxygen and call an ambulance. I don't want to be responsible for leaving him here."

"Why? You examined him and everything was all right."

"How old is he?"

"Twenty-one."

"What makes you think so?"

"We were in the Army together."

"Were you lovers?"

"My God, no!" Shocked by the presumption and suddenly furiously angry. "God damn it! I don't know what you think I am. I may be a fairy, but I'm not some sort of sex maniac. You stand there smugly making judgments as if the fact you're a hetero makes you better, wiser and more ethical than I am. I wouldn't dream of touching a boy who was under age. And furthermore, what are you thinking? That I'll do something obscene to him while he's too sick to defend himself? I think it would be best if you left now. I'll simply have to find another doctor if you won't treat him. I promised Dan I'd keep him here, and I've no intention whatsoever of breaking my word."

"Hey, easy." The doctor's attitude had shifted.

He was appalled at himself for losing his temper the way he had, but he meant what he had said, he was not going to back down.

"You're right. I was out of line," Solomon said. "But please, would you tell me what your interest in him is? I'd feel more comfortable if you would."

"All right. In the Army I taught him to speak good English. He's got an excellent mind, and I wanted to see him get educated, have a chance at something better than stevedoring and drinking himself to death. He's self-destructive, and he's bleeding psychologically. Why, I don't know. As Simon put it, I want to save his soul. That's why Simon left, so he wouldn't come around and louse things up. His idea, not mine. Secondarily, I think Dan may be a latent homosexual. If he is, that's something else—and none of your god-damned business."

"I see," Solomon said in a neutral tone. Then more warmly, "I believe you, and thank you for being honest with me."

"Did I have a choice?" he asked bitterly. Then, anxiously, "Are you going to treat him then?"

"Yes, and now that I think about it, he probably is of age. The lack of beard and body hair made me wonder." Solomon was explaining, his tone no longer at all hostile. "But certainly his bone structure and muscular development are mature."

"Thank you, Doctor."

"Please call me Ben. I'd prefer it. We'll have to be working together for a few days." Then, becoming businesslike, he began giving detailed instructions on how to care for Dan. When he was finished he looked at his watch. "Too late to go back to bed. I'll stick around and help you start the oxygen. It will be here soon. Got any coffee?"

He made coffee and breakfast. He regretted having lost his temper and wanted to make up for it.

Ben apparently also felt apologetic. He said that Simon had helped him find his apartment. Then, explaining how he had come to know Simon, Ben said, "Simon was almost the first patient I had after getting out of the Navy. I'd been on an aircraft carrier in the Pacific and I was only in the service six months when I lost my leg. Of course, I'd talked to the Navy squirrel-doctors and all that. I wasn't shattered about it, but . . . losing a leg at my age. I didn't feel like much of a man somehow. Then Simon tried to seduce me. I'm an amateur photographer and I'd admired his work long before I met him.

"Two things happened. He made me feel attractive again and, more important, scared the hell out of me. He damn near seduced me. He'd been talking me around for days, and there's something very appealing about him—a childlike directness—and he's so unique, so physically beautiful that he seems an exception to all the rules, as if trying something like that with him wouldn't count. I actually found myself considering it.

"I'd been afraid to talk about my leg to Ruth—my fiancée—and then suddenly I had to face it with her. She let me know she doesn't mind. She loves me." Ben smiled. "When I told Simon I was engaged and thanked him, he struck one of his poses and said, 'That is *not* the outcome I had in mind.' But I could tell he was glad for me."

"It might even have been the outcome he had in mind. I think sometimes that Simon saves souls in his own way." If Ben had been seduced by him, would Simon have been pleased about it?

Ben nodded. "I'd have liked to be friends with him, but . . . I'm still a bachelor and frankly he's— Well, I have to think of my reputation. In the hospital he seduced a male nurse, two orderlies, a thoracic surgeon, and the executive officer before he was discharged."

"At least that's what he told you."

"He wasn't kidding about the surgeon. Do you think he was about the others?"

"Probably. Simon loves to shock people." Haakon wondered why Simon had been hospitalized and why he had never mentioned it.

After Dan was in oxygen, Ben left. He watched Dan for a while until he was sure he was resting comfortably. Dan's breathing had already improved. Then he went to the bathroom and was forcefully reminded by the stench that he had to do something about Dan's clothes. They were still wet. He picked them up. Jeans, a work shirt, jacket and shoes. That was all. No underwear, no socks, not even a belt. He cleared the pockets, laying the items on top of the toilet tank. A worn bent wallet, sixty-one cents in change and a silk scarf so dirty its apparent color was dark gray.

He looked at the scarf. Dan had in his possession nothing but the most minimal necessities, therefore it was logical to assume that the scarf was a necessity too.

In the Army Dan had had a dark green silk scarf that he had passed off as a lucky charm. Not hard to do, considering how many men carried all sorts of things for luck. But he had noticed something furtive about the way Dan handled the scarf. And Dan always took it with him when he went into town, folding it small and stuffing it into his pocket. One night in occupied Germany Dan had discovered his scarf was missing and had gone into a rage.

Dan had been about to go after the man he thought had stolen it, when he had stopped him. They were alone in the barracks. He said, "Polecat, if the other men find out what that means to you, how are you going to live?"

Dan stared at him blankly for a moment, then he went pale and nodded. A few minutes later Dan left, and he did not return until the following morning during inspection, looking as if he had spent the night in hell. Later that day he noticed that Dan had replaced the scarf with a piece of parachute, and several days later Dan had another scarf, brown this time.

Not a lucky piece at all. It could only be a fetish. He made up a bundle of all the dirty laundry in the apartment with Dan's clothes in the middle, hoping the smell would not leak through. He should not send the scarf to the laundry or cleaners. Dan might want it. But it had to be washed. He felt almost embarrassed to be handling it, but there was nothing else to do. After washing it in the kitchen sink, he hung it over the dishtowels to dry. He had not been able to get all the stains out. He hoped they would be less obvious when it dried. It was long and narrow, pale blue with a white design at the ends.

He cleaned the bathroom and tub, pausing frequently to check on Dan, then went to the kitchen for another cup of coffee.

God, the time! This was a school day. He had to call the university and cancel his seminars, classes and appointments. He would not be able to leave the apartment until Dan was out of danger. He called the university, made arrangements for instructors to take over his classes, then called the laundry and asked them to pick up the dirty clothes. He made out a grocery list and called the market.

He took his coffee cup back to the kitchen and glanced at the scarf again. So maybe Dan was not a latent after all. That desperate searching could have been looking for a way to free himself of the fetish.

He rinsed and dried the cup. Most probably he would never know what Dan did with the scarf. Not likely he'd ever have him, and Dan sure as hell would not tell him.

In love with a heterosexual fetishist. God damn it! How about all the plans and altruism? All right, he would do what he could to educate Dan. Just have to settle for that.

By the end of the afternoon Dan's care was sufficiently routinized so he did not have to think back and double-check everything he did. Dan's breathing improved steadily, and he stopped muttering in German. Around dusk he woke.

Haakon unzipped the oxygen tent. "How are you feeling?"

"Professor?"

"Yes."

"You came and got me."

"Don't you remember?"

Dan thought a minute, then shook his head. He glanced around. "What's this thing?"

"An oxygen tent."

"I don't like it." He began to cough, automatically reached to hold his side.

He caught Dan's arm. "You're on IV. Take it easy."

"Oh." Dan looked down at the needle taped to his forearm, then up at the bottle of glucose.

"Dan, would you tell me your real name? I'd like to know it."

"Daniel . . . Heydrich . . . Reinach," he said unwillingly, lapsing into Teutonic gutturals. "Heydrich after my father."

"How old are you?"

"Twenty-one. Go look in my wallet. I've got my Army discharge, California driver's license, union card. Go look."

"No, I believe you." He felt better to hear the confirmation. Ben's doubts had worried him. Dan had no trace of beard, just a shadow of fine hair on his upper lip. But some men had little hair, and some developed beards late. He had not had enough to mention until he was well over twenty.

January 25, 1946

He gave Dan his midnight shot of penicillin and set the alarm for four, then lay down on the couch. He felt old and tired. He had never learned to sleep well fully dressed, even in something as comfortable as chinos and an old Army shirt. He loosened his belt and tried to relax.

He was being absurdly overcareful; he ought to put on pajamas and then he could rest better. No, take no chances. He had to make every effort to be as he had been in the Army. He had some influence on Dan now, but if Dan discovered he was queer, he would leave. There would be no chance to get him educated.

Thank God for Ben. If he had not had him to talk to from time to time he would have been up the wall. Not accustomed to being closed in with one person like this, unable to leave. Did Ben like him or was he only curious about fairies? No way to know, but he was a pleasant enough young man.

Only three and a half hours until the alarm. Relax. Not easy to go to sleep waiting to be jarred awake by Dan's screams. Maybe he wouldn't have a nightmare tonight.

Tomorrow he could go and buy clothes for Dan. Pajamas. He was getting better so rapidly, he would soon need them. After less than an hour's sleep the alarm woke him. His eyes ached, but tired as he was, he had difficulty getting back to sleep again.

The following afternoon he saw that Dan was comfortable and then went out to shop for him. He liked buying things for him and had to stop himself from going overboard. Could he take Dan to his tailor later? Nothing ready-made could possibly fit those massive shoulders properly. Dan would look magnificent in clothes that fitted him. No, inappropriate.

Back in less than an hour, he went to the bedroom with the packages. The bed was empty. He dropped the bags on the chair and looked on the floor on the other side of the bed. Nothing. He called, "Dan." No reply.

He searched the apartment and finally found Dan on hands and knees in the kitchen, shivering, and trying to get up. "What the hell are you doing here?"

"I wanted to take a leak. And I'd have got back if you hadn't come home so fucking soon."

In the kitchen? He was lying, but there was no point saying so. Get him back to bed and get him warm. "Come on, let me help you."

In the bedroom Dan refused to be put back to bed. Sounding like a small child, he said, "I don't like it there. I wanna sit in your chair."

"Please, Dan."

"No, too many nightmares in that bed."

He was physically unable to put him where he did not want to be. Dan was at least as heavy as he was, and he could not be rough with him because of his broken ribs. "All right. Let's put on your pajamas anyway." After he got him into them and got him to sit on the edge of the bed, he asked, "Will you go to bed now?" Dan was shivering and swaying with fatigue.

"No."

"What do you want? You damn well weren't in the kitchen to take a leak. Why were you there?"

Dan shook his head.

"God damn it, if you'll tell me what you were looking for I'll get it for you. Now what was it?"

"Where's my stuff?"

"Your clothes are back from the laundry and put away in the dresser. Your wallet, change and scarf are in a drawer in the living room. Do you want them?"

Looking away, almost in a whisper, Dan said, "Yes."

"Get into bed and lie down. I'll get them."

He did as he was told.

Haakon covered him and went for the things. He had ironed and folded the scarf some time earlier. When he returned to the bedroom Dan was pretending to be asleep. He put scarf and wallet by Dan's hand, on top of the red blanket, and left the room.

A half hour later the scarf was nowhere in evidence and the wallet was on the bedside table beside the ice-water pitcher. Dan had gone to sleep.

At dinnertime Dan was uneasy with him, would not look at his face. He did not know what to say to put him at ease, and after some thought he decided he would do best just to get it all out in the open. "Listen, I know you didn't want your wallet. You were hunting for your scarf, weren't you?"

Dan stopped eating, turned his head away and did not reply.

"I guessed about that in the Army, Dan. The way you always had to have it when you went into town. And the time you found out it was stolen. I don't think any less of you for it."

Still looking away, Dan said, "It's not like that right now. I mean, I thought maybe it'd keep the dreams away, like back when I was living with my old man. You know?"

"I think so. I used to have a book I took to bed. My father's. It had a brown leather binding and a special smell all its own. Gold designs of leaves and spirals all over it. I used to think the nightmares got trapped in the spirals."

Dan glanced at him, smiled and began eating again. "That's it," he said. "Hey, what was your father like?"

"I don't know. I can't remember him at all. He left the States when I was less than two and went back to Denmark. I never saw him again. He died there not long after."

"What'd he die of?"

"My mother said it was tuberculosis."

"You ever been there? To Denmark?"

"After my father died my mother went back to settle the estate. We lived there until I was seven. I've been back half a dozen times since then too."

"What happened to your mother?"

Dan had never before asked him personal questions. Why was he now? "She's been dead for almost sixteen years. She'd been an invalid for a long time."

"What was she like?"

He could not answer immediately. The first thing that had come to mind was that she had been a warm talking corpse those last years. His memory of her prior to her first stroke was so vague he could not be sure of any detail of what she had been like. "Intelligent," he said. "She read a lot. She was beautiful before she became ill." A banal, lifeless description, but the best he could do. Dan seemed satisfied.

The following morning Dan was markedly better. He was more alert and ate his breakfast with enjoyment rather than just to be accommodating. His chest was clear now, and though he was still weak, he was over the pneumonia. Ben dropped by at noon to check him over. The doctor was worried because Dan's temperature had remained at 101. He took blood samples, left a prescription for sulfa, and said to continue the alcohol rubs and aspirin, that the only thing to do was treat symptoms until he found the cause of the fever—or it went away by itself.

The fever usually peaked around four-thirty. He decided to give the alcohol rub at four to see if he could at least keep it below 102. He smoothed a handful of alcohol down over Dan's bare back. His tan, from the waist up, was beginning to fade. Afternoon sunlight crosslighted Dan's body. His skin texture was like a child's, his body hair fine, almost invisible, even on his buttocks.

He was still too thin, all his ribs showed. The adhesive tape was getting grubby, sticky and rolled up at the edges. The scrapes and bruises had healed, leaving new pink skin and washes of green and yellow. Incongruous, the hardness and strength of the musculature under that fine-grained skin. The contours were beautiful, accentuated by the light. Lovely the way Dan was put together. As Simon had said, a body worth dreaming about.

He took his hands off. Somehow he had stopped taking care and had begun to make love. And to make everything more difficult, Dan was breathing faster too. He could not touch him again now. Trying to sound businesslike, he said, "All done," and held out the pajama top.

Dan stayed on his belly, not looking at him, and said, "OK," in a muffled voice.

He pulled the covers over Dan, left the pajama top on the bed beside him and escaped to the living room. He had to rearrange his emotions, find his way back to the paternal attitude of yesterday.

His hands remembered the shape of Dan's shoulders, the heat and smoothness of his back. He wanted to go to him and caress him with his hands and mouth, explore him and kiss him. Taste him. Good god, stop it! He opened his eyes and only then realized he had had them squeezed shut.

Take a cold shower, walk around the block, go scrub the kitchen floor. Finish reading that book on the battle of the Coral Sea. He had had hours of time free to work on the revision and he had not used any of it.

Talk to Ben next time he came. Surely now that Dan was so much stronger he could take a bath or a shower instead of having alcohol rubs. How in hell could he give him another one?

He was overtired, that was the problem. At least he no longer had to give a shot of penicillin every four hours. He would be able to get an uninterrupted night's sleep. Put pajamas on and make up the couch as a bed.

Dan was almost his usual self at suppertime, and from all appearances had not noticed, or perhaps had not understood, his upset in the afternoon. He told himself he had been making something out of nothing, that he was unstrung because he was exhausted. In the morning, after a night's sleep, he would be all right.

After seeing that Dan was taken care of for the night, he worked on World War II for an hour, reading and jotting down notes. Then he made up the couch as a bed, got into pajamas, and lay down. He fervently hoped that Dan would not have a nightmare. He automatically began organizing a paragraph in the book. Did the Coral Sea deserve only one paragraph? The turning point in the Pacific war?

He woke at eight the following morning. The room was bright with reflected sunlight, and outside he could hear snow shovels, like iron mice digging. It must have snowed during the night, but the weather was clear now. A good day. He felt rested; his eyes no longer felt sandy. He stretched luxuriously, then lay quietly, appreciating the silence, aware of his body pressing on the cushions of the couch, supported and comfortable.

He liked this room, the two walls of books, the rich carpet, the waxed wood surfaces and warm brown leather. He contemplated the seascape over the fireplace. Though the scene was calm, it somehow looked as if a storm was brewing. There was a tension in the way the gulls were placed, something slightly sinister about the quality of the light.

After a time he got up and went to check on Dan. He was sleeping quietly, mouth open.

He got his black silk kimono out of the closet, being careful not to make any noise, and took it into the bathroom with him. He hung it on the hook behind the door. The gold dragon glittered on the back. He would be all right today. He was sure of it. Maybe even be able to manage the alcohol rubs. First a long hot shower, shave, then have a cup of coffee in peace. He deserved the respite.

He had just turned on the fire under the coffee, half an hour later, when Dan began screaming. He turned off the gas burner and hurried to the bedroom.

He braced his knee on the edge of the bed, grasped Dan's shoulders and shook him. "You're all right. Wake up."

Dan was struggling and thrashing ineffectually, tangled in the bedclothes. His eyes opened, but he obviously was not really awake.

"Dan, Dan, it's all right." He pulled the sheet down so he would not be constricted by it. Then Dan's arms were around him, clinging.

"Professor."

"Yes. You had another dream." He held him, stroking his head, then held him away. "It was only a dream."

62

"A dream," Dan repeated, seeing him now, finally awake. He rubbed his eyes, then said, "Christ, I feel stupid! I mean, I'm not a little kid any more. I used to have nightmares a lot, but . . . that was before . . . back when I was little."

"Do you remember any of it?"

"Not really. Being lost in some kind of maze, or building, or something like that. All dark. Looking for someone, don't know who. I'm real little in the dream. But being caught or tied up in something is part of it—and that's about all." He looked down. "Look, I'm sorry."

"No, don't be. It's the fever."

Dan lay back down. His hand stayed on the kimono sleeve, and he began stroking it absentmindedly.

"What is it, Dan?"

He shook his head. "I was just thinking."

The hand moved slowly down from the sleeve to Haakon's thigh and lay there inertly. He could feel its heat through the thin material of the kimono. Dan had closed his eyes and was lying very still with a puzzled frown on his face.

The heat of Dan's hand seemed to spread up his leg. He could not ignore it, and felt a pulsebeat of desire. No good. But he could not keep himself from responding to the touch. Dan was still sick, and whether he was straight or queer made no difference. He could not allow anything to get started now. He stood. "Come on, why don't you go to the john and then we can have breakfast."

Dan did as requested. He was markedly stronger. He brushed his teeth, washed his face and hands before going back to bed. He got in and lay back.

Haakon followed him into the bedroom, then stopped just inside the door. He thought he was all right now, but he was not sure. Better to stay away from Dan, to collect his clothes and get dressed. He was acutely aware of the texture of the Bokhara rug under his bare feet, of the strong shadowless light that filled the room. The blanket on the bed was almost the same shade of deep rich red as the carpet. Dan's torso was dark against the white percale sheets, his blue pajamas light against the blanket. Red, white and blue. White stripe of hair. But the eyes were green.

Green eyes watching him. Dan was lying on top of the bed, making no effort to get in. Not posing the way Simon did, but displaying himself. Dan knew. He could not help measuring the breadth of those shoulders. Then, with regret, pretending he had not understood, he turned away toward the dresser. Not now. Dan was still feverish.

"Professor."

"What is it?" He took T-shirt and jockey shorts out of the drawer, closed it and opened the one above to get socks.

"Please come here."

"In a minute." If he dressed first, he would be safer from himself. He got out a clean shirt and went to the closet for chinos. He would go and dress in the bathroom.

He turned and found himself in Dan's arms. Holding him tightly, looking directly into his eyes, Dan said, "I love you." He sounded as if he had just finished doing a complicated sum in his head and was proud of himself for arriving at the correct answer.

"No," he told him gently. "You're sick, you have a fever. And you've just waked up from a nightmare. You're grateful." It was too sudden, he could not believe it.

"Of course I'm grateful. What's that got to do with it?"

"Maybe everything."

"Nothing, that's what. I really do love you."

"Dan, you're still sick, you don't know what you're getting yourself into." He could feel Dan's body against his, and controlling his reactions was becoming less and less possible. He tried to move away, but Dan held him, apparently without effort.

"You want me," Dan said. "I knew it yesterday."

"No." He was beginning to shake. When had he dropped his clothes? They were lying on the floor in a heap, white and khaki. "No." He could feel Dan's fever and struggled again to break away.

"I love you and you love me."

"You don't even call me by my name. In a way, you don't even know me."

"Haakon . . . Hawk." Dan pulled his head down and kissed him on the mouth, at first tentatively, almost virginally, then with assurance, sustaining it until there was no way he could keep himself from kissing him in return. Dan's mouth was hot, tasting of toothpaste.

His heart was racing and the shaking was worse. Instead of embracing Dan as he wanted to, he drew on some source of determination he had not known he had available and broke away. "God damn it, Dan, you don't know what you're doing." When he had thought Dan was heterosexual he had daydreamed he was not, but now he knew that he cared enough about him that he did not want to have him committing himself to a homosexual future. "Dan, you've got to give yourself time. I don't want you falling into my arms out of gratitude and because you're wound up and feverish. Don't do this to yourself. At least wait. Please. It's too soon." He was shaking all over and could not control it.

"I know what I'm doing." Dan moved quickly, caught hold of him and kissed him again. He found himself exploring Dan's mouth. Dan's cheek was smooth under his hand.

"You love me," Dan said, tugging at the end of the belt of the kimono, untying it. His hands were hard and callused on his back and sides.

"Yes . . . yes . . . but . . ." He was dizzy from holding his breath in an effort to control himself. He had to breathe, and in taking a deep breath he no longer could struggle against what he had wanted for so long.

Gently, insistently, Dan moved to the bed, then fell on it, pulling him with him. Dan's lips on his throat were dry, rough, peeling from the fever. He wished he had shaved more carefully. Too late. He should not let this happen; he was the older one, the responsible one. Too late. Although he had not stopped shaking he knew he was committed. There was no turning back.

Dan was markedly hotter than he. His skin was tight over the muscles, silky under his lips and hands. Dan's hands were gentle on his back. Dan was responding, not initiating. Not passive, but unsure. He knew that Dan had never before made love to a man. The thought was intensely exciting, but at the same time the part of himself that loved him like a son grieved.

His hands explored the strong S-curves of Dan's collarbones, the softness of the hollow of his throat, the dense hard muscles across his chest and shoulders, curving into each other, complex, more marvelous than any work of art.

Dan's belly was still hollow, the points of his hipbones prominent. Sparse brown pubic hair. Testicles a soft handful, flowing, conforming to the shape of his palm. Sensual, musky odor. Hot. Flaring head to the circumcised penis, almost without taste, responding to his mouth. Bigger erect than he had expected, beautiful.

He had thought only of making love to Dan. He had not expected him to reciprocate, novice that he was. He was surprised, almost shocked, when he felt Dan's lips on him. Tentative at first, kissing, then licking. Hesitation, then the heat of Dan's mouth on him. Everything disappeared except the intensity of physical sensation, time and consciousness dimmed. The taste of semen, the texture of it in his throat. His own fulfillment and momentary blankness.

He found himself holding Dan in his arms, Dan's head resting on his chest. He was overwhelmed and grateful.

Dan gave a long shuddering sigh, snuggled close and was almost instantly asleep. He lay there for some time while his heartbeat slowed, needing the closeness, feeling both tender and afraid, wondering what would happen now. After a time he got up carefully so as not to wake Dan, worked the kimono out from under him and put it on. It was warm in the places they had been lying on it, cool in the others. He covered Dan so he would not get chilled.

Dan looked younger than he ever had before, vulnerable and helpless. He wanted to take care of him, help him get educated, but he remembered Simon's warning and wondered what he had gotten himself into. A bit late to worry about that.

He picked up his clothes off the floor and got dressed. There was a long scratch on the underside of his penis. Those broken teeth. Get Dan to a dentist as soon as possible. He went to the bathroom for antiseptic. One whole shelf of the medicine cabinet was taken up with Simon's shaving lotions.

Put them away? Why? Dan had already seen them. No point in putting any of Simon's things away. They were all over the apartment, everything from monogrammed towels to clothes that were obviously not Haakon's size. He had never thought about it before, but Simon had a passion for putting his initials on things. When Dan asked, he would handle it then.

He put the coffeepot back on the fire and went to check on Dan.

He was awake and smiled when he saw him.

"Would you like breakfast now?"

Dan nodded, then said, "Business as usual?"

He went into the room and sat down on the edge of the bed. "I didn't know what to say."

"I know what you mean," Dan agreed. "But I gotta talk to you. Explain."

"Explain what?"

"Look, Hawk. Nothing was ever quite like that for me before, but all the same, I wasn't exactly cherry, you know. So stop blaming yourself, will you? I mean, in a way, I'm a JTO."

"What does that mean?"

"Jailhouse turn-out. You didn't know that? You're not very gay, are you?"

"I don't know the jargon, if that's what you mean. You were in jail?"

"Couple of times. D and D, and once for assault, on the Coast. You know how I get when I drink. Jail's bad, Hawk. There were these fucking faggots—I'm sorry. I'm not calling you that."

"That's all right."

"Yeah, well . . . I mean, there were these big jockers that would rape the new fish. Really hurt them too. One kid had to go to the hospital to get his asshole sewed back together. Well, me, I'm not

66

big, but I'm strong, and I'm mean. Besides they prefer the girlish ones anyhow, so after I rearranged one guy's face for him, they let me be."

That was easy to believe. He remembered his first impressions of Polecat, how dangerous he had seemed.

"I never did turn into a gutstuffer myself, but I was afraid I could. I could just feel myself turning mean. Look, I know I'm a prime bastard when I'm drunk, but I never thought I'd be like that sober. And it was happening.

"So when I got out of the jug I headed East. I'd missed too much of my bookkeeping class to be able to catch up, and my foreman at the docks was pissed off with me—so there was no reason to hang around. And if I'd of got busted again, they'd have thrown away the key. I got as far as Chicago."

Dan looked down and became interested in rolling up a corner of the sheet. He needed a question to be able to continue. "What happened in Chicago?"

"Couldn't find work, ran out of money. Hungry. I was standing there on one of those bridges over the river when a guy came up and wanted to buy me dinner. I knew what he was after all right, but I thought, What the hell, a hole's a hole. Wanted to give me fifty bucks if I'd let him blow me. Think how long it would take me to earn that on the docks."

Dan looked up from the rolled corner and said defiantly, "I mean, I never took my belt off, you know. I ain't pretty, but I'm built good, you know. I even got more'n fifty a couple times."

"Oh." He felt numb.

"So I got busted for hustling, and after paying my fine came to The City. I was thinking about you on the train, how you'd said to look you up and all.

"So I got a job on the docks. Got busted once for D and D, but pretty much kept my nose clean. I wanted to phone you, kept looking up your number, ended up memorizing it. I even put a nickel in the phone a couple times and sat there listening to the dial tone, but I couldn't call. I mean, I never felt so rotten inside myself. It was like . . . I dunno. I'd think, What would somebody like you want with a shit like me? And I didn't wanna hear you tell me to get lost.

"I tried to have some fun, but nothing was any damn fun, and nothing was any damn good. And I'd work all day and then spend all my dough getting smashed or renting a snatch. Then I got sick and couldn't work. Spent my last couple bucks on rotgut. I don't remember phoning you."

"I'm glad you did."

"Even with everything?"

"Yes." Dan needed him more than he had thought. And he felt guilty. Dan had obviously understood his interest in him, had figured it out. There was no way of knowing to what extent that had influenced him to turn in a direction he might not otherwise have gone, but he felt responsible.

If he had not been important to Dan, Dan would not have come to him. And under that street hardness, he was vulnerable. Dan was still watching his face, apparently not convinced. "I love you," Haakon reassured him. More than before: not only sexually, but paternally, protectively. And he could also see the promise of a new kind of relationship based on friendship, mutual respect and honesty.

February 22, 1946

After his last class, he went looking for George Van Zandt in his office. To his surprise, George was not there, and after ten minutes' wait he decided to go home and phone him in the evening. He was on his way down the broad steps of the Arts Building when he saw George coming toward him, head down, hurrying as usual.

"Hi, I was just at your office looking for you."

George smiled. He looked wonderfully solid and burgomeisterly in his overcoat and hand-knitted scarf. "I was just at yours looking for you. I wanted to tell you I talked Ralph into letting that young man, Reinach, into his Freshman English class. He'll have to go non-matriculated of course, can get credit later if he does matriculate and gets a B or better. But you know that. Ralph said to tell you he'd better be an improvement on that Doris Rollins."

"Some work out, and some don't. I'd rather try and fail than worry about what I could have done and didn't."

George nodded agreement, then said, "By the way, congratulations."

"What for?"

"That article of yours, 'The Horror Factor,' was mentioned in an editorial in the *Times*. They even spelled your name right."

"Oh? I didn't see it. When did it appear?"

"Yesterday. I thought you always read the editorials."

"I've been busy lately." Tricky title, but the article had not taken him much effort. He had written it on the troopship on the way home, to kill time. He had simply made the point that a weapon does not have to be cheaper or more effective; it only has to be new and frightening. He had supported his argument with examples: Dresden, Hannibal's war elephants, and the fact that early musketry was less effective than crossbows. When he got back he had checked his dates and sent it off to the *Journal of Modern History.* He was surprised that anyone had been impressed enough to refer to it in an editorial.

As he talked to George he gradually became aware of a girl hovering nearby. One of his students. She was wearing a tweed skirt and a leopard coat, standing on one foot and then the other, impatient for him to finish his conversation. Interruptive. A prep school girl, with polished manners but no real sense of politeness. Big, strong-jawed, beautifully groomed, daughter of a trustee and very aware of it. What could she be wanting so near the beginning of the term? Perhaps permission to drop his class?

After he had said goodbye to George he turned to her. "Yes, Miss Grey?"

"Mr. Hvitfelt, I don't want to bother you."

She had just spent at least ten minutes waiting to bother him. Annoying how some of these kids automatically disclaimed their intentions. Sad too, because they were so unaware of their behavior. "What is it?" he asked neutrally.

"Mr. Hvitfelt, I can't understand why you gave me such an awful grade. What was wrong with my paper? You gave Binky an A and she can't spell anything."

"The course is in history, not spelling." Her imperious tone rubbed him the wrong way. She apparently thought she had not deserved her grade. Hadn't she read his marginal note? He had taken pains to be certain he was both clear and specific. He did not like her and did not want to bother with her, but he reminded himself that she was a product of her background and did have a fairly good mind—if she ever learned to use it. "That paper won't count against your final grade if you improve your work."

"But I don't understand!" she wailed. "Binky got an A!"

"All right. In the first place, I asked for two pages and you gave me six. In the second, all six pages, well-spelled as they were, added up to perhaps half a thought. I expect more than that from my seniors. I thought I had made that clear in the note I wrote at the top of the paper."

Her mouth tightened. She gave him a look of undiluted hatred, said politely, "Thank you, Mr. Hvitfelt," and stalked off.

Walking home along Broadway, he thought, Binky? He had not

heard the nickname before, but Binky could only be Frances My-
tych. The only other A in that class had been Tom Silbart. Binky.
That suited her far better than Frances. She was round, bouncy
and dark. Sloppy. Always had Coke and coffee stains down the front
of her tan all-weather coat. Her shirttail hung out under her sweater,
and her grubby socks were collapsed in folds around her ankles.
He could always hear her coming because the backs of her loafers
were stepped down and the heels dragged behind her, clunking
with each step. She did not look like the best brain in class. Charming, gentle sense of humor. He had to make an effort not to let it
show that she was definitely teacher's pet. Perhaps that was why
Grey's comment had irritated him so much. Have to watch that.
He had been too curt with her.

A fine drizzle was falling, neither mist nor rain but something
in between. Pleasant on his face, but the hand holding the briefcase
was getting cold. He tucked the case under his arm and put his
hands in his pockets. Binky. Like a little soft teddy bear. Cuddly,
huggable. And that marvelously misspelled paper had been one of
the best pieces of student thinking he had seen since his return
from the Army. When he had asked her why she didn't look words
up in the dictionary, she had said with comic dismay, "I can't spell
them well enough to *find* them." Probably true for someone who
spelled imperial with an e at the beginning. At least her spelling
was phonetic enough so he could figure it out.

Reminded by his discomfort, he thought, Thank god Dan has a
dental appointment tomorrow. He had gotten nicked again last
night, and it had been bothering him all day. But Dan was inexperienced, and with those sharp broken teeth . . . Never felt it at the
time; he only became aware he had been hurt fifteen or twenty
minutes later. Last night he had had a hell of a time getting the
bleeding stopped. The worst part of it was feeling self-conscious
all day long.

Dan was really going to be all right. He would be in Ralph's
class, and Ralph was the best. A hell of a good teacher. Emil Breiden-
bach had room for him in Faust. Junior-senior level, but not too
advanced for a man who was bilingual. Good thing he had taught
Dan some German grammar in the Army.

Dan's German was not particularly literate, and he did not have
the vocabulary for Goethe, but with a dictionary and a little help
he would do well. He became aware that he was smiling. Dan had
gotten practice in translating after Coston brought back that footlocker full of German pornography from an SS headquarters.

He himself had flatly refused to translate the garbage. It was

70

repetitive, boring and embarrassing. Much of it sadistic and grotesquely perverted. Dan, who had gotten himself deeply in debt with his weakness for inside straights, had initially agreed to do it.

One day, however, he had stamped into the barracks followed by Coston and several others: ". . . and eating shit! What's sexy about that? No, I ain't gonna read any more. It makes me wanna puke. Go jack off on the pictures, but leave me alone."

"God damn it, Polecat, we made an agreement."

"You suckered me, you mean. That *Fanny Hill* was OK. I thought it was all gonna be like that. Now go fuck yourself." And nothing Coston said could change his mind.

Haakon turned into his building and collected his mail. It had been a long day.

Now that Dan was better they could go out to eat. He still wished he could have taken Dan to his tailor, but Dan was right. Only the older professors and newly arrived foreign students wore tailored suits.

The mail did not look interesting. Bills. He would have to set aside time to pay them tonight. A pink envelope with no return address, postmarked Seattle. Rather elegant script, written with a fine-pointed pen. He didn't recognize it. As he opened the letter he got a faint whiff of perfume. Familiar, but he could not place it.

Dearest Professor,

I have started to write you many times, but I've promised myself that this one is going to be sent. I want to tell you that I'll always be grateful to you, and I'll always love you. I can't possibly begin to thank you enough for what you did for me—not just the money, but the way you listened. I suppose that mostly I wanted to let you know that casting pearls before swine isn't always a waste. I'm going to school. I'm going to be married. He knows all about me, and he understands. That's really all. I'm going to mail this now before I lose my nerve.

All my love,
Jenny Hanover

He held the paper to his nose, inhaling the faint fragrance. The lobby door opened. Startled, he turned his back and hid the letter. Guilty reflex. Shame. Irrationally afraid someone might think he got letters from men on scented pink stationery.

Jenny Hanover. He had met her one night in a London whorehouse. She had been standing to one side looking like a waif, too thin, hollow-cheeked. And she seemed exhausted, her dark hazel eyes shadowed and held too wide open. Her breasts were small, and he could see the ribs on her chest. Yet she reminded him a little of Simon. Perhaps because she had olive skin and short curly black hair. There was something beautiful about her face even though she was not pretty. He had gone over to her when the other men began choosing women, partly because of that resemblance and partly because he thought no one else would pick her.

She smiled up at him and said by rote, "Hello, dear heart, my name is Jenny Hanover."

He was immediately fascinated, for the name was an obscure medieval term for a fraud. "Did you choose that name knowing what it meant?"

Her smile changed and became real. The tiredness dissolved in an instant. "You're the first one who's noticed."

Now at his apartment he unlocked his door. Dan was dressed, lying on his stomach in the middle of the rug. All the lights were on. He had been reading Haakon's world history text. "Hi, Hawk." Dan took a spent match from the ashtray beside him and used it to mark his place, shut the book and sat up. He looked happy and sure of himself.

"Have a good day?" Haakon asked.

"Un-hun." Smiling. "I'm beginning to feel good. Hey, that cleaning lady came and I paid her like you said to. She sure looked at me cross-eyed." Dan thought it was funny.

Her reaction was not unanticipated. "She'll get over it."

"Oh, she's all right. I teased her some and got her to giggling. She's a nice old lady. She fixed me lunch."

He hung his coat on the closet door to dry and went to put his mail on his desk. He envied Dan his ease with women. As he set down the letters he was reminded by the pink envelope and said, "Do you remember Jenny Hanover?"

"Sure as hell do. You had a real case on her in London. At least that's what we all thought."

"She wrote me from Seattle. She's in school and about to be married."

"Hey, that's great! Giving her that dough wasn't pounding sand in a rathole after all then." Dan picked up the book in one hand, the ashtray in the other and got up in a single easy movement. He set the things down on the coffee table and started toward the kitchen. "Wanna drink?"

"Thank you. The usual."

Dan returned with brandy for him and a bottle of beer for himself, went over to the couch and sat back with his bare feet on the table. "Would you explain, Hawk? I mean, you don't have to,

72

but back then I thought you had something big going with her. I mean, you took her out of that whorehouse and spent a week with her and gave her all that dough."

"That was what you were supposed to think." He remembered the night he had met Jenny. It had really started in the afternoon. He and Simon had made love and then, too soon afterwards, Simon had informed him that he would be gone overnight, at the country estate of a member of Parliament.

He had been hurt and jealous, particularly upset because the invasion was close and his leave could be canceled at any time. He knew he would be in an early wave and did not expect to live through it. He asked, "Do you have to?"

"Of course I have to! If I don't butter up the old boy he won't help me with the admiral. Never mind the details. I've simply *got* to be in on the invasion. The possibilities for pictures will be endless. I *can't* miss it."

He had not said any more, believing it to be of no use. He wished Simon a good trip, dressed and left. Then, after he was out on the street, he was overcome with depression, and instead of eating dinner, he began to drink.

During the course of the evening, Dan, Morrie, and half a dozen other men from his outfit came into the pub, and he was glad to let them talk him into joining them.

His memory of much of the evening was hazy, but he vividly recalled standing on a rain-slimed street in the blacked-out city after the bars were closed. A rasping Southern voice drawling—not one of his outfit but someone they had acquired, god knew how, in the course of the night—suggesting, "Hey, y'all. Ah know this place where the pansies collect. Whyn't we go step on some flowers?"

Ashamed and afraid, telling himself that if he went along he might be able to warn the homosexuals, confusedly thinking that he was a sheep in wolf's clothing, he had been ready to agree. And simultaneously he felt Dan, who was almost too drunk to stand, leaning against him for support. He did not remember putting his hands on Dan, but they were there on the barrel of his chest, feeling the rhythm of his breathing. He wanted him desperately, unexpectedly. Almost caressed him.

Suddenly almost sober, he pretended to stumble in order to move away, reeled into a wall. He remembered the wet grittiness of bricks and mortar under his hands.

Then Dan's voice behind him: "I sure as hell ain't gonna fuck around with no fuckin' fairies in the fuckin' damn rain. I'm gonna go get laid at Big Betty's."

Morrie, Coston, and the others seconded the motion, and he went along. He did not know what happened to the Southerner. He was not with them when they got there.

Now Dan said, "Hey, Hawk?"

Recalled to the present, he said, "What? Oh, about Jenny. What did you want to know?"

"That first night, I saw you looking at her. I was just wondering. You *were* interested, weren't you?"

"Yes, partly because of her pseudonym." Dan didn't know what he was talking about. "In the Middle Ages Jenny Hanover was a term for a fraudulent 'dead monster.' People believed in basilisks and such things, and there was quite a demand for their bodies. They were generally constructed in India, using dead skates that were molded and doctored to resemble the fabulous beasts. When I discovered that she had chosen that name knowingly, I was interested."

"And she went for you. I saw her perk up. I remember thinking, Shit, she's not half bad after all."

"Yes, I was the only one who understood the name."

"How come she wanted a name like that?"

"She never really explained. But among other things, her father had been a scholar and teacher. He'd been killed by a buzz bomb. Her mother had been dead for years. She let me know that if she told me his name, I'd know it, but I didn't want her to tell me. It didn't seem right somehow." He could see that Dan was still curious. Understandable. "I went up with her," he said, "and told her all I wanted to do was sleep, that I'd had too much to drink. She . . . well, we got to talking, and she offered to get me a boy."

"Huh?"

"It's a standard service at a lot of whorehouses."

"Go on."

"I told her no. I didn't want that—didn't dare and wouldn't have in any case. I liked her, Dan. In her way she understood me. I could talk freely with her, be myself. She became a good friend. I was having a tough time right then." Because Simon had not returned the next day as promised. He had not come back until the last day of his leave. He told Dan, "I was not unaware of the impression the rest of the men were getting. I was grateful to Jenny for helping me to put it across."

"No sex?" Dan sounded disappointed.

"No." A lie? Not really a lie. To have said yes would have been more of a lie, for he had pretended she was Simon. But he had to be honest with Dan. It was important. So he amended, "Not really."

74

Then added, not wanting to explain, but wanting to be clear, "I didn't screw her."

"Hey, Hawk! Stop it."

"What?" He didn't understand.

"You don't have to turn yourself inside out like that."

He had not been aware that his discomfort showed. "I just wanted to be truthful."

"Yeah? Yeah, sure."

Disbelief. Deserved. He had left out so much it amounted to a lie. But he did not want to mention Simon, or his shame over using Jenny. That whole incident was like a knot, and he did not know what was in the middle of it himself.

Dan drained the last of his beer and stood up. "Let's go eat."

"Good idea." Dan's tendency to move out of uncomfortable situations simplified things. He was glad not to have to think about any of that any more.

May 28, 1946

The morning was bright and cool. Carrying a briefcase heavy with corrected term papers, he walked uptown above the park, wishing he dared walk to class with Dan. Dan had to be at the university the same time he did Tuesdays, but they left separately and took different routes. God, he was fed up with the everlasting need for caution.

He put his hand in his topcoat pocket and was reminded of the letters he had shoved into it as he left the building. He glanced at his watch. He had time. He set down the briefcase and looked through them.

A letter from Chicago. An invitation to a doctoral graduation. William Jacobs—yes, Jacobs was a junior when he left for the service. Dark, chunky, Semitically handsome, a sensual curve to his mouth. Bill wrote that he had enclosed the invitation to prove he really had made it. He was touched to be remembered, but did not recall having been particularly useful to this student. Bill was a good logical thinker. All of his good grades had been earned. Oddly unsure of himself though, doubtful of his ability. Had the support and encouragement he offered been that important? Apparently.

A letter from Simon. He was glad Dan was not with him. Postmarked Mexico City, and the return address was a hospital. Was

Simon ill? Clumsy with anxiety, he tore the envelope. A portrait of Simon looking raffish and piratical in a black eyepatch and unbuttoned white shirt. The background was a pillow and part of a bed. Simon had obviously not made the print; there were white specks on it caused by dust on the negative. How serious was it? He unfolded the letter.

Darling,

I wanted you to see how sexy I look in my eyepatch. Don't worry, the doctor says I won't lose the eye after all. I suppose you want to know what happened? I hope so, because I'm going to tell you. I've been lying in this utterly ridiculous hospital for weeks feeling dreadfully sorry for myself, and have come to the conclusion that it's all your fault. Without your steadying influence, my life tends to get downright tacky.

If I hadn't missed you so much I never would have got involved with Eduardo, and if I hadn't got involved with him, he wouldn't have tried to kick me to death when he caught me with his Japanese houseboy.

Simon was exaggerating as usual. And blaming him for the trouble he got himself into.

I assume it's still all roses between yourself and Wolf Boy, otherwise I'd have heard from you by now.

Why should he have written? This was the first letter he had received from Simon. He could have gotten Simon's address from his agent, though, and in the past he would have done so.

Seriously, I miss you, my darling, and hope you'll write. I'll be here for at least two more weeks. Did I forget to mention that Eduardo is a 235-pound ex-wrestler with, it was rather forcefully brought to my attention, a perfectly vile temper. He did a remarkably thorough job on me.

I expect to come home when I get out of here, so don't say I didn't warn you.

Love and kisses, S.

He looked at the picture again. Even if Simon had not held the camera, he had directed whoever took it. The lighting, the perfect focus, the composition were his. Simon had posed for and taken it in order to manipulate him, and was doubtless fully aware that the camera had caught the sadness under the bravado. But Simon asking for a letter? He must really need one. Simon did not ask for things. He either took them or went without.

He glanced at his watch and continued uptown. No, he did not believe Simon. He would not be made a fool of again, the way he had been that time Simon had dictated a letter implying that his hand had been crushed. He had taken the first train that time, only to find Simon with a sprained finger.

Even if Eduardo had done more than just give Simon a black eye, Simon probably deserved it. He remembered again a time when Simon had brought another man to his apartment. Over six years ago, but he could not eradicate the memory. He had walked in to find Simon standing naked in the middle of his living room with what at first glance appeared to be a fully dressed woman crouched at his feet. A corseted, padded transvestite. Long blond wig, false eyelashes, drawn-on eyebrows so far above the plucked brows that the face was a mask of surprise. Black stubble showed through the heavy makeup. The sort of queen who turned his stomach, and made him ashamed of being homosexual.

Simon, who never forgot his schedule, said, "Darling, I didn't expect you home yet."

The creature simpered, with remarkable lack of tact. "Thweetheart, I *thaid* we thould use my plathe." It lisped too. God, what a caricature!

He was so angry he only said, "Out! Now." And the transvestite, showing fear, was briefly human. Then it gathered up its mink stole and flounced out, slamming the door.

Simon stood there posing. "I don't understand why I do things like that," he said contemplatively.

"You too. Out!"

Simon left without arguing. If he was afraid, he neither showed it nor admitted it, but he did not return for three months. He came back full of the usual easy, meaningless apologies, but by that time Haakon had missed him enough to be willing to listen.

Simon's only explanation—"For I am the cat that walks by himself, and all things are alike to me"—was no explanation at all. Perhaps a partial one. Simon's picture of himself as the clever cat who agreed to do this if he could get that in return, who gave nothing out of love, wanted no love, sought only warmth and comfort, was bleak. Simon was better than that. "Not quite" a priest? There were times when that side showed.

And Dan was so different. Honest, blunt. Uncomfortably blunt, but far easier to live with. He had worried how to tell Dan about Simon, but he need not have. He had simply told the unadorned truth and Dan had accepted it, commented that he remembered meeting Simon in London, then dropped the subject.

Dan had not asked any more questions, except once. An embarrassing moment for him, though Dan seemed mainly curious. Dan had gone to the linen cupboard for towels and turned around holding an inlaid box. "What's this?"

He glanced at it. "I don't know. Probably something of Simon's." He did not remember ever having seen it before.

Then Dan opened it. When he too saw what was inside, he felt himself flush. The box contained a bulb-type enema, Simon's "douche," and a tube of lubricant.

Dan said, "Un-huh," closed the box and put it back. Then a few minutes later Dan asked, "Hey, that stuff of Simon's—do you go for that?"

"No," he said flatly, feeling his face go hot again.

"That's good. Don't think I'd like it. You know, I worried about that."

"I don't understand."

"Not before I phoned you, but later, after I was sure you wanted me. I mean, it's no big deal to screw a man, but to have it done to me? I don't like the idea."

"How did you figure me out?"

"Didn't. I just made up my mind that if I loved you I'd just have to put up with whatever you wanted. And there's a lot of ways to do it, and I hoped you'd go for something else—like it turned out." Dan shrugged, "I don't know if I could've gone through with it, but there was a trick in Chicago that told me that if the other guy's gentle and all, it doesn't have to hurt. And those johns sure as hell seemed to enjoy themselves. I mean, you don't pay somebody fifty bucks to do something you don't like. You know?"

"I suppose not."

"Me a cocksucker—shit!" Dan sounded surprised, as if he had not put it that way to himself before.

"How do you feel about that?"

"Dunno. Well, that first time I was so damn glad you didn't want to screw me . . . and while we were making love, it was so damn exciting, I wasn't thinking at all. I never do think much when we're making love. There doesn't seem to be any right or wrong then, I just do it. So, well, yeah, I do feel funny about it, and I wouldn't want anyone to know. But I don't think less of you, so how can I think less of me?"

Dan always tried to simplify, but it was not that simple. Dan's entire background militated against his accepting a label as pejorative as "cocksucker." It had been one of his favorite curses in the Army, generally preceded by "stupid" and certainly used with a fine disregard for its meaning. He applied it as readily to a bulldozer as to a person.

Haakon remembered the guilt and shame he had felt those first years with Jim and wondered if Dan were similarly troubled. He did not appear to be, but that might only mean that he was hiding it. Dan seemed happy, was even beginning to enjoy going with him to museums, concerts, opera.

And Dan's lack of sophistication gave Haakon a new perspective. That performance of *La Traviata*, for example. He had explained the plot to Dan and during the last act Dan began to laugh. The hefty soprano was throwing herself about the stage with enormous energy and enthusiasm, singing at full volume. Dan whispered, "Do you call that fading away?" And it was funny. Dan's attempts to stifle his laughter were funnier, and suddenly everything was hilarious. He had begun laughing too, and could not stop. They kept setting each other off, and the angry shushing from all around only made stopping impossible. A bad case of the giggles. He had behaved childishly, recklessly, and had not cared. Still did not. He had never giggled with anyone before.

He remembered sitting in the living-room window, between the glass and the heavy velvet drapes, watching other children walking home from school together on the snowy street, talking together, giggling. Above his head the canary chirped in its cage and he wondered if it envied the busy brown sparrows that squabbled in the gutters.

He was always kept in, away from other children. Because in winter he had "weak lungs," and in summer asthma. The few times he had ventured out on his own he had not been accepted by the neighborhood children. They didn't know him and didn't want to. They didn't even tease him; they ignored him.

He went up the steps into the History Building. The first friend his own age he had ever had was George, and he had met him in college.

Dan had made friends of his own at the university. Funny kind of vicarious pleasure he got out of Dan's excursions, as if Dan were living out for him the kind of heedless good times he had missed.

Last Saturday night Dan had gotten back late, his face windburned and hands chapped. "You know Tex? The skinny guy with all the hair. Always talking about kites. Would you believe that the son of a bitch went and made the biggest fucking kite you ever saw—all on the quiet. So we took it to Far Rockaway on the subway. Had to put the thing together on the beach. Damn near put out this crabby old lady's eye as it was. I wish you could've seen it, all big and ruby-colored up there. It was pulling and tugging as if it wanted to fly to the moon."

Taking off his grubby clothes, laughing when he tipped sand out of his shoes. "Looks like I brought half the beach back with me. And then we were down in the Village. There's this little Italian guy there with a pushcart and he had these sausage sandwiches with peppers and tomatoes and crusty bread. And then we found a pushcart uptown someplace where you can get sauerkraut and chili on your hotdogs— Christ! I even got sand in my underpants. Bart had that creepy Chichi along, but Tex called Alice and she brought along this real neat little blonde—Ruthie—and she took us to a place that had kasha knishes, and then we had raw cherry-stones with all kinds of sauce . . ." Dan's version of a gastronomic tour of the city. He must have the digestion of a goat. Haakon could no longer remember the entire list, but it had included roasted chestnuts, cotton candy, orange soda, beer, hot chocolate and some kind of Armenian pastry that "tasted like lamb chops and honey."

On time for class now, the last student slipping into her seat. Today's subject Oliver Cromwell—a fanatic. His head ended up on a pike on London Bridge. How many of his troops, or the King's, had known or cared what they were fighting for? Most of them were dogfaces, men with hopes and dreams. But they died nameless and were buried by strangers. Only the statistics were important, because the general with the most men usually won.

The students were waiting for him to begin.

Later that day, after his two o'clock history class, Miss Grey but-tonholed him in the hall. Not unexpectedly, since he had returned the corrected term papers that day. "You gave me a C minus," she said accusingly.

"That's right," he agreed. Binky came out of the classroom, loafer heels clunking, grinned and waved to him. He waved back and she hurried off down the hall, the corner of her coat, which she had under her arm, dragging on the floor. He had wanted to congrat-ulate her on her paper, let her know that he appreciated the effort she was making with her spelling.

"But why?"

"Because that was what you deserved," he said patiently. He disliked failing with a student, but he had given up on Grey. He wondered if he had initially overestimated her mental capacity. She certainly had not responded to any of his suggestions. She was still staring at him demandingly, so he said for at least the sixth time this semester, "I don't want you to feed back facts to me. I want to see some evidence of original thinking."

"Is that what I'm going to get for the year?" she wailed. "It will keep me off the Dean's List."

"That's too bad, but I feel that your grades in my class are, if anything, overgenerous. I've allowed you to rewrite two papers. It's possible that the course is too difficult for you, but if that's the case, you should have taken my suggestion to drop it."

"But I needed the three credits."

This was getting nowhere. "I'm sorry," he said and turned away. She grabbed his sleeve. "But I don't *want* a C minus."

Gently he disengaged himself. "I'm sorry," he repeated and walked away. Behind him he heard her stamp her foot and mutter, "Damn!"

After his last class he reread Simon's letter, sitting at his desk in his office. He was going to have to reply. He tore up three drafts and ended up with a colorless recounting of what he had been doing. A letter suitable for the eyes of anyone's maiden aunt. He knew how cold it sounded, but could think of no way to improve it. In an effort to compensate for the tone, he signed it, "Love, HH," instead of simply initialing it as he ordinarily would have.

He was startled by a knock on his office door. Hastily he dropped Simon's letter and his reply into his top desk drawer and closed it. "Come in."

Peter Randall, with a smile pasted on his face, came into the room and crossed to his desk. "Dr. Hvitfelt, may I have a minute?" Randall was much shorter than he, about five feet, seven inches. He had dark hair, not showing any gray. He looked innocuous, kindly. But there was a hostile watchfulness in his small dark eyes if one looked closely.

"Of course." What could Randall want? The smile was insincere. Their relationship could be summed up by the fact that—although they had had adjoining offices and shared a secretary for four years before he went into the service, and did so again now—they had never been on first-name terms. Randall's false teeth were even and shiny, the pink plastic gums brighter than real. First good look he had had at them. Randall looked as if his smile were beginning to hurt.

Randall cleared his throat several times before saying, "I've been talking with Betsy Grey. She's terribly upset over her history grade, and appealed to me to intercede on her behalf. After all the extra work she's put into rewriting papers for you, couldn't you give her a little more credit? She spent weeks on this last term paper."

He wondered how to respond. He didn't want to get Randall's back up. It was difficult enough now sharing quarters with him.

He held out his hand for the paper, playing for time. At the top, "C—" was written quite large, and just below it, diagonally, "No evidence of original thinking." He said, "Unfortunately that grade is the best I could give her. I had considered giving her a D." He attempted to return the paper-clipped sheets. Twenty, and he had asked for ten. When Randall made no move to take them, he laid them down on the far side of his blotter.

"Are you aware that her father is Clement D. Grey?"

"Yes."

"Doesn't that mean anything to you?"

"The fact he's a trustee can't affect her grade. I'm not grading her on her pedigree." He was becoming annoyed.

"You won't reconsider?" Randall's face was red.

"No."

"Thank you for your time," Randall said in a sarcastic voice and left, forgetting the paper.

He got up and went to stand by the window. The grass was spring-green and the new elm leaves were bright against the darkening sky. Students hurried down the narrow paths clutching books. He wished he did not find Randall so irritating. Pleasant as this office was, he would gladly have switched it for a cubbyhole on an airshaft if by doing so he could get away from Randall.

The phone rang. He seated himself and picked it up. "Hvitfelt here."

"Hello, Haakon, how have you been?" Dean Grimes, sounding a shade too cheery.

"Fine, Bill. And you?"

"Oh, fine, fine."

"What can I do for you?"

"Could you fill me in on the situation with Betsy Grey?"

Her father must be applying pressure. "What is it you'd like to know?"

"Clem called me just now, says the girl's in tears because she won't make the Dean's List. I was just wondering if you might have made a mistake. Clem says she's worked like a Trojan on your course, rewritten papers . . ."

A tap on the door. He put his hand over the mouthpiece. "Come in."

Lucy, the secretary. Randall had unkindly described her as "a rag, a bone and a hank of hair." Randall had a way with cutting phrases that were just accurate enough to be remembered. She was very thin, and her clothes hung on her, but she had a sweet, shy smile. And behind her glasses, her eyes were dark and beautiful.

"I'll be with you in a minute." He motioned her to a chair. She perched on the edge of it.

"Yes," he said to Grimes, "I'm aware of the time she's put in. Unfortunately, she deserves no better grade than the one I gave her." While he was explaining his reasons he noticed that Lucy was staring at the term paper.

"Yes, yes, I understand," Grimes was saying. "Don't worry about it, I'll explain to Clem." Grimes would too. He always backed up his teachers.

After hanging up he asked Lucy, "What is it?" indicating the paper.

"I typed that for Mr. Randall." She sounded puzzled.

"He wrote it?" The grade and comment jumped out at him.

"No, not exactly. He made a lot of changes though. A lot of the handwriting was his—the last three pages."

Randall would never forgive him for that grade or that comment. No wonder he was upset. "Well, never mind," he told Lucy. "It's not important. You wanted me to sign these?" Reaching for the letters she had brought in with her.

After she had left the room he sat playing with his paper knife, watching the light shine on the damascened blade. Yes, Randall fancied himself a close friend of Clem Grey's, was always dropping remarks about their golf dates. So he had helped Betsy Grey with that thoroughly mediocre paper. To get in Grey's good graces? Could Randall be shacking up with Betsy? No, not likely. She would not be interested in a middle-aged associate professor with no publications to his credit. Married too.

He ought to flunk her, and what Randall had done was at the least unethical. What a mess! Confront Randall? Do nothing? Give the paper a zero and grade her on that basis? Allow her to rewrite it?

It was possible that she had led Randall on, one way or another, and that he had led himself on to do far more work on it than he originally intended to do, or even wanted to do. He had no desire to get Randall into trouble, because that would hurt Winnie Randall and he was fond of her. He suspected that she was far brighter than she pretended to be, and in any case, she was a kind, gentle woman.

He looked up Grey's telephone number and pulled the phone toward him. A perfunctory knock and Randall pushed open the door and came across the room. He picked up Betsy's paper. "I forgot this." He scowled at the grade. "Are you sure this grade should stand? It didn't seem a bad job to me. I've read it, you know."

"I almost gave her a D."

"You say you object to the thinking. Frankly, she didn't understand that at all and neither do I. I thought the last couple of pages were very well reasoned."

"They were a rehash of what I'd said in class."

Randall's face reddened. "She never said a word! How was I supposed to know what you'd said—" He cut himself short, then burst out furiously, his voice rising in pitch, "All right! I helped her with it. There's nothing wrong with helping a student."

"Nothing at all." He had meant to sound neutral, but he realized he sounded sarcastic.

"You needn't be so damned superior."

Randall had a talent for bringing out the worst in him. He could not think of anything to say that would not make matters worse.

"What are you going to do?" Randall demanded.

Instead of telling him it was none of his business, he said, "I have decided to give the girl another chance. I'll phone her and let her know that if she wants credit for the course she'll have to write another paper on a different subject."

"I wouldn't advise that. You'd better watch your step, Hvitfelt. You and your so-called protégé. Need I say more?"

Blackmail. But when he tried to look Randall in the eye, Randall looked away. If Randall had any facts to back him up he would be far more arrogant. But he was the worst gossip on campus and he would certainly talk.

Certainly Haakon had no choice now. If he gave in, that would confirm Randall's suspicions. He picked up the phone and dialed while Randall watched unbelievingly.

Betsy answered.

"This is Mr. Hvitfelt. I've been getting a good deal of static about your grade."

"You'll change it then?" A pleased sigh.

"No. I called to tell you that if you don't want a zero you will have to write a new paper on a different subject. And do it without help. Do I make myself clear?"

There was a long silence, then, "Oh. Yes, I see." She did not sound arrogant and he was glad he had decided to give her another chance. She might even learn something from this incident. "You have exactly a week."

"Oh, yes, all right." Her voice was small.

"You'll be graded without prejudice," he reassured her.

Randall, looking swollen with rage, stamped out of the room and slammed the door.

He finished his call and said aloud to himself, "Now what?"

Now that he was safely alone, his stomach was knotted with fear. He held out his hands and watched them shaking. Thank god his physical reactions usually delayed themselves until after the crisis was over. He lit a cigarette, having to hold one hand with the other to keep the match steady.

What might Randall have on him? Certainly nothing specific. But he had been careless. Eating most of his meals with Dan, paying for them. Going everywhere with him. But Dan was not like Simon. He acted straight, and they had so often been together in the Army it had seemed natural. Nobody in the Army thought it was strange if buddies went places together. No big deal about that—especially since your life might depend on a friend.

And while Dan was not exactly dating, he usually had a girl with him when he and his ex-GI friends went out together.

"You and your protégé," Randall had said. A guess, that was all. Nothing to worry about, but he would have to be more careful from now on.

June 3, 1946

He reached out and turned off the alarm, lay with eyes open until he was sure he would not go back to sleep, then closed them and began the slow process of waking up. Monday, a nine o'clock class. No class for Dan until eleven. He became aware of Dan on the other side of the bed, of his weight on the mattress, his warmth a few inches away under the covers, the sound of his breathing. Let him sleep. He sat up and reset the alarm to wake Dan for class, moved the clock across the room to ensure that he would have to get up to turn it off, then picked their pajamas up off the floor and hung them in the closet.

As he did so he realized that he had been picking up pajamas for weeks now, that neither of them was wearing them to sleep in. More comfortable. Funny, not long ago he would have felt insecure without them. Now he liked the freedom, the lack of encumbrance.

He went to look out the window before dressing. The air was warm. Light summer suit then. Beautiful day. Sky pale Delft blue, enough breeze to be comfortable. The park looked clean in new leaves, bright and inviting. He thought he could hear the leaves rustling, seeing them fluttering in the light wind. Too bad he had to go to class. Not much longer now though. In a couple of weeks he would be free for the summer.

Almost as soon as he walked into the History Building, half an hour later, he became aware that he was the focus of too much attention. Sudden silences as he walked down the halls, titters almost outside of earshot, students watching him, only to turn hastily away when he looked in their direction. It was starting. Randall.

His shoulder hurt. He straightened, glad the scar forced him to maintain what was by now his usual posture, prèvented him from hunching over in self-protection.

As he entered the anteroom to his office, Randall passed him on the way out. Randall did not greet him. Not unsurprisingly. Randall had not spoken to him since last Tuesday. Randall's face was smug. He seemed swollen with satisfaction.

In his office he collected his notes for his first two classes. This sort of thing had never happened to him before, though he had always feared it. What would his best defense be? Behave normally and try to ignore it insofar as he was able. Nothing to do but try to weather it. What in god's name had Randall said?

His morning classes were not as difficult as he had expected. After an initial silence and feeling of strain, the students behaved much as usual. But after all, he had a relationship with them, they knew him and most of them liked him. At least he thought they did. But by noon he felt stifled, and bolted from the building, walking as fast as possible.

He felt hollow and empty with dread. His stomach was like a knot. He would not be able to eat. As he was about to cross Broadway he heard George's voice. "Hey, wait up!"

He turned. "Hi."

George was with Tom Enfield. Tom reached him first, "Come and have lunch with us." Tom gripped his elbow and he found himself crossing the street with George on one side and Tom on the other, going toward the coffee shop.

Tom was several inches taller than he, even bonier and lankier. As always, Tom set a fast pace and George was having to trot to keep up. He tried to slow his walk, but Tom took hold of his elbow again and propelled him along, then suddenly began to talk animatedly about his forthcoming trip to Italy. He would be leaving with his wife, Abby, as soon as the term was over. "First real vacation we've ever had."

When they got to the restaurant Tom was still talking, so rather than interrupt to make his excuses, he went in and seated himself at the table with them. He would have a cup of coffee.

". . . over twenty years," Tom was saying confusingly. He had apparently changed the subject. "And what a honeymoon! We were broke, of course. Went to that place of mine on Rupert's Island. I'd had it about six months then, and it wasn't fixed up. No stove, no fireplace, no electricity. We'd both given up our apartments and didn't really have money for rent anyhow. Abby was a saint. It *rained*. For forty days and forty nights. I built a lean-to over the outdoor fire and was about to start on an ark."

Tom paused and picked up the menu, flipped it open, then immediately shut it. "I always have a Western. What am I looking at this for?" He laid it down. "I still haven't rented it for this summer, but I don't want a stranger in it, so I didn't try very hard. Funny how you get about a house. I've hated it so long I love it. It's owned me ever since I fell off the roof and broke my leg when I was building the chimney." He grinned. "Besides, without it what would I have to complain about? No, I've had a lot of fun with it."

Tom's hands were bony, as long as his own and narrower. Tom made a production out of relighting his pipe, black brows contracted, brown eyes intent and slightly crossed behind his thick horn-rimmed glasses. Craggy face, Lincolnesque, but with a stronger jaw.

Next to him George looked even rounder and more cherubic than usual. George was watching him, two unusual worry lines between his brows.

He put down the menu. "What's the matter?" he asked flatly.

"What do you mean?" Tom said immediately, glancing at George, who returned the look.

George hesitated, then said, "We'd heard Randall's rumor earlier and thought perhaps you needed cheering up."

"What rumor?" he asked dishonestly, then added truthfully, "I haven't heard it."

"That figures," Tom said.

"What's being said?"

George hesitated, then said, "Is it true that Dan Reinach is living with you, and that you paid his tuition?"

"Yes." No point in denying that, it could be easily checked. How in hell could he have been so careless? Paid by check, and Dan's address was the same as his. So goddamned obvious. Randall must know someone in the registrar's office. He would just have to try to brazen it out. "So what?" he said in a harder tone than he had intended. "We're old Army buddies. He saved my life. He needed a hand up."

"So nothing," Tom said, shrugging. "But Randall's making it sound like a real can of worms. You know the kind of mind Randall has."

"And so does everyone else," George put in. "Don't worry about it. It'll blow over."

The waitress came to take their orders. He decided he ought to eat something to prove he was not upset, and asked for soup, hoping he would like it, not wanting to reconsult the menu after spending so much time pretending to read it.

The vegetable soup was well flavored, the crackers fresh, but he could hardly choke down a mouthful. He felt harried, closed in on, beset. He appreciated the fact that Tom and George had gone out of their way to align themselves with him, be seen with him, but he was troubled because they believed in him, thought he was straight.

Tom, who was uncomfortable with silences, had gone on talking. Apparently he was still on the subject of his cottage, describing a view out over the sea. It occurred to him that if he could get away for the summer he would be free enough of pressure to finish the textbook, get it over with. He had already refused to teach summer school this year. A full professor could do that.

If he could rent Tom's place he would be away from everything that was bothering him. No phone. No pressure from Higgins at Meadows Press. No Randall. No rumor. No suspicion. By the time he returned, this ugliness would be ancient history, of little interest at the beginning of a new term. Of course it would never quite be buried and could follow him the rest of his life. But it would not be so dreadfully oppressive. Dan would have to move out. No help for that. At least he would have to have a different address, even if he did not sleep there.

And Simon would never follow him into the country, assuming he came back. Simon was phobic about small American towns. He would drive all night for two nights rather than be in one after sunset. He had mentioned once that some yokels had dragged him out of his hotel bed in the middle of the night years before and hurt him badly.

And to have two months with Dan. Swimming, lying in the sun. Be free. There would be no neighbors to watch or wonder or disapprove. Tom had said the place was totally isolated. A honeymoon? All right, why not? Wasn't he entitled to be with the man he loved? Heterosexuals were allowed to enjoy themselves, take time to cement a relationship.

"Tom," he said into a brief silence, "will you rent me your cottage?"

Tom looked startled, then said, "Sure, why not? I guess you know all about it by now. How primitive it is. I sure as hell talk about it enough."

"Good." He discovered he was going to be able to eat his soup.

When he left the restaurant he had in his possession a key to the place and a snapshot of it with a map of how to get there carefully drawn on the back. Tom had his check for the rent.

On campus he was again aware of being on stage. He tried to ignore it, but became increasingly uncomfortable. He did not think he was going to be able to get used to it. He found himself studying all his gestures, his walk, wondering if he might have picked up one of Simon's mannerisms, worrying about the expression on his face.

At twenty of two, instead of going to his office, because he knew Randall would be in his then, he went to the room he would be using for his next class. It was always empty the period before his on Monday. He was desperate to find solitude, even if only for five minutes. As he approached the wide-open door he heard Grey's voice.

"He said he'd *flunk* me! But Mr. Randall told my daddy—I was right there in the room. He said, 'What can you expect from a queer like that? He simply doesn't like girls.'"

Whom was Betsy talking to? Her voice continued, sharper now with annoyance. "You needn't sit there shaking your head at me! It's all true. Every single word of it. You'll see! Mr. Randall even saw the check and everything." Her tone shifted, became confidential. "And you know something else? They go everywhere together, and eat together, breakfast even. Mr. Randall says that Reinach is Mr. Hvitfelt's catamite."

Catamite! he thought. Jesus Christ! But the word did apply in a sense. Randall must have consulted a dictionary to find that archaism. He wanted to run away, skip the class. He also wanted to go in and confront Grey, but he was immobilized, caught halfway between fear and anger. He could not allow himself to act on either one.

Then Binky's voice. "All the same, you got that lousy grade because you turned in a lousy paper. If what Mr. Randall says is true, how come Ann and I are getting A and it's two of the boys who are flunking? Answer that. You really don't think very well, do you? That's obvious."

It was by far the unkindest thing he had ever heard Binky say. She was defending him. He should not be eavesdropping. He had to do something—either go in or go away.

"Well, you're teacher's pet. Everybody knows that!"

"In case you hadn't noticed, I'm *not* a boy."

"Oh, really!" Grey sounded furious. Then she said airily, "You just hang on to your innocent little illusions if you want to. But *every*body knows Mr. Hvitfelt is nothing but a fairy godfather."

And that appellation was pure Randall. Fairy godfather! Not too libelous, because he had a reputation for helping students out— both sexes. But with that pejorative emphasis, deadly. He would never be rid of it.

He went into the room. Grey stared at him, wide-eyed with surprise. Clear gray eyes, they looked honest.

Binky smiled up at him. "Hi!"

"Hello, Binky," he said to her, then to Grey, "How is your new paper coming along?"

She stared at him defiantly. "I don't think I'm going to have time to write it."

"That's too bad," he said evenly. "Since you need the three credits to graduate."

"You wouldn't dare flunk me!"

He thought a moment. Why pretend he had not heard? He said quietly, "If Mr. Randall's slander were correct, I would not dare *not* to flunk you now. If it is incorrect, I have nothing to keep me from it, do I?" He paused to let this sink in, then said, "You still have four days left. I suggest you get to work on it."

"But I'll have to break two dates!"

"It's entirely up to you," he said. He was relieved that only her social life would be interfered with; he had been concerned that her other course work might suffer from this unexpected demand on her time.

Several other students came in, cutting off the conversation. He went over to Binky and congratulated her on her paper, as he had been wanting to do since last week. He told her he was pleased with the improvement in her spelling.

After his last class he got his briefcase from his office and said good night to Lucy. She was looking at him wonderingly, seemed about to ask him a question, but he left precipitously, not giving her a chance to speak. He simply could not deal with any more that day. He had to have time to think.

He was on Riverside Drive a block from home when he heard Dan's voice. "Hey, wait up, damn it!"

He stopped and turned, watched Dan hurrying toward him, then glanced nervously around. He had to stop that. He must behave more normally. "Are you crazy?" he asked.

"You mean that shit on campus? Seems to me we ought to act like we always do. Come on, let's go home."

Dan was probably right. He walked along beside him, a little farther away than usual. He wondered what to say, and realized he had not thought of Dan's reaction. Somehow he had assumed Dan would be left out of it, but how was that possible? Obviously he would be in for unpleasantness too. How could he have been so heedless of Dan's welfare?

"What the fuck's a catamite?" Dan asked abruptly.

"The word is derived from the name Ganymede. He was cup-bearer for Zeus—"

"Stuff the lecture," Dan interrupted. "What's it mean?"

"A boy kept for unnatural purposes," he said bleakly, quoting Webster's dictionary, unable to think of any better way to put it.

"Oh." Dan was silent for a moment, then said, "Yeah, I see. Sort of like I'm your mistress, huh?" He said nothing more until after they were inside the apartment, then he said, "It's funny I never noticed or thought about it, but you do pay for everything."

"I have more money than I know what to do with," he protested. "I like spending it on you, and I didn't think you'd mind." But he had been afraid Dan would mind if he noticed. He knew how proud he was. Suddenly he was terrified of losing him and searched for some way to soften or change the definition, make it sound better. He could think of nothing.

Dan looked up at him, then clapped him on the back in a comradely way. "Shit, don't look like that. I'm not gonna leave you. I know it isn't that way with us, no matter how it looks. So do you. Now relax. It's all right."

"Thank you." But his throat was not working right, and it came out a croak.

"Hey there. Take it easy." Dan gripped him a shade too tightly by the upper arms and gave him a little shake. "Come on now." Then, moving rapidly away toward the kitchen, "What we both need is a drink."

When Dan returned with brandy for both of them, he saw that the knuckles on Dan's right hand were skinned. "Dan? What happened?"

Dan looked at his knuckles. "Yeah, well. You see . . ." He paused, then said, "These two big bastards in football sweaters came up. I didn't even know 'em. Not really, that is. I've seen 'em around. They both go out with that stuck-up broad with the leopard coat. The one with blond hair and a big jaw. Her old man's some kinda big-shot. You know her."

"Betsy Grey."

"Yeah, that's her. Well, they came up acting mean and saying stuff. Like calling you a fairy godfather. And me a catamite. Didn't even know your name and one of 'em was going on about how it sounded like a cat sneezing. And laughing because he thought he was pretty fucking clever. Well, I didn't know what the fuck a catamite was, but it sure as hell sounded like an insult. And I don't take that kind of shit from any-fucking-body. Besides, they were moving in on me, so I flattened 'em both. Kicked one in the knee and socked the other one in the face. Christ, they were stupid! I mean, they looked at my size and couldn't see any more'n that, but both of 'em were slower'n hell and didn't know shit about fighting. They never touched me. Hey, Hawk? You think there'll be a lotta static? I busted one's nose, and I might have wrecked the other one's knee."

"Were you on or off campus?" It was a relief to be able to turn his attention to a practical detail like this.

"Off. Me and Bart and Ruthie were coming out of the pizza place on Amsterdam after lunch. Bart would've helped, only it was over before he could."

He had seen the two football players walking Betsy to and from classes. They were over six feet tall and bulky. One was a tackle, the other a fullback. The smaller of the two outweighed Dan by at least fifty pounds. "How could they complain?" he said. "They'd have to admit you took them both single-handed."

Dan grinned. "Yeah. You shoulda seen their faces." Then he said seriously, "I thought about it after . . . you know? What if getting mad like that made it look like they were right or something. But then I thought, Shit! In the Army I'd of taken apart anybody that called me names. So that part's got to be all right."

"I should think so." He hoped others would see it that way too.

"Hell, I wasn't even that mad. I just gave it to 'em. You know?"

Half an hour later Dan got a phone call. After he hung up, he reported, "Bart says I put 'em both in the hospital. Jeez! I didn't mean to ruin them. Oh, well, they asked for it. Anyhow, Bart says they're madder'n hell at that Grey for telling them I was a faggot. They feel like she set 'em up." Then wonderingly, "People are kinda dumb, aren't they? I mean, why should loving you make me any different?"

"No reason, but it's that kind of prejudice that enabled me to get by in the Army, you know."

"Yeah, I see what you mean."

II

June 30, 1946

The secondhand green La Salle fled down the winding road in the late afternoon sun. Shadows of leaves and branches slid across the shine of the hood. The motor was quiet, sounding better now that Haakon had driven it long and fast enough to clear the engine. It handled easily compared to an Army truck. He was satisfied, even pleased with it, and with himself for having chosen it.

"Look there," Dan said, pointing.

He glanced to his left and saw only a wooded slope much like all the others they had been passing.

Dan asked, "Did you ever get the feeling you've been a place where you know you weren't?"

"Once in a while. I think it happens to everyone, one time or another." Dan had kicked off his moccasins and was slumped in the seat with his feet on the dashboard. The wind through the wide-open windows ruffled his hair, white and red-brown like a new not-quite-ripe horse chestnut the moment after its shell was removed, before the white spots began to yellow in the light. Shiny. His hand twitched on the steering wheel. He would have liked to reach over and stroke Dan's head, but that made no sense, would have surprised Dan, and perhaps even required an explanation, though not necessarily.

The tires hummed as the road curved abruptly toward the sun, then turned again, back east again toward the Massachusetts coast.

Dan said, "When I was a kid, my dad used to borrow a gun and go get rabbits. Deer and pheasants too, in season. Once or twice out of season, when we didn't have food. You can swap deer meat for other stuff. Usually he was very law-abiding though. My mother'd make *Hasenpfeffer*. Is there English for that?"

"No, I don't think so."

"You know, I'd forgotten until I looked up into the woods back there. We'd go out together and I'd follow him. He never let me touch the gun because it was borrowed and I was too little. Never taught me to shoot—shells cost a lot—and he only hunted for food. I mean, if there was a rabbit, he sure wasn't going to let me take a shot and miss. And he wouldn't waste a shot on a target, because that could mean another rabbit. You know?"

"Yes," he said, because Dan needed assurance that he was listening. He had not previously been aware of how poor Dan's family had been.

"He didn't miss often. Six shells, six rabbits," Dan went on. "He had sharpshooting medals he'd gotten in the German Army. It was great, going with him, walking quiet. And after he'd got the rabbits and we were on the way back, he'd talk—talk like he hardly ever did. About everything. His job at the mill when he had one, how he was trying to get one when he didn't. About his medals, how it was when he was a boy. He had four brothers, and they lived beside a pine forest on the side of a mountain. He'd had a pet goat named Heidi, and he said that every time she had a male kid they'd slaughter it for Easter. He hated Easter." Dan paused and then went on. "You know? I'd forgotten that—most of it—until now. Like the good part got swallowed up in the bad. Am I making sense?"

"You are to me." Then, "What happened to your father's brothers?"

"They all got killed in the first war. My dad was wounded. He limped. Left leg, same as me, only in the knee. You know? It was great going hunting with him. He didn't treat me like a little boy when we were out in the woods. Then in the late afternoon we'd come back down the mountain and go return the gun to Mr. Rodenmeyer. My father always tried to give him rabbits in exchange, but he'd only take them sometimes. Said he didn't like rabbit all that much. And Mr. Rodenmeyer and my father'd sit there in that big kitchen drinking beer and talking. They had a black stove with shiny metal, chrome I guess, on it, and white china oven doors. I never understood half what they said. I just liked to listen to their voices rumbling. I'd go curl up in this big rocking chair in the corner and almost go to sleep. Mrs. Rodenmeyer always gave me a cookie and a drink of something—lemonade in summer, cider in fall, hot chocolate in winter—and if it was cold or rainy. But then we always hadda go home, and my mother was always pissed about some damn thing or other. If she couldn't think of anything else, she'd bitch because the rabbits were too thin or too old or something. And I'd stand there and watch my father sort of shrink up, and feel like dying. But the good part that came before that was really good."

"Yes." Feeling as if he understood Dan better.

Abruptly Dan took his feet off the dashboard and sat up. "Hey, let me drive for a while."

"All right, as soon as I find a place to pull over."

After the car was stopped they heard running water. At the foot of the bank, a small mountain stream rushed foaming between smooth rocks. Not two feet wide at that point, it spread out farther down the valley behind a beaver dam. They climbed down the grassy bank to it, and Dan squatted and drank from cupped hands. Then he stood, chin dripping, and wiped his mouth on his sleeve. They both lit cigarettes. Dan looked around and stretched. "It's nice here. I'm glad we aren't going to stay in the city."

"I was worried after I made the decision to take the cottage. I was afraid you'd miss your friends."

"You mean Bart and all? No, and anyway they're all going home for the summer. All of them have folks." Then sounding as if he had just discovered it, "You know, most people do."

"I guess so." He climbed back up to the car, suddenly and irrationally sad.

"One of these days I'm gonna go see my sister," Dan said, following him. "If only Aunt Freda wasn't around! Oh, well, that old bitch can't last forever. When I was home that time at the end of the Army, the druggist told me she has a bad heart." Dan gave a bark of mirthless laughter. "He doesn't know the half of it."

The cooling car ticked quietly to itself. He paused to inspect a piece of loose chrome, tried to force it back into place. It broke off in his hand. He looked at it. "Shit!" To hell with it, the car would work just as well without it. He threw it into the bushes.

"Don't you have folks in Denmark?" Dan asked, going around to the driver's side.

"Distant relatives. I hardly know them. And the Norwegian branch of the family all lived in the same small town. They were wiped out during a Nazi reprisal. But I didn't know them well either."

"Shot?"

"Machine-gunned." Like the women and children at the concentration camp. Then he felt Dan's hand on his shoulder and looked at him, almost startled.

"Don't, Hawk. I didn't mean to bring that up. Come on, let's get going. I'm getting hungry." But he kept his hand on him and did not move away.

Strange blend of mental and physical pain, guts in a knot. And sweeping through it, diminishing it, the love and desire for Dan. Impulsively, he pulled him close and kissed him fiercely on the mouth, heedless of who might see, though also aware that the road was not heavily traveled, and that no cars had passed for some time.

Dan's arms were strong around him, his mouth warm and responsive, then Dan moved away. "C'mon. We ain't got all day."

"Yes, of course." He got awkwardly into the passenger side and slammed the door, feeling embarrassed. His hands were trembling.

Dan started the engine, adjusted the rearview mirror, put the car in gear and pulled smoothly out into the road. "This thing handles nice," he commented after a few minutes. "It's like dreaming about driving."

He had to say, "I'm sorry, Dan."

"What for? Oh, back there. Why? Nobody was around."

He shook his head, more to himself than Dan, frustrated because he could not find words, even for himself. "I shouldn't have" was all he could come up with.

"Forget it. Shit, Hawk, you sure make a lot out of nothing sometimes."

He was both disillusioned and relieved by Dan's lack of understanding. It was not "nothing." His hands had stopped trembling but his mind remained uneasy, at odds with itself. They drove in silence through a medium-sized factory town, past stony farms and back into wooded valleys.

"Hawk?"

He looked at Dan, who was watching the road. "What is it?" There had been an intensity in Dan's tone.

"I'm gonna ask you something. I've been thinking . . . and listen. You can't go around being eaten alive by that damn camp full of dead people. You've gotta stop it. Can't you see it's no use? It's been a long time now. Can't you leave it be?"

"It won't leave me be."

"Do you remember it? I mean, do you know what happened after that first half-hour, after you found that kid and told off Lieutenant Travis. I've always wondered."

"I remember telling off Travis . . . the pile of bodies. Looking for . . . Not finding . . ."

"Do you remember that you were gonna try and sort through a heap of real dead ones? Do you remember that?"

He felt a shudder of disgust and dismay, but his memory was blank. "No," he said slowly. "The next thing I remember is running a bulldozer, digging." Then, when Dan did not say any more, "Tell me."

"Morrie got in your way and stopped you, and you began swinging at him. So I came over and took hold of you. I mean, you were already in trouble up to your fucking ears for calling Travis an asshole. You remember that he went bitching to Captain Hogarth and wanted you court-martialed for insubordination and inciting to mutiny? Only Hogarth blew his stack and called him an asshole too, so he hadda drop that. Hadda content himself with busting you all the way down from corporal."

He had been peripherally aware of that, though he had taken no interest in it. Dan had gone off on a bypath to give him time. He asked, "What happened when you took hold of me?"

"I got my arms around the outsides of yours. I was sort of off to one side. You weren't fighting so much as trying to get away, but hard to hold. Then all of a sudden you turned toward me and held on to me like you were drowning." Dan stopped, then said, "You gotta understand this part. At the time I didn't think about it, hardly noticed. It wasn't until lots later that I realized you'd kissed me—here." Dan touched his temple. "Then you said, 'I'm all right now, lay off.' And you sounded OK, so I let go and you went off and climbed onto a dozer."

"And then?"

"That's all. Except you didn't speak a word to anyone for three-four days, past 'yes sir' when it was necessary. And you walked around like a fucking zombie for a couple of weeks, until all of us were beginning to worry that maybe you'd cracked up. And then all of a sudden you began to come around . . . and that's all."

"How much later was 'lots later'?"

"Dunno. Sort of gradual. In jail, I guess. Yeah, I was lying there on this fucking iron bunk scratching flea bites. In jail. And thinking that Jeanie probably thought I was dead by now. And thinking that nobody on earth cared if I lived or died. And then it came to me that you cared. That time I was wounded you cried for me. Nobody ever did that before."

Dan stopped talking and concentrated on passing a dilapidated truck piled with burlap bags. The road wound downhill. He kept getting glimpses of a flat valley, golden in the late sun, carpeted with dense green and divided by a small river. The road followed the course of the water in gentle curves, then turned sharply to cross a bright orange bridge.

"My old man used to cry a lot," Dan went on thoughtfully, "but I think he cried for himself. Every fucking time he got really smashed he'd get down on his knees and beg me to forgive him. But I must have told him a million times that I did, and he never believed me."

"Did you?"

"Dunno. I suppose so. Have by now certainly. Shit! I loved the old fart, even if he was a fucking drunk. The poor bastard never had half a chance. And then he ended up dying of DT's, screaming. What a way to go. I was there. He kept calling me Emil—that was one of his brothers who'd been dead God knows how long. Thought he was back in the Old Country. I joined the Army three days after he was buried."

"Dan?" He wanted to convey some of his concern.

"No, let me finish. Where was I? Yeah, in jail scratching fleas. There was this kid in my cell. Just barely twenty-one. Blond all over like you. Not at all like you really. Little skinny guy, maybe weighed 125. They'd gang-banged him that afternoon, and I was feeling kind of wormy because I hadn't done a goddamned thing to stop it. Telling myself all the goddamn reasons why it wasn't good sense. But you see, little as he was, it took four of them to hold him down, and a blanket over his head too. And he didn't make a sound. His lip was fat from his biting it. He wasn't crying like most of them do, just lying there still and stiff.

"And I began to wonder what it would be like not to be strong. I mean, strong isn't something you get for being good, it just happens to you. And I was wondering how the kid felt. Just then this creep they called Pigshit came by and made some kind of crude remark about how they were planning a double feature."

The car turned sharply and crossed the orange bridge, tires whirring on the metal mesh flooring. A sound like an enormous zipper.

"I didn't stop to think," Dan went on. "I just tried to look mean and said, 'Lay the fuck off him, he's mine.' "

The road wound uphill again, around granite outcroppings. "Pigshit didn't like that one damn bit, but the punk was my cellmate, which gave me rights, and besides, nobody wanted to mess with me. I had it made as long as I didn't cross Big George.

"So anyway, the kid just looked at me. Not scared or grateful

98

or anything. Just sort of sad. Resigned. Poor kid was only in for shoplifting. He'd been stealing for his mother from the time he was old enough to walk. So there I was staring back at him. His eyes were dark blue, almost as blue as yours. And I could see— Well, it was like a fork in the road. If I went one way, I'd end up like Pigshit or Big George, because that way it's safe. You're so hard nothing can get to you. The other way was you, and good English, all that stuff. But not safe.

"I wanted to go to sleep, because I didn't want to think about it, but I began remembering all kinds of stuff. It was like putting a puzzle together.

"Like the time I got hit. You came out and got me, cried because you thought I was dead. And I'd thought I was dead too for a minute there. Then I saw you leaning over me. And then you were carrying me, and I looked back at the dozer and this shell came in and wiped it out. But you didn't even break stride. You acted like nothing had happened."

"I didn't notice."

"Jesus! And then the fuel started to burn orange. Orange with black smoke, like at Schwartzgarten. Then I remembered how you had kissed me, and how you sort of pulled yourself together and I was sure you cared about me. Maybe more than I cared about myself. Were you in love with me then?"

"Yes. I didn't know how I felt until you were wounded though. I wouldn't let myself know."

The side of the hill was bathed in pink light, the shadows of the rocks long and dark, stretching ahead of them, pointing toward the coast.

"And I never guessed."

"Except you did guess," he reminded him.

"Not really, not then."

"When did you decide to come to New York?"

"In jail that time. You see, I had to pretend to use the kid. The way I felt about him, like he was my kid brother or something, for Christ's sake, I couldn't have got it up if my life had depended on it. But he helped me fake it. It was after he got out. You see, I'd liked having him in my arms, holding him close. It helped the loneliness.

"And the more I thought about it, the more sure I was that you had to be gay. All that about looking you up. And the time in the pine forest when we both got smashed on schnapps, and you went bolting away from me as if the devil was after you. None of it meant shit at the time, but it all added up."

He remembered the night in Bavaria. They were alone together, the others having gone off to do god knew what. Lying on the warm grass looking down a slope at a small mountain lake, silver in the moonlight. The sound of the wind soughing in the pines behind them, the scent of the needles. A feeling of cleanness and space, the stars thick overhead, an owl calling in the distance. A timeless moment of peace in the middle of horror, as if this segment of time were lifted free of context, as if there would be no tomorrow, had been no yesterday. Death an ugly story made up to frighten children, unreal, not to be taken seriously.

Dan was curled beside him, sleepy and warm. His head was heavy on his shoulder, a source of comfort that spread over him like a safe blanket, keeping away the world. Neither had spoken for some time.

Then Dan lifted a schnapps bottle and inspected it critically, holding it up to the full moon. He said, "Empty," and threw it away. It struck something in the dark and shattered loudly. He was startled by the crash, then relaxed again, but he was no longer numb with alcohol and fatigue. Dan's head on his shoulder, his presence near him was overpowering. Without thinking, almost without meaning to, he began stroking the soft hair. And Dan did not object, he snuggled closer and seemed to go to sleep.

He discovered he was murmuring Dan's name aloud, over and over, that he had forgotten to call him Polecat, and he heard the yearning in his voice. Dan, much more than half asleep and very drunk, snuggled closer and rubbed his cheek against his shirt. For a moment love seemed easy and possible, and he almost reached out to embrace him. But a noise—what? Perhaps a branch breaking, or a fish jumping in the pond below, some small night sound—reminded him that there would be a tomorrow. That there had been a yesterday, and that Dan's closeness meant no more than that of a sleepy child pillowing its head on a handy shoulder. Panicked by what might have happened, he jerked away and ran, leaving Dan sitting astonished in the moonlight, staring after him.

He said, "You never referred to that. I'd thought—hoped—you'd been too drunk to remember."

"I damn near was. The next day, it seemed so unlike you, I figured I had to've dreamed it or something. It wasn't that important to me. I just didn't think about it again. Until later, of course."

"I called you Dan," he said.

"Yeah. And you know, that was what made it seem so much like a dream that I figured it hadda be. It was like when I was a real, real little kid and my old man'd carry me, and I'd go to sleep listening to him say my name, and everything was good then. Even my mother. So it all got mixed up together and I forgot about it."

The light had faded to gray. The road topped the rise and dipped down into another valley. Abruptly they were plunged into evening. Dan turned on the headlights.

He remembered that Dan had said he was hungry over an hour before. "We'd better find a place to eat soon."

"Yeah, I'm starving."

The car sped on down the narrow black road, past far-off farmhouses. The shapes of the hills could still be made out against the last wash of light in the sky. The first star was out. There seemed to be no towns, and he did not know where they were, for he had paid no attention to the names of the last few they had passed. He realized that they were going to have to stop for the night. He would never be able to find the cottage after dark. The map was complicated.

Dan was attending to his driving. It was a tricky road, narrow and with unexpected turns. Dan drove well, better than he did, for his reaction time was far faster. The engine did sound smooth. There was an odd intimacy in the dark, in the confining space of the front seat. The car seemed to be following its lights, as if drawn forward by the beams on the road.

He did not want to stay at an inn with Dan. Could not sleep with him in such a place. Danger? Yes, but not that. That was not the real reason, it was an excuse. What then?

Simon. He almost said aloud, "Simon, go away," but saying it would not dispel his image, or any memories. A few months against more than ten years. He almost said, "Dan, talk to me," but could not do that either.

Hotel rooms, pensions, all transient places. Impersonal, all different and all the same. Shuttered windows in Italy, mosquito netting and bolsters in France. In France, in a better inn, a girl asking if the gentlemen preferred pillows.

Simon seen through mosquito netting, Simon complaining and making a joke of the bolsters. One hotel room after another. Some good, some not so good. Simon laughing about "waterproof" French toilet paper. Laughing in Normandy because the toilet was a square porcelain affair on the floor with raised places for one's feet. Like a flush cat box, Simon said. Edinburgh, Scotland. The bathroom scale weighed in stones. Vegetable marrow for dinner and thick wet bacon for breakfast. Simon's waspish comments making it funny.

Carcassonne before that, a huge room over the city wall. In a shopwindow pictures of St. Nazaire with a dog, reminiscent of the Fool in the Marseille Tarot. Simon saying with an edge to his voice that since the saint had been cured of his ulcers by the dog licking them, it was obvious that the wrong one of the pair had been canonized.

Simon taking pictures. Always taking pictures. Climbing onto walls, borrowing flimsy ladders, lying on his belly, stopping in mid-stride so he would find himself talking to the air. Amused by his annoyance. Simon talking about the light, rearranging schedules so he could come back when the shadows were right. Always carrying at least one camera, usually two or three, and a bag of lenses and equipment.

That first week they had spent together in Greece, Simon had sneaked a camera into a monastery and gotten a portrait of a monk that looked like a medieval carving. Later in Rome he had gotten them both up before dawn and driven out to the Appian Way to take pictures of the Italian pines and the chariot-wheel grooves worn into the smooth stone blocks. In 71 B.C. Caesar had crucified hundreds of Spartacus's followers along that road. Miles of them had been left to rot in the sun and be eaten by crows. And no one remembered their names.

Nameless dead. His mind flinched again. It was like taking a step back from quicksand. He looked at Dan, his face faintly illuminated by the light from the dashboard. He had to touch him and reached out.

Dan glanced at him. "What?"

Ashamed of his weakness and not wanting to mention his obsession—for he had to admit that was what it was—he peered ahead into the darkness and said, "A light, I think." As if mentioning it had conjured it into existence, they rounded a curve and found an inn in front of them, dimly lighted by guttering gas flames, dark and low to the ground, almost part of the landscape.

"Hey, great," Dan said, turning onto the graveled area beside the building and pulling in beside a black Cadillac. "I'm so hungry my stomach thinks my throat's cut."

The Tory Inn, with a picture of a redcoat on the sign, after the style of old pub signs in England. He had never heard of it, but it looked inviting. Not that it made any difference. He was going to have to feed Dan. He wished his memories would leave him alone, that he had a better-disciplined mind and could turn them off before they led him into difficulty.

The interior of the inn, as he had expected from the sign, was decorated in unsparing Early American throughout. The dining room was small, dark enough so the candle on the table was needed for illumination. There was no menu, no choice of food, but he realized with his second spoonful of mushroom soup that they had stumbled onto a gourmet restaurant of the first order. The soup was followed by lobster newburg and a green salad. Dessert was rich homemade vanilla ice cream. Dan was happy because he could have all he wanted to eat. Haakon had never had better coffee and he was tempted to ask the brand and method of preparation but lacked the nerve. Simon would have dared, and would no doubt have charmed the chef into parting with half his secrets too.

What did Simon want out of life anyway? He seemed to be trying to store up the world in his photographic files. Pictures of everything: people, always people, animals of all sorts, birds, insects, art, architecture, everything from castles to hovels—and yes, walls, ruins, construction sites. His war pictures had made him a worldwide reputation. A perfectionist and an artist. Dedicated. A different person from the faun who made love.

Why was he thinking of Simon now? He looked across the table at Dan. Simple, complicated; beautiful, ugly. And he loved him. Yet he felt unfaithful to Simon now as he had not before.

He had taken a room at the inn when they arrived. There were two double beds in it; no reason to share a bed with Dan. He finished his coffee and they went up the wooden stairs. Their room had a heavily beamed ceiling and claustrophobic wallpaper in a dark green with a small all-over design. The casement windows had bull's-eye glass panes. Perhaps the building was genuinely old.

He got ready for bed and got in, wondering if he hoped Dan would join him or if he hoped he would not. When Dan got into the other bed and turned out the light he felt bereft and lost and knew what he had wanted.

He could not ask Dan to come over, because he was afraid he would think he wanted to make love, and he did not want to have to explain that he only wanted him close enough so he could touch him if he needed to, that he was afraid of his memories. He heard Dan rustling around in the other bed, then five minutes later Dan got up and came over, got in with him.

"I'm afraid to be alone," Dan said, uncompromisingly honest as always.

Because Dan had been honest, he had to be too. He said, "I felt the same way."

He felt Dan's hand touch his cheek. Dan said, "Tonight let's just sleep. OK?"

"OK." Had Dan read his reluctance or was it Dan's mood?

July 31, 1946

Haakon was wakened by the intense red of the sun on his eyelids. He rolled onto his back and turned his head away from the brightness, hoping to be able to go back to sleep. He could feel the sun's warmth across his chest and on the side of his head. He told himself to be grateful that today was clear. He had not liked those last two days of rain and wind.

He could hear gulls crying over the house, the hum of the exhaust fans in the roof peaks, the crash and suck of the waves. Still some sound of rolling gravel, but the tide would soon be high enough for the swimming to be good. He opened his eyes and looked up at the golden beamed ceiling that slanted down to the book-lined walls. All the wall studs had shelves between them, crammed with books, and artifacts brought by the sea.

At the foot of the bed was a chest of drawers, and dominating the wall beyond was Tom's fireplace. Rupert's Island was the last remnant of a lateral moraine, the local rocks were an index of all the places the glaciers had been. And all were rounded by the ice, not wave-worn as he had at first assumed. The facing of the fireplace contained as many kinds of stone as Tom had been able to find: marbles, granites, basalts, sandstones, schists. All put together with quantities of cement. The first day he had walked into the cabin, he felt the fireplace was an old friend, for Tom had talked about it endlessly during the three years he had worked on it. He had collected yellow firebrick from an abandoned factory to line it, found the iron pothooks in a barn. The lion-faced andirons were antiques he had discovered at a local auction.

Jutting out from the wall to the left of the fireplace, away from the bed and near the only door, was a bookshelf that defined the kitchen area with its stove and sink. He wondered whose day it was to get breakfast, but could remember no detail that made yesterday stand out enough for him to be sure.

Timeless here. At first it had made him uneasy, but now he liked the freedom from schedules and clocks. Why was he uneasy, unhappy? Nothing had happened. Dan was asleep beside him.

He looked over at him. Dan was on his back, hands at his sides, palm-down, one leg drawn up. The white fishook-shaped scar on his thigh was sharply marked against the deep bronze of his skin. His mouth was half open. Dan usually slept with his mouth open. Doubtless a habit remaining from the years when he had not been able to breathe through his broken nose.

Dan's face was relaxed, no harsh lines. The sunlight sparkled on the down on his upper lip. His cheeks and powerfully muscled neck were still child-smooth.

He reached out to touch him and saw the lightness of his hand in contrast to Dan's darkness. He paused and withdrew his hand. He had always been ashamed of his paleness, his fair complexion. It seemed somehow unmasculine to him. And though he had more tan now than he ever had before, it was light gold, not the dark, almost blackish color Dan had acquired within two weeks. Yet he had spent so much time in the sun that his body hair was bleached pale, as it had been when he was a teenager, and the hair on his arms and legs was almost white.

Nothing effeminate about being blond, he told himself, yet he did not believe it. Phrases like "fair young maid" and "lily maid of Astolat" were his associations. If just once he could have a lover lighter than he! But he was not attracted to blonds. He was excited by men with olive skins and black or dark hair like Simon and Jim. Even though Dan's hair was chestnut, now sunstreaked almost blond in places, he had the dark complexion of a so-called "black German." Bavarian. Jim's hair was gray when they first became lovers, but it had been black before that. Jim had been swarthy, his body thickly furred with black. There had always been a bluish cast to his jaw even when he was freshly shaved.

Suddenly restless, he got quietly off the bed, pulled on chinos and went to the kitchen corner. He pumped water for shaving and, while he was at it, filled the coffeepot too.

He was measuring coffee into the perforated metal basket when he caught peripherally the movement of Dan sitting up and heard him yawning as loudly and elaborately as a dog. Something almost puppyish about Dan of late, a playfulness. Yesterday when he had been plowing through *Mein Kampf* in German as part of the research for his text, Dan had come over and tickled him until he almost lost his temper. Then had wrestled with him and teased him like a teenager. Infuriating, yet charming. He would have been content to spend the day reading, but Dan needed more movement than that, and a brief foray outdoors had proved too uncomfortable because the rain was cold. Certainly it had been much more pleasant spending half a rainy afternoon making love in front of the fire than it would have been reading Hitler's rantings.

Dan padded across the room, paused behind him, noticed he had on pants and asked, "You making breakfast?"

"I thought I might as well." So it had been Dan's day. He took bacon and eggs from the refrigerator, unhooked the frying pan from its nail and put it on the stove. After the first few days they had been here he and Dan had stopped wearing clothes when it was warm, but cooking in the nude was foolhardy. Especially bacon.

Dan pumped water to wash his face and brush his teeth. The bacon was in the pan, and his shaving water was hot. Dan was in his way, leaning over the sink inspecting his face in the small round mirror that hung over it.

"Do you think there's something wrong with me?" Dan asked. "There's lots of men younger'n me with beards. How come all I've got is this dumb fuzz?" he said, rubbing his upper lip with his forefinger as though he hoped massaging it would encourage the hair to grow.

"Some men have hardly any beard, and you could just be late getting one."

"Did you ever grow a beard? I mean like in the pictures in books."

"I had a mustache for about two years once. But one day I was trimming it and ended up without it. I decided it was too much trouble to grow another. Besides, it got butter in it when I ate toast."

"Why don't you grow a beard in the month we've got left? I bet it'd be a good one," Dan said enviously.

"I don't want to." He wished Dan would not ask questions before he had had his coffee.

"But then you wouldn't have to shave, heat water. Why do you shave twice a day? Why not just mornings?"

"And have you bitch about me being prickly?" He didn't know why he felt so irritable. "Now move. I need the mirror."

Dan went around to the other side of the shelves and leaned on the top, watching him intently. "Why do you shave mornings?"

"I don't feel right if I don't."

Dan was quiet for a time, then observed, "You sure make funny faces when you do that."

He finished the area under his nose. "Didn't you ever see anyone shave before?" he snapped, feeling self-conscious and even more irritable.

Dan ignored his crossness. "Couldn't in the Army. The guys'd of thought I was a nut if I'd stood around staring. And I can't remember watching my old man." Dan straightened and went to the front door, saying as he passed, "You'd better turn the bacon over." Then he stood looking out the screen at the sea, hands braced on the frame. "Nice day," he commented contentedly. "Looks like the tide'll be just right in about half an hour."

He turned over the bacon. "We have to clean the place."

"Yeah, I noticed. OK," Dan agreed.

"Before swimming," he specified. For a week they had been intending to sweep first thing in the morning and then had not gotten around to it.

"Yeah, OK." Dan sounded amused and he glanced at him. "Sometimes you're a real crab before breakfast," Dan observed, obviously not taking his mood seriously.

While he finished preparing breakfast, Dan shook out the bottom sheet and made the bed. Dan objected to sand in the bed far more than he did, so he had taken over this chore, claiming he did a better job.

After they had eaten, Haakon found his mood considerably improved. Dan was right. Breakfast did have a good effect. They swept the floor, dusted, cleaned ashtrays, laid a new fire, then together gathered up the surprisingly heavy rag rug from in front of the hearth and took it out to shake it. It was twenty by fifteen feet, the center more faded than the outside edges, as if it had taken years to complete. He wondered again where Abby had found it. Abby had to have discovered it. If Tom had, he would have talked about it.

The rug seemed dense with memory, for every strip of braid had once been something else, a dress, a necktie, a shirt. Had belonged to someone, been worn, perhaps liked, perhaps disliked. The stitches were tiny, tight, and even. Someone had spent years putting it together. He knew something about sewing, for his mother had taught him to embroider when he was ten and in bed with asthma most of a winter. "What a lot of work this was to make," he said.

"I suppose," Dan responded without interest.

He dropped the subject. He never would have admitted to knowing how to embroider, to having completed a sampler that read, "Truth is beauty and beauty is truth," with birds and leaves around the sentiment. In 1931, after his mother's death, when he had been clearing the house prior to selling it, he had come across the sampler among her things. He had burned it in the furnace with enormous satisfaction, and still did not know why this childish act of destruction had pleased him so much.

They swept the area where the rug had been and put it back, then finished up the cleaning. No dustpan was needed; they could brush the sand out the door. Dan left the broom leaning against the outside of the house and started down the beach toward the water. He watched him walking, the economy and grace of all his movements, the play of muscles in his thighs and buttocks. Dan paused, half turned. "Hey, move it!" Stood waiting.

He left his pants on the back of a dining chair and followed Dan down. The water was green, slightly turbid from the storm. Bits of seaweed floated on the surface. He waded slowly out, wary of the rocks on the bottom, gasped when a wave slapped him in the belly, then plunged in and swam. The top layer of water was thinner and warmer than usual. He could feel the cool of the layer below when he kicked.

They swam slowly out together, then Dan stopped, treading water, and gestured toward the boulder that stuck out of the water some yards down the shore. "Race?"

"Sure." The first day they had arrived, Dan had swum like a puppy, splashing inefficiently and energetically. He had taught him how to kick, then the various strokes. Dan swam well now, but he could still swim faster. Partly experience, but partly that he was better built for it. He could run faster too, though in every other way Dan could easily outdo him physically.

He was already sitting on the shelf of rock when Dan touched it. Dan pulled himself out and sprawled beside him looking over the edge into the water. Waves washed past, swelling and dropping. Gulls called, and a dozen of them bobbed on the water like bathtub toys.

He reached into the water and hooked out a cluster of rubbery brown seaweed, sat pinching the air bladders along the strands. "We should get some supplies today," he said idly. "We're getting low."

"It's gonna be hot," Dan said, then, reconsidering, "Yeah, why not? Maybe I can talk that blonde in the drugstore into the movies Saturday. You know the one? Got curly hair and nice big tits?"

"Susan, the druggist's daughter?"

"Yeah, her." Then Dan sat up. "Hawk? Tell me the truth. You really don't mind me taking girls out?"

"No, I'm glad to see you with friends your own age." Dan continued to look at him, so he added, "Besides, it's good camouflage."

"Why don't you?"

"Why don't I what?"

"Go out with women. Like you said, camouflage."

"I do."

"Big deal! Wives of friends to a concert."

"Others too. You know that."

"Yeah, and shake hands good night."

"They're friends."

"Safe," Dan said scornfully.

What was Dan after? He knew Dan enjoyed kissing girls, he

had said so. He had seen him in the Army feeling up whores with obvious enjoyment and excitement. Dan found women exciting, no doubt of that. Could Dan turn around again and go back to being normal? He wanted him to have a happier life than he had had, but the thought of losing him made his stomach hurt. Dan had asked him a question. "What?" Then recalling the question, answered it before Dan could restate it. "Yes, I've been out with women who wanted more than a handshake, but . . . It's hard to explain. Some seem to feel my lack of interest and either become friends or drift away entirely. Once or twice women have become fond of me and been hurt. I try not to get involved. I can't kiss them on the mouth, and women always seem to feel it's because there's something wrong with them."

"Can't, or don't want to?"

"I begin to feel panicky. But I suppose you could say I don't want to."

Dan was silent for a long time, then he asked thoughtfully, "Was it always like that, your whole life?"

"Yes." Then, surprised by his lapse of memory, "No. There was a girl, Leda, when I was around seventeen or so." He remembered long hair the color of tea, her quick gesture of pushing it back from her face. She liked yellow and wore it often, looked like sunshine in it. Hazel eyes, greenish but not green. Near-sighted, large-pupiled like many myopic people. Long, slender, delicate hands, very white. Not pretty, but beautiful with the kind of fine-boned beauty that would always last. Her face was like a good poem, the features harmonious and clear. He had written poems to her, though he had never showed them to anyone, and later on had burned them.

"What happened?" Dan's voice was gentle, almost like a prompting from inside his own head.

"Nothing much. It took me forever to ask her out. I was horribly shy. I thought I loved her. I don't know any more if I did or not. My mother didn't like her and made me promise not to see her any more, but I kept right on seeing her. Then my mother found out, and we quarreled. She got so angry she had a stroke. I always felt it was my fault."

"And Leda?"

"First there was the uproar over my mother's illness, and after that she was an invalid. I never made a decision not to see Leda, but by the time I got around to contacting her, she had become engaged." He remembered that last meeting. She was in love, and seemed almost to glow with happiness. She had been kind and regretful, sitting there, half turned toward him, beside him on the red plush sofa in her parents' living room, occasionally reaching over to pat his hand consolingly. Her fingers had been cool on his skin. He did not want to think about that any more.

He stood up and dived down into the opaque water, plunging through layers of coldness until he felt the give of sand under his fingers. His hand encountered a smooth stone about the size of an egg. He grasped it and rose slowly up toward the circle of light on the surface.

The stone was black, diagonally bisected by a band of slightly crystalline white quartz. A lucky stone. He swam to the rock, laid it down and got out of the water.

Dan picked it up and looked at it. "Hey, this is the best one I've seen. Do you want it?"

"No."

"Can I have it?"

"No." Without pausing to think, he took it from Dan and threw it as far as he could out to sea.

"What'd you do that for?" Dan asked, seeming hurt.

He said, "I don't know." He did not know exactly enough to state it, even to himself, and he did not want to attempt to explain to Dan. It had something to do with the soapstone dragon and with the wish that he could throw that into the ocean and in this way divest himself of his past. Inadequately he said, "I'm sorry."

"Shit! It was only a fucking rock," Dan said, accepting his apology. But he looked hurt, and a moment later he dived into the water and swam back the way they had come.

He expected him to turn and come back, but instead Dan went ashore in front of the cottage. He watched him until he disappeared behind the nearest dune.

Then he sat for a long time, hugging his knees and staring unhappily at the horizon. He should have let Dan have the goddamned stone. It did not mean to Dan what it did to him. His bones began to ache from the hardness of the rock and he was lonely. He swam back to shore and returned to the cabin.

The room smelled strongly of scorched coffee and Dan was at the round table eating a peanut butter and jelly sandwich, a cup of black dregs in front of him. He had put on a new pot, but it had not yet begun to percolate.

Dan took a drink from his cup, made a face, then drank some more. "Want to go into town now?"

He discovered that he did not want Dan to go into town at all. He wanted to go to East Rupert alone and leave Dan safely here. Simultaneously he did not want to let Dan out of his sight. Perversely, to spite himself, he said, "Why don't you go in alone? I ought to be getting something done on my book." He picked up the box of notes he kept in the corner, set it on a chair and began taking out file cards and arranging them on the wooden table. "That is, if you don't mind," he added, hoping desperately that Dan would say he did.

"No, why should I? Where's the grocery list?"

"Beside the sink."

Trying to ignore Dan, he bent over the yellow blue-lined legal-sized paper and began rereading the manuscript, putting notes in the margins to indicate which points he should double-check when he had access to a library.

Dan had come over near him, buttoning his shirt. "How about I stop at the fish place and get a couple of boiled lobsters? If I pick them up on the way home they'll still be hot when I get here."

"You're planning to stay in town all afternoon?" Dan unzipped his jeans to tuck in his shirt. Half-dressed, glimpsed, his body was intensely exciting. Haakon's hands began to tremble. He hid them under the edge of the table and gripped them together.

Dan shrugged, "Why not? Suzie said something about showing me where to dig clams. Or maybe we could go swimming if she isn't too busy."

"Hadn't you better take swimming trunks?"

"Why bother? I can swim in my pants."

Dan finished tucking in the long-sleeved blue work shirt and zipped himself up again. Then he went over to the chest of drawers and rooted around in the second one down for a minute before opening the top one and taking out a twenty-dollar bill. He put the bill into his wallet, commenting, "There's only fifteen left now. You'd better cash a check next time you go into town."

"Remind me." He felt unreal, talking so naturally and calmly while eaten by rage and desire.

"OK, then. I'll see you around six at the latest. If I come back sooner, I'll pick up lobsters anyway. They're good cold. See ya."

Dan had noticed nothing. He listened to the car start and move in first gear up the dune. Then the sound was abruptly cut off a moment after it was shifted into second. He listened to the silence and stared at the manuscript with unfocused eyes. After a moment he screwed the cap onto his fountain pen and laid it down. He was not going to be able to concentrate.

He went over to the stove and poured himself a cup of fresh coffee and stood drinking it, then slowly went over to the dresser and, disgusted with himself, groped around in the drawer Dan had

111

had open until he found Dan's blue scarf. He held it in his hand a moment, then guiltily put it back exactly where he had found it.

He had not really thought Dan would try to sleep with the girl anyway, but now he had proof. Why didn't he feel better? This jealousy of Dan was new and disturbing. He had never felt it before. A good thing he had stayed here. He would not have been able to bear watching Dan's head snap around when they passed a pretty girl, seeing him smile at the pharmacist's daughter. Yet he had watched a week ago and felt nothing but an almost fatherly enjoyment of Dan's ability to be happy.

His black silk kimono was hanging on a hook by the bed. He found himself staring at it. Yesterday when they had made love in front of the fire, Dan had left him to go and get it.

The first few weeks they had been lovers he had hardly been aware of the silk. Dan had kept his scarf clutched in his fist and was not obvious about it. But then, as time passed, the scarf had been more in evidence. Dan would wind it around his forearm, holding the end in his hand. He had told himself that Dan felt comfortable enough with him so he no longer had to hide it. Now he wondered if that was not it at all, if instead Dan needed it more.

He had asked about the fetish once, and Dan had left the apartment, gone for a walk, and not come back for two hours. He was curious to know how Dan's attachment to silk had gotten started, but he had lived with his curiosity about Simon long enough so he was used to being denied satisfaction.

When had Dan started wanting him to wear the kimono? Some time ago, back in New York. He had thought he could get used to it, but each time they made love he found himself wondering if Dan were caressing him through the silk, or the silk he happened to be under. The damn stuff was almost like a third person in bed. But he had no right to complain, since he had known from the outset that Dan was a fetishist.

Dan had left his blue scarf behind, but did he have another one stashed in the car? Or another one he did not know about that had been in the drawer? Could Dan make it with a woman without silk under some circumstances? What was wrong with him? He had to stop thinking like that. He either trusted Dan or he did not. He could not allow himself this sort of emotional binge.

In love with a heterosexual fetishist. He remembered thinking that back at the beginning. What was the matter? He had always known that he could not keep Dan forever. He had hoped he could, but he had known it was unlikely their relationship could last.

Dan was in town by now, no doubt flirting with Susan. Dan

112

would leave him and marry. Should Dan marry? Jim's life had been hell because of his marriage.

He remembered the scene Martha had made a month after Jim's death. She had arrived at his apartment unannounced and had charged in gesticulating with a leather-bound diary. The lock was still in place, but the strap that had held it shut was cut cleanly, as if with a razor. She perched on the edge of a chair, refused to take off her coat, and refused the coffee he brought her.

As soon as he saw the diary he thought he knew what had brought her. And he had been correct up to a point. He had thought she was angry with him, but it developed that she was angry with Jim, and that it was even more complex than that.

"You were a boy of nineteen," she said. "He debauched you. Oh, Haakon, I'll never forgive myself for keeping silent, for letting him go on like that. I brought him into your house, and you the son of my dearest friend."

She waved away his attempts to explain, did not listen to him. Then she began to cry and appealed to him for help. Her son, James Jr., had come to her for money to pay blackmail. Jim's son had married well, had three daughters and a son, and cruised parks at night, picking up men. He was glad Jim had not lived to find out that his older son was homosexual, for one of Jim's prides had been that he had raised his sons to be normal.

He had not been able to be of any real help. He knew nothing about that sort of thing. He told Martha this, and offered her the only help he could, money. She was indignant and left in a fury, pausing only to throw the diary at him.

He had read the entire diary carefully. Much of it concerned Jim's law practice, his observations about clients, co-workers, judges he dealt with. There were notes about points of law, often with comments on the paradoxes that were so prevalent. There were some philosophical speculations. Jim had copied aphorisms from a variety of sources and commented on them pointedly and aptly, with a turn of dry bitter wit that was very much Jim.

Then there were pages of long sentimental, passionate descriptions of himself and their relationship. "My golden god, my salvation." That sort of thing. Things Jim never would have said to him, even in the tenderest of moments. Alien, touching, tragic, for he had never known he meant that much to Jim. And he had been hurt too, for even though he knew Jim wore a mask for the rest of the world, he had always thought he wore no mask with him.

Now he could be glad he had not known this side of Jim, for back then he would have been embarrassed. Distressed by unmerited adoration, he probably would have put up barriers against it. A good reason for Jim not to have shown it, for Jim knew him well enough to have foreseen his reaction.

The most touching part of the diary had been the seldom mentioned but pervasive sense of loneliness. There were brief references to Martha's lack of understanding, her distaste for him, the ways in which she made him feel castrated and ugly. But the loneliness went far beyond that.

He had felt it himself. He knew more about it than he wanted to. Dan ought to have a better life than that, ought to live with the world's approval, be smiled at for loving.

But ought-tos were not always possibles. He remembered the night he had met Jim's son. That was more than four years ago, before the Army. In fact, he had been walking, trying to think out what to do, having just gotten his draft notice. He wanted to be in the Army, not only out of a feeling of patriotism—a strong enough factor—but because of an urge to play what he saw as a masculine role. Yet the fear of exposure weighed on him like a nightmare.

He had been crossing Central Park on his way home. Simon out of town. Feeling lonely.

An almost-familiar shape approached him in a shadowed area of the path. He recognized the walk and head carriage, but something was askew. He stopped short and the man approached, stopped just in front of him.

Jim's voice propositioned him. Some form of double entendre. He no longer remembered the words, but the manner had been slick and practiced.

Befuddled by the voice and a feeling of recognition, he asked, "Jim?"

"Do you know me?" The voice was wary.

"Do I?" Still confused, trying to understand, wondering who this was, even—momentarily—on the verge of believing in ghosts.

A car had passed, temporarily blinding him with its lights, and Jim's voice—not quite Jim's, though the inflections were his—said, "Oh, God! It's Haakon!" The hand that was not Jim's but his son's clutched his sleeve and the voice pleaded, without dignity, "Please, please, I don't want my wife to know. I *promised* her."

He shook the hand away. "I haven't seen you. I don't know you. Leave me alone." And he walked on without glancing back. Tried to forget the incident, and had up until now.

But looking back now, he knew that that was what had decided him to let himself be drafted. Had influenced him not to attempt to be transferred into Intelligence, where—according to Simon— all the *intelligent* fairies were going.

114

But all that had nothing to do with Dan. Maybe all day had had nothing to do with him. Maybe he had been making something out of nothing. He had woken up out of sorts. Perhaps a dream?

He wished again he had not thrown away the damned lucky stone, hurt Dan's feelings for no reason. He realized he had been behaving oddly, not like himself. He did not do things like that, yet he had.

Still feeling unreal, he returned to his manuscript and forced himself to get to work again. After a time he became engrossed in it and was surprised when Dan returned at six-thirty with groceries, lobsters, and a battered pail full of cherrystone clams.

Dan was smiling, proud of the clams, explaining how they had to be kept in water overnight to get the mud out, but that they could be eaten tomorrow. "Susan says they're really called quahogs."

He discovered he was smiling and suddenly everything was all right again, his bitter mood wiped away, almost forgotten.

August 21, 1946

He lay on the warm solid flank of a dune in the dark, looking out over the quiet sea. The tide was low and still going out. Waves crashed softly on the beach. From the rocky area to the south came the sound of pebbles rolling each time the water withdrew.

A new moon tonight, thin and curved like a surgical needle. Why had that comparison occurred to him? He had not seen a surgical needle more than once, when he had been wounded, and he did not remember looking at it closely. He had only given it a glance.

The stars were bright and cold, the Milky Way spilled across the sky. The Milky Way could not be seen from the city. It was blotted out by the haze and glow, and the stars were fewer and more distant. Only a week left, then he and Dan would have to go back.

Back to Randall's rumor, Higgins's nagging. Suspicion and carefulness. Dan would have to have a different address. They could no longer be seen together so often. He would miss Dan's companionship, his clear-sighted comments that made familiar things new.

He deeply resented being forced into a kind of paranoia simply in order to survive professionally. He always had hated hiding.

When he had complained to Simon once, Simon had been unsympathetic. "Survive?" he said. "You don't *need* a job. You inherited a quarter of a million. With that kind of money you can live any way you want. You aren't being forced to be a closet queen."

He had said, "I'm a teacher. If you get into the papers for being arrested the way you did last week, the worst thing that happens is that you may lose a couple of assignments. Nobody takes your cameras away."

"You do have a point there," Simon admitted.

Where was Dan now? Dan had wanted to finish a book he was reading, but he had seemed only a few pages from the end. He should be done by now.

What in hell was he going to tell Higgins when he got back? He had done very little work on his book, and he did not propose to waste his last week working on it in an attempt to catch up. There was a temptation to come out of the closet. He could imagine Higgins's face if he walked into his office at Meadows Press and announced, "I didn't have time. I was honeymooning with the man I love." He could understand the delight Simon sometimes took in shocking straights.

Dan had grown; his wrists stuck out of his sleeves, and his jeans were a size too small. He would need all new clothes when they got back in the fall. In the fall. In a week. Only a week, time running through his fingers like dry sand. Back to clocks and doorknobs, back to time dependent on the schedules of others. Back to school. Randall, and fairy godfather. Too apt a label—he'd never be able to shake it off.

And catamite. That ugly word with its ugly implications. He had never been able to spend half as much on Dan as he would have liked. He wished Dan had let him buy him good clothes, but Dan would only accept jeans and work shirts, necessities. He understood, but still felt frustrated. Yet he loved Dan partly because of his pride, his ability to draw a line and state, "No further."

Dan had grown. At least an inch, perhaps more. Did twenty-one-year-olds grow an inch in two months? He doubted it. Of course, he told himself, on a normal curve there were always a few individuals out at the ends.

Dan could be childish, but what did that mean? In some ways he was more mature than Simon. Why did he find himself attracted to childish men? In a way Jim had been immature, had not grown much past adolescence emotionally. Or was Dan not a childish man at all, but a mature child? He had a child's skin. And Dan was changing, growing up. He was far more sure of himself now. More assertive, and at the same time more gentle. How old was Dan?

"Hi." Dan was right beside him. He started; he had not heard him approach.

"Hi," he replied, looking up.

Dan sat down saying, "There it is again," gesturing out toward the sea.

"Yes." Near the horizon a passenger ship, like a cage of light, silently and slowly moved across the darkness. The first night they had sat here there had been a ship like that. Probably the same one, for it passed once a week on a regular schedule.

That first night—not two months ago, a lifetime, a few seconds— Dan had said, "Hey, look out there! Now I know the war's over." And after Dan spoke, he became aware that he too had felt a shock to see a ship at sea so blatantly lighted up.

It seemed as if no time at all had passed since then, yet they had both changed. Dan more than he.

Dan lit a cigarette, hands cupped around the flame of the match. His face was briefly lit from below, his eyes deep in shadowed sockets, his bones seeming heavier and harsher than usual. The face was a man's. Also the physical strength and powerful laborer's body.

But when he had thrown away the lucky stone Dan had been as hurt as a child. He had seen the disappointment, even though Dan had shrugged it off. Dan had changed, and not only that, but that apparently trivial incident had cleared Haakon's own vision so he could now see him more clearly.

The foul-mouthed crust of maturity Dan had shown in the Army had not been quite real. It had been like a carapace to protect him. Now the maturity was real, but tentative and new. Unstable because unpracticed.

For the past three weeks he had been refusing to react. Refusing to pay attention to his own doubts, but now all his observations and worries were coalescing into a picture he could no longer ignore. Dan was younger than he claimed to be.

He remembered the Freudian analyst he had gone to for three years in his twenties, that great black grasshopper of a man in his funereal suits. He remembered him without fondness, but with respect. Dr. Stein had finally told him he could be of no further use to him, and said, "Perhaps, had you come to me sooner, before you had a lover, I might have been able to help. As it is, you're getting too much out of the relationship to be willing to give it up. Therefore, you will not change."

After Jim's death he had considered going back into therapy, but he had known that by then it was too late for him. He wondered at what point it had become too late.

And Dan? No, not too late for him. Would Dan have to change much in any case? Dan had never given another man a second glance, but he could not keep his eyes off a pretty girl in a bathing suit. Dan was not like him. Dan was not queer. He was sure of it.

Dan's world was not the same. One afternoon when they had been walking he had been struck by the sensual curves of the dunes and had thought they resembled the blanketed bodies of sleeping men. A few minutes later Dan gestured around. "Just like a bunch of girls," he commented, "lying there all soft."

Then why had Dan come to him? Been willing to become his lover?

Dan threw away his cigarette and moved closer, rested his head on his shoulder. He automatically put his arm around him as he always did. And there was part of the answer. Dan could lie in his embrace all night and never become sexually aroused. Like a child with a parent. Mother? Father? Both? What difference did that make? And for comfort, Dan was willing to pay any price.

So far Dan had not been hurt by their relationship. At least he thought not. When Dan had been a child of twelve he had been forced to father his father, care for him. Now he needed to be young for a while, be cared for. But it was time for him to go beyond that now, to finish growing up into what he should be.

He almost asked Dan then how old he was, but did not. If Dan was nineteen instead of twenty-one, then he would have to send him away. If he was that young, there could be no doubt he was not homosexual, and he could not take a chance on turning him into something he was not. Living beyond the law, in constant fear of discovery—or alternately, like Simon, always disapproved of, on occasion beaten up simply for being oneself—was no kind of life. Blackmail, entrapment and harsh laws. Not right to wish that on anyone. The sexual relationship would have to end if Dan was young, but he wanted one more night. Only one.

They made love later in the warm room, the light of the dying fire flickering across the walls of books, the bed, Dan's body. He had never before been so intensely aware of how many shades darker Dan's skin was than his. Guiltily, he tried to memorize him, to store up his scent, his essence, feeling tenderness almost like pain.

August 22, 1946

He was awakened at dawn by Dan getting out of bed. He pretended to be asleep until Dan had left the cottage, then dressed, for the morning was chill, and went to look out the door. The sun was a burning bronze coin on the horizon, the path of light on the sea too bright to look at, seeming solid enough to walk on. Dan was down on the wet sand digging in it, silhouetted against the brightness, a tide pool blazing at his feet.

His eyes watering from the glare, he turned away and stood in the middle of the room staring blindly at the oval rag rug, remembering the care that had gone into its stitching. What wasted life had gone into that rug? What lost dreams? Perhaps it had not been like that at all. Perhaps someone had worked on it while waiting for a baby, while a husband was away. Perhaps it was full of happy anticipation or memories of children studying by lamplight. Perhaps some old lady had made it, counting over the reminders of a full, happy life, living a little longer to get it finished.

He shook his head to clear it. "I must ask him," he said aloud. "I can't put it off. I must stop lying to myself." He forced himself to go to the door, open it, and walk evenly down the beach to where Dan was playing in the sand.

Dan had built a system of canals from the edge of one tide pool to another, digging with a shell, putting in floodgates and bridges with chips of wood he had gathered on the beach. Dan looked up. "Gonna be a nice day."

"I suppose so." He squatted near him, at an angle where the sun did not shine into his face. Dan's hair was tousled and shaggy, hanging in his eyes. He looked relaxed, happy and young. Young. A boy. The cold chill that had been building in his gut since the night before intensified. The haunted expression that had made Dan appear old in the Army was gone now. He looked like a teenager.

Gulls were crying to one another, wheeling over the water's edge. The shadow of a bird slid over the sand at his feet and was gone. The sun was higher, its path of light had disappeared. He could begin to feel its heat on the side of his face. Dan's project kept expanding and getting more complicated.

"Dan?" he said finally.

Dan looked up, shaking back his hair. "Yeah?"

"How old are you?"

"You know. You've seen my Army papers."

"No, Dan. Not the age you gave the Army. Tell me your real age."

Dan squatted back on his heels, wiping his hands on the legs of his rolled-up jeans. "What difference does it make?"

"Please tell me."

Dan was watching him alertly. He hesitated, then said, "I'll be eighteen pretty soon."

119

"You're seventeen?"

Dan nodded.

"Oh, my God!" Dan was younger than he had guessed. Years younger. "You were fourteen when you joined the Army?"

"Almost fifteen."

"I never guessed."

"The whole fucking Army never did. Why should you?" Then he asked again, this time intensely, "What difference does it make?"

"You're under age."

"So what?"

"You don't understand. You're under age." He could see that he was not making any sense to Dan, but he could not seem to organize his thoughts enough to explain.

Again Dan said, "So what? I was supporting my old man hauling ice when I was twelve, and I've been cutting it ever since. What was I supposed to do when he died? Go live with my mother?" Then he frowned as he had another thought. "Hey, Hawk? Are you trying to tell me I'm not enough of a man for you?"

"No. God, no. You're more of a man than most."

"Then what the fuck's eating you?"

They had both stood up and were facing each other a few feet apart. "You're too young," he said. "None of this ever should have happened." He felt ill with guilt, especially for deliberately not asking the night before, for embezzling one more night.

Dan stepped forward, destroying his canals as he did, grabbed his shoulders and shook him. "You stupid prick!" he raged, "What the fuck do you think I am? Some kind of shitty-ass college kid? Too fucking stupid to know which end is up? I knew what I was doing, god damn it! And I know what I'm doing now, and I want to do it. So you just shove that under-age crap and talk sense."

Dan's fingers were digging into his flesh, hurting him. He made no effort, however, to pull away or defend himself. He felt passive, immobilized, uninterested in his own well-being. "I should never have let it happen," he said aloud to himself.

"You didn't let anything happen," Dan said. "*I* made it happen. I made *you*, you didn't make me. Keep it straight, Professor!"

That was true. He probably never would have gotten around to seducing Dan. He had never seduced anyone in his life. The pain of Dan's grip was beginning to get through to him. "You're hurting me. Please let go."

Dan dropped his hands to his sides. "I'm sorry."

"Don't be." He wondered why Dan had called him Professor, but he did not ask. He turned away and walked back toward the cottage, not knowing why, just needing to go away from him.

120

Dan followed him, then walked along beside him. "Hawk?"

"Yes?"

"Look, maybe I'm not twenty-one like you thought, but I've been around. You know I have. More than you have in your whole life."

"I know," he agreed. "But that doesn't alter the fact that you're not an adult. I'm to blame. I should have seen. I should have stopped—"

"Stopped!" Dan interrupted. "What in hell are you talking about?"

"That first night, Ben asked me how old you were. I convinced him you were of age, citing your Army papers. Simon calls you Wolf Boy. Even Randall. That word 'catamite.' A *boy* kept for unnatural purposes. Don't you see? Why didn't I see?"

Dan grabbed him and swung him around to face him. "Now you listen to me, you stupid cocksucker! I'll tell you what you've done—since you seem to have forgotten. You saved my life. I'm not talking about not being dead, though you did that too—twice. Have you ever thought about what would have happened to me if I hadn't known you?"

"Yes, that was why I wanted to teach you in the first place."

"I don't mean just that either. It's the same thing you did for Jenny Hanover."

Confused, he said, "But all I did was give her some money."

"Are you *trying* to be stupid?" Dan demanded angrily. He went into the door ahead of him, over to the stove and slammed the coffeepot down on the burner, broke two matches before he got the fire lit.

Haakon sat down at the round table and stared at his hands. He was going about this all wrong. He had to find a way to explain. Dan came over with two cups of coffee, thumping the mugs down on the wood.

"Listen, Hawk," he said, leaning toward him. "I know a lot about whores, was one myself, right? And I've heard one hell of a lot of sad stories. But it all adds up to one thing. It's a matter of . . . well . . . giving up. Most johns treat you like a piece of meat, and you accept it because that's how you feel about yourself. Jenny didn't write that letter saying she'll always love you because you gave her money! Somebody else could have given her twice as much and it wouldn't have turned her life around. You gave her self-respect. Now do you understand?"

"Yes, though I think you're giving me too much credit." He took a drink of coffee. Halfway down it seemed to develop corners and stick crossways in his throat. He set down the cup. It had a discolored line on it, the beginning of a crack. The sun glinted off the surface of the coffee and cast the shadow of the cup on the warm wood, the handle a loop. He looked away and saw the shelves of books. English Lit, Tom's subject. He had read many poets this summer he had never before looked at. Books drew him, demanded his attention. "And a crack in the teacup opens/A lane to the land of the dead."

His mouth was dry, but he did not want another throat spasm. He said flatly, "Unfortunately, all that is beside the point. The point is that you are not homosexual and never were."

"What the Christ do you think I've been doing with you all this time?" Dan demanded. "Are you crazy?"

"No," he said slowly, feeling the beginning of grief because he was going to lose Dan. He could not look at him, kept staring at the shadow of the coffee mug. "You've only been able to make love to me because you have the silk. You're becoming far more dependent on it than you were before."

Dan's chair crashed to the floor as he jumped to his feet. Standing over him threateningly, fists clenched, he shouted, "You heartless fucking damn prick!" Then he turned away abruptly and walked away, stood near the fireplace with his back to him. "Oh, shit!" he said quietly after a moment, "I don't blame you. It's just that you knew about it back in the Army—that time that bastard stole my scarf—and you warned me. It's just that I thought you loved me anyway."

"I do love you."

"Then why do you want to send me away?"

"*Because* I love you."

"That doesn't make any fucking sense at all."

"You're not queer, that's all."

"Oh, shit! Back to that again. I *love* you, you asshole, I've got to be queer."

"Like a father—and that doesn't make you queer. You're too young—"

"Back to that again!" Dan interrupted, sounding disgusted.

"And," he continued doggedly, raising his voice, "the most immoral thing a man can do is get a boy too young to be sure of himself involved in a homosexual relationship. There are times in everyone's life when there are choice-points, when if something happens today you'll go one way, if it happens two weeks later you'll go another."

"You're talking about something that happened to you," Dan said.

"No, I'm not," he denied, "but I've seen it happen."

"Bullshit!"

"I've always been queer—"

"Bullshit! How about Leda, huh?"

"Oh." He had forgotten about her, had forgotten mentioning her to Dan. "Yes, I don't know about that." So long ago. He felt confused. And Molly too, red hair and clear skin. When he was ten she went back to Ireland to marry. The lilt of her Gaelic accent like a caress. He had cried himself to sleep for weeks after she left.

"Who was your first lover?"

"Jim Harrison."

"How old was he, how old were you?"

"That's got nothing to do with it. I had been worrying about myself for months, reading everything I could find: Krafft-Ebing, Ulrichs, articles in *Archiv für Psychiatrie*. Dreaming about men, and frightened. So many books said that one was born that way, defective genes."

"Ages, Hawk," Dan reminded him.

"I was nineteen, he was . . ." Could Dan be right? Was there a parallel?

"Go on."

"Fifty-three." He shook his head, "No, Dan, it was not the same as us at all. I'd already made my choice before I met— No, not met, because I'd known Jim all my life. It happened because I was queer, because we recognized each other. I didn't meet him and need a father so goddamned much I'd take anything as part of the package. Set about convincing myself after the fact."

Dan came back toward him, stopped by his chair and put his hand on his shoulder, "How can you be so sure you know what's in my head?"

"I know you'd rather have women."

"I'd rather have you."

"No, not really. You'll get over that. It's not as if I'd never see you again. I want you as a friend. When we get back, you'll find a girl, and you'll be glad—"

"Now what are you talking about?" Dan's hand was suddenly hard and tense.

He thought he had explained, but had he? He had not spelled it out. "We have to stop sleeping together. It's not good for you."

Dan let go of his shoulder. Not replying, he left the cottage, letting the door slam behind him.

Dan had gone off without eating breakfast. He was sure he would be back within the hour, but he was not. The day became interminable. He tried to work on his book but could not. He spent several hours doing nothing but smoking and drinking coffee. He went looking for Dan three different times but found no sign of him. He did not even know in which direction he had gone.

At six Dan returned. He walked into the room, letting the screen slam. "All right, you win. What's for dinner?"

He could not believe that Dan was convinced, though it was possible that he had come around to his way of thinking. He did not want to argue any more, and set about making dinner. Over dinner Dan was cheery and no longer seemed upset. Dan was intelligent; apparently he had seen the truth and agreed with him. He washed up after dinner feeling sad and happy at the same time.

A half-hour later Dan said, "Let's swim. The tide's about right now. Come on."

Why not extract what little pleasure there was left in the summer? "Yes."

He followed Dan down to the beach. Dan walked easily, relaxed. Broad, sloping shoulders, narrow hips. A man's body. Not like a young athlete either. He carried himself differently, and the muscular development was different. A workman, years of hard physical labor hauling ice.

They swam out from shore together as always, raced to the rock and back. Everything as always, only totally different now. He felt old, as he had not all summer. He was aware that he would never be young again.

The sun was hidden behind the dunes backing the cottage when they came out of the water, but the sky was still bright with daylight, the clouds white. He picked up the towel he had left on the beach and dried his head, then draped the towel over his shoulder and went up toward the cottage.

He could not sleep in the same bed with Dan any more; he still wanted him too much. It would be too difficult. There was a steamer blanket in the car. If he wore pajamas he would be warm enough, and the wool wouldn't itch. He could sleep on the couch. Better if he took the couch, because then there would be no room for Dan to crawl into bed with him in the night. He was not convinced Dan had accepted his decision. He had given in too easily.

The handle of the car door was warm as flesh, the air inside hot. He picked up the folded blanket. Larger than most steamer rugs, tan on one side and plaid on the other, with a fringe at each end, it was long enough to cover him. He stepped back to close the car door and almost ran into Dan. He had not known he was so close behind him.

124

"What are you doing with that?" Dan asked.

"I thought I'd better sleep on the couch from now on."

Dan dropped his towel and took hold of him. "You really did think you meant it, didn't you?"

"I meant it."

"No, you didn't."

"Dan, cut it out! Let go of me," he snapped, annoyed, anticipating the tiresome process of having to explain all over again. And there was a part of himself that wanted Dan more than ever. He not only had to resist Dan, he had to resist himself.

Dan snatched the blanket out of his hand and tossed it aside, then suddenly threw his weight against him, trying to knock him down. He was slammed up against the side of the car, recovered his balance and shoved back. For a second he thought this might be an ill-timed bit of playfulness, but then he saw the anger in Dan's face.

Simon had said, "Can you imagine what he could do to you if he became disappointed in you?" He refused to let himself imagine, but he had seen Dan break a sailor's arm.

He was not afraid and wondered if he ought to be. Dan was stronger than he, no doubt of that, and outweighed him by about twenty pounds. As they struggled in the dry yielding sand between the cottage and the car, he became keenly aware of Dan's quickness and coordination. He could not possibly win a wrestling match with him. But there was no need to win. He was as lean and hard as he had been in the Army. All he had to do was contrive to break away and run. Dan could never catch him. He would run him into exhaustion, run the anger out of him.

He had begun to sweat, but not quite enough yet. Wait a bit until he was slippery enough to be hard to hold. No hurry, he had confidence in himself, his capabilities.

Dan had hold of his left arm and, suddenly shifting his weight, twisted it behind him. He felt the scar on his shoulder blade tear, and the unexpectedness of the agony almost buckled his knees. He was held by Dan's forearm across his throat, choking him.

Dan forced his arm higher, and there was no strength in him to resist. The tearing continued, the pain became worse. Then he became aware of Dan's body against his back, pressing against his buttocks. Panic erased all caution, and heedless of the fact that he was injuring his shoulder further, he wrenched away and began to run.

He did not get far. Dan brought him down with a flying tackle. He twisted as he fell so as to land on his back. Immediately Dan was on top of him weighting his chest so it was difficult to get a breath. Then, to his astonishment, Dan leaned over his face, hair still dripping an occasional drop of seawater, and tried to kiss him.

He turned his head away. "Dan, stop it!"

"You love me," Dan said grimly. "I know you do. I won't let you send me away."

"I have to send you away because I love you."

"I won't let you. I can give you what you want. I'll do it without the silk if that's how you want it."

He had misjudged him. Dan had not intended to rape him. But what in hell was he talking about now? The pain had diminished slightly. Dan was now holding his wrists so his arms were crossed. He felt helpless and didn't know what to say. He tried to pull away. Keeping hold of his wrists, Dan moved abruptly down so his chest weighted his thighs. He found he could not even sit up, for the long bones of his arms acted as splints.

He tried to squirm away, but the pain increased. Sand slid under him, providing no traction. Dan was too strong and he had leverage. Then he felt Dan's mouth on him.

"Dan, don't do this to me."

Dan lifted his head to spit sand, then went back to what he had been doing, ignoring his plea.

His back felt as if it had been ripped open. It hurt more than it had when he had been hit, as much as it had when Morrie had probed for the piece of steel and cleaned out the wound. But that had only lasted for minutes, and this was going on and on. His wrists ached in the tightness of Dan's grip. His skin was scraped raw in places by sand.

Impossible to respond sexually under such adverse conditions— or it should have been. But he was responding. Dan's mouth was warm, loving. His tongue caressed him skillfully, patiently, and he could not shut out the sensations. He felt outside himself, strange. Remembering all the times they had made love in tenderness, knowing this might be the last time he would feel Dan's mouth. And after a moment the sexual excitement blocked the pain, made it less, unimportant, and thus drew him into it further as an escape. He heard himself moaning and felt as if he had been raped after all. His humiliation was greater because he could not deny the element of his own acquiescence.

Dan held him a few more minutes, then stood, went over and picked up the blanket, threw it into the car, and slammed the door so hard the car rocked. Then Dan went into the house and the lights snapped on, painting yellow trapezoids on the sand.

He lay where Dan had left him, feeling destroyed. Slowly he

uncrossed his arms and brushed at the sand on his forearms. The sky was dark now, the first stars were out, blurred by tears. He brusquely wiped his eyes on the backs of his hands.

Then he sat and gingerly reached back to feel the scar on his shoulder. It felt swollen, but he was not sure, and touching it made it hurt. He held his hand out into the light to look at it. No blood, it only felt that way. He could feel sand dropping from his hair. He found that if he held himself just right, the pain decreased.

Carefully he stood and went down to the water. He waded in. After an initial sting, the salt water soothed the abrasions. He rinsed out his hair and stood chest-deep in the water, looking out toward the horizon. He could swim out now. Never have to face Dan or deal with him. Never have to get any older. Never again have to live alone. The water was warm, buoyant, tempting.

But Dan was only a boy of seventeen, not a responsible adult. He had thought of him as a man for so long, it was hard to remember he was not. Dan had enough problems without adding guilt to them. He turned back and waded slowly toward shore.

Halfway there he paused again, looked back at the dark water. The air was chill on his wet skin. He shivered, and went back up to the cottage.

The room was bright and empty. No sign of Dan. Dully, painfully, he dried himself and got into pajamas. His left arm was useless. He was cold and could not stop shivering. He went to the fireplace and touched a match to the paper under the driftwood, watched the flames lick up.

He heard Dan come in but did not turn. He didn't know what to say to him, or even how he felt about him now. The pain was making it difficult to think.

"Where were you?" Dan demanded.

"I was washing the sand out of my hair." The salts in the driftwood streaked the flames with purple, green and rose-red. Once, years ago, Simon had brought some powder to his apartment and sprinkled it on birch logs to give this same effect.

"I'm sorry," Dan said.

He did not reply. He felt he had nothing to say.

"I'm so very sorry." That did not sound sincere.

"All right," he said shortly.

"You don't understand."

"No," he agreed, "I don't."

"Please, Hawk. Please don't be mad at me. I'm sorry."

"All right, accepted. Now why don't you stop apologizing and go read a book, or eat, or something." He felt harassed.

127

"I didn't mean to—"

That made him angry. He turned, still on one knee by the fire. "Dan, you did mean to. And you know it. Now shut up and leave me alone." The pain was so bad it was upsetting his stomach. He stood up, caught himself reaching to hold his shoulder and dropped his arm. He did not want Dan to know he was injured, whether to spare Dan guilt or preserve his own pride, he did not know. He found it necessary to steady himself against the fireplace. He felt lightheaded and cold inside.

"You don't understand," Dan persisted.

Why couldn't Dan leave him alone? He simply was not up to dealing with him or his demands. It was all he could do to stay on his feet. "I agree," he snapped.

"God damn it!" Dan shouted, coming closer, looking somewhat threatening. "I don't understand you either. You must've liked it! You came, didn't you?"

Explain the difference between hunger and love? How could he when he did not know himself. Dan was too young to be aware of some of the complexities. He found he could not frame any sort of reply, even a totally inadequate one. He shook his head, more to himself than Dan.

"You did so come. I oughtta know."

But he had not disagreed about that. Suddenly his face was covered with cold sweat. "Dan, it's all right," he said with difficulty. "Really. I'm not angry with you." The room got darker and began to buzz.

Dan was closer, reaching. "Hawk! What's the matter?" He felt his hands holding him.

He tried to reassure him that he was all right, but it was too dark and the buzzing was too loud. No word for the quality of pain. None at all. It was simply, flatly unbelievable. He felt himself beginning to fall.

August 23, 1946

Haakon moved his pillow so he could lie with his head toward the foot of the bed, looking out into the room with his hurt shoulder up. The weather had turned hot, and he felt mummified in the thick bandage, his left arm strapped across his chest, immobilized. He was still wearing the dark blue silk pajama bottoms he had put on the night before, and wondered if he would be cooler with them off. Then discovered he would no longer feel comfortable naked, as he had all summer. A sense of sin had crept in, the world was breathing on the back of his neck. Lilith, that apocryphal snake, had found a hole in the fence and entered Eden, bringing with her opprobrium, and the smell of smoke. Eight centuries of churchly burnings, stonings and mutilations.

Dan was clearing up after lunch. A narrow rectangle of sunlight lay on the counter and reflected off the unemptied dishwater, casting intricate shifting patterns of light high on the peaked ceiling. He could smell coffee.

Dan poured coffee into the thick white cups and brought them over, set them down on the chest at the foot of the bed, and sat next to him on the corner of the bed. Dan had said little today. The night before, on the way home from the doctor, he had said, "I didn't mean to hurt you, and I'm sorry. But I keep saying that. I won't any more."

He had replied, "I know you didn't mean to, and in a sense you didn't do it." But he had been too exhausted and drunk with morphine to say more.

He felt fairly well now, the pain tolerable. He had had some canned soup for lunch and his stomach felt better. He said, "Dan, I wanted to explain why my getting hurt wasn't your fault."

"It was," Dan said. "I did it."

"Not purposely. No, listen. I wouldn't have had such a badly healed scar if I'd gone to the hospital the way I was supposed to— either in the first place or later when it got infected. And last night you didn't know you were doing any damage. Neither of us could have anticipated that. And in any case, I injured myself when I broke away."

"Why did you walk out of that aid station?" Dan said. "And don't give me that shit that you didn't want to be separated from the outfit."

"That was the truth though. Not all of it, but nothing but. You remember the stories about Army hospitals, about homosexual orderlies. I didn't believe most of it, but where there's smoke, et cetera. Besides, in a strange place, with different men, forced into idleness . . . I couldn't take the chance. I was far more afraid of being found out than of pain or anything else. I was safe with the outfit."

"Christ, Hawk! Do you let your whole life be run by that?"

"It's necessary," he said bleakly. "I wish it weren't."

Dan was silent and thoughtful for a time, then said, "I kinda thought the hiding was fun. You know, cops and robbers." Then, looking at him, "But I can see how it'd get you down after a while."

"You never get used to it," he told him; then, remembering back, "When I was still in college, I thought hiding was exciting too—getting away with something forbidden. It was only after I discovered how much I like to teach that I began to worry. Any suspicion could have cost me my job."

"You rode out that fairy godfather thing all right," Dan objected.

"That's now. I'm a full professor and have tenure. It would take a scandal to get me fired. You don't know what I was like before the war. I was timid, somewhat effeminate. I remember an elderly professor once characterized me as 'neurasthenic,' not a bad description. A mama's boy: thin, pale, undermuscled, asthmatic, and with horrible posture."

Dan shook his head, then commented sarcastically, "So the Army made a man of you."

"That's very accurate. It forced me to exercise until I learned to like it, provided me with a whole new set of mannerisms." But that was just the surface, not the important part. "And I found out I was as much a man as anyone. I had always told myself that queerness doesn't imply a cowardly streak, but I'd never been sure until I found out for myself."

"Is that what made you do crazy things?"

"I didn't do any crazy things."

"You did so. Like the time that asshole Travis drove his fucking jeep into a minefield because he didn't know left from right, and then sat there shaking and yelling for help. And Coston said, 'Leave'm. I hope the bastard gets his ass blown off.' So we all just stood there, but you hadda go get him. More guts than brains." Dan shook his head. "Like I said, crazy. The bastard had been riding you for weeks, after he couldn't get you court-martialed for that business at the camp."

"I didn't care if I lived or died right about then," he admitted. He did not say that he had not cared very much at any time during the war. Instead he tried to trivialize the incident by adding, "It was worth it, got Travis off my back and got me a pass to Munich."

"To meet Simon," Dan said with an edge of jealousy in his tone. Then abruptly, "You gonna have an operation now?"

"I don't see any need to."

"But the doctor said your back's a mess and ought to be fixed right."

"I don't think he believed me when I told him it hardly ever bothers me. To me it's not worth the time—among other things."

"Ummm. Well, drink your coffee before it's stone cold."

He sat up to drink it, then lay down again. Hot as the day was, Dan had been wearing cut-off jeans since he had gotten up at dawn. Did Dan too feel the presence of the world? Or was he somehow responding to him? No use asking. Though Dan often did the right thing intuitively, he was rarely aware of his reasons, since he did not think them out. Dan finished his coffee and took the cups back to the sink, then came to sit crosslegged on the corner of the bed, leaning against the two-by-four at the corner. The Army had done a nice repair job on Dan's wound. The scar was a narrow line, a J with neat stitch-marks along it, not a wide irregular gouge like his own. Perhaps if his own scar were where he had to see it, he would be more inclined to do something about it.

Behind Dan hung the black kimono. Dan readjusted his position, and as he leaned back the corner of it brushed his face. Dan glanced up and tucked the silk around the side of the post so it would not touch him.

Dan and silk. He had been curious for a long time. If he asked now, Dan would probably tell him. Doing penance. No, that would be unfair. Too much like blackmail.

Dr. Stein had been a man who had answers. Sitting there in his big armchair, sinking lower and lower during the session until all that could be seen of him was his long black-trousered legs, black socks and big well-shined shoes. Like an undertaker. And the great beak of a nose, the high forehead, the sensual, rather thick lips. He had dreamed about that mouth and duly reported the dreams. "Ye-es, and what are your associations?" Viennese accent. Big hands washing each other like an insect rubbing its forelegs together, or Uriah Heep, or the stereotype of a Jewish pawnbroker. Why did he remember him with such singular lack of fondness? Dr. Stein had helped him, had enabled him to live with himself, had alleviated the guilt and fear that had driven him there in the first place.

"Dan, would you consider going to a psychiatrist or analyst?"

"Huh?" Dan sounded astonished.

"Just for a little while, to help you." No, he must not mention the silk. He finished lamely, "Ah . . . think things out."

"What in hell are you talking about? I'm not crazy."

"Neither am I, but I spent three years with an analyst."

"What for?"

"I was upset about being homosexual."

"A fat lot of good he did you!"

"I learned not to be upset about it."

"Yeah, sure."

131

"Would you at least consider it?"

"Boy, are you full of shit," Dan said affectionately, patting his forearm. Then he slid down and stretched out beside him and began stroking his hip. The readiness and intensity of his response shocked him. Having decided there was to be no more sex, he had not expected to be more vulnerable to Dan than he had been before. How could he expect Dan to listen to him when his actions and reactions contradicted every word he said. He pulled up his knee to keep Dan from moving closer. "Stop it!" he said too strongly.

"C'mon," Dan said coaxingly. "You want to. Why not?"

"As a start, any rise in blood pressure hurts too goddamned much. And the doctor said I should rest. And I've explained why not until I'm blue in the face."

Replying only to the first half of his statement, Dan withdrew his hand and sat up. "Yeah, I'm sorry." He got off the bed, went to the sink, washed the cups and dumped the dishwater. Then he said, "I'm gonna go put the chemicals in the latrine. That has to be done this week. Back later." He went out, letting the screen slam.

Why not? Live for the moment and let the future take care of itself. A question Simon often asked. There was not always a satisfactory answer either. What difference did once or twice more really make after all this time? Was he being stubborn or was he right? Easier to say no to Dan now, while he was still in pain, but difficult even now. How would he resist when he felt better?

Time running out, and nothing would ever be the same again. Could not, must not be. Perhaps Dan would accept his word. When they got back to the city Dan would have to move out. That had been agreed on in the spring, when the rumor had started. He would have to find a way not to give in to Dan and himself. But he had doubts. In the past he had given in to Simon many times after resolving not to. His mind was always being double-crossed by his desires.

Ten years ago—no, eleven now—in Glasgow with Simon. Dingy city, specks of grit on the windowsills, on the sheets and pillows in the morning. Clydesdale horses with huge hairy feet pulling carts in the steep cobbled streets. A long bridge over a wide river with ships anchored below.

They had gone to see an Anglican church, Simon taking pictures. Then in a dark corner of the empty church Simon had kissed him, caressed him, seduced him. The same feeling of his mind being completely at odds with his body. If he gave in to Dan now he would not be doing it to please Dan but himself. Passive, yes. He always had been. But actively seeking seduction.

132

That day in Glasgow he had not seen his own responsibility, but he could now. He had not thought of that incident in years, but now it came back to him in detail. The unlit church, windows dark because it was raining outside. A smell of old wood, dampness and beeswax candles. Simon's arm around him, his hand caressing him. The scent of Simon's shaving lotion, the taste of bourbon in his mouth.

Simon had seemed desperate, as if only he could save him. Yet he had made a cleverly phrased joke about kneeling at the altar as he went down on one knee in front of him, deftly opening Haakon's fly as well as his own. Then the warmth of Simon's mouth on him, the smoothness of Simon's tongue against the underside of his penis. He leaned against the cold stones of the buttress, eyes closed, and gave himself over to sensation. His hands still remembered the softness of Simon's curly hair, the hard contour of his skull. The element of danger had made it doubly exciting.

He had been ashamed afterwards, not only because such behavior was against his principles but also because his enjoyment had been so intense. That had been a turning point in their relationship, in his own life also, for he had been brought fully awake. After that he was able to enjoy sex more than he ever had before. As if he had accepted himself on a new level and therefore could give up layers of inhibition. Yes, now he remembered thinking right afterwards, as he awkwardly buttoned his fly, that only a real fairy would do a thing like that. And for the first time the word fairy was acceptable, not a means to torment himself with name-calling.

Simon had changed too. Up until then he had been a shallow, charming companion, negligently good-humored on all occasions. After that Simon became more intense, lost his temper with him sometimes, seemed at times almost to hate him, but at other times gave of himself, was tender and loving with a passion and commitment he could not quite match.

That day, before he had his own clothes straight, Simon walked jauntily down the center aisle taking flash pictures of the altar, the groins and arches.

A lanky Anglican priest with small deep-set eyes had appeared, it seemed from nowhere. He greeted Simon by name. Simon introduced them, but he did not catch the name, Simon's speech having suddenly gone excessively British. There followed a disjointed, almost surrealistic conversation with the priest. Simon and the priest referred to places and events he knew nothing about, using a kind of shorthand of phrases that made it impossible for anyone who had not been there to follow.

He had glanced down then and discovered that Simon had come

all over his shoe and the cuff of his pants. In the dimness of the nave the white gobs of semen seemed almost luminous. Face burning, he edged away into a pew, where he cleaned the stuff off with his handkerchief, trying to look as if he was not doing anything at all. He was convinced that the priest had not only noticed but knew what it was.

Then the priest had asked Simon to sing at mass the following day, said the soloist was ill and there was to be a special service. Instead of replying, Simon glided up the steps toward the altar in an exaggeratedly ecclesiastical walk. He genuflected, then turned and stood with his hands folded, looking angelic, and began to sing a cappella. His baritone was clear, true and carrying. "Love that wilt not let me go, Let me rest my weary soul in thee." Adding innuendo with pause and emphasis so the lines became totally obscene. The priest flushed almost purple and screamed, "Stop it! Stop it!"

Still smiling beatifically, Simon came back down in the same slow walk. In a loud, hysterical whisper the priest said, "Simon! I'm a married man."

Putting on his most exaggeratedly faggish manner, Simon said, "How *nice.*"

As they went down the church steps into the foggy drizzle, Simon said between his teeth, "That bastard!" He had subsequently refused to discuss the incident, explain any detail of it, or even tell him where and when he had known the priest.

Now here in the quiet cabin the fans still hummed. The cricket was chirping more slowly as it cooled off. The sea breeze was stronger, plucking at the kimono on its hook.

He wished he had not remembered that day in Glasgow. Now he had to ask himself how much of what had happened last night had been his fault, how much his mind, and how much his body. He had to deal with Dan's question, "You came, didn't you?"

Was he really that helpless? Admit it. No, he was not. He had wanted Dan and had half-hoped Dan would find a way around him so he could enjoy him without too much guilt. And Dan had come through magnificently, overwhelmed him. So much for noble motives and principles. He was disgusted with himself.

The pain had been gradually worsening, becoming more insistent. Why hadn't he taken a pill? Was he punishing himself? He got up and took a codeine, washing it down with half a cup of cold coffee. He looked out the door. No sign of Dan anywhere. He went outside. Dan was not anywhere in sight. He walked down toward the water until he could see past the dunes. Where was

Dan? Probably walking. When Dan was upset he had to move, work, walk, exercise in some way.

He went back into the cottage and lay down again. Gulls were calling to one another outside. The room was bright with reflected light. The rectangle of sun had moved, touched the wall and shone on the stones of the fireplace. Mica glittered in some of the schists and granites. He began to feel drowsy as the pill took hold, dulling the pain.

He was going to have to watch himself very carefully from now on. Use every means at his disposal to outwit his body, to master his sexual response to Dan.

III

October 24, 1946

In his office, he evened the edges of the sheets of handwritten manuscript, double-checked to make sure all the pages were in order, and put them into a brown envelope. He glanced at his watch. After five. Too late now, he would have to take it down to the typing service in the morning. He would have time before his ten o'clock class, then the service could hand-deliver the original to Higgins before noon.

He was dissatisfied with the chapter. He had been rushed into completing it, and was not at all sure it was weighted properly, that he had paid enough attention here, not too much there.

Higgins was upset with him. "For heaven's sake, Hvitfelt, what's holding you up? We're going to press at the end of November. So help me, if you don't have that last chapter in my office by the end of the week, we'll get along without it."

Higgins probably did not mean it, but the threat was an indication of the pressure he was under. "Finish up World War Two." Just like that! Still too close in time to know what had been truly important, what only seemed important now. A few obvious things like the atomic bomb, but how about Berlin? That seemed crucial, but was it? If only it were possible to wait a hundred years for all the returns to be in.

Almost dark out. Days getting shorter. End of October. Pumpkins, black cats and witches in the window of Woolworth's. A rack of masks in the drugstore. He collected library books and piled them on his desk so he would remember to return them tomorrow. He was beginning to have difficulty reading fine print. He would need reading glasses soon. Not yet, but soon. Getting old.

Desk neat. What would he do now? Would he ever get used to being alone again? Loneliness like a toothache that would not go away. Dan was doing better in English. Were they both using the tutoring sessions as an excuse to see each other? Or was Dan being kind and coming because he recognized Haakon's need to see him? Pain? Or the perverse pleasure of biting down on a sore tooth? Seeing him here in the office was not too difficult. He set the times and was braced and ready, his feeling turned off for the half-hour. Ever since that ugly episode with Simon, Dan had stopped using his apartment to study in. Would he ever stop wanting him?

He should find something else to think about. Start that new world history he had been considering. And this time take due account of the Far East and the New World. Much of the New World part would necessarily be prehistory, but why not? At least make an effort to fill in what had been going on there.

He stubbed out his cigarette and checked to make sure he had everything he wanted in his briefcase. He was due for dinner at George and Mary's tonight, something to look forward to. Good friends, both of them. Without them the past two months would have been intolerable.

A volume of *Oliver Twist* on the corner of his desk. He opened it. No name was written in it. Whose? Dan had been there during the afternoon, but so had several other students.

He turned out the light and was on his way out the door when he ran into Dan. Dan caught him, held him long enough so he would not lose his balance, then stepped back, saying apologetically, "I forgot a book."

"On the corner of my desk. I wondered whose it was."

Dan went and got it, "Yeah, well, if you put your name in they don't give you as much when you sell it back." A wave, "Well, see you," and he was off down the hall.

He locked the door to the outer office, wishing his hands would not shake every time he got upset. Dan holding him even so briefly. Don't think about it. Dan was dating, happily drooling over every pretty girl on campus. At least last year's rumors were taken care of.

His footsteps echoed in the empty hall. Nuremberg trials. "I was only following orders." International judgment. More important than squabbles over Berlin. A change in the direction of world thought. No city was as important as an idea, even though cities are embodiments of ideas, and sometimes it seemed as if Berlin could lead to World War III. What could be more important than that?

Outside he saw Dan with Steve Miller, Bart Oliver and Tex, laughing with them, joking with some girls. They did not see him. The group split up as he watched and the young people went off by twos and threes. Steve, Dan and a girl together, Steve gesturing broadly, apparently explaining something. Dan's easy, coordinated walk, his back, broad-shouldered and slender-hipped, going away, white stripe bright in the half-light. Haakon's hands had not forgotten Dan's shape and texture, the quality of his skin. He had tried to memorize him before the summer ended, and had done the job too well.

He was tired of daydreams that went nowhere, and even more tired of waking at night empty-armed, or thinking he heard Dan coming back. Dan would not come back, should not, could not. That was over. Done with. Believe it! Believe it! And toothache loneliness, nagging.

He had succeeded in what he had originally set out to do. Dan was in school now and doing well with his studies. And Dan was free of him now, as he had wanted him to be. That ought to be happiness enough.

If only Simon had not interfered, come and made trouble after everything was settled and Dan had moved out. Not only that, but he had done it at precisely the wrong moment. Only the day before, over lunch, Dan had said, "Remember Ruthie? I met her last winter. We've got a big date planned. Dinner, show—the works. So I'm going down to the docks Saturday and start earning some dough."

Then, Friday, he had come home from a faculty meeting to find Simon and Dan in his living room. At that time Dan was coming over to his apartment to study, to use his reference library, which was extensive enough for Dan's purposes. Dan had a key, but always checked with him first so he was not unprepared to see him. Before Dan left, they would talk briefly. He looked forward to seeing him; yet, again, his pleasure was mixed with anguish. Nevertheless, there was a bitter satisfaction in seeing him to the door and saying good night to him. "Inhuman self-control?" Not funny, not at all funny. And he knew that Dan would have been willing to go to bed with him, even though Dan had accepted his decision, for Dan still hoped to come back and be fathered and loved.

That Friday night he had heard the sound of Simon's voice before unlocking his door. A sudden feeling of dread, wondering what Simon was up to. After briefly acknowledging his arrival, Dan and Simon had gone back to arguing.

Simon was posing by the fireplace, leaning on the mantel as he so often did. All the lights were on, flooding the room with brightness. Simon was elegant in his Savile Row suit, playing lord of the manor, slightly effete, decadent, baiting Dan with his wit. Dan was in denims, new enough, bought the day after they had returned from the shore, but already faded and worn-looking. Dan looked the peasant boy, and was being made to feel ignorant and crude.

Dan was pacing in an odd pattern, like a dog on a tether, in a sort of semicircle, as if he dared not approach Simon too closely for fear of striking out at him.

He blamed himself for talking to Simon, trusting him. Shortly after his return to the city, Simon had phoned, and Haakon had told him Dan was not gay and had moved out. No more than that—and he had done it hoping Simon would come back to him. Simon was using that call, making it sound as if he had discussed Dan at length with him, tormenting Dan, playing on his jealousy.

"Haakon's right," Simon said, "you're not gay at all."

"I am too," Dan retorted angrily, in an odd about-face from his interest in the girl the day before. "What the fuck do you know?"

Simon smiled. Then, like a picador approaching a bull, he crossed to Dan, took his face in his hands and kissed him on the mouth. Simon's timing was precise. He sustained the kiss until just before Dan's astonishment allowed him to react, and was back out of range when Dan swung at him.

"Cut it out!" Dan said, stopping to scrub at his lips with the backs of his hands. And when Simon laughed at him, he said, "Shit, I don't even like you. That doesn't prove a fucking thing."

Then he had seen the nature of Simon's challenge. Simon was daring Dan to prove he was gay, and Dan was being forced into trying to meet it by pride, tempted by his wish to be taken care of, to not have to grow up yet. Dan was not certain of himself. One night with a woman now, and Dan would have a new source of comfort.

Simon invited Dan to a gay party with him. Probably what Simon had been leading up to from the outset.

He objected, tried to explain to Dan what was going on, but Dan would not listen, and Simon said scornfully, "Don't let your imagination run away with you, Haakon. You don't know anything about it. You've never been to one."

"No, but you've told me enough to let me know what they're like. Dan, for Christ's sake, don't go!"

By then Dan could not back down. Dan had left with Simon and been gone all of Saturday and most of Sunday. He even went over to Dan's apartment building after he could not reach him by phone. He spent a large part of Sunday on the phone trying to locate the party through a chain of Simon's friends and acquaintances. He had no luck, and all that his calls netted him were five propositions and two invitations to other parties. He gave up eventually, telling himself that it made no sense in any case for him to go charging into a party to rescue Dan.

Sunday night, just as he was cradling the phone after trying to reach Dan at his place, Dan walked in. He hurried over to him and put his arms around him. Dan let him, then pulled away. "Don't touch me. Hawk, I was so . . . bad. Why would I act like that? Just because everybody else was? One of them called me 'fresh meat' and that's all I was to them. Christ! But I went along with everything, and kept drinking and drinking. After a while it was like I wanted to see how bad it could get, how low I could go. Hawk, listen, I'm sorry. And I don't wanna tell you this, but I better, because if I don't he sure as hell will, and it's better you get it from me. I screwed Simon too. I was drunker'n hell, but that's no excuse."

"It's called group pressure," he had said, trying to explain, and knowing he sounded colder than he felt, unable to sound warmer because he was hurt and so angry with Simon. "Don't blame yourself, it could happen to anyone."

"Look, Hawk, I've been walking for a couple of hours, thinking. And well, I gotta go home now and take a bath. That won't wash off how I feel, but I gotta take a bath. And look—I dunno how to put this—but I missed shape-up, and I have that date with Ruthie tonight . . . and can I borrow some dough? I'll pay you back."

"Of course!" Dan was going to be all right after all. The party had not swayed him. If anything it had made him more certain of himself. He tried to give Dan a hundred dollars but he would only accept fifty.

It was clear by Dan's behavior that he didn't want to be touched. He couldn't tell whether this was due to revulsion or shame.

At least Dan had gotten over that weekend. The next time Dan came over, he had given him a brief comradely hug before leaving, warm and unembarrassed.

Thank God he had been right about Dan. A woman had been what he needed. But what if he had been wrong? What would have happened to Dan then? He hoped he never saw, heard of or heard from Simon again. Simon had not contacted him since. Simon knew that this time he had gone too far.

Get over all of that. Find something else to do, to think about. Find someone else? Not yet.

That damned chapter was not good enough. Maybe he could do a little more work on it tonight. Nuremberg, Berlin, Hiroshima. Add up cities and try to find their sum. Dresden, Königsberg, not counted yet. How important was an uncounted city, an uncounted corpse? How many Freuds, Mendelssohns, Semmelweisses, how many Einsteins had he shoved into mass graves in Germany? Don't think about it. It's done, over. They'll never be alive again. They're dead. Forever.

The bulldozer blade dark and sticky with rotten protein, the incredible mind-filling stench. The handkerchief over the face a useless comfort. Perhaps it might have strained out a few molecules of death. All of them retching, driving the machines. So thin, those corpses. Pitifully shrunken. Children like little hide-covered skeletons. How many inventions, concertos, books had he buried? Had one of those dead brains contained a workable plan for peace?

He walked rapidly through the October dusk, under the yellow trees on campus, down the gray streets. Leaves swirled and rustled around his feet in the eddying wind, like scuttling brown rats, followed him in relays on dry pattering feet. The smell of death was in his nostrils. He could not divest himself of the memory. Driving forward, shifting gears, backing, lowering the blade and then forward in low, feeling the machine take the weight of death. Rat-gnawed fingers, and clear fine profiles, not objects, people. The other men had wept too. Coston, who seemed to have no feelings at all most of the time, had commented, "The stink sure makes your eyes water." Everyone had nodded and somberly agreed to the fiction.

He had thought he was over it, but he cared as much as ever. He remembered all of it now, minute by minute, day by day. All of it. The stench, the color of burning buildings, the roar of motors, the pain in the gut. And the indifference of those who had not been there.

Had the Nazi mentality been catching? Like some obscene virus? Before the war the British had turned back shiploads of Jewish children from Palestine, sent them back to die. U.S. relocation camps for Japanese. Americans talking like Nazis, paranoid about communism, hating and baiting whatever minority was handy and fashionable this year.

History was nothing but a catalogue of endlessly repeated mistakes. Take a head count for the records, then shove the dead into

142

holes like diseased sheep. Put up statues to killers. Generals on horse-back gracing town squares, surrounded by gardens.

George's house. He had to cheer up. He walked around the block first, to collect himself, to prepare his face, his smile. He went up the narrow stone steps and rang the bell. Mary let him in. She was plump and welcoming, seemed glad to see him. She was as beautiful now as she had been twenty years ago, when she had been a slender dark-haired girl full of fire. Now she was gray, and there was less fire, but her intense joy in living, her concern for people, were as strong as ever. He hugged her, grateful to her for being herself, for not having changed in any important detail.

"New dress? Pretty." He shook George's hand. "Hello." Their acceptance of him was like salve on a raw wound.

Mary's specialty was simple food, well prepared. Tonight pork roast, baked apples, potatoes, peas. He was not particularly hungry, but found himself cleaning his plate, drawn on by the flavors.

After dinner George suggested a game of chess. He agreed almost too eagerly, thinking that this way he could have companionship without having to talk. He sat down across the chess table from George and began the game with a standard pawn-to-king-four opening. George was frowning at the board, looking somewhat tenser than he generally did, but not enough so he felt he should comment. George was comfortable to be with, comforting, and he wanted him to stay that way tonight. Tonight he did not want to know if George had a problem.

He looked away from George's round Dutch face and moved another pawn. A few moves later George said, "Haakon, what's the matter?" He sounded concerned.

"What do you mean?"

"You've never played so badly in your life. You just castled into check."

He had thought he was paying attention to the game. Now he discovered that the arrangement of pieces that he himself had moved was totally unfamiliar. "I can't understand it."

"What's the matter?"

He shook his head. Maybe he could deal with the concentration camp if he could stop wasting so much energy grieving over Dan's loss. He wanted to blurt out, I'm in love with a heterosexual boy. And I think and think, and I can't get over him. I can't see a way out. I can't stop seeing him, and I can't stop wanting him. "It's hopeless," he said. "I concede this game." George would not understand. He could not expose himself. If he did he would lose George and Mary's friendship, and he needed it to survive.

"All right." George turned the table around and began setting up his pieces, putting each one deftly in the center of its square with his short pudgy fingers. He was frowning more, his bushy eyebrows drawn toward each other. Finally he said, "I count you my best friend. You're certainly my oldest friend. I care very much about you, and I can't help worrying." He looked down at the board, the lamplight reflecting off his bald head.

Haakon glanced guiltily at the hairline scars on the insides of his wrists, then turned his hands so they were hidden. "I'm all right!" he reassured him hastily. George was one of the few people who knew about that suicide attempt he had made shortly after his thirtieth birthday.

George understood his gesture and said, "No, not about that."

"I don't understand then." Setting up his knight, long narrow hands, bony fingers. Different from George in all respects. His cuff brushed a bishop. It fell soundlessly on the thick rug. He bent to look for it, located it and picked it up, sat staring down at it, not knowing what to say.

Mary came in with cups, brandy and a pot of coffee on a tray. "Did you tell him yet?" she asked. Then reading George's expression, "No but you were about to." She set down the tray on a table near the fire. "I've still got a few things to finish up in the kitchen."

Tell him what? He found he was frightened, a knot in his stomach. Mary looked concerned too, but in no way hostile. Both of them were watching him. Clutching the chess piece, he sat very still. They looked alike in a way. Randall had called them Tweedledee and Tweedledum, and the name had stuck. Brown eyes, short, plump, they seemed to look more alike every year. On occasion they seemed to be able to read each other's minds.

He looked from George, comfortable as a teddy bear in his heather-colored sleeveless sweater and shirtsleeves, to Mary, neat and pretty in her new blue dress with its crisp white collar. "Mary, please don't leave." He set down the bishop. "Tell me what?"

"We decided we ought to talk to you before things go any further," Mary said. "You see, Hawk, Randall is after you again."

"Still," George amended. "Luckily the Reinach boy is so obviously interested in girls nobody believes he's, ah . . ." George was searching for the correct word, concentrating so hard his expression was almost comical.

"Anything but normal," Mary finished for him.

"But you've got to stop moping around," George went on.

He felt panic first, then surprise. But they were not rejecting him, they were both watching him with concern. "How long have you known about me?"

144

They exchanged glances and George said, "For years."

"But you never said anything."

"There was no reason to," George said.

"We didn't want to upset you," Mary said.

"And now we'd like to help, if we can. You weathered the fairy godfather thing, but a repetition could be disastrous."

Their concern was genuine. He was astonished. Too many questions crowded in on him at once. He didn't know which one to ask first. "Have I been that obvious? What's been said?"

"Randall claims you spent the summer with him. Is that true?"

"Yes, but how could Randall have found out?"

"We think it's only a guess," Mary said.

And George added, "He showed up at our table at lunch the other day. Tom Enfield told him flat-out that you had spent the summer alone working on your revision. We think he believed him."

"Tom too?"

"Don't look so horrified, Hawk." Mary sat down near him and reached over to pat his hand. The light flashed a brief rainbow of colors in the diamond of her engagement ring. He remembered helping George pick it out.

"After all, Tom's known you almost as long as I have," George said.

"What is the problem this time, Hawk?" Mary asked. "You've always been moody, but you were never careless before—and you did manage all right in the Army."

A log fell in the fireplace, sending up a shower of sparks behind the brass-edged screen. The madonna with the monkey he had brought George had turned out to be authentic. It was framed, in the place of honor over the mantel.

Moody? He had never thought of himself as moody. "I remember the day I came home," he said. "When we collided on the library steps, you asked me if it had been difficult for me, and I thought there was too much concern somehow, but I convinced myself I was being oversensitive."

"Yes, I saw you flinch."

"I can't believe it," he blurted. "You like me anyway."

They both nodded together, looking owlish. It was almost funny. He could talk to them, be honest, and not be so goddamned cut off and isolated.

"I don't know what to do," he said. "In the Army there was some sort of mental shift. A kind of balancing act. It worked, but I never did understand it. The men in the outfit were just people— whom I disliked or liked or felt neutral toward. They were not a problem, any more than students are. To resort to a cliché, I felt like a man among men for the first time in my life. I didn't want to lose that, and I knew I would when I got home again."

"Do you think you could get back into that frame of mind?" Mary asked. "Or somehow remember it so you wouldn't feel so bad about Dan?"

"I've tried," he said with despair. "But . . . I had to send him away. There wasn't any choice. I found out he's only seventeen, not twenty-one as I'd thought, and realized he was normal, just— Well, he had a crush on me. Yes, that's really very accurate." Mary and George exchanged glances. Mary might as well have said, "I told you so."

He said, "I'm not being noble. He's the nearest thing to a son I'll ever have. I never thought sending him away would be easy, but I never guessed it would be this bad. I've never been so lonely in my life, never been so at the mercy of my emotions. I can't switch myself off. I have everything clear in my head, but I can't seem to make myself let go."

Unexpectedly George said, "What connection is there between that and the concentration camp?"

He almost said, "Nothing," but reconsidered. "I don't know. Please tell me why you asked?"

George said, "I noticed a change in your letters then. Not a coldness . . ." He looked at Mary.

"More cerebral," she said.

George nodded. "Yes, intellectual, as if you were writing for publication."

"Yes," he said. "Looking back, I think I may have been close to cracking up. You see, there was a child. She died in my arms. She smiled at me and she died, and there was nothing I could do about it. Absolutely nothing." To his horror tears were running down his cheeks. Mary leaned toward him, but he held up his hand. If she touched him he might begin to bawl. He took a deep breath and wiped his face with his hands.

"You're right, George," he said abruptly, almost coldly. "It was then that I began to think about Dan all the time. An obsession. And now, if I'm not tying myself into knots over him, I find myself back there burying bodies, rooting through heaps of corpses looking for one that is alive—another obsession. One or the other, I seem caught between them. I can't live with either of them. Is it cold in here?"

"Oh, my! I brought coffee and forgot to pour it." Mary hustled over to the tray and filled three cups with coffee and brandy. He noticed she gave him a healthy slug of liquor. She brought him his cup. "That should help warm you up."

146

"Thank you." He took it gratefully. "But, please. I can't talk about that any more now. Please."

"Of course," George agreed.

November 2, 1946

In the shower Haakon scrubbed his elbows, the backs of his heels, and his finger- and toenails with a nailbrush. He then wondered why he was washing so carefully, as if he were planning on going to bed with someone. All he was going to do was take Ellen O'Connor to Dean Grimes's November party, an annual function that, on a graded scale of pleasures, fitted somewhere between a visit to the dentist and breaking in a pair of new shoes.

Why did he feel uneasy? The simplest, most effective way to deal with suspicion had always been to start dating, to be seen with women. It had always worked in the past, and should work equally well now.

After he had left the Van Zandts' the week before, he had realized that if he had been so obvious they had felt the need to warn him, he would be well advised to find a woman in a hurry, preferably in time for this party. He had thought about all the women he knew. Many of the women he had dated in the past were good friends, but all the ones who lived in New York were long since married, so none of them would do. He knew a few unmarried women, but he had no idea which were available and, furthermore, was sure he would never be able to line one up in time for the party. In desperation he decided to ask Mary for help.

When he phoned her the following afternoon, she said, "I'm in the middle of my Christmas fruitcake, but come on over. Just walk in, you'll find me in the kitchen."

She had installed him on a stool by the counter and given him a cup of tea. The almost black dough was in an old-fashioned blue enamel roasting pan with white speckles. The kitchen smelled of brown sugar, vanilla and brandy.

Mary, enveloped in a white apron, was cutting a half of a sticky green citron into cubes. "Let me think," she said after he explained his problem. Outside the window sparrows squabbled over crumbs and seed in the tray bird feeder.

Mary laid down the knife and ate a piece of citron. "Ellen O'Connor," she said, smiled and nodded to herself. "Yes, definitely. You'd like her, and you'd be doing her a favor too."

"Who is she?" Reaching for a piece of candied fruit but then hesitating until Mary's smile told him it was all right. The flavor was pure and sugary on his tongue. It tasted as green as it looked.

"One of George's new instructors. Been here less than a year. She's working for her Ph.D. in medieval architecture. Not churches—houses and shops. She was planning to go to Bill Grimes's Halloween party alone."

An old joke, but it never failed to amuse him. The party was so relentlessly old-fashioned and formal that calling it a Halloween party, even though it had fallen on Halloween a few times, was an incongruity. Mary gave him an answering smile, scraped citron into the dough and laid a bright candied orange rind on the cutting board.

"George can send her over to see you," Mary said, mincing with precise, even strokes. "He can think of some question, I'm sure. Haven't you made something of a specialty of medieval woodcuts? I know Ellen has been looking for any with houses in the background."

He stole a cube of orange and nodded. Mary scraped the pieces into the dough and started on another half rind.

"Then you can look her over," Mary went on. "I know you'll like her, because we do. She's one of our favorite people. And she's a beauty. One of those Irish redheads with that flawless white skin. A knockout." Looking at him, she added, "You'll make a striking couple. You're so handsome and distinguished-looking, and tall enough for her."

Slightly and pleasantly embarrassed, he demurred. "I don't want to get involved in something I can't handle."

"Don't worry. She's lonely, but what she needs is a friend. She's been having a bad time of it, trying to get over a love affair. She needs someone safe and kind to get her mind off it—no strings and no demands." And reading agreement in his expression, "I'll ask George to send her over tomorrow."

The sun came out from behind a cloud and filled the kitchen with sudden brilliance, struck sparkles from the heaped red candied cherries, and illuminated the pale translucent grapefruit rinds that lay on the waxed paper like exotic sea shells. He became aware of a rhythmic thrumming and, after a glance around, saw Winston crouching placidly on a chair with his eyes closed and realized the cat had begun to purr. "Yes," he agreed, "that's a good idea."

Now he finished drying himself and looked in the medicine cabinet mirror. "Handsome?" He had been told so before, but his head was too narrow and he always looked worried. Bright blue eyes, straight nose, strong-enough jaw, not unmasculine. An unremarkable face—not bad-looking, he supposed. There was nothing wrong with it anyway.

White hairs in his eyebrows. He noticed one on his chest and pulled it out. Immediately he saw dozens more. Too many; to hell with them. His body hair was still pale from the summer's sun and a shade of tan was left, though almost gone now and somewhat yellowish.

Body getting stringy, too thin too. He could see his ribs. But not a bad body. It was in fair shape anyway, better than a lot around campus, including much younger men. The muscles of his abdomen were taut and hard, no trace of pot. He was glad he had kept up the twice-a-week swimming originally suggested by Ben as therapy to get his left arm and shoulder back in shape. It had kept him trim. But nevertheless old. Definitely getting old.

He turned and inspected the shrapnel scar in the mirror. It was even uglier than it had been before—again adhering to the bone, a deep gouge, varying in width from an inch to over two. At the outside lower end there was a discolored puckered area where blood had collected. But oddly enough, the injury had improved the scar; it pulled less than before, ached less often. When he had gone to Ben to have it treated after his return to the city, Ben also had suggested he get it "fixed properly." He was glad he had not. It had been bother enough being unable to use his left arm for a month, first bandaged, then in a sling. And he did not have to look at the thing if he did not want to.

He turned around and opened the cabinet door and got out his shaving equipment. Half the shelves inside were still occupied by Simon's lotions. He was going to have to do something about that, get rid of all of Simon's stuff. Simon's agent would know if Simon was in the city, but if he talked to the agent, the agent might talk to Simon. Damn! he didn't want anything to do with him at all, not even that much.

He was taking extra care shaving. Why? He certainly did not expect to kiss her. On the forehead or cheek perhaps, by way of good night, but no need to shave carefully for that.

Certainly she was an attractive woman, but he could not be attracted to her. Absurd. He had never been attracted to women. But when he had said that to Dan, Dan had said, "Horseshit! How about Leda?" And, he asked himself now again, How about Molly?

He had nicked himself. He said, "Shit!" and stuck a dab of toilet paper on it to stop the bleeding.

His first glimpse of Ellen had stayed with him with unusual clar-

149

ity. She had come into his office with a long easy stride, confident but in no way overbearing. A tall, slender young woman wearing a short-jacketed dark gray suit with a full pleated skirt that swung as she walked and fell in pleasing folds when she seated herself. Long well-shaped legs, slender wrists and ankles. Rather big strong-looking hands. Bitten nails, but not down to the quick. He rather liked the bluntness of her nails; they gave her hands a childlike look, and certainly they were far more attractive than the painted claws many women affected.

Her hair was like sun after a month of rain, shining and clean, red-gold and silky. Why did she pin it back?

Molly had pinned hers up in a bun. Molly from Ireland, with her soft voice and lilting brogue. He had learned to wake early so he could go down to the kitchen to watch her prepare breakfast. While the oatmeal cooked she combed and pinned up her hair, sitting in the sun by the window, a warm summer breeze bellying the white curtains, a carefully tended red geranium on the sill near her elbow. A country girl, unused to pavements, she loved and needed plants. She had spent some of her free time weeding the tiny walled garden behind the house. His mother had not approved, had called Molly a peasant.

His mother would have approved even less had she known of his watching Molly comb her hair. But his mother ate breakfast in bed, and Molly understood that his trips to the kitchen were secret.

Ellen's hair was as bright as Molly's. The color was the same—not red and not gold, not orange either. An impossible color to describe. Titian had painted it. And once he had seen a horse that color.

Ellen's skin was clear, thin, white, grainless. There were traceries of blue veins flat under it on her temples, faintly on her throat, and crossing the line of her jaw at the sides. A beautiful woman. Mary had not exaggerated. But there had to be more to his preoccupation with her than an evocation of nearly forgotten childhood love. He had liked her almost on sight. She had a warmth and courtesy he could respond to. He was not at all afraid of her. Why, then, was he so anxious about tonight? He dressed carefully.

Ellen had a lower voice than most women. Pleasant. A slight Boston accent, a tendency to flatten a's and drop r's in some words. During the course of that meeting she had asked. "Were you named after Prince Charles of Denmark?"

"No," he had replied, "it's an old family name. I was six when Charles was crowned King of Norway in Trondheim and took the name of Haakon VII." Discovered he was sounding like a history lecture and overcompensated, saying, "There was a big celebration and I was allowed to stay up late to see the fireworks. Everyone was laughing and saying 'Haakon,' and I thought they meant me. My Uncle Björn carried me around on his shoulders and called me a king. The rockets were like flowers, and I could feel the boom of the explosions in my stomach." Then, suddenly shy, he had fallen silent, embarrassed by his openness. He could not remember now what she had done or said, but a moment later he had been talking with her comfortably again.

Now he realized that her question had been quite a compliment. She had taken him for six years younger than he was. Had she looked up his name? No, there was no reason for her to have been interested prior to meeting him. She had just happened to know, probably had picked up the information in a history course.

The night of Charles's coronation had been intensely exciting, good and happy, yet he had not thought about it in years. Because his mother had spoiled it for him, made him ashamed of how he had felt by ridiculing him.

He had asked her once, years later, why she had gone out of her way to spoil his pleasure, and she had replied, "You were insufferably vain. Children shouldn't be encouraged to believe such things. Björn should not have led you on like that. But then, he was always a disruptive influence on you."

But the night of the coronation she had dressed him in a velvet suit and had basked in the attention along with him, played queen mother. She had even had a miniature painted of him in that blue suit with its wide lace collar. His hair was long, in flaxen curls. The locket that contained it was stored now, with all the other jewelry he had not known what to do with, in a safe-deposit box.

Those curls. He remembered the day he had decided he did not like them. He had gone under the dining-room table, where the pile on the carpet was long and bristly because it was never walked on. The heavy linen cloth hung down all around, creating a safe shadowy cave. His mother's sewing shears were huge, cold and very heavy. His heart thudded in his chest, and he made an effort to silence his wheezy asthmatic breathing.

Using two hands, he cut off the long sausage-shaped curls and laid them side by side in a row, counting in a whisper, *"En, to, tre, fire, fem, seks, syv."* They were the color of summer cream against the burgundy carpet, and once they were no longer part of himself, rather interesting objects. They were shiny and springy, felt nice, and looked solid. When he was done, his head felt light, the back of his neck cool, and he shook his head hard from side

151

to side, enjoying the novelty of having nothing attached to it to flap in his face. He felt grown up.

He had known his mother would be angry, but she was far angrier than he had expected. She was more upset over that than she had been when she caught him in the stable with Ingrid a few months earlier. Ingrid was a big girl, perhaps all of seven. Blond like him, and with curls like his. When his mother found them they had been comparing belly buttons. He remembered the delighted thrill he had felt on seeing her protuberant abdomen and finding out for sure that girls were like boys in that respect. Back then, had he taken that for a sign that girls were alike in all respects? He must have had his doubts, for he had been terribly disappointed to be interrupted just as Ingrid was about to take her pants down. (I'll show you mine if you'll show me yours.) After that both her mother and his had watched them so closely they had never had another chance to complete the investigation.

Uncle Björn had been summoned to talk to him. His uncle had laughed at his mother's outrage, called him precocious, and given him a hug and a pat when his mother was not looking.

Now he found himself striding rapidly down the street toward Ellen's apartment house. The afternoon's puddles had turned to ice. His breath smoked in the cold air.

Strange, he thought, his mother's reaction when he had cut his hair. She had hit him repeatedly with a belt, screaming at him over and over to say he was sorry. Suddenly he remembered all of it clearly. He had been hunched up on the floor, ashamed because he had no clothes on, but not at all sorry, and determined not to say he was. He remembered how his lips had felt pressed against each other, the muscular strain in his chin, the pressure of the carpet against his forearms and knees. But the blows had not hurt. Could it be that he did not remember correctly, or was it that he had really felt no pain? He ought to have. The next day the welts had been sore. And if he had not felt pain, why had he finally given in and screamed he was sorry? He had hated himself for betraying himself. Then he knew why. He had begun to feel as if the scene would never end, and he had had to make her stop yelling at him, even at the cost of his self-respect.

Uncle Björn had come, sent for by his mother, to take him to the barber. As soon as they were around the corner, out of sight of the house, his uncle rubbed his shorn head, then lifted him onto his shoulders, called him a man, and joked with him until he was laughing. After the haircut his uncle bought him ice cream. With his uncle's approval for armor, he had not minded too much having to pretend penitence with his mother.

152

He had never seen Uncle Björn again after he was seven and they left Denmark. Therefore he remembered him as altogether larger than life, as a big warm giant of a man. Björn had been broad-shouldered and burly, with dark curly hair and deep-set brown eyes. He was well named, for he was gruff and clumsy as a bear. His laugh was a deep rumble that seemed to roll around in his barrel chest before it came out.

Why was he thinking about that now? He tried to retrace his train of thought, but could not. Beside the point anyway. An odd thing though, that he had not remembered before that his mother had hit him with a belt. That should have stuck in his memory, since she had never done anything like that before or after. She had rarely even slapped him lightly. Another bit of evidence that Dr. Stein had been correct in saying that his mother had not wanted him to grow up and become a separate person, but he had agreed this was true years ago.

Ellen's building was much shabbier than his own. The hall was painted dark dull green. The threadbare carpet had blobby beige flowers on it, and all the doors and woodwork were dark shiny brown, repainted so often that the surfaces were slightly bumpy, the edges of the molding thick and clumsy-looking.

He found himself standing in front of Ellen's door. In the center of the cross between the panels was a white card fastened with a green thumbtack in each corner. In neat black block letters, it said, "322, Ellen O'Connor." He knocked. No answer. He looked for a bell—none. Below the fluted knob was an old-fashioned keyhole, above it a bright round brass Yale lock. He knocked again. From inside, her voice: "Wait a sec, I'm coming."

The door opened. He was startled. Her hair was loose around her shoulders and she was wearing a bathrobe. What had he gotten himself into? Mary had not led him to expect anything like this. His greeting got stuck somewhere short of utterance.

"I'm sorry, I didn't mean to shock you," she said quickly, taking a step back. "My toilet overflowed, and I just now finished unclogging it and cleaning up the floor. I just hate waiting for people, and I didn't want to leave you cooling your heels in that hall, and—" She shrugged. "You see?"

"Of course," he said, feeling inept and shy, wondering if she found him ridiculous.

But her smile was warm and welcoming. He was sure she was not laughing at him. She said, "Please come in, sit down and let me get you a drink. It won't take me long to finish getting ready. I've got brandy, scotch and bourbon—soda and tap water."

"Brandy and soda, thank you."

She brought him a drink and disappeared through a door. He looked around the room, seeing it for the first time. The furniture was nondescript, sturdy and somewhat battered. It had probably come with the apartment. He could pick out her additions: a bookcase constructed of boards on bricks, full of art books, and a regular bookcase full of miscellaneous books that ranged from poetry collections through Dos Passos, Dickens and Tolstoy to books of cartoons. The window curtains were green and blue-green stripes, and on the couch a matching pillow. On the bookcase was a brass bowl with figures in relief on it, and an oddly shaped blue glass vase with a single fresh white carnation in it. On the wall were framed prints of Dürer animals. A pleasant, comfortable room. Not hers, but she had put her stamp on it.

She came back into the room in a dark green velvet dress, still pinning up her hair. She held bobby pins in her mouth the way Molly had held hairpins all those years ago. Impulsively he said, "Don't do that."

She took the pins out of her mouth. "Don't do what?"

"Pin it up. It's so beautiful loose." He wanted to say, "Like a cascade of sunshine," but was too shy. What was the matter with him? He had never had trouble giving women compliments before.

"But . . ." Then she smiled broadly. He liked her smile. "All right. And thank you for the compliment." Taking bobby pins out of her hair, she went back through the door.

When he helped her on with her coat he pulled her hair out from under the collar. It was warm and surprisingly heavy in his hands.

In the elevator he discovered that his supply of small talk had evaporated. Ellen rescued him, saying, "I hear the Dean's party is a real tradition."

"It's a colossal bore," he said. "I've never enjoyed it, though this time should be different." Not entirely rescued, he was being too stiff.

On the street she said, "It's such a nice clear night, and it isn't far. Do you mind if we walk?"

He looked down at her spike-heeled shoes. "I'd like to, but are you sure you want to?"

"Yep." She tucked her hand in the crook of his arm. It rested there lightly, comfortably, as if it belonged. She said, "George said you were in the service. Drafted. I was wondering how come. I know your age from your telling me you were six when Charles was crowned."

"They were taking them up to age forty-five that year. You've

heard the joke: 'If he's still warm, pass him.' And I was a bachelor."
Then amended, "Am," and felt awkward again.

"Branch of service?"

"Engineers, European theater."

"I was a WAC. England first, then later France and Germany.
Before coming home I was able to go and see Denmark and Sweden
and take a week in Italy. What was your rank?"

"Buck private."

She looked up at him in surprise, one eyebrow raised.

"I made corporal once, but got myself busted. And you?"

"Second lieutenant."

He could think of nothing to say. After a few minutes, she said,
"What are you thinking?"

"Wondering how old you are." Then realizing he should not
ask that sort of question, "No answer required."

"Thirty-one," she said, then, "I like you, Haakon. I know you're
not supposed to say that sort of thing to a man you're meeting for
the second time, but I decided a long time ago that too much time
is wasted being cagey and polite. Life's too short. And if there are
any questions you feel like asking, go ahead. I won't promise to
answer, but I won't be insulted."

He could feel himself relax slightly. "All right. And that goes
both ways."

"Why did you ask my age?"

"You look younger. I just wondered."

"Afraid of robbing the cradle? You know what? I've got eleven
brothers, half of them older than you are."

"You do come from a big family."

"Youngest of twelve and the only girl. And spoiled rotten, according to my mother and multitudinous aunts."

"How so?"

"It isn't fitting or proper for a young lady to run off and join
the Army . . . or go to college . . . or go for higher degrees. But
I decided when I was nine years old that I wasn't going to spend
my life being a brood mare. There's a lot more to living than tons
of dirty diapers and one damn kid after another."

"Don't you want children?"

"Oh, yes, eventually. I just don't want to drown in dishwater,
you see?" She checked her stride and looked up at him. "What
did George and Mary tell you about me?"

"That you are beautiful, working on a dissertation on medieval
architecture, and that you need somebody safe to go out with."

"And you're safe?"

"What do you think?" he said, surprising himself.

"Don't know yet. Ask me later."

They were half an hour late to the party, and therefore made more of an entrance than he would have planned, but he found himself enjoying the envious glances he was getting when some of the men saw his date. Dean Grimes came charging over and greeted them both enthusiastically. Then Haakon became caught up in and distracted by the round of amenities, and the necessity to introduce Ellen. After the first ten minutes he discovered he had his arm around her. He did not recall putting it there, but she felt good and did not seem to mind, so he left it.

She even helped him leave it there by picking up a punch cup and holding it over the bowl for him to dip punch into it, and then held his for him. She took a sip, grinned and said, "They did it!"

He tasted the pink liquid that had always before been bland and kickless. "Who spiked it?"

Ellen gestured toward two poker-faced students in short white monkey jackets who were soberly serving canapés. "They're ex-GIs, and one of them has a brother still in the Navy. They got a couple of gallons of torpedo juice."

"I won't embarrass them by mentioning it now," he said, "but next time you see them, pass along my compliments. This is the first time this bug juice has been fit to drink."

Randall and his wife were coming toward them. Far shorter than Winnie, he looked innocuous as a stuffed animal. But his shoe-button eyes did not miss anything; and of the two, Winnie, so tall and hefty, carapaced in her corset, was the innocuous one. Winnie had done something strange with her hair. It was almost a violet color and looked as if it had been applied to her head with a pastry tube. Her eyes were shadowed and unhappy, and her face was set in a kind of permanent half-smile of greeting.

Suddenly he remembered the day he had met Winnie, more than fifteen years before. What had happened to that lovely long-legged coltish girl? He remembered talking to her on a bright fall day. Her long brown hair blowing in the wind, cheeks pink, eyes bright and happy. She had been free and alive then.

Now Randall paused, said something to Winnie, and moved off at a tangent. The rather hard-looking blonde he was heading for gave him a smile of welcome and linked her arm in his.

Winnie looked at them, then doggedly came over to the punch bowl and dipped herself a cupful. That was one thing that had happened to her—Randall's affairs, so blatant that she could not pretend to ignore them.

156

He had never understood what women saw in Peter Randall. He usually found men who were particularly attractive to women somewhat exciting, but Randall was physically repellent to him. Just not his type, perhaps.

"Why are you smiling?" Ellen asked.

"Was I?" He certainly was not going to explain that private thought to her. Winnie had drunk her first cup of punch. She raised her eyebrows, inspected the cup a moment and with a trace of a genuine smile dipped out another. The slight defiance in her gesture, the trace of old sparkle, aroused his compassion, and reminded him of the affection he had always felt for her.

"Come and meet Winnie Randall," he said to Ellen. "She looks as if she needs company."

"Is she a friend of yours?"

"No, but she could have been if she had only been married to someone else. Peter Randall and I do not get along." That was the understatement of the year.

"I've heard," Ellen said laconically.

When Winnie saw him her face lighted up, then she glanced around to see if Peter had seen. The dullness settled back. She made small talk with them for a few moments, drank her punch and dipped out more. He thought he saw a trace of fear behind her mask, but he was not sure. He got a whiff of her breath and realized she had fortified herself before coming. A smell of gin. Winnie reached again for the ladle. He touched her arm gently. She looked at him, and he shook his head very slightly.

For a moment he thought her face would shatter, then she had the mask back in place. She said softly, "Oh, Hawk. Yes, thank you for caring. You're right." Then she seemed to gather herself, turned and sailed off across the room, a juggernaut swathed in yards of purple lace, to inspect the buffet.

By way of explanation to Ellen he said, "She drinks too much." It was no secret.

"I know."

There was something about the warm, quiet tone she used that made him want to talk about his concern over Winnie. "Randall's destroyed her," he said angrily, keeping his voice low. "She used to be . . . like a bird. I can't explain. But he's turned her into a stuffed owl."

"He's a nasty little man. I can't imagine what anyone could see in him," Ellen said. Then, "Hawk?"

"That seems to be my nickname now. It's odd. Before I was in service I never had a nickname, and in the Army I was always called Professor, but this past year everyone—or, anyway, nearly everyone—has called me Hawk. I like it."

He was feeling alien, not like himself. He had some more punch. He circulated, talking to people, and the whole party turned into a blur.

Then he found himself out on the cold street, wind cutting his face, and his arm around Ellen. Without discussion they walked to her building and he took her up to her apartment.

She said, turning on the living-room light, "I don't think I ought to offer you a nightcap, but I rather think you could use a cup of coffee."

She was right. He was definitely unsober. He felt reckless and outside himself. But Ellen was nothing like Jenny Hanover.

Jenny? What had made him think of her? And it was as if that knot had unraveled slightly. At the time he had convinced himself that he was able to enjoy her because of her resemblance to Simon. But now he had to remember that Jenny had been exciting, her body had aroused him. How could he have forgotten that? Or not noticed in the first place?

God damn it, he was queer. Always had been. What was the matter with him tonight? All right, why not prove it to himself once and for all. Ellen was right there, looking up at him. He took her in his arms and kissed her, felt her lips part. Nothing. Not nothing. His heart was pounding. Her mouth was warm and accepting, sensual.

Then a blinding wave of pure terror, and he pulled away shaking. "I'm sorry," he blurted, feeling as if he were choking. "It's not you. I'm homosexual."

"That's all right," she said soothingly. "Come and sit down, I'll get you some coffee."

By the time she was back with the coffee he had himself under better control. His hands were still unsteady enough that he had to concentrate on not rattling the cup, but at least he was able to do it. "I'm sorry," he repeated, feeling utterly stupid and gauche.

"Don't be. I still like you just as much." A pause. "More, in fact."

"Huh?"

"And at the risk of upsetting you further, I think I have to tell you that you are definitely not homosexual. AC-DC maybe, but not one hundred percent homosexual."

"Huh?"

"I felt your reaction, Hawk. So did you. Now . . . I'm not going to say any more about it tonight, and I won't bring it up again unless you want me to. Drink your coffee."

Later he could not remember what they had talked about during the next half-hour, but he had felt reasonably comfortable when he was ready to leave. Then, shaking her hand, not daring so much as a kiss on the cheek, he had been as overcome with shyness as if he were asking a girl for a date for the first time in his life. "Will you have dinner with me tomorrow?" he asked carefully, having to pay attention so as not to stammer.

"I'd love to." Her hand was soft on his cheek. She closed the door.

November 12, 1946

After they had ordered lunch, George said, "How are things going?"

A serious question, not to be answered with an automatic "Fine!" so Haakon said, "I wish I'd met Ellen sooner. She's a delightful person."

"I've thought so. And Dan?"

"Dan?" Surprised because he had not noticed when he had stopped thinking about him all the time. "I seem to be over him," he said. "George, thank you. And thank Mary for me. You really helped."

"We didn't do anything."

"If it weren't for you, I might never have gotten to know Ellen." They had spent most of last weekend together, had gone to the Museum of Modern Art, walked in the park, and talked endlessly across restaurant tables. About everything from Truman (he had turned out to be a better president than either had expected), the implications of the Nuremberg trials (he had not mentioned the concentration camp), her dissertation (he had been able to direct her to some sources she had not considered), to telling each other mildly dirty jokes. They had laughed and held hands. He had not tried to kiss her again. As promised, Ellen had not mentioned the subject, but her AC-DC remark still worried him. He was, however, becoming more used to feeling like an adolescent. He could even enjoy his own uneasiness to some extent, for it was exciting.

"It's the damnedest thing," he said to George. "Suddenly everything is going right. My students are turning in excellent term papers, even the weather's been good, and I finally seem to have at least diminished my problem with the concentration camp. I wrote it all down exactly the way it happened and sent it off to a magazine. They probably won't publish it, of course, but writing it was a help. Putting it on paper."

"You look happier."

"I am. Yes, I'm happier than I've been in some time. And George, I don't know quite how to say this, but . . . well, a part of it is that you and Mary know about me and like me anyway. I can feel better about myself. I never realized how important other people's opinions were to me."

"What a man does in private shouldn't be anyone's business but his own. As long as he doesn't do anyone any harm." It sounded like a credo. As if embarrassed at sounding pompous, George changed the subject. "Did you see the reviews of Tom Enfield's new book?"

"One in the *Times*. It looks as if it'll be a popular success. I like the title, *Accents and Attitudes*. I've not had a chance to read it yet."

A pleasant lunch. Strange how much more comfortable he was with George now. Aside from a few minutes' conversation about himself, they had not talked about anything they would not have formerly, but knowing that George accepted his homosexuality made the friendship mean more.

He stopped by his office to pick up his notes and went to his one o'clock class, Modern European History. An average class, perhaps a bit better than average. He had managed to interest three students enough so they were no longer just in it for credits. And there was Ann DeCamp in the back row, as she always was. Overweight, looking like a loaf of unbaked bread. Stringy hair, small eyes. She never asked a question or made any contribution in class, but her term paper had been a jewel, well reasoned, well written and creative. With a mind like that, it was a pity she was so goddamned unattractive. She probably knew it too. That would explain her shyness. She could at least wash her hair. Perhaps she had given up? He ought to make an effort to help. Schedule a conference before vacation? Yes, why not? Last student in his seat, time to start.

At five minutes of six he left the university to walk home. Having eaten a larger lunch than usual, he was not hungry enough to want a full dinner. He knew that there was a good chance he would find Dan at the T & T, where Dan had a part-time clean-up job in exchange for a small wage and all he could eat. When the proprietor made that bargain, he could not have known how much Dan ate. Haakon had avoided the T & T recently, but now he felt he could comfortably go there. Furthermore he wanted to check himself out and see how he did feel. He ordered a hamburger and had begun to eat when Dan came in.

"Hi, Hawk, how're things?"

"Fine, and you?" Dan stood hesitating. "Sit down?"

Dan slid onto the bench across from him. "Good." He reached out and caught the waitress as she passed. "Hey, Sal. Do me a favor and get me three big ones?" Dan's smile was as beautiful as ever. He felt an odd blend of regret, tenderness, loss and happiness, but no desire.

Sal slapped Dan's hand playfully to make him let go of her skirt. "Aren't you always in a rush though!" She was back almost immediately with three large hamburgers. A young girl, plain, flat-chested, with a pretty smile.

Dan said, "Hey, I got another letter from the Army today. I told you how they've been having fits about my age. Well, I wrote 'em that I did my stint right along with the big boys, and that I want my Purple Heart."

"I never did understand why you never got one."

"I was in the VD ward, and they weren't passing them out there. I must've picked up a dose the night before I was hit. Coston told me to go to the pro station. Should've. And then, before transferring me into surgery for the nose job they gave me a weekend pass, and I did it again. Got a dose and then came down with chickenpox. The nose doctor was purple." Dan grinned and said through another bite, "Anyway, that made 'em sit up and take notice. I think it's straight now." He swallowed. "Oh, I've got myself a job in a department store, stockboy. Lousy pay, but the damn docks are colder'n a witch's tit this time of year. Hey, don't worry, I'm not overscheduled. I've got time for school too, and even enough so I can go to shape-up weekends if I need dough. I don't need a hell of a lot of sleep, you know?"

"Stockboy?"

"Yeah, well, Personnel said something about managerial trainee, since I'm an ex-GI and going to college and all. Start at the bottom and work up. You know? And the guys at the top are richer'n God." Dan paused to gobble another half a hamburger. His table manners were still appalling. "Steve, Bart 'n' a couple of chicks and me went to the Bronx Zoo yesterday. That's some place!" he said with his mouth full.

"It's one of the best zoos in the country," he agreed. He had been there with Simon many times. Simon liked to photograph the animals. One winter afternoon Simon had climbed over the guard rail and almost put his head into a cage in order to get a picture of a cougar with no bars in it. He had waited until the big cat charged, spitting and snarling, before he snapped the shutter and jumped back. The cougar had swiped at him, torn his overcoat and jacket, scratched his arm deeply enough so there were still two faint scars from shoulder to elbow. The photograph was a prizewinner, and it was frequently reprinted. He had seen it again just last week. The focus was perfect, every barb on the arched tongue clear and sharp, the big canine teeth gleaming, the whiskers spraying back from the wrinkled snarl.

"What?" Dan said.

"Off on my own tangent."

Dan had arrived after he had, had ordered three times as much, and was done first; then he went to the counter and came back with a triple ice cream cone—strawberry, pistachio and chocolate. Licking around the side of it, he said, "Is it OK if I walk partway home with you?"

"Of course." He had considered mentioning Dan's table manners to him, but had decided that feeling fatherly would be carried too far if it degenerated into nagging. He reminded himself that Dan could eat politely if he had to. He felt easy and relaxed, settled inside himself. Now that the internal struggle was gone, he could begin to enjoy Dan in a different way, appreciate his energy and enthusiasm, his new self-confidence.

They walked down Broadway toward his apartment building. Dan said, "I didn't want to say anything in there, you know? Someone might overhear. But you're OK now, aren't you? You aren't hung up on me any more."

"No, I seem to have gotten myself straightened out."

"That's good. It's easier to be friends. It really bothered me, seeing you. I didn't want to make you feel bad, but I wanted to see you, and you wanted to see me . . . well, you know."

"Yes, I do."

They had reached the corner of his street. They both stopped. Dan said, "Well, that's what I wanted to say. See you around. G'night, Hawk." He sketched a wave and turned back uptown, walking rapidly through the pools and splashes of light, his streak of white hair colored by the neon signs as he passed under them.

Haakon turned the corner and continued home. That was the end of one part of his life. He still felt the sadness of loss, though he was glad that everything had worked out as well as it had.

He had Dan's affection and friendship. Dan was going his own way, taking care of himself, planning his future. Not the future he would have chosen for him, but it was not his choice to make. Dan had to be himself. A businessman. Yes, with his brains and energy he should do well.

Why did he still feel guilty? Obviously Dan had no regrets. They had both gained from the relationship, and Dan had needed those months of being fathered and taken care of. Too bad sex had gotten into it, but no harm had been done. It was even possible that Dan could not have been saved any other way. What other form of love could he have accepted? What other form could have been intense enough, offered the hours of physical cuddling?

At home he sat at his desk drinking a brandy and soda. The blotter was empty now that the book was finished. Time to think about another. What other? A completely new world history? But he had been over that ground so recently doing the revision that he was sick of it.

There was always *Fairystory: A Study of Persecution*. He had not even thought about it in months. What good was it working on a manuscript he would never dare publish? Assuming he could get it published. Of course he could, there were always the vanity presses. He took the key from under the papers in his top desk drawer and unlocked the lower left-hand drawer.

After some hesitation he lifted out the thick wad of manuscript and placed it on the desk. It looked more like a cat's bed than a book-to-be, and bore little resemblance to any other manuscript of his, for he usually worked directly from outlines and notes, turning out a neat almost-final draft that needed minimal editing.

Although the bulk of the manuscript was written on the blue-lined yellow paper he had come to prefer, it included typing paper, legal foolscap, blue-lined white pages torn out of notebooks, even a few opened-up envelopes and brown wrapping paper trimmed to fit. There were portions that dated back to 1929, so some of the pages were discolored with age. File cards, scraps and news clippings were taped and stapled to some pages, and many of the margins were filled with notes and afterthoughts. It was frazzled, bent, dog-eared, lumpy and warped. Many pages had been cut apart, rearranged and pasted.

He began looking through it. Near the beginning there were twenty pages of closely written legal material in Jim's hand, mainly listings of court cases and anti-homosexual laws. Immediately after this was a section in his own minuscule overly neat prewar handwriting dealing with castration laws. Jim had written in one margin, "You're not paying enough attention to the fact that a so-called hereditary degenerate could be anything from an epileptic to a

163

chicken thief to a cannibal. You will find that yearly income has more influence on the application of sterilization laws than the nature of the disability or crime." This was followed by a dozen legal references.

Jim had married and fathered two sons. What about Ellen? A beginning? He looked at the soapstone dragon but did not touch it. It threw a long oval shadow on the green blotter. Unborn, petrified, wound in and around itself—the way he felt. But in China both red and dragons were considered to be lucky. "About to be born," Jim had said. There was also that diary, witness to the tragedy Jim's life had been. But he was not Jim, and Ellen was certainly nothing like Martha. No, what was he thinking?

Of marrying Ellen? Ridiculous. Perhaps it was not too late? But when he'd kissed her he'd had one hell of an anxiety attack. He felt a faint wash of fear at the memory. Why, for God's sake? There was no sex difference in mouths. Smooth skin, but no smoother than Dan's.

Ellen. He could almost recreate the faint clean scent of her. His hands remembered the texture and weight of her hair. Hazel eyes, and that marvelous skin so transparent he could see the veins under it. Delicate and strong. He remembered the pressure of her breasts against his body when he had kissed her. How would it feel to touch them with his hands?

Too late? He picked up the paperweight. Too late. Years too late. But he was tired of slamming doors in his own face. He set down the stone and turned several more pages idly, not reading. Suddenly a phrase in Jim's hand jumped out at him: "How narrow do"—his hand was over the last half of the sentence and he automatically completed it—"you want your life to be?" That was not how the sentence ended, and he knew it. He turned the page without reading the rest, taking the question as a valid one for him now, preferring to pretend, and half remembering a conversation with Jim about goals in life.

He turned more pages and came across a comment in Simon's hand: "Ordericus Vitalis implies that William Rufus, son of William the Conqueror, was gay. Probable reason for his not having been buried in consecrated ground?"

Several pages further on was another note of Simon's: "Edward II, murdered in 1327(?). Assassins put a hot poker 'thro the secret place posteriale.' Q. Would Thomas of Canterbury be a saint, had he died with a red-hot poker up his ass? Not only do they murder us, they allow us no dignity in our dying." A point well taken.

Simon had also been helpful in obtaining illustrative material.

Medieval woodcuts, etchings, old handbills and pamphlets, photographs of pages of old books. He had them in a safe-deposit box in the bank because much of the material was irreplaceable. He had obtained the box in the first place because he had not dared keep a series of a dozen rare and intensely beautiful homoerotic etchings in his apartment. Another of Simon's gifts. He did not know where Simon got such things and had never asked, because he did not want to hear if it was from or through a lover.

Something symbolic about that, amusingly typical, that the only pornography he owned was in a bank. What good was it there? He could hardly jack off in the vault. He seldom resorted to masturbation anyway. He found it too lonely and unsatisfying. After Jim died, he had not felt any sexual need. His feelings were so muted he was hardly aware he had any. Now he could not seem to get away from need. He was no longer the same person at all. Even his former handwriting seemed unfamiliar and alien. His signature had changed so much the bank had questioned it, and he had had to go in and give them a new one. He would rather feel alive, even with this almost constant ache as the price. Not that he could go back, even if he wanted to.

Simon? Not after what he had done with Dan. He was tired of being tormented, betrayed and lied to. Tired of being teased and laughed at, tired of hearing about Simon's liaisons. Simon was in town now, embroiled in a grubby minor scandal that had gotten his name into a gossip column. He could phone him and tell him to come and pick up his things. But imagining talking to him, remembering his voice, he dared not, because he still loved and wanted him.

If Simon came back, he would begin by recounting an affair. They would quarrel and then make love. Haakon shivered.

No, he did not want to go back. Simon offered a lot, but not enough. He was getting old and running out of time and choices. What options did he have? Celibacy—uncomfortable, but perhaps the easiest. Also the loneliest. Simon—assuming that Simon would come back. Simon might not. Ellen—too much doubt about that to call it a real possibility, and no need as yet to make any decisions. Enjoy the relationship as it stood, see where it went. Ellen would be patient with him; she had made that clear.

AC-DC? Women? Impossible! But there he went slamming another door. Remember the students. He never felt any desire for male students because his automatic censor did not allow it—except occasionally in retrospect, after a man had left the university. However he had always allowed himself mild interest in some of the girls. Binky for one. He had wanted to hug her and cuddle her. He had felt strongly enough about her so that he'd had to keep a lid on his favoritism. Her intelligence? Yes, but DeCamp was equally bright, and he would almost rather kiss Randall than her. Physically repellent—but not because she was female.

Go cruising? Absolutely not! From a practical point of view, far too dangerous: blackmail, police entrapment, fairyhawks and VD. Not what he wanted anyway. He wanted a relationship, not a blow job.

Find a new lover? A possibility. Difficult though, and perhaps dangerous. His standards were too high. He wanted a mixture of Simon and Dan, of excitement and honesty. He wanted high intelligence and he wanted physical beauty too.

Endings and beginnings. A future of sorts in Dan—real friendship, almost a son. A kind of love. He was not entirely over him. It was not going to be that quick and easy. Nevertheless, the problem was under control now. He could live with it and not betray himself in public or to Dan.

His mind seemed made up of compartments. Some with doors that would not open, others with doors he could not keep shut. Exceedingly uncomfortable to have his compartments leaking as they had been of late.

And this mess of paper on his desk was not a book. It was raw material for perhaps half a book. He had ignored too much. All persecuted minorities were important. Consider the categories: sodomites (including heterosexual sodomy), heretics, witches and Jews. Heresy-sodomy. A linked charge, one almost meaning the other. So closely linked that the commonest English verb for anal intercourse, "bugger," was derived from an old word for "heretic."

And how did he propose to have a relationship with a woman if he could not even bugger Simon? Or would it be somehow different with a woman? And even if he couldn't have intercourse, other things were possible. Because his own pleasure depended to a large extent on that of his partner, he had learned to satisfy Jenny with his mouth, and that relationship had been both enjoyable and rich.

He flipped through the manuscript, paused to read a passage dealing with Nazi Germany:

In 1933, when homosexuals were marked with a pink triangle and put in concentration camps along with the other heretics (now renamed . . . "political undesirables," "religious objectors," etc.) and Jews, destined for the gas chambers, Röhm, an obvious and well-known fairy, was head of the SA. His lieutenant, Edmund Heines, had Storm Troopers scouring Germany to keep him supplied with lovers.

On another page he came across a recent newspaper clipping:

Children of tender years were invariably exterminated since by reason of their youth they were unable to work. . . . Very frequently women would hide their children under their clothes, but of course when we found them we would send the children in to be exterminated. We were required to carry out these exterminations in secrecy, but of course the foul and nauseating stench from the continuous burning of bodies permeated the entire area and all of the people living in the surrounding communities knew that exterminations were going on at Auschwitz. [Affidavit of SS Oberstürmführer Rudolph Hess. April 5, 1946. Nuremberg.]

Jews and heretics—anyone whose thinking was a little different. Call it *The Sin of Being Different?* Certainly by the time he was done *Fairystory* would no longer apply. Yes, he would begin work on it. An enormous amount of research would still be needed.

And by deciding to make a better book of it, he had neatly solved the publication problem. Fairies would be one of many. He would probably come under some suspicion, but no more than he could weather. He had been narrow before, and as it stood the book was no more than an indictment of straights, of little real value. Jim had tried, gently, to tell him that.

The bibliography was on file cards in the back of the drawer. He got them out, then glanced at his watch. Where had the time gone? It was nearly midnight, and he had tomorrow's classes to prepare for.

Leaving the file cards out, he carefully gathered up the manuscript and replaced it in the drawer. The pages were unnumbered, and if he ever dropped them it would take him days to put the material in order again. He closed the drawer but did not lock it.

Strange, now that he thought about it, both Jim and Simon had helped him with this book, but he had never even shown it to Dan. Dan did not know of its existence.

He pushed the rubber-banded cards to the back of his desk, opened his briefcase, got out papers and books and set to work. He was not finished until almost one o'clock. He ate a piece of buttered toast, washed down a vitamin capsule with a glass of orange juice, showered, brushed his teeth and went to bed.

The radium dial of his alarm clock on the bedside table showed

167

one-thirty. And he had to be up at eight. Why did he need so much sleep of late? He never used to need more than five hours. Getting older? Mental turmoil? Both? Time to turn off his head and go to sleep. He rolled onto his back, stretched, and allowed himself to relax.

November 13, 1946

He dreamed of the stench of death and burning. He was trying to wash blood off his hands, and a woman's voice proclaimed, "No, this hand will rather the multitudinous seas incarnadine." Unable to speak above a whisper, he said, "But I'm innocent." The voice replied like a gong, "Nobody is innocent, you least of all."

He woke shaking, and had to turn on the light to look at his hands, even though he knew they were clean. The dream was familiar, a variation on one of the nightmares that had plagued him after the concentration camp. A little after two. He had not been asleep more than half an hour, at best. Something familiar about that phrase "multitudinous seas." He could feel himself falling asleep, almost like being overcome by anesthesia, but he kept worrying at the dream, the phrase. Then it came to him. Yes, Lady Macbeth's speech. He relaxed and went to sleep wondering why identifying the quote made him feel better.

He was awakened some time later from another dream by a small noise that did not belong. Breathing? A footstep? Hope and panic combined, and still more than half inside the dream, he thought, Ellen. But she would not come to him like this, like a thief in the night. She had no key. She would not come in any case. It could not be Dan, not after their conversation earlier.

The bedsprings gave under someone's weight, not as much as they would have for Dan. He smelled after-shave lotion. An exotic scent, rather like sweet fern with an underlying muskiness. A whiff of bourbon. A finger traced his backbone. He did not move or turn his head. "Simon, go away."

"I didn't surprise you."

"No." Simon had come back like this before.

"When did you stop wearing pajamas?"

"I don't think that's any of your business. Now go away."

Simon was silent for some time, then he said, "Oh." He felt

Simon's hand flatten on his back and begin stroking him. Then it moved to his hip and started to reach for him.

He caught Simon's wrist and held it, feeling the links of a bracelet under his fingers. He had awakened with an erection and had no intention of letting Simon find out. Pavlov's dog? The dogs salivated when the bell rang, even if they had just been fed, and he had been hurting with hunger for months, ever since summer.

He could not seem to wake up. He felt drugged and heavy. A fragment of verse ran through his head: "Some say the world will end in fire, some say in ice. From what I've tasted of desire, I hold with those who favor fire." Around the world with Simon. The need for sleep was almost painful. Sex and sleep. Allow himself to indulge?

Simon had disengaged his wrist and was caressing Haakon's shoulder with a kind of slow appreciation that made him aware of his entire body as he ordinarily was not. Simon's hand on his collarbone, tracing its curve, his lips on his neck, his breath against his skin. Simon's nude and lithe hardness pressed against his back full-length. Familiar cues, familiar excitement.

Simon's lips on the rim of his ear, then Simon's whisper: "Darling, I love you."

If only Simon had not said that, if only he had not used that whore's tone, had sounded sincere. "No, you don't." He reached out, turned on the light and, blinking and squinting against the glare, threw back the covers and got out of bed. His eyes felt sandy. "Get out of my bed and go home."

Simon propped himself on his elbow. "Why are you so mad at me?"

Posing, always posing. No expression on his face but watchfulness, relying on his beauty to beguile. Too damn many reasons for being angry. "You woke me up! Now go away."

"You can't make me," Simon said sulkily, defiant as a small child.

"Yes, I can, but I don't want to have to." He was cold, and in any case did not like standing around naked arguing with Simon. He got pajamas from the dresser, put them on, then went to the closet for a bathrobe. The black kimono was back from the cleaners. The only bathrobe he owned that had not been given him by Simon. No choice there. It smelled aseptic and neutral. Neat creases were ironed into the tops of the sleeves. He put it on and tied the belt. And remembered Dan untying it, remembered Dan's warmth and scent, the feel of his hands.

"Haakon?"

He turned. "What?" Simon was still posing.

"Please can't we talk? Please?"

A new tack. Apparently Simon had seen that his last one was not working. He looked at him. God, he was beautifully put together. Altogether desirable. But his mind stood aside from his body, uninvolved, wary and cold. "I'd rather you'd just go away."

"Please? I'm sorry about Wolf Boy. Really I am."

"You always say you're sorry. I'm tired of it. I've had it with you, Simon. I've had it up to here. All I want you to do is go away and leave me alone for the rest of my life. Do I make myself clear?" After he had said it, he discovered that he meant it. He wanted Simon as much as ever, but when he had given up Dan he had learned a great deal about withstanding his physical desires. He was running out of time and choices. He wanted a chance to have more from life than Simon either could or would give.

Awkward with tension, he turned and blundered out into the living room. Simon's clothes were carefully laid out on a chair. He collected them.

Simon was leaning negligently against the doorframe. He went to him and held out the things. Simon took them, then dropped them. "Haakon, please. Please. You've got to listen to me." He took a step toward him, stepped on his suit, and kicked it aside. Unlike Simon to treat clothes cavalierly; he hated to be in any way wrinkled or less than perfect. Simon did not just dress, he adorned his body.

"Simon, just put on your clothes and go away. Please? Don't make a scene. I don't need that either."

Simon came closer, then put his arms around him and, in the same movement, went down on his knees in front of him, rubbing his face against him, holding his buttocks so he could not move away. "I love you." Nuzzling, reaching with his mouth.

No longer feeling any desire, he pried Simon's arms loose and backed off. "Jesus Christ! Will you stop that shit?" There was nothing remotely pleasant or sensual about being attacked like that. Why was Simon being so gauche? What was going on? He needed time and a cigarette. He got a Lucky from the pack on the coffee table, lit it and sat down in his leather armchair. So goddamned tired. Simon was still on his knees, spotlighted by the lamp near him. He had sat back on his heels, hands lying loosely, palms up, on his thighs. He looked young and small.

Why didn't Simon age? He was over thirty-five but he did not look twenty. He looked younger than Dan. Wasn't there a fairy tale or a folk belief that a person without a soul—or was it a heart?—could have eternal youth? He could not recall. *Picture of Dorian Gray*, that sort of thing. The "Snow Queen," and a story about a giant who kept his heart in an egg? A jewel? What the hell difference did that make? Three o'clock in the morning. No sleep to speak of so far, and it looked as if it was going to be a long night.

Simon shivered. "It's cold in here. Shall I light a fire?"

"No. Get dressed."

Ignoring him, Simon went over to the fireplace, got a match from the cloisonné box on the mantel and moved the fire screen. On one knee he lit the paper under the wood, and when the fire was well started, replaced the screen and stood leaning on the mantel. "Please let me talk to you?"

How many times had he watched him stand in that same spot in that same pose? "It won't work, Simon. Not this time."

"But I only want to talk."

"If you only wanted to talk, you'd have gotten dressed." And oh, god, he was tired.

"Please? I'll go quietly then. But listen first."

That was the best offer he had had yet. "All right."

"You'll listen?"

"Yes, if you'll leave then."

"It was what happened in Mexico City," Simon said. "I have to explain, because I *have* changed. Really, Haakon."

Crawling into bed with him? Taking Dan to that obscene party? Posing, throwing around the word "love" and not meaning it. Some change!

"Really," Simon insisted, responding to his expression. "I almost *died*. Not only that, but I was almost a John Doe." He held up the arm with the bracelet. "That's why I'm wearing an ID now, with my name and blood type on it."

"How badly hurt were you?" he asked, concerned. Then wondered if Simon were exaggerating.

"Well, I almost lost an eye." Ticking off on his fingers: "Concussion, ruptured spleen, perforated intestine, kidney damage." He had run out of fingers, dropped his hand and added, "Nearly bled to death internally in the first place. Peritonitis after that. The broken leg was the least of my problems. And I got this perfectly *horrid* scar." Pointing to his abdomen.

He could not see any scar. It was hidden by the midline strip of hair that extended up to Simon's navel. "I can't even see it. God, you're vain!"

"I'm not vain, I just don't like to be mutilated. And I was on the critical list for a week and a half. Even got last rites. Catholic, because they assumed I was Mexican. But that's all right, it's within the apostolic succession. And worst of all, my face was such a mess that nobody recognized me, and I was unconscious and couldn't give my name. I don't want to be buried in an unmarked grave."

Fighting off sympathy, he said, "I'm sorry you got hurt, but you did get yourself into it."

"But Eduardo wasn't supposed to be back before midnight! How was I supposed to know he'd come home early? And it was such a glorious afternoon."

Standard Simon, giving details and telling a story. He felt exhausted and was having difficulty paying attention. That was strange. Usually—no, always—Simon's tales of his lovers were something he had to hear, that he could not block out. Now he had missed a big portion of it.

". . . on my hands and knees on Eduardo's exquisite jade green Chinese Oriental, when suddenly Kiki froze, the little fool. If he'd had sense enough to pull it out and let go of me, I could have gotten away. But there he was clamped onto me like a crab . . ."

Why was Simon doing this? Surely he knew this was no way to show he had changed. What was going on?

". . . Kiki let go and scuttled off, and Eduardo *ignored* him, kept on kicking me . . ."

He found himself suppressing a yawn. He thought longingly of his bed, imagined stretching out and relaxing, going back to sleep. But he had said he would listen.

". . . I did enjoy cranking him up to watch him spin, made me feel wanted. But how could I know Eduardo would be so *utterly* uncivilized? He actually threw me out naked into the street, and it was so ridiculous—" Simon stopped abruptly. He shook his head and after a silence said in a puzzled tone, "Why do I say things like that? It bloody well was not ridiculous. It was terrifying. The pain . . . I thought I was dying. I could hear, but I couldn't see or move or speak. I could feel myself falling and couldn't do anything at all to catch myself. Like a nightmare. I hit the cement sidewalk like a lamb's carcass. And then the voices gabbling. I couldn't even ask for help. And trying to hold on so I wouldn't die, and wanting to let go to get away from the pain." A pause, a flicker of remembered suffering in his expression. "And all because I'd been a bit bored and thought, Why not? and Kiki was willing. I guess the question Why not? sometimes does have an answer."

"You've been incredibly lucky up till now if you just discovered that." Was this apparent openness just another act? Simon had come here as arrogantly heedless as ever, crept into his bed naked assuming he could not resist him. Just now Simon had been telling one of his standard stories, filling in details of a liaison that were in no

172

way relevant to what he claimed to be explaining. Yet he had, apparently, not exaggerated how badly he had been hurt. If anything he had played it down.

"I know," Simon agreed. "I suppose I have led a charmed life. Unfortunately, no charm lasts forever. The world can be horrible, Haakon. And I've discovered that I'm probably mortal."

Simon having intimations of mortality? High time. But the thought made him sad. He did not want Simon's self-confidence to develop cracks. He wanted Simon whole and hard, so he would not have to care so much. Why had Simon gone on about Kiki like that? How had he encouraged it? Yes, much as he had objected in the past, the details that hurt him also excited him. He had to admit it. Simon was trying to put things back into the familiar pattern, so they could squabble and make up, make love. Oh, god! And he wanted to. All he had to do was stay here and Simon would come over, begin kissing him. So easy, so goddamned easy. Run down the corridors of his life slamming all the doors. No. If Simon had really changed, then . . . But Simon had not explained taking Dan to that party. He said, "How about what you did to Dan?'

"*To* him! *Really*, Haakon! I didn't hold a *gun* to his head. He didn't do anything he didn't want to."

"I didn't ask about that, and I don't want to hear about it. What I want to know is why you came here and deliberately set out to fuck him up. And after I'd told you he'd moved out."

"I was jealous," Simon said. Immediately, seeing that this pseudo explanation would not do, he added, "All *right!* I came back from Mexico truly meaning to be good, be different, turn over a new leaf—all of that. And where were you? Off with Wolf Boy, that's where. You'd run away to East Overcoat to scamper about in the undergrowth together." Simon shrugged. "I had no choice. I had to go back to being the Cat That Walks by Himself again. And then when I phoned you in September, you were so *bloody* cold, so bloody goddamned *cold*. You let me know you wouldn't mind *too* much if I came back, since you had nothing better going. Since he had left. I was beside myself." For once Simon looked angry. "Haakon! I love you. I've never loved anybody else."

It sounded more like a declaration of war than of love. "You didn't answer my question."

"I was furious! I decided that I either wanted you back right then, or I wanted to be free of you forever. I didn't care which— at least that's what I told myself then. Haakon, if it weren't for you I wouldn't even *want* to be human. I knew that if I got to Wolf Boy you'd hate me for it—because he is your precious jewel, the love of your life, your magical creation. You kissed the frog and turned it into a prince, after all!"

"Knock it off, Simon! I don't feel like being mocked. Now I've listened. Please get dressed and go away."

"Well aren't you just so bloody self-righteous! You sound just like the Bishop. You're so pure your shit doesn't stink. I didn't *do* anything to Wolf Boy. He *liked* fucking me, and he can *do* it too, which is more than I can say for you."

Thank god Dan had already told him about that. Even already knowing it, he felt shaken. Did Simon hate him? Why was he being so venomous? Attacking him this way. Out of hurt, certainly. But what other reasons? He ought to be angry, but he found that he felt almost nothing, just detachment. He was a spectator. "Dan told me about it," he said, hoping to short-circuit the details.

"You think I 'debauched' him, don't you? Oh, I can see why you wanted him for yourself! That body—like a gladiator's—and skin like a woman's. Your beautiful beardless boy-child. *Seventeen!* I didn't know his age when I took him to that party. Believe that, Haakon. I never would have done it if I had. You're the dirty pervert in the picture, not me. You'd been sucking his cock for six months by then, wining, dining and sixty-nining . . ."

Simon had been coming closer and closer. Haakon did not remember standing up, but he found himself facing Simon a foot away. He had thought he was past anger but he was not. He slapped Simon's face. Even though he pulled the blow at the last moment, Simon's nose promptly began streaming blood.

"Now see what you've done," Simon said reproachfully, as if he had not been trying to instigate him into striking out. Pressing the edge of his hand to his upper lip, hand cupped to catch the blood, Simon went into the kitchen.

The refrigerator door opened and closed. Simon got nosebleeds easily. He knew exactly what to do. He was putting ice on it.

He stood with his hands hanging heavily at his sides. After a moment he took a deep breath and closed his eyes. God, God, when would Simon be done and go away?

He could throw him out bodily. He was more than strong enough. Throw his clothes out after him. But he did not want a scene in the hall, and he had no idea how far Simon was prepared to go. Clever of him not to have dressed. That gave him an enormous advantage.

He would not, could not beat Simon up. Threatening to would be a waste of time. Simon would call his bluff. How in hell was he going to get him to leave? He felt old and exhausted and could not think of anything to do. He would have to wait and see what Simon said. "Simon Says." In the game, everyone was supposed to follow suit. But this was no game. He sat down by his desk.

Simon came back into the room, nose pink with cold. He went directly over to his clothes and, after picking them up off the floor, hung his jacket on the back of a chair and put on his pants and shirt. He left the shirt unbuttoned down to his belt and the sleeves with their French cuffs hanging loose. He looked like Sydney Carton on the way to the guillotine and almost certainly knew it. Even when they had been making love in that mirrored bedroom of Simon's, Simon had occasionally paused to check out an expression or pose. Simon was his own best audience.

Simon came back toward him and sat on the arm of a chair. "I'm sorry," he said. "I didn't mean that. I shouldn't have said it. But you don't understand. For me, being jealous of you is like being threatened with . . . not quite death. Disappearance, perhaps. You just don't understand."

"No, I don't." Simon sounded sincere, but he always did.

"If it weren't for you, I wouldn't want to be human."

"You said that."

"That makes me resent you, because I want to be free, so I'll not have to care. Be impervious, never bleed again. Listen, I've already paid the piper, overpaid. I never ought to have to pay another farthing for the rest of my natural life. I don't want to suffer, or be sorry, or have regrets. I just want to enjoy myself and take pictures. You don't understand me."

"No, I've agreed I don't. How could I? You've never once told me the truth about yourself."

"Truth?" Simon proclaimed. "What is Truth?" Then pettishly, "Don't sit there feeling up that chunk of rock. Sit here in your chair where I can see you."

Haakon reached out and switched on the desk light. "Now you can see me." He did not put down the paperweight but, suddenly self-conscious about it, stopped turning it in his hand.

Simon stood up and began pacing. Apparently bothered by his flapping sleeves, he paused to put in his cufflinks, then continued pacing, his bare feet silent on the thick rug. "Truth!" he said furiously. "Truth! You make me want to *scream!*" Then he whirled suddenly and came to stand a few feet away, glaring at him. "All right, you son of a bitch, truth then. What do you want to hear about? How I got thrown out of divinity school a week before graduation? Or what it feels like to be the only American in a stinking bloody British choir school and be raped by a dozen boys twice your age?" A pause, and Simon swallowed hard. The breath he took had a slight catch in it, but then he said with incongruous lightness, "Every night. For weeks."

"Simon, I didn't know—"

"Of course not! You with your Ph.D. and honorary degrees. It never crossed your mind that maybe for me a trip down Memory Lane is more like being lost in Nightmare Alley."

Simon's eyes were too bright. He was struggling to keep his mask in place, to hide his feelings. Simon would go to almost any lengths to avoid showing hurt. Simon did not cry.

Years ago Simon had owned a blue Persian cat. He had been there while Simon nursed it for days, heard him talking to it as if it were a baby. It finally died of pneumonia, in spite of Simon's care. When he knew it was dead, Simon had stuffed it roughly into a paper bag and shoved it into the garbage can with a show of callousness. He had put his arm around him trying to comfort him, and Simon had pulled away, glared at him, and announced, "I've not cried since I was nine years old. I never will again."

Now he said, "Simon, don't . . . I didn't know what I was asking."

"Oh, no!" Simon said calmly. "You've made me remember now, and the least you can do is pay attention." He resumed his pacing and after a moment began talking in an emotionless voice, as if reciting dull facts. "My father and mother died when I was nine. They went sailing on Long Island Sound and managed to drown themselves on a calm blue day, the week after my birthday. My father was a Navy man. He never made a mistake up until that one. All he would have had to do to become an admiral was live long enough. I'm told he was well liked, highly thought of." A pause. "He gave me a Leica for my birthday and I still had film with pictures of him in it. You've seen the one in my living room."

He remembered it well. A handsome naval officer in full uniform. He had thought it a lover and was glad now that he had never commented. "You took that when you were only nine?" Simon had had an early and extraordinary gift.

"Oh, well, that print was the result of hours in the darkroom. The negative left a great deal to be desired." Simon the artist, sober, reasonable, perfectionist. Simon stood still, staring pensively at the floor. His silence was so long it almost seemed as if he had decided to say no more about himself. Then he made a faggish gesture of negation, shrugged, and said crisply, "But I was telling you about my happy childhood. After my parents' funeral I was shipped off

176

to England. The American relatives didn't want to be bothered, and my mother's father, the Bishop, was willing to take me in out of Christian charity—than which nothing is colder, with the possible exception of the ninth circle of hell. I lived in the Episcopal residence for one whole fortnight before he put me in the choir school. I was to live there, he said, to learn to act like a proper British gentleman instead of a wild Indian. Get a proper Christian education.'"

As he talked, Simon's accent became increasingly British. He began pacing again, and an edge of anger crept into his tone. "Some Christian education! The Bishop had been in such a rush to get rid of me, he couldn't wait for there to be room for me with the younger boys. I was put in the only empty bed, with the teenagers. Now it's fairly common knowledge that the British are so obsessed with preventing homosexuality that they give children the idea even if they might not have arrived at it themselves. Furthermore, if one is taught that masturbation will drive one mad, turn one into a drooling idiot, cause leprosy and tuberculosis—but never given a hint that reaming boys will do one the slightest harm—the results are foreordained." Simon stopped a few feet away, cocked his head to one side and asked in a tea-party voice, "Are you enjoying this? I *do* hope so."

Simon's face was stiff, overcontrolled, but his eyes were wide with pain. The expression did not match the tone, and the tone did not match the words, as if Simon were trying to use all his masks at once. He understood the sarcasm as a diversion and said, "Simon, you don't have to—"

"But my darling! You owe it to your education. And we're just getting to the good part. There I was, small for my age, an American and the Bishop's grandson—a lamb to the slaughter. A total innocent. I didn't know such things were possible, I didn't even guess what they were going to do to me until the first one penetrated and I thought it would kill me." Simon shivered and looked away into an upper corner of the room, standing very still and stiff. His suffering eyes were the only part of his face that seemed alive. He took a deep breath and went on. "The thing itself was bad enough. One after another, more and more pain. I believed I would die of it. But then afterwards the humiliation, and ridicule too. They teased me for walking funny, imitated me, and howled with laughter at their cleverness." Simon took a ragged breath and closed his eyes. Tears ran down his cheeks, and he said in a shamed voice, "I could not stop crying."

He felt as if he were watching Simon cut out his own heart, and wanted to comfort him. He reached out, would have stood

177

and gone over to him, but Simon, hearing the rustle of his kimono, opened his eyes and, looking him in the face, shook his head, took a pace back.

Simon had abandoned his mask. His face matched his words, but his tone remained, for the most part, emotionless. "Blood," he said. "And no way to forget for a moment what had been done to me. Carrying the sensations in my flesh, the feeling of utter violation, each step a new agony. The next day I crossed that endless soggy lawn to the Bishop's house and rang the bell, naïvely believing that my grandparents would rescue me. My grandmother opened the door. She did not let me in. She told me not to bother her with little schoolboy problems, to stop sniveling, act like a man and go back where I belonged. Then she softly and firmly closed that big oak door and left me standing in the rain."

Simon looked away again with a gesture like a tied animal turning away from something painful. He had seen Dan do the same thing once or twice, as if memory were fire, physically wounding, and right in front of him. Compassion was like a stone in his chest, and he ached to offer comfort.

As if Simon had read his intent, he gestured for him to stay where he was. Tears were still running down his face, but when he resumed speaking, his tone was cool, his voice under control. "It was nasty and cold, drizzling the way it always is in England. And there I was in the middle of a cathedral close surrounded by a wall with broken glass set in the top and spikes on the iron gates. In the middle of a strange country where everybody talked so funny I could hardly understand. And nobody was going to rescue me. Nobody! Though for a time I hoped. I was far too afraid and ashamed to complain, but I kept hoping. Then one day the master in charge of the dorm noticed the blood. For a moment I thought— But no. He smirked and said I must be constipated from the change in diet. Smirked! And then I knew that he had known about the whole thing, had sat back and done nothing. Foul little man! We called him Putrid Pulfer behind his back, and I think now that it was his influence that made the boys as beastly as they were. He probably had watched everything through his spy hole and enjoyed it all. He forced me to drink a huge dose of castor oil, and it burned. I thought my guts would turn inside out."

"Oh, Simon . . ." He had to reach out to him.

Simon looked at Haakon as if he did not quite recognize him. "They never broke me," he said—a simple statement. "I came out of it with my pride. For a short time I think I went a bit mad. I attacked the largest bully and they had to pry me off. He had marks on his throat for days, but I wasn't punished for trying to strangle him. Pulfer knew he'd gone too far. They all did. Then they let me alone. And the loneliness was far worse than anything that had gone before."

Suddenly, shockingly, Simon's face shifted. He smiled impishly, looking as calm and faunlike as if they had been talking about nothing more distressing than a menu. But the tears were still running down his cheeks and neck. "And then," he said in a light, cool tone, "I learned how to make things go the way *I* wanted. I had the world by the tail—pun intentional. They fought for my favors, they stole milk for me. I'd never gotten over my American passion for milk, and the school wouldn't give it me. I got Putrid Pulfer sacked. Saw to it that we got caught together in the chapel. I had his cock up my ass and crocodile tears on my face. The new master was a decent sort, and dim enough so he was easy to get around. And to top it off, the choirmaster discovered my voice, and I became the prize canary." Simon struck a pose. "I sang like an angel and looked like an angel. Little girls slipped me sweets during the recessional. I should have looked angelic; I practiced every night in front of the mirror. And because I drank milk I was considerably healthier than the others, and didn't have rotted British teeth." A pause. "Haakon, don't look so horrified!"

He felt like weeping for him because Simon could not weep for himself. The only thing Simon could do with his tears was ignore them. They were still running down, but Simon's face was in repose now, utterly beautiful. He did not know what to say, how to respond. He no longer was at all sure he wanted Simon to leave. Simon had changed.

"I was *glad* when Wolf Boy turned up," Simon said. "I hoped I could be free of you—because I love you, and I don't want to love anyone, ever. I want to be wanted, not loved. I don't want anyone to know me, to see past my flitty nonsense and clever monkey tricks. But you don't laugh when it isn't funny. You're the only person who's listened to me or cared a damn how I feel since my parents died." Simon's face suddenly screwed up like a small child's. He covered it with his hands and said through his fingers in an overcontrolled voice, "I love you. I love you so much I hate you. 'The desires of the heart are crooked as corkscrews,' and all that. I *want* you to send me away, but I don't know how I'll survive if you do."

Even now there was a bit of playacting in Simon's honesty. A touch of dramatization. He could begin to understand many of the things Simon had done and said, and forgive them—yet, even though he knew he loved him, even though he yearned to hold him and comfort him, he could not forget that he owed himself his own life. He believed Simon now, but he also knew that tomorrow Simon was perfectly capable of being as cruel as ever. He wanted more than that. And there was the promise of Ellen. The faint possibility of living like the rest of the world. He could not bring himself to shut that door.

He looked down at the soapstone egg, turning it in his hand, becoming lost in the shine of the stone. What was he to do? He felt raw inside.

"What's the verdict?" Simon's tone was cool again.

He looked up. "Verdict?"

"Will you give me one more chance?"

He had to swallow twice before he could speak. "That's not the point," he said with difficulty, feeling almost ill because he needed Simon and wanted to drown his own loneliness in lovemaking. "I do love you, Simon. But I also have to live . . . live my own life, at least for now."

"What do you mean?"

"I can't allow myself to be owned by you any more. I must be free. Am I a person to you, Simon? Or some sort of magic talisman to keep you feeling secure? I don't know, and I doubt if you do."

"Oh." Simon looked thoughtful and did not say anything for a long time. Heat clicked in the steam pipes, and far away in another part of the building water was running. A truck rumbled past outside. Finally Simon said, "If I don't play your way, you won't play at all. All right, I'll take what I can get. Fair's fair. It's your turn to call the shots." Then, starting toward him, hands out, "Look, can we go to bed now?"

"No!" Not only for his own sake, but for Simon's too. Simon had been honest, had turned himself inside out, but he was already beginning to deny himself, to pretend to himself he had only been acting, to tell himself that the price had gone up but that the game was unchanged. He understood how important Simon's pride was to him, why he needed to maintain it at all costs, but he still could not live with it. He said, "Perhaps we can start over. I don't know. But we can't go on from here. Our relationship as it has been in the past is over. Finished. I want you to come here tomorrow and pack all your stuff and take it home. I also want my key back. If you want to see me, phone first." He was sounding too hard and brusque, but could not be otherwise, he was hurting too much. "Now please go away? I'd like to try to get in a little sleep before morning."

"Oh." Simon turned away and went to his clothes. "All right," he said icily, "whatever you say."

December 24, 1946

The day before Christmas. Haakon sat down at his desk to drink a cup of coffee. In the middle of the blotter, ready for him to start work, was a ragged section of the book he had begun to think of as *Persecution* rather than *Fairystory*. On top of it was a neat pile of file cards filled with new information and references. Beside it was a new pad of yellow paper with his pen lying on top of it.

All set to go, but now, at only nine o'clock in the morning, he could hardly read his prewar handwriting. Why on earth had he written so small? And what kind of idiotic pride or vanity was keeping him from making an appointment with an optometrist? Owning glasses would not make him a day older, and not owning them sure as hell would not make him a day younger. If he had a magnifying glass— But that was even worse, the picture of himself peering through a lens. He really had no choice now; he could no longer read a phone book without great difficulty.

He remembered Tom Enfield joking about poor eyesight, saying he could see perfectly well, but his arms were not long enough. At the time Haakon had laughed, but it suddenly was no longer funny. Only a year ago his vision had been 20/20. Why was it deteriorating this fast?

His cup was empty. He went for more coffee and paused to look out the window on the way back. A slender girl was hurrying down the sidewalk above the park holding her upturned collar against her ears with red-mittened hands. Her blond hair was bright as a flower in the morning sun. Why did Dan always seem to go for blondes? Dan preferred them petite. He felt as if he had stumbled mentally as the thought occurred to him that he himself was a blond. The boy in jail Dan had spoken of was too.

A new category to find himself in—one he didn't like. It made him feel uncomfortable almost to the point of anger. The girl disappeared around a corner. The street was empty. Frozen gray and black snow was heaped lumpily at the curbs, hard as stone. In the park, black skeletal trees groped hopelessly toward the far-off winter sun, as if begging for warmth.

He turned his back on the view. "And all our yesterdays . . ." went nowhere, did nothing. Had Dan been hurt by their relationship? Had he been made more dependent on the silk? Wasn't it about time he stopped belaboring that? It was done, past, irretrievable. Nothing to be learned from it either, for he would never get involved in a relationship remotely similar again. No way for it to happen.

If only that could have been different, if only his whole goddamned life had been different. If only, if only—exercise in futility. Gear spinning. He ought to get to work on the book.

He began wandering aimlessly around the apartment. God, what a mess. Old newspapers, rolls of fuzz under the furniture, dust all over everything. The cleaning lady had been ill, or so she claimed, for three weeks.

"Dusty death." Deathly dust. If the place were clean it would not be so goddamned depressing. He could clean it. But he ought to be working on the book.

He was not working on the book. He was standing in the middle of the damn room feeling sorry for himself. "Go out in the garden and eat worms." Only he had no garden, and the ground was frozen—and the thought was not amusing.

He finished his coffee and stared at the sludge in the bottom of the cup. There was a small crack along one side of it, and the entire inside was coated with brown scum. The rim was slightly sticky on the side he drank from. How long since he had even rinsed it out? Days. When had the crack appeared? He did not know. "And a crack in the teacup opens a lane to the land of the dead."

He could see the end of his life in the dark residue, could imagine himself years from now standing in the same spot, staring into an identical cracked cup. Alone. Old, selfish and queer. He was already, in Simon's phrase, between forty and death.

The one time Simon had told him the truth he had sent him away. Selfish, and stupid too. What else was there for him? Better Simon at his worst than no one at all. But Simon had not come back to him, had not called. Simon had merely collected his things as requested, left the key on his desk without even a note.

Simon was always out of town on Christmas. In Morocco, Algeria, with Jewish or Arab friends. He could not have kept Simon here under any conditions, nor could he have gone with him. The first year they had been together he had asked to go along, after it became clear he could not persuade Simon to stay. And Simon had said, "You're joking! You'd be like old Death at the carnival, like a monk at a whores' picnic. An albatross around my neck. Besides, you'd hate it. You're the one with a Ph.D. Figure out your own good time."

Simon was right. The gay world was not for him. He was as offended by the word "gay" as Simon was by his use of "queer." But "gay" had always seemed too ironic to him.

Maybe he did not have to give up seeing Ellen after all. Not altogether, though he should see less of her. It was not right of him to take up her time when she could be going out with a man she could have a future with.

He, make it with a woman? What a joke! One drunken kiss did not open any doors. He had kissed her cheek when he saw her off on the train the day before, unable to bring himself to even brush her lips with his. But her hair had been warm and heavy over his hand, a sharp contrast to the scratchy tweed of her topcoat. She had looked up at him smiling.

A matronly woman looked approvingly at them as she stepped into the train. He glanced up and saw, mirrored in the polished glass of the train window, a striking couple. But the reflection was false, the implication totally untrue, void of the content assigned it by the woman.

If only he could have met Ellen twenty years ago. No, twenty years ago he would not have noticed her, could not have reacted to her even this much. He had been living an exhausting nightmare, a prisoner to his mother's paralysis.

There had been pleasure and comfort in teaching, forgetfulness in studying and writing. Most of the time he had existed in a limbo of waiting out the hours and minutes between assignations with Jim. Short hours of love and companionship separated by deserts of loneliness and longing.

If most of the year had been purgatory, Christmas season had been one of the lower circles of hell. That recording of Schumann-Heink singing "Silent Night" playing and replaying itself in his head hours after he had left his mother's room.

The day Christmas recess started she always gave her two nurses a Christmas vacation. He had total care of her, and could only leave the house for a few hours at a time, during the day when the maid was available.

He had to buy a Christmas tree, and always agonized over which to choose, hoping that this time he could please her. But he never could. It was always too thick, too skimpy, too small, too something. It never matched the image of perfection she had in her mind.

"That's my scholar," she would say, sighing. "My absentminded professor. You just don't care, do you? You'll get anything just to get it over with. Grab the first thing you see. If only I . . ."

He tried not to listen, and after the first two years, he gave up trying to defend himself. He would set it up in the corner of her room an arm's length from her bed, feeling like a condemned criminal building his own scaffold, knowing the scenes that would be replayed.

While he trimmed the tree she lay propped on her pillows instructing and criticizing. Each day thereafter she demanded that he shift around the bright balls, birds and trumpets every time he came into her room.

One day he brought her lunch—vegetable soup, crisp crackers, a ripe red apple—laid out as attractively as possible on the tray. She lifted the silver cover from the soup bowl, then asked him to move one of the birds. Knowing she would not taste her food until he was done, he went over and replaced the cover to keep it warm. As soon as he turned away, she took it off again, put the spoon in as if to begin eating, then did not raise it, but left it in the bowl.

The bird was green, blue and silver, with a long white spunglass tail. He unclipped the metal foot from the branch and tried to follow her instructions. She was vague. She said right when she meant left, and then denied she had done so. Finally he located the spot she had in mind and stepped away. She looked critically at it and shook her head.

"No, it was better where it was before. Put it back."

He did so. It was in the same spot exactly, the needles were still bent from the pressure of the foot clamp.

"No, that's not where it was. Up a little."

Until her soup was cold. Then she ate a little, grimacing. She refused to finish.

"It wouldn't be cold if you'd left the cover on," he protested.

"How could I know you'd be so slow?"

"Because I always am," he said with despair.

"Now don't be surly," she chided.

"Let me go and reheat it. You must eat more."

"No, I haven't time. I have to get ready, Martha's bringing Jimmy with her today. Something about investments. I want to look my best. And he's such a bore about money! Martha and I— You're not listening. You've got that glazed look in your eyes."

She pressed the sharp fruit knife into the apple slowly, as if killing it with leisurely enjoyment. "That gold ball near the top, would you move it down?"

By then his hands were shaking, as they always did after he had been with her for a while. He was awkward anyway, too long-legged, hands and feet too big. Always stumbling all over himself. The knobs of his backbone were still scabbed and sore from falling down a flight of stairs at the university. He was desperate not to break the ornament. So far this year he had not broken one, and he dreaded what would happen if he did now. He reached carefully, watching out for his elbows so he would not knock off another that way as he had the year before. It was a huge ball. He could see his distorted reflection in it, big hand, little buglike body. Just as he grasped it she shrieked, "Watch your feet! Be careful!"

As he looked down his hand contracted on it and crushed it. Bits of glass tinkled to the waxed parquet floor to lie there dead. The top third still hung from the bough. He looked stupidly at his hand, the palm sequined by flecks of silver and gold stuck in the sweat. A drop of blood gathered on his thumb and dripped, splattering on the floor.

When he looked at her he thought he caught the tail end of a smile. She cut into the apple again. A clear drop of juice caught the light and sparkled like a jewel as it slid down the knife blade. He thought, What she really wants for lunch is my heart, still hot and beating on that Limoges plate. Perhaps he ought to drape his entrails on the tree like a Druid's sacrifice. Maybe that would please her at last.

"Give me the pieces," she said, pushing her plate away, leaving the apple uneaten.

"No." He knew what was coming next.

"Give them to me." And when he did not move, "Such a little thing, and I can't get up to do it myself. Please. Please?" A tear slid easily down her cheek, then another. "It's so dreadful to be so helpless."

His hands were shaking badly. He had only nicked his thumb, but it was bleeding with a slow, regular drip. He wrapped his handkerchief around it. His chest had constricted, and if he did not take his medicine immediately he might be in for an asthma attack. "I need my medicine," he told her.

"Oh please," she wailed.

He could not deny her what she wanted. With clear despairing knowledge that every time this happened he was assisting in his own destruction as a man, he unhooked the top of the ornament from the tree and collected most of the fragments from the floor. She took them from him and cupped them lightly in her small hands. She leaned over the silvered hollow, tears dripping into the shell of glass, collecting them there as if in a medieval weeping cup. She recited a litany of the years she had owned the ball, implying that its destruction had somehow robbed her of some of the essence of her happier past.

He had not been able to escape until the Harrisons arrived. While Jim was talking to his mother he took his medicine and bandaged his thumb. Then he went to his room to wait for Jim to come to him, lying on his bed naked, covered by a blanket in case the maid happened to look in.

Jim knocked on his door a little later, came in and closed and locked it behind him. "We may have as much as an hour," he said. "Your mother said I was to ask you to 'entertain' me."

Laughing with relief as much as at the double entendre, he threw back the blanket and held out both arms. Jim crossed to him and knelt beside the bed, kissed him. Jim's clothes always smelled of cigar smoke. It was an odor he had never liked, but on Jim, because it was associated with him, it was exciting.

Before leaving his room half an hour later, they kissed once more, lingeringly, clinging to each other. Then Jim opened the door and they went sedately, not touching, down the narrow stairs to the living room. He got out glasses and poured two brandies.

"One thing I'll say for your mother, she gets good liquor," Jim said, tasting his. That was in 1928.

"It's not bootleg. She has several prescriptions."

"You're going to have to talk to her about her investments. All her money is in Torrington Steel. I'll grant you it seems solid enough, but it doesn't do to have all your eggs in one basket. I can't seem to get through to her. God knows, I've tried."

"Yes, of course." He had not been paying attention. He had been watching Jim's mouth, listening to the rumble of his voice, and wondering how soon they could meet again.

"You didn't hear a word."

"Yes I did. I can repeat it back if you like."

Jim set down his glass and came over and shook him. "Damn it, Haakon! You're a man, not a foolish woman. You have to learn to take an interest in finances. I won't be here forever. You must learn to take care of yourself."

"I don't want to be rich, and I have a profession. I really like to teach."

"You're talking like a fool. You need a buffer—money in the bank." Lowering his voice carefully, "Men like us can never be sure we won't lose our jobs overnight. You can't afford to forget that." Now he thought, It was a funny thing the way his lack of interest in finances had worked out. Torrington Steel had not only survived the crash the next year, it had not missed a dividend. Furthermore, it had been the stock in this company that had prevented Jim from being wiped out.

Was that the day? Yes, he remembered. Jim had been standing close to him, and he had reached out to him impulsively and kissed him, standing there in the living room beside the liquor cabinet. The only time he had ever broken Jim's rules for caution.

Jim pulled away angrily. "You damned fool!" he said under his breath. "What if someone had walked in?"

"Nobody did."

Jim looked at him a long time, then said, "Haakon, I'm worried about you. You're in worse shape than you were last year. Every Christmas it gets worse. Please don't let your mother destroy you. Put her in a nursing home, or move away. Save yourself. Don't let her torture you like this."

"She can't help being paralyzed. She doesn't mean it."

"She does mean it."

He knew Jim was right, even though he would not admit it aloud. He said, "She needs me," and changed the subject.

Had the next year been worse? He did not know now. The years ran together into a blur of misery. He had managed to endure until the year he was thirty. He remembered that year as separate from the others.

That year he had begun not only to wish she were dead, but to think about how easy it would be to kill her. She was small and frail, he much stronger. It would not be difficult at all to smother her with her pillow. Put her out of her misery. But he knew he could never do it.

He went through days of caution, moving ornaments, avoiding all the traps she set to startle him into carelessness. He could no longer deny the knowledge that she enjoyed tormenting him, but he could not leave her.

She blamed him for her paralysis, and, even though he knew there was no logic in that, he had to accept the guilt.

But he was thirty years old, and he could not remember having been happy for a full day in years. She would never die. She would lie there year after year for the rest of his life, becoming uglier, more malignant, more difficult to care for. She seemed to feed on his misery, his manhood, his very essence. In the end there would be nothing left of him but an echoing shell that had the appearance of life but nothing at all inside.

The ornament he finally dropped was plain silver. He watched it break, heard it shatter, and felt as if his chest were full of broken glass. Without waiting to be asked this time, he gathered up the shards and presented them to her. Then stood and listened to her paint a picture of how he had cheated her of another bit of life.

187

He went downstairs and telephoned Jim at work. Jim was in court. He should have known that; Jim was always in court on Wednesday. Four o'clock, and no possibility of seeing Jim for hours at best. He stood in the high narrow hall looking up the stairs, and suddenly he said aloud, to no one but himself, "I'm tired of being unhappy."

His mother could not be left unattended for long, but the doctor would be coming at six. Enough time for him, and she would be all right. He felt the broken glass in his chest dissolve, and there was a feeling of peace that amounted to happiness. No tomorrows, no more having to answer to anyone for anything.

He went to the bathroom and filled the tub with warm water because he had heard that was how to do it. Then he carefully stropped his straight razor and slashed both his wrists.

Now he became aware that he was still standing in the middle of his living room staring into an empty dirty coffee cup. He set the cup down on the nearest table and looked at the almost invisible white scars on his wrists.

There had been little pain at first, less than he had expected, and the blood had run thickly. Kneeling by the tub, he immersed his arms halfway to the elbows and watched the red skeins curling slowly through the clear water, watched the water turn pink. He felt utterly content.

He yearned for that ecstasy of contentment now. For the freedom from suffering, loneliness, decisions, obligations and tomorrows. Perfect peace, unobtainable at any lesser price.

And that day, when the realization had come that he was not bleeding enough, that he had missed the artery and would have to cut deeper, he had not hesitated. It was difficult to manipulate his hands because he had severed most of the tendons. He could use his right hand, but not his left, and his fingers felt stiff with pain. He picked up the razor, braced his left hand against the edge of the tub to open the wound, and carefully cut again. He was immediately rewarded by spurts of bright arterial blood.

But he had taken too long, and the doctor came early that day. He was discovered by the tubful of red water, still conscious. He struggled grimly with the doctor, trying to fight off aid, until he fainted.

The doctor arranged for a specialist to repair the damage, did his best to cover for him, listed it as an accident, and had him put on the general surgical floor. He understood why when the doctor apologized, saying, "I should have seen that she was too much for you to handle alone—too much for anyone. I've put her in a hospital, and I shall insist that she stay there. I'm sorry I didn't have sense enough to do it sooner. You've no idea how sorry."

Everyone was kind to him. He was helpless for days, both hands in casts, unable to even feed himself. But he didn't mind. He was at peace, cheerful, cooperative, a model patient. Waiting serenely for the day when he would be discharged and could get on with the job. Do it properly this time.

He read a good deal and became adept at turning pages with his elbows. One day an intern came in with a volume of Grey's *Anatomy*. He asked to see it, paged through the section on the nervous system, and asked to borrow it. The intern said he could for the afternoon. As soon as the young man left he turned to the circulatory system.

His mistake became immediately apparent. He should have cut the insides of his elbows where there was no gristle to get in the way and the arteries were larger and nearer the surface. Jim walked in then and found him smiling over the diagram.

Jim slammed the room door and came over to him, shook him fiercely, saying between his teeth, "Selfish, selfish. Oh, damn you, how can you think of that?" Then embraced him, heedless of danger, and said, teeth still clenched, "God damn you to hell, don't you know how much I love you?"

"I'm sorry," he said, because that seemed appropriate, not because he meant it.

After Jim had left he discovered that his serenity had begun to develop a crack. Later he asked the nurse he liked best, a dark young intense girl, if she thought he was selfish.

"I don't know you well enough to say," she replied immediately. Then, as she often did, understood the question under the question and responded to that. "You mean what you did? Yes, I suppose it is in a way. Yes, very."

"Why?"

She wrung out the white washcloth into the metal basin, then gently washed his face. When she did it he always felt better afterwards; it was a talent no other nurse had. She had enough fur on her upper lip so that he was sure she would have a mustache when she was older, but she was more beautiful because of the shadow, at least to him.

"Because," she replied slowly, after stopping to think, "if you're dead you're out of it. But all the people you've left behind have to get along without you. And some of them need you."

189

"Would you care if I were dead?"

"Yes, of course, now I've met you," she said with conviction and without hesitation.

Then the next day George came to visit. The crack widened enough so that he admitted to George that he had not had an accident, wanting to see how George would respond.

"Why didn't you let me know, Haakon? Maybe I could have helped—done something. I would have liked to try anyway." Then later, just before leaving, "Please don't do it again."

He said, "Don't worry, I won't." And felt the weight of all his tomorrows settle back on him like a doom.

Now he stood looking at the hairline scars. One scar per wrist, no hesitation marks. Heavy veins crossed through them under the skin, and the knots on the tendons had long since disappeared. With his hands in a normal position they could hardly be seen at all.

He understood now, for the first time, that although he had agreed not to kill himself he had never made any real commitment to living. To some extent he had seen the war as an opportunity to have someone else do the job for him. A part of himself had never given up the serenity of suicide, because for him it was always a very real alternative, not a remote and alien one as it seemed to be for other people.

He unbuttoned his cuffs and carefully rolled up his sleeves above the elbows. He owed no one now. Jim was long dead. Dan had picked up his own life. Simon would make out, Simon always did. He regretted going back on his word to George, but George could hardly blame him for breaking a promise made that long ago. Ellen? That was hardly started. Surely she would not miss him for long. No one would miss him long or deeply. His friends would be upset for a little while, but he was not an important part of anyone's life. Why not be selfish for once? He was tired of being unhappy.

He supposed he ought to write a suicide note. It was expected. But there was nothing he wanted to say, no one he wanted to communicate with.

There was no hurry. No one would interrupt him this time. Had he forgotten anything? Damn, his will. He had not changed it since he had left for the service. His entire estate, except for a few odds and ends, would go to set up a scholarship fund. But now he wanted to leave some money to Dan.

He would have to see his lawyer. Those Danish cousins were a greedy lot, and he wanted any codicils to be ironclad. The cousins did not need the money, and Dan did. Better to make sure. All right, he could wait a few days, and he probably would have to. Christmas tomorrow, then New Year's.

But he did not want to wait. Even deciding to put it off was like having to decide to live all over again. A week was like eternity, his life was so impossibly empty.

Maybe he should get a dog. He had seen a sign in a shop window: "The only love money can buy." Under the sign, black and tan puppies with floppy ears pressed their noses longingly against the glass, wagging short tails. But he had never had a pet of any sort. What did one do with a dog? Things like housebreaking.

He wandered over to his desk and looked at the manuscript. He had wanted to write this book. He really ought to. He had completed the first chapter and done all the research for the second. A shame to let it go to waste.

He looked around the living room. God, what a mess! Half the reason he was depressed was probably the dirt and clutter. No, it was the other way around. When he felt depressed he made no effort to pick up or put things away.

The last thing he wanted to do was clean, but he was going to have to occupy himself somehow. Phone a friend? On the day before Christmas? He would be an albatross. He sure as hell was not going to be able to do any writing today. But the job of cleaning was too big. Where could he start? Toss a match in the middle. Move out?

No. Begin with one thing and do it. After all, his sleeves were already rolled up. He got the dirty coffee cup, then picked up the overflowing ashtray beside it. Do it! He took them to the kitchen.

The sink was full of foul-smelling dishes. Three weeks' worth. No room for the cup or ashtray. He almost turned and walked out. Job too big. Too big? What was the matter with him. He had washed hundreds of dishes in the Army, enough to pave a road from here to Istanbul. He filled the sink with soapy water and set to work. He scraped hard-dried egg off plates, scoured greasy pans, and after the third washing finally got the milk film off the glasses. At one point he seriously considered smashing all of them. But he felt satisfaction when they were finally clean and he could put them away.

He cleaned the sink, stove and counters. What next? The floor was so cruddy his shoes stuck to it in places. He got a mop and pail of water and began working on that, now swearing under his breath and banging things around. In an odd kind of way he was beginning to enjoy himself. He realized that he had never before cleaned his apartment. Somehow it made it more his own.

While waiting for the kitchen floor to dry he paused for a cigarette. His shoulder was beginning to ache. Was that from bending over or a drop in barometric pressure? It seemed to him occasionally that it bothered him more before a storm. And Ben had mentioned that on those days his leg bothered him. He looked out the window. If a storm was on its way, he could see no evidence of it. The sun was bright, the sky blue and cloudless. The Hudson sparkled and pigeons strutted in the park. An elderly lady, cocooned in layers of clothing against the cold, appeared with a brown paper bag. Within moments she was surrounded by birds greedily eating bread.

He waxed the kitchen floor. He would probably break his neck the next time he walked in there, but it did look nice. In the bathroom he discovered black stuff on the grout between the ceramic tiles. He could find no tool to clean it with. Scrubbing with a rag did not work. He found himself looking at his toothbrush. Why not? He could always buy a new one. He spent a peaceful half-hour sitting in the bathtub scrubbing the right-angled cracks. Hardly thinking at all, just working.

When he finished the bathroom he went to work on the living room. Even as he worked, comfortable for now, not fighting with himself or wanting to die, he knew that this solution was temporary, that the entire problem was still there as big as ever, and that he was going to have to deal with it one way or the other. He was not at all sure he would be alive tomorrow, much less a week from now, and wondered if he were doing all this cleaning partly because he did not want the police to think he was a slob.

Back from dinner, he hung away his overcoat and scarf. His face still stung from the cutting wind and his nose was running from the change in temperature. He put his new toothbrush in the bathroom, blew his nose, then went to the kitchen to put away the bottle of brandy he had bought.

He paused in the kitchen doorway to look around. He could derive some satisfaction from his clean apartment, but he was restless. He would have liked to walk, but the weather was too unpleasant. He crossed to the fireplace and stroked the neck of the bronze lioness. There were few objects that were important to him, but this was, and he never would have bought it if Simon had not prodded him into it.

Ten years ago in Paris. The bronze had been in a dusty shop on a narrow cobbled street. He saw it standing there, between a grubby porcelain shepherdess with missing fingers and an elephant-foot umbrella stand containing a bouquet of canes. In front of it were dirty demitasse cups and a conglomeration of odd silverware, meerschaum pipes and statuettes.

The day he bought it, Simon was in an effervescent mood. That morning Simon had picked up a new suit from the tailor, and he was full of childlike delight with it, looking at himself in every reflecting surface they passed, admiring the cut of the jacket.

The street was still wet after an afternoon shower. The sun had come out and cast his and Simon's shadows on the dusty glass. From the narrow entrance to the neighboring grocery came the smell of fresh coffee beans and the sound of the hand-operated mill grinding them. He could hear the summer sounds of shrill children's voices and the flat rhythmic slap of a rubber ball being bounced. A fruit wagon rattled down the street, bringing with it the smell of horse sweat and overripe peaches. The window was so dirty they could only see through the film where their shadows fell on the glass.

"It's the bronze, isn't it?" Simon said.

He nodded, saw his shadow bob.

"At first I thought it might be that silver-headed cane, or the pipe with the dragon. You can't pass here without stopping. Buy it, for heaven's sake!"

"It's bound to be heavy. I'm not sure I want to carry it all over Scotland."

"You could have it sent."

"No, it might get damaged or lost."

"Which will you regret more? Lugging it about for a month, or not having got it when you could?"

He saw his shadow nod again, and turn away from the window to take a step toward the door. A bell on a coiled spring rang and reverberated tinnily long after the door shut. The shop smelled of incense, old leather and sour Turkish tobacco. It was so dark and crowded that he hesitated about going farther in for fear of falling over the furniture or breaking the china objects that covered every flat surface. He stood there wondering why he had hesitated so long over buying something he wanted so much.

He still did not know why he had procrastinated, and he was grateful to Simon for urging him to get it. Simon did understand him in many ways. He wished Simon were in town now. He wanted to see him, to hear the sound of his voice.

He turned away from the lioness and noticed that the wrapped gifts he had left on the record player were rearranged. The Dürer—authenticated, and much more expensive than George would approve of, but easy to lie about since bargains were not unknown—

193

was still there. The blue vase for Mary, to replace the one he had broken that summer. The first edition of *Varney the Vampire* for Tom and Abby. He had read it and enjoyed it, but found Tom's tastes in books strange. The chessboard he had bought for Dan was gone, and in its place a small box and a wrapped bottle.

Dan had been here while he was out. He unwrapped the bottle first. Haig and Haig. The box contained a watch band. He was touched that Dan had noticed he needed a new one. He went to his desk to take off the old one and replace it, and found a note from Dan, written in his childish script on the top page of his pad of yellow paper:

Dear Hawk,

Merry Christmas. I couldn't wait because people were waiting for me, but I hope we can see each other maybe day after tomorrow. I'll call. Thanks for the chessboard, it'll look a lot better with my chess set than the cardboard one did. I'm glad you kept the set for me, because if you hadn't, I wouldn't have it. Love, Dan.

Admonishing himself not to get sentimental, he set about replacing the watch band, but he would have given almost anything to hold Dan in his arms right at that moment, just to feel his solidity. He tore the page off the pad, folded it, and put it in his top desk drawer.

Could he work on the book now? No, he was too restless, too much at odds with himself. He could not think of anything else he wanted to do either. He could hear the wind whistling in a cornice of the building. In the park the tree branches tossed in the wind. Except for cars and an occasional bus, the city seemed deserted.

He poured himself some of Dan's Haig and Haig and sat at his desk sipping it, trying to savor it. Tomorrow . . . Christmas dinner with George and Mary, then around four drop over to the Enfields' for a couple of hours. After that, what? How was he going to get through this night? He picked up the file cards and riffled the corners, then threw them down.

He was wandering aimlessly around the apartment, trying not to think when the phone rang. Who would be calling him now? Dan? It was after ten. "Hvitfelt here."

"Hawk? I didn't wake you, did I?"

"Ellen?" She was the last person he would have expected to hear from. "Are you calling from Boston?"

"No, I'm back. And, well, look . . . I know this is a big favor to ask, but could I come over? If you aren't busy, that is."

"No, not at all. Do come. I'd been wishing for company."

"Great. See you." She hung up quickly as if she were afraid he would change his mind.

After he had put down the phone he realized how strange it was that she was back in New York. She had been eager to go home. "It's been three years," she said. "I was overseas in the Army, you know." Enthusiastically she told him how she looked forward to "a real family Christmas." What on earth could have impelled her to leave Boston tonight?

When she arrived, not much later, face pink with cold, she thrust a chilled beribboned magnum of Piper Heidsick champagne into his hands, then took off her coat, not giving him a chance to help her out of it. "Merry Christmas." She was smiling. She rooted through her purse and got out two paper snake whistles. "See? I brought a party."

He looked at the big cold green bottle. "Merry Christmas to you too, and thank you." He was pleased, touched. He set it down to take her coat and hang it in the closet.

He did not know what to make of her mood. It seemed too exuberant, a shade out of character, as if she were covering something up. "I didn't expect you back until after the holidays."

"Things don't always work out the way you expect them to." She laughed. "To quote Thomas Wolfe, 'You can't go home again.' But let's drink and be merry. I never saw you dressed like that before—in khakis. You look different. Sort of beautiful."

He glanced down at himself. He had put on old Army pants and shirt to go walking before he had discovered how cold it was. He was glad he had not thought of changing before she came.

Ellen was upset. She was talking too much and too brightly. Something must have gone seriously wrong at home, but she clearly did not want to discuss it. She wanted to be happy and so did he. Give it a try. It would be far pleasanter cheering her up, and perhaps himself too in the process, than spending any more time alone. He picked up the bottle. "I'll get glasses. Let's get the party started."

When he came back from the kitchen, bottle in his silver champagne bucket, draped with a blue-checked dish towel (Simon would disapprove of that), with two hollow-stemmed glasses, Ellen was over by the fireplace inspecting the lioness. He put down the things, reflecting that it was fortunate that he had decided to clean earlier. The lioness had been very dusty.

Her back was turned, so he could take a good long look at her. He tended not to look too closely at people, often did not know where to look. Her hair was loose. She had worn it that way ever since he had asked her not to pin it up. Her white turtleneck sweater looked soft and was just transparent enough so he could see she was wearing a white bra. He had never seen her in slacks before. They were dark green wool and showed off her slenderness. No girdle, she obviously did not need one. A sensual curve to her buttocks.

She smiled at him over her shoulder. "This has that cat-mother feeling, the apparent neglect that isn't neglect at all, but letting the cubs alone so they can squabble and play, learn to fight and grow up strong. Getting her paw washed while they're busy with each other. And that one looking over her back, about to pounce— you can almost see the tip of his tail twitching. Beautiful! Where did you get it?"

"In France, a long time ago." He was struggling with the cork. She crossed to him, watching his hands. The cork popped and he poured the foaming wine into the glasses. She had put her finger on one of the reasons he had wanted the bronze, as well as a reason why he had hesitated to buy it. The lioness portrayed the loving indifference that allowed children to grow up, be themselves, be ready for the world. Some of the important if-onlys of his life.

An oval enameled locket hung from her neck on a thin gold chain, resting in the hollow between her breasts. The same old problem of not knowing what to do with his eyes. Should not stare, that was not polite. At least his hands were occupied with the wineglasses.

The wind seemed far away. The room was quiet. He watched the bubbles rising from the bottom of the stem of his glass. He could hear them as they broke the surface of the pale wine. He handed her a glass, held his up. "Merry Christmas."

She took her glass soberly, looking into his face. Her pupils were dilated, making her eyes seem almost black. "Yes, merry Christmas," she said, then touched his glass with hers and took a swallow. "Here!" She held out a whistle. "You get the one with the red feather because you're brave. I'm the one that's yellow, so I get the white one." Before he could respond, she blew her whistle at him, tickling his nose with the white fluff on the end.

He dodged, almost spilled his drink. He grabbed at the diamond-patterned paper tube, but it had rolled back up. She laughed.

Then she held her glass up again. "To friendship." She waited until he repeated it and drank, then drained her glass in one long draft. She held it out for more like a little girl with a punch cup.

He poured it full again. She took it to the couch and sat down, then patted the cushion beside her on seeing he was about to take his usual chair. "Sit by me?"

"Yes." The cold wine tasted like spring sunshine; it prickled his tongue and went down smoothly. A good vintage. He knew little about wines, but Simon had taught him enough to be discriminating. He sat down a foot away from her.

"I was thinking about you on the train coming back," she said. "And about Christmas. It was snowing in Boston, and the tune of 'I'm Dreaming of a White Christmas' kept running through my head. You know how it was in the Army. The nostalgia. And remembering the night we heard that Patton was raising the siege of Bastogne. You could hear the planes overhead, wave after wave of them, roaring. And everyone went wild, jumping up and down, singing, dancing, hugging and kissing each other. Where were you that night?"

"Outside Bastogne clearing roads, with half the Third Army waiting. Truckloads of troops."

"Was that when you and Dan were wounded?"

"I wasn't. I got hit on D-Day. Dan was, though, early in the day. We lost quite a few men during that barrage."

"I can't quite imagine you operating a bulldozer."

"I'm very good at it."

"I bet you are. I'd like to see you do it someday."

"I'd love to show you, but I haven't one handy just now."

She laughed. She was overready to laugh tonight.

He finished his glass of champagne and poured more for both of them. "I can repair them too, at least to some extent," he said, still trying to go along with her wish to ignore her upset. "That's how I spent Christmas day—trying to haywire one working dozer out of the pieces of three shot-up ones. Me and Morrie and Roger." He was slipping back into his Army speech pattern. Ellen had noticed, smiled when he said "me." "And I never had such cold hands in my life. They were stiff and ached all the way to my elbows, like an impacted wisdom tooth."

"Go on," she said when he paused.

"The supply sergeant didn't have gloves or mittens big enough for either me or Morrie. His hands are bigger than mine. We tried socks, but they were too clumsy to work in."

She reached for his hand and held it, turning it over, stroking it. He thought she was using this as an excuse to hold it, and appreciated that she could so smoothly contrive it. "I like big hands," she said. "What did you do?"

"It was quiet that afternoon. There was artillery all around, but where we were, nothing—just snow." Like a lunar landscape, pockmarked, empty, populated by the shrouded bodies of all the broken tanks—and smaller mounds. Together he and Morrie had walked among the mounds, kicking snow away from them on a treasure hunt for a means to warm their hands. At the time—until just now—he had not thought about the fact that those frozen forms had once been men with thoughts and wishes. All of it had been unreal, almost outside time. "We went looking for gloves on the battlefield," he said, "and ended up robbing German corpses to get them. At the time it didn't seem wrong."

"You needed them worse than the dead. I don't see that it was wrong."

"Yes, our efficiency was impaired by the cold."

"Don't back off from me like that."

She was still holding his hand, playing absently with his fingers. Yes, he had been backing off. "I didn't mean to." Her smile was ready, but it wavered, and her expression did not match even so small a smile. He said, "Ellen, what is it? What went wrong?"

"Nothing—everything. I left in the middle of dinner. I had to get out of there before I killed somebody. Aunt Tessa as a start." She laughed brittlely. "Aunt Tessa is insufferable. Imagine a matchstick with a dried-up yellow raisin on top. That's her. Maybe weighs ninety pounds in her sealskin coat. And you'll never see a lion tamer get the results with a whip and chair that she gets with that sticky voice of hers. When she tells her kids or husband 'frog,' they jump." An even less convincing laugh. "But I'll tell you about her on Halloween. She's not a fit subject for Christmas Eve." She drained her glass and held it out for more. "Tell me about yourself." It was a formula, but also a plea.

He would have talked about himself if he had thought it would help, but he could see that her attempt to be cheerful was not working. "Ellen," he said gently, "I know you're trying to be happy—be 'good company,' whatever that is. But it's not working. Please let me try to help."

She let go of his hand and held her glass in both of hers, staring into it. Her chin was quivering. "I don't want to ruin your Christmas Eve."

"I've had a very bad day, Ellen. I need your company. You can't possibly do or say anything that would ruin my evening."

"Really?"

"Really. Cross my heart. All right?"

Her smile was tentative, but genuine. "All right." Then, with concern for him, "What went wrong with your day?"

"Let's just say that I finally had to face up to the fact that I'm going to have to get reading glasses."

To his surprise she nodded. "Yes, that's a tough one. My brother

Mark was depressed for days over getting bifocals. But you know, getting older isn't a sin." She paused, looking at him. "Or a tragedy either. You're handsome, distinguished-looking. I bet you're handsomer now than when you were younger. Some men improve with age."

"By the time I'm a hundred I'll be gorgeous," he said bitterly.

"Stop it. Hey, you did have a bad day, didn't you? A lot worse than you're letting on." She was looking at him intently. "You don't want to talk about it though," she said almost to herself. "You don't want to think about it. All right. I guess I want to talk a little. Get some of it out of my system."

She paused as if waiting for permission, then reading his willingness to listen in his expression, went on. "I think I told you about my brother Matt. The priest. He was unfrocked five years ago for falling in love and getting married. My oldest brother, and closer to me than my father. When I was little I didn't know he'd wanted desperately to be a chemist, but the family pressured him into the priesthood. They were bound and determined to have their own priest. He made the best of it, and he was a hell of a good man. Are you sure you want to hear about this?"

"Yes."

"He died last year of diabetic gangrene."

"Oh."

"When he was dying his wife and I were his only visitors. There he was, rotting away by inches, and in terrible pain, and not a single one of them would come to see him. From the time he was unfrocked his name was anathema at home.

"Until today. Today Matt was all they would talk about. Saying they were glad he was dead, that it was a good thing that the 'disgrace' was decently buried. Aunt Tessa and my mother talking, and everyone else nodding like a bunch of those obscene little china Buddhas with wiggly heads.

"And I sat there and didn't say a word. Like Judas. Selling my soul for approval. Lack of disapproval. And keeping quiet was the same as agreeing.

"Until finally I couldn't help crying. And then I stood up and told them that I loved Matt and that they were a bunch of pious buzzards, and walked out. All the way back on the train I was thinking of all the things I should have said. I should have said that Matt was a man, a person—not a tinsel ornament to pin over the front door to make the family look good."

He said, "There were a lot more of them than there are of you. Not many people can stand up to family pressure. Too many years of childhood, doing as you're told, believing what they tell you—"

"I was a goddamned coward," she interrupted.

"Not at all. You spoke up."

"Too little, too late. Oh, damn." She had tears in her eyes. "I just know I loved him and didn't speak up."

There was no logic that would make her feel better now. What she needed was physical comforting. He put his arm around her and pulled her close.

For a moment she was stiff, then she suddenly kicked off her shoes and shifted around so she was lying across his lap with her arms around him. She was warm and soft and smelled clean and fresh. Her body felt right against his, as if it belonged. A stirring of interest that caught him by surprise. Her hair was silky under his hand, the texture of her back softer than he could have expected, the tenseness of cloth as his hand crossed the back of her bra was fascinating. But he had meant only to comfort her.

What was going on? Women did not interest him. Well, *had* not. Fear gnawed gently in the pit of his stomach, not so much as to be distressing. Rather, it was exciting, like the thrill of the first long downgrade on a roller coaster. Expectation of disaster along with the conviction that nothing bad could really happen. Disaster? Men slept with women every day, every hour.

Might she go to bed with him? And if she did, would he be taking advantage of her upset? Exploiting her vulnerability? Matt had been around his age. She had mentioned that. Had, according to her, looked somewhat like him, been going white, had blue eyes, was tall and thin.

She shifted in his arms and lifted her face. "Would you mind kissing me? I don't want to put you on the spot, make you uncomfortable. Just say yes or no. You won't hurt my feelings."

Instead of replying he kissed her. At first with anxiety, waiting for the fear to swell up and take possession of him. But the fear remained quiescent, merely adding excitement. She kissed more gently than a man. There was no undercover competition, no implicit struggle for dominance. Her response was cautious but warm, accepting, not pressing. She did not probe or penetrate. A kiss was not necessarily more than just that. She was stroking his side now.

Then with her face against him, her lips on his throat, she asked softly, "Will you go to bed with me?"

Holding her tightly, feeling her against him, he said, "I want to. But I'm afraid it wouldn't work." Nothing of his experience with Jenny was of any use. The expectations were too different. With Jenny he had started out as a customer to be pleased. There had been no hint of mutuality until several days later, and by that time he was used to her. And Jenny had been very boyish, not at all like Ellen.

"Listen, Hawk. I need you with me. That would be enough. I need to be held. I can't bear the thought of being alone."

"But I don't want to disappoint you. I need us to stay friends."

"Hawk, that couldn't happen," she said earnestly. "I like you so much I almost love you. In a sense, you could call it love, I suppose. If it doesn't work, all right. Do you understand?"

"Yes."

"I know I'm asking a lot."

"No, not asking, offering." She shifted in his arms, holding him closer, and he realized that she could not avoid being aware of his excitement. Mightn't it work? Then he felt himself blushing as another thought occurred to him. He did not own a condom, never had. The drugstore was closed. "But . . . ah . . . I don't know— I mean . . ." he stammered, feeling utterly inept and tongue-tied.

"You're a virgin."

"Ah, only in a sense. I suppose you could say that. But . . . ah . . . well . . . don't women get pregnant?"

She laughed and hugged him. "Don't worry about that." She kissed his cheek. "I'm safe."

"Safe?"

"Yes, really. Don't worry about it."

He did not know what she meant, but he was willing to take her word for it. She should know. "All right." He kissed her again, both to allow himself the enjoyment and to assess the extent of his fear. It was still there waiting. He would probably have to deal with it later, but he was willing to.

She picked up his hand and laid it on her breast. He had never felt anything like that before, though once he had caressed a marble statue in a museum when no one was looking. Not at all the same. Jenny's breasts had been so small he had been able to ignore them, had tried to. Now he wanted to undress Ellen and explore her, but he was too embarrassed. Even if she were nude he would not be able to look at her in the bright light. Why hadn't he had enough sense to turn off some of the lamps before she arrived?

"Could . . ." He had to clear his throat. "Do you want to go to bed now?"

"Of course."

He wanted to scoop her up in his arms and carry her into the bedroom like some knight of old, but more than likely he would hurt his shoulder if he tried that. Too bad. It would be a nice romantic gesture.

He felt flooded with gratitude and tenderness. He wanted to

please her. Do everything right. She was helping him to pry open a door he had thought closed and locked forever.

He left the bedroom door open. Light from the living room spread across the dark red Bokhara in a wide wedge. Standing beside the bed, he kissed Ellen again. Taller than Simon, she was easy to kiss without having to stoop. Her breasts were pressing against him, her body was slender and strong in his arms. Stroking her back he became aware of the narrowness of her waist, the flare of her hips as he had not been before.

He wanted to get her into bed, but if he let go of her he would not know what to do or where to look. Why in hell was he so inept? If only he could wish them both under the covers and skip the preliminaries. He could not even figure out how to get around to pulling down the spread. Thank god he had changed the sheets.

He wanted everything to go smoothly. There should be no rough transitions, no unfortunate nudgings of necessity. But anxiety and the somewhat cooler temperature of the bedroom had made him aware that he was going to have to make a trip to the bathroom. Characters in novels never had to stop in the middle of a love scene to take a leak—but he could not take the chance of having mechanical difficulties. He caught his train of thought and reflected that it would be comical if it were not so important.

Not knowing what to say, he held her away, then blurted, "Do you want pajamas?"

A look of amusement, quickly gone. A smile for him. "Yes, thank you."

He was making a fool of himself. Damn, what had inspired that stupid suggestion? Now he could only go through with it. He got silk pajamas out of his dresser.

"Just give me the top, you take the bottoms. All right?"

A neat solution. He was grateful. "Ah . . . would you excuse me a minute? I'll be right back." She nodded and he escaped to the bathroom, clutching the pajama pants with a hand so sweaty it left a damp spot. He stood in front of the toilet. Nothing. To give himself time, he undressed and put on the pajama bottoms, then tried again. After some difficulty he finally got his valves unstuck and was able to relieve himself. He paused to feel his chin. Far too prickly. He ought to shave. Ellen would be wondering what was taking him so long, but shaving would not take that much longer.

When he got back to the bedroom Ellen was in bed as he had hoped she would be. He got in beside her. She sniffed and touched his cheek. "You shaved." She sounded pleased. "I like your shaving lotion."

It was Simon's, and suddenly he wished he had not used it. In the bathroom he had only thought that since he liked the scent Ellen might too, but now all he could think about was the smell. He wished she had not mentioned it, though he was glad to have pleased her.

He put his arm around her and she rolled closer to him. What had happened? Not fifteen minutes ago he had been interested, even eager. Now he was lying there trying grimly to relax. All his excitement had vanished. He was sure he could never revive it and was not at all certain he wanted to try.

The silk was slippery under his fingers, her shoulder under it round and warm. For the first time he found himself envying Dan his fetish. If only he could have some object to excite himself with and know that with it available he could not fail. But there was the other side of the coin, the total helplessness without it. No, that would be ghastly.

He was beginning to tremble and, knowing she could feel it, was ashamed. "It's no use," he said, feeling old and bitter. "I'm queer, that's all. It's no use."

"Hawk, it's all right. I told you, I need you close. Just to hold me, no more."

A few minutes later she said quietly, "But you don't really want to give up, do you?"

"No," he admitted, "I don't. But you don't understand." Then, angry with himself, hating himself for his limitations, "I'm a fruit, a faggot. God damn it, I've been a fairy all my life. It's too late for me now. I can't even screw Simon properly, I'm not even that much of a man. Don't you see? I'm nothing but a damned mouth queen. It's hopeless."

"Hey, take it easy. And stop calling yourself names." Her hand was soft on his cheek, not bony like Simon's or calloused like Dan's. "Listen, it's all right to be afraid. It's normal to be afraid. The first time I went to bed with someone I was scared out of my wits. And it has to be worse for a man. So much less is expected of a woman." Her lips brushed his face as swiftly and undemandingly as a butterfly's wing. "Listen, making love isn't a task. Not like grading an airstrip or organizing notes for your next chapter. There's no timetable, no need to 'get on with it.'"

"Oh, you read minds too?"

She chuckled. "I do know you fairly well by now. I know you tend to think in terms of a job to be done. Now, I don't want to push you or make you uncomfortable, but I'd like to try to help. Would you mind if I tried to seduce you?"

"I wish you could," he said despairingly. "I don't think it's any use though."

"Maybe not, but let me try. You don't have to do anything. And I won't be disappointed, no matter what. All I wanted was for you to let me stay with you."

"That's not all though," he said bitterly. "You're kidding yourself. You want to 'save' me. If I fail, you fail, and then maybe we won't be friends any more. I don't want that to happen."

"I don't think you need saving. And I can't imagine not wanting to be friends." Abruptly she propped herself on her elbow, looked in his face. "I'm going to put all my cards on the table, Hawk. I wanted to get you into bed because I want you, but everything else I said was true too. I won't be upset if we don't have sex. I promise. Furthermore, assuming you're as queer as you keep claiming, even if we did make love, you might not like it."

That had not occurred to him. "Oh."

He must have looked surprised, because she smiled and said, "That never crossed your mind, that you might not like it, did it?"

"No, it didn't."

"Then the fact I'm female doesn't disgust you."

"God no! I've always liked women . . . only—"

"I know, you're a fairy. How important is that to you?"

"Huh?"

"You've defined yourself as queer. How important is it to stick to that definition of yourself?"

That was what had upset him about her AC-DC remark, but she was coming to it from a different angle. Put this way, it seemed easier to deal with. "Not all-important, but perhaps too important. I've thought I'd like to change."

"All right." She snuggled against him in the crook of his arm, her head on his shoulder, and began stroking him. In a short time she said, "No good. You're only getting tenser. Let's try something else. Hug me."

"What?"

"Come on, just do it." She took hold of his arm and put it around her. He rolled toward her and hugged her tentatively. "Harder. I'm not made of glass." He tightened his arms. "Yes, nice. More." He did feel less tense, held her even tighter. "Oh, yes, strong. More." He could feel her arms around him.

He had always found the weight of someone on him exciting. Why not start easily with something familiar, see how it worked? He rolled onto his back, still holding her. She was as heavy as Simon, a good armful. The familiarity of breath tickling the side of his neck

204

was reassuring, and the unfamiliarity of hair across his face, warm, sweet-smelling, feminine, was exciting.

Molly's hair had smelled like that, had been almost the same shade of red. She had bitten her nails, and took her tea with milk and two spoons of sugar. He felt himself become warm with embarrassment as he remembered feverish afternoons of guilty, love-struck ecstasy spent in her empty room, the intoxicating perfume of her flannel nightgown, her pillow. He remembered wild romantic daydreams of being big and strong, of carrying her off to a castle on a moor, a mountain, or an island. He had not remembered that in years. And there had been a dream horse named Lion. Sometimes black, sometimes gold, sometimes with wings, but always faithful to him only. Mobility, freedom, and power—all the things he had yearned for.

"Hey, don't go away," Ellen said.

He gave her a squeeze to let her know he was with her, but it was not easy to stop thinking. There had not only been Molly, but Leda too. He had kissed her shyly, one afternoon, and walked on air the rest of the day.

He was glad for Ellen's weight on him. He trusted her. He discovered that he had been stroking her to reassure himself and now, gradually, he began to appreciate her shape, her softness. The fear receded again and became an extra source of excitement rather than a hindrance. He kissed her recklessly, defying it, and it remained quiescent.

His pajama tops were so loose on her he could pull them off over her head without unbuttoning them. Her skin was smoother than the silk, smoother than Dan's. Her breasts were soft, yielding yet solid. He felt her nipples harden against his palms. He did not know when or how he had loosened his half of the pajamas, but he found them binding his ankles and kicked them off.

His body seemed to have taken over, but there was no reason not to let it, since it apparently knew what to do. Her hands caressing him were almost too exciting. He wanted to look at her, but could not. It was almost as if a part of his mind were shouting "Danger!" Touching was safe though, and he could explore her with his mouth. The valley between her breasts tasted pleasantly of salt.

Did she mind? He glanced to her face for permission. "Anything you want is all right," she said. She was pleased that he had asked. His confidence increased. His instincts seemed to be in working order.

Her breathing was faster, a familiar cue. Recklessly confident, unaccountably sure of himself, he almost stopped worrying. After all, he was not totally inexperienced. He had been inside Simon. A woman couldn't be so very different. But what if he had the same problem with her that he had with Simon?

Her thighs were satiny around his hips. Inside she was warm, ridged, slippery. Almost shockingly different from the single ring of sphincter and hint of dryness he had expected. It was pleasant and the novelty was exciting.

He was larger than most men. Simon had told him this often enough. "I don't want to hurt you."

"I'm fine. Don't worry." She moved so he was all the way in. This passageway did not go on indefinitely. It ended, providing pressure and stimulation. He had not imagined it would be like this. And inside, beyond that extraordinarily exciting knob of spongy flesh, babies grew. And here was Ellen in his arms, warm and real, a person. He felt he loved her, but could not say it because Simon had cheapened the word too much.

He had never before had to make any effort to control his reflexes. There had been times when he had thought he did not have any. Now restraining himself was making him tremble. "Are you all right?"

"Yes, don't worry."

"Really?"

"Really! Please shut up?" She pulled his head down and kissed him. Then as if she understood what was bothering him, she said, "Don't be careful. Just let go."

Although he believed her he tried to be careful. He also wanted to savor and enjoy her, to be sure he would remember all of it. Her muscles contracting on him were too much. He heard her moan with pleasure and felt himself spiral away from consciousness.

He surfaced slowly. He was amazed at himself. He had done it. He had really done it.

Strange to be breathing easily, not to be as short of oxygen as he was with a man. Not unpleasant but too strange. A little frightening. He missed the texture and flavor of semen in his throat and mouth, but that was not what was bothering him.

Lying beside her with his cheek against her shoulder, the scent of her in his nostrils, he gradually became aware that he felt strange all over. His body felt alien, spent and empty. He was defenseless, as if he had lost some kind of armor, not only mentally but physically as well. The muscles deep in the small of his back felt lax and disconnected. He had never before been this relaxed after sex, and although he told himself that it ought to be pleasant, it was not. It was frightening.

Ellen was stroking the back of his head and neck. "My love," she whispered.

"You're all right?"

"Of course."

"I didn't hurt you?" He was worried about the way he had completely lost control.

"No, listen, Hawk. I didn't know sex could be so gentle."

"Oh?"

"Yes, it was wonderful for me. I've never before enjoyed it half so much. You're really special. Thank you. God, that's inadequate! Hawk? How was it for you? Was it all right?"

"Yes."

She hugged him. "Sometimes, when I first knew you, the way you say just 'yes' like that sort of irritated me. But it can mean more than a long explanation. And now I like it because it's you—and I like you. Maybe love you."

The fear had begun to gnaw again. "Don't say that."

She must have felt his tension. Instead of apologizing or explaining or insisting she meant it, any of which would have made him more uncomfortable, she said lightly, "How about a change of venue? I shouldn't think the champagne would be flat, it's been on ice."

"Yes." Going to the living room might be a help. Then remembering what she had said, he added, "Let's." A shade too much pause, too self-conscious. Gauche. Sex with a woman was not a magic charm against awkwardness. He still could not look at her. Why should looking be more dangerous than touching, than making love? It made no sense.

He sat up and felt around under the covers for the pajama pants, got into them before standing. He felt defiant about his squeamishness and told himself he had a right to cover himself if he wanted to. Nevertheless he felt unmasculine for it. He wished he had the nerve to parade around naked the way Simon did, or that he had some of Dan's innocent unself-consciousness. If only he could feel half as comfortable with her as he could with a man.

He still wanted to look at her and, feeling furtive, stole a glimpse. "It's gotten chilly," he told her. "Let me get you a robe."

She had started to get out of bed when he did, then, as if she understood his problem, had picked up a corner of sheet and held it to her. "Yes."

Several years before the war Simon had given him a yellow Chinese kimono. He had only worn it a few times, to please Simon, but it was too gaudy with its huge embroidered flowers and bright colors. He had felt foolish in it. He got it from the closet and handed it to her, then put on his old black kimono with the dragon on the back.

"Is this new?"

"No, but I've not worn it. It makes me feel like a refugee from *A Thousand and One Nights.*"

"It's lovely. You can look now."

The sunshine colors suited her, and seeing her in something different made her new again. "You're beautiful!"

"Thank you." She held out her hand, waited until he took it. "Let's get that drink."

The champagne had not lost its effervescence. As he poured it he heard church bells, chimes playing, "Hark the Herald Angels Sing."

"It's Christmas." She took her glass and held it up to clink against his.

"Yes, merry Christmas." Where was Simon now? Probably playing belle of the ball with his faggoty friends. He refused to think about it.

Ellen was dancing a minuet to the sound of the church bells, holding out her wineglass like a libation to some god. She was perfect and wonderful. Lovely as a bird in flight.

She danced over to him and held her glass to his lips. Her face was happy and serene, her hair like fire. He sipped her wine, wanting to tell her he loved her, but unable to do it.

She set down the glass and put her arms around his neck, hugged him, then, taking his hand, wanted him to dance with her.

As he started to follow her, he stubbed his toe on the table leg. "Shit!" The word was out before he could stop it. He sat on the arm of the chair holding his foot. She was not offended though. She looked as if she were trying not to laugh. "Nothing like that ever happens to Clark Gable," he complained, and laughed with her.

IV

February 3, 1947

Haakon tore the January page off the wall calendar in his office, crumpled it into a ball, and lobbed it into the wastebasket on the other side of his desk. He could tell by the sound that it had gone in.

A strong gusty wind slapped rain against the windows. Lucy was typing in the outer office—a fast steady clicking, punctuated by the bell and the zip of the carriage being returned.

Next year he would have a new office. He would be assistant head of the history department. No surprise to be told that. He had taken over most of the duties in January when Brampton died.

That had been a shock. Brampton had been going to retire in the spring, and the day before his death he had been talking about the house he had bought in California, about how he was going to plant his garden. An austere, kindly man, he had been enthusiastic about gardening, about plants. He had loved sunshine. And now he was dead in the darkest months of the year.

People beginning to die—no, nonsense! Not surprising that some of his older friends and acquaintances were beginning to go. They were at that age.

He looked at his watch. Weimerschlage was late. When he was through with this interview he'd be done. If this young man shaped up as he expected, he would hire him. He had the best credentials and the most experience, but Haakon could not decide definitely without seeing him. Wouldn't do to have an instructor he couldn't tolerate, since he would have to work with him.

Dinner with Ellen tonight, at her apartment. He looked out the window. A few students hurried along the paths, hunched against the wind. Since he would probably be spending the night there, he would have to remember to buy razor blades. She kept forgetting, and last time he had shaved at her place he had butchered himself. What did she do to razor blades anyway? Sharpen pencils? How could shaving her armpits wreck the things so thoroughly?

He took a deep breath and discovered he felt good. He had been feeling good lately. Confident, free, energetic. And yes, attractive. Women were making passes at him lately. Always a surprise, and always pleasant. He had asked Ellen about it last weekend after a party, startled by the intensity of the play a young faculty wife had made for him.

She had laughed. "Hawk, you nearly fell into her decolletage. Of course she thought you were interested. I'd be jealous if I didn't know you were just making up for lost time."

Yes, he could look at women now, and women liked to be looked at. So it was all right to, of course. An enjoyable pastime. A shame he had missed so many years of it. They were all marvelous. What would it be like to sleep with a skinny one like Lucy, or a chubby one like Mary? No, watch it! No passes at wives of old friends, co-workers or students. He might feel like a randy teenager, but he would be a fool to act on it.

Yet it would be easy to be promiscuous with women, the amount of his commitment was so much less somehow. Ellen would not like that though, and he did not want to hurt her.

A knock at the door. "Come in?"

Lucy in tears. What had Randall done now? "Mr. Hvitfelt, what . . ." Weeping too hard to talk.

He grasped a handful of Kleenex as he passed his desk, went to her and put his arm around her. "There, there." He handed her a tissue. Funny how she always called him Mr. Hvitfelt when she was upset, and never seemed quite easy about calling him Haakon. "What happened?"

Wordlessly she held out the sheet of paper she had been carrying. A letter. He took it and looked at it. Errorless, except that she had left out one of the l's in Randall. "I didn't even see it," she wailed. "I reread it a dozen times to make sure he'd have nothing to complain about."

He soothed her and patted her until she got hold of herself, then said, "I'll be moving to Brampton's office at the end of the term, and you'll be coming with me. Can't you put up with him until then? Remind yourself that you won't have to deal with him after June."

"I do, but he's so nasty to me."

"If you like, I could proofread his letters for you."

"Oh, no! He'd say you were spying on him, and hate you worse than ever."

"I didn't think of that. I suppose you're right." He gave her a last pat and stepped away. "Do try not to take him so seriously."

"I'll try." She blew her nose. "Thank you, thank you very much," she said and left his office.

Did Lucy have a case on him as Ellen thought? She did have a way of looking at him. At least she was keeping it platonic; he couldn't ask for more than that. It might be interesting to go to bed with her, but he had no intention of doing so, especially if she cared about him. He had no desire for the kind of emotional complications that would surely follow, and furthermore it would be unfair to her. Women seemed to take these things very seriously.

A knock on the door. Lucy put her head in. "Mr. Weimerschlage is here."

"Thank you, send him on in."

Weimerschlage was a beefy young man with a deep tan and crew-cut hair. Almost too clean-cut, and saved from being too pretty by a slight jog in his nose, as if it had been broken. Almost as tall as he. Weimerschlage was carrying a wet topcoat and his pants legs were damp to the knees. "I'm sorry I'm late," he said. "But the hotel told me to take the Seventh Avenue subway. I took an express, and when I got off I was in Harlem and couldn't find a cab. I walked up here through the park."

"Morningside Park, yes. You should have taken a Broadway local. They should have told you." He took the coat and hung it on the tree in the corner. His first impression was that he liked the young man, that he would do nicely. But then he shook hands with him and found himself wondering if there was something slightly off about the handshake. It was warm and firm, but the index finger was on his wrist. A pass? Or was he being oversensitive.

Then, a little later in the interview, the young man was too eager to be called by his first name. He looked through the folder to gain thinking time. Was Bruce homosexual or not? He could not be sure, and there was no way for him to check it out without taking a chance of exposing himself. This man was the best of the applicants. Was it fair to take second-best only because Bruce might be queer?

He, of all people, should be tolerant. But he could not afford to be. His own neck was at stake. If he could see through Bruce,

211

it was quite possible that Bruce would see through him. Not yet, but eventually. He was going to have to think about it. He said, "Your qualifications are excellent. I do have one more interview. How long will you be in the city?"

"Another week."

"I'll be able to let you know by noon tomorrow."

"Thank you, sir."

After Bruce left, he went to the window to watch him walk away from the building. He walked like an athlete, not surprisingly, for it was in his record that he had played football and also been on the swimming team. Unusual combination that. No hint of effeminacy in his walk, but he had not expected there to be. Could he afford to hire him? He might not be queer. But what if he were, and made a slip? That would be a mess, if the first man he hired turned out to be a fairy. No good, he could not take the chance.

Of all the other applicants, one woman stood out. Her academic record was not quite as good, and she had less experience, but he had been impressed with her when he had talked with her. She would do. He would play it safe and hire her. Prejudice? Yes, no getting around it. Perhaps after he had hired a few more people he could then afford to take the chance, but not now. When he phoned Bruce tomorrow he would suggest he try again next year. That would give the young man time to foul up somewhere else—or acquire a better cover.

He began clearing his desk preparatory to going home. He had a full briefcase tonight. He would go home first and change, get in some time on his manuscript, then go to Ellen's apartment. She had a late class today, no hurry. Funny little ceremony she had made of exchanging keys, almost like getting engaged.

In the outer office Lucy was looking pink around the eyes as if she were trying not to cry. "What's the matter?"

"I don't know what to do," she said pathetically. "I know I'm being foolish, but I'm just so scared of Mr. Randall. These letters—they're supposed to go out tonight, and he left without signing them. I'll just have to take them to his place before I go home, and he'll be so angry."

"It seems to me it's his fault for not attending to them before he left."

"He was angry about his name being misspelled and just slammed out—and that was my fault."

"Do they really have to go out tonight?"

"Not really, I suppose, but he thinks so. And I don't want him mad at me."

212

Her timidity annoyed him. He wanted to shake her. Instead, he offered, "Give them to me. I'll drop them off for you."

"You will?" Looking at him as if he had said he would kill a dragon for her and bring her its pelt.

"Of course. It's no trouble. It's on my way home." He held out his hand for the half-dozen envelopes, took them, and tucked them into his briefcase.

When he left the building he discovered that the rain had stopped. The wind was damp and brisk, smelled of the river. He took a deep breath and squared his shoulders. He didn't feel like stopping at Randall's place. Randall was sure to be in a foul mood. But he could understand Lucy's panic at the thought of going there, and was glad he had taken on the task. He did not take Randall's venom personally as she did.

The Randalls lived in one of the newer buildings a block uptown from his own apartment. He walked down Riverside Drive, turned into their building and looked at the nameplates by the door. Fifth floor. He pressed the doorbell and waited. No response; he tried again. The door to the lobby buzzed and he pushed it open.

The elevator was noiseless, and his footsteps made no sound on the thick dark blue carpeting in the hallway. He knocked on the door. It opened immediately.

Startled, he took a step back. Winnie Randall looked so different from her usual groomed and corseted self that he hardly recognized her. Her hair was not curled. It was still a violet shade and she had it fastened in a little tuft on each side of her head with green rubber bands. She had no makeup on, and without the fierce boning of her corset, he could see that she was pleasantly and roundly dumpy. There was something totally and vulnerably human about her. She was wearing scuffed bedroom slippers and a navy-blue bathrobe with, apparently, nothing under it but a pink slip. She clutched the collar to her throat when she saw him. The venetian blinds were closed, making the room behind her dark.

An indrawn breath, almost a squeak. "I thought Peter'd forgotten his key."

She had been drinking and crying. Her eyes were red, and he could smell gin on her breath. Awkwardly he opened his briefcase and reached for the letters. They were not in the pocket he thought he had put them in, and he had to hunt for them. Finally he found them and held them out. "Peter forgot to sign these, and the secretary says they must go out tonight. Would you give them to him?"

"I didn't mean to imply you weren't welcome," Winnie said, not taking the envelopes. "I was just surprised, you know. Please, come in. Please." A tear ran down her cheek. She sniffled and wiped her nose on the back of her hand. A childlike gesture, oddly appealing. She took hold of his sleeve and stepped back from the door, drawing him into the room with her.

He remembered the bright-faced stunning girl who had married Randall. What had happened to turn her into a caricature of the woman she might have been? But she was still pretty.

"May I give you a drink?" she said in a formal party voice.

"I doubt that Peter would approve." He laid the envelopes on the nearest table. He did not want to get her into trouble. Randall was unkind to her in public, and probably worse in private.

"Peter! He won't be back all night. I don't know what got into me, thinking he might come back. He's on a tear—something at the university. He wouldn't say. But he told me he's going to spend the night with Virginia Lee McElvain. She is, he informs me, everything I'm not. Young, beautiful—and she understands him. By which he means that she agrees with everything he says. What would you like to drink?"

"Brandy?"

"Yes, we've got it. Soda?"

"A dash."

"Please take off your coat and sit down." Her party voice again. She brought him his drink and poured herself another martini from a sweating chrome shaker, then sat down beside him on the couch. "Thank you for staying," she said.

He did not know how to respond. He said, "You're welcome," and felt stupid. Her breasts were like eggplants. Big, full and probably soft. He wanted to feel them.

"I'm not stupid," she said unexpectedly. "I know everyone thinks I am, but I'm not. It's just that that's the only way I know of to get along with Peter. To let him think he's as brilliant as he wants to be. I'm sorry I was crying, but sometimes he hurts my feelings. He's good at that, as you know."

"Why do you stay with him?"

"Because we're married." She tossed down half her cocktail. "Besides, where else would I go?"

"Do you love him?"

"I used to. No, I don't think so. Not any more. But, you see, I'm sorry for him. He's spent his life not quite making it, not quite succeeding. Every time *you* publish, *he* writes something, but he's always turned down. He's not much of a thinker, I'm afraid, and what makes it so hard for him is that he's just bright enough to know he isn't quite bright enough. Poor thing." She drained her glass and poured herself another. "And anyway, now it's too late for me. I'm old and fat. No chance to find another life now. 'So soon old and so late smart.'" Abruptly her face crumpled and she began to weep silently. "Got to stop feeling sorry for myself," she mumbled, reaching for her cocktail glass.

He prevented her. Held her hand. "Don't, Winnie. Getting smashed won't help. You'll just get sick."

"Or have a hell of a hangover. And he'll look at me as if I make him want to vomit." She tried to laugh. "No wonder. I'm old and ugly. Ugly and fat. But you remember, don't you? How pretty I used to be, once, a long time ago. I was pretty once, wasn't I?"

"You're pretty now."

She looked at him with astonishment. "Why . . . you really mean that, don't you? You're not just saying it."

"Yes."

She smiled, "You know, you're the first man who's looked at me like that in God knows how long. You make me feel like a woman again."

His hands felt twitchy. He wanted to take hold of those marvelously full breasts, feel her softness, bury himself in her. He did not think she would reject him. Impulsively he pulled her close and kissed her.

Her response was immediate and passionate. She not only did not mind, she was enthusiastic. How drunk was she? His hand was inside her bathrobe and she had nothing on under the pink slip. She was softer than anyone he had ever felt. No bones. He was frantic to get out of his coat and tie, all the confining barriers of clothing, to feel her belly against his, to wallow in her femaleness. Her newness made her more exciting than Ellen. "Please, let's go to bed?" She looked doubtful. "Please." He kissed her again.

"All right," she whispered against his cheek, and led him into the bedroom.

He was no longer embarrassed about getting undressed in front of a woman, and he was not afraid to look either. She reached up to pull the rubber bands off her hair, and the shape of her breasts changed. Fascinating. Her navel was very deep in its pad of fat. She pulled back the bedclothes and sat on the edge of the bed looking at him. "My God!" she exclaimed, "you're Peter's age and you've got a better body than most of the college kids." As he came over close, she put her hand on his belly. "All muscle." Randall was not obese, but now that she brought it to his attention, he had developed quite a pot lately.

He rather liked being admired, but he was impatient to have

her. He knelt by the bed to kiss her, then she lay back, pulling him onto her.

She was now in more of a hurry than he was. He wanted to appreciate her. He felt tender toward her, and he had always liked her. Finally she said, "Please, now."

She made love more aggressively than Ellen, almost desperately. There was an unexpected tightness at first. He hesitated, wondering if he were hurting her, but she thrust with her hips so that he was all the way in before he was quite ready for it. She was with him all the way, more quickly than Ellen.

Afterwards she lay beside him breathing heavily, stroking him. He had to take hold of her hand to make her stop.

Suddenly Winnie laughed. "Peter'd never believe it. He thinks you're a pansy."

"I know."

"I'm sorry, I didn't mean to insult you. It just struck me as such a joke. I'm afraid I'm a little drunk."

"I'm not insulted." He wanted to stay with her but he was going to have to leave soon. Ellen expected him at six. There was also the possibility that Randall might come home. It would not do to get caught. He propped himself on his elbow to look at her face. "I rather think he might believe it if he saw us right now," he said. "And I think I'd better leave soon. I don't want to get you into trouble."

She giggled. "Yes, he'd be a mite peeved, I suspect."

After all he had put up with from Randall, there was satisfaction in getting back at him.

Later, on his way to Ellen, he was not pleased with himself. He should not have taken advantage of Winnie, and he hoped she would not regret what had happened. He didn't think she would though.

He should not be unfaithful to Ellen. She would be upset if she found out. But she wouldn't find out. Winnie certainly would not tell anyone.

June 27, 1947

He got to his office early while it was still cool. He had not expected to see Randall, but felt relief on finding he was not there. He set down the cardboard boxes he had brought with him and

216

went to his desk to clear it out. Today he was moving to his new office.

Thank God. Away from Randall, who had been worse than usual these past weeks, ever since discovering that Dean Grimes, instead of promoting him, had hired someone from the University of California over his head.

Poor Winnie. He hoped she was not getting too much flak. Last time he had seen her she had looked trim and cheerful, had given him a happy wave as she stepped onto a bus.

He tipped his chair back and looked at the ceiling. How many hours had he spent here, staring and thinking? He knew the cracks by heart. Green walls, dark bookcases. Comfortable, but a bit shabby. It would be repainted for the new man.

In his top desk drawer he found the picture of Simon in his eyepatch. Beautiful, raffish and, underneath, lonely. Could Simon change? He had not heard from him since November. But just last week Simon had been named corespondent in a Miami divorce suit—by the wife. Simon was just famous enough for an item like that to hit the gossip columns of the New York papers.

In another drawer, a package of condoms. He put them in his pocket and told himself he was going to have to do something about women. But he had been telling himself that ever since he had slept with Winnie and had not done anything so far. He was not being predatory; he was simply gathering the rosebuds that fell around his feet. Where did they all come from?

What was he doing? No woman had given him a second glance for most of his life. He stood straight now, but he had done that last year too, and women had not noticed him.

Odd that he never wanted to go to bed with anyone but Ellen more than once. Some were not much fun, but others were good enough, and some skilled at making love.

Why couldn't he learn to say no beforehand? He had no difficulty turning down a return engagement, and smoothly enough to remain friends with the woman. What if Ellen found out?

His life was getting far too complicated, and he was not progressing as fast as he should on his book. He had not been swimming in weeks, but he was staying trim and had even lost weight, in spite of the fact that he was eating more.

Somehow he could not forgo the promise of a new body. Smorgasbord. Breasts like eggplants, half-melons, Gouda cheeses, apples. He had read in a book once about pear-shaped breasts but had not seen any yet. The author had not specified the type. D'Anjou, Seckel, Bartlett, winter? It could make a difference.

Bottoms were wonderful too. The way big soft ones jiggled, the tightness of little round ones. Girdles spoiled everything, no woman should ever wear one.

Best of all was the way everything fit together—the narrow waists and full hips, the smooth skin and lack of apparent muscles. Legs were a good place to start, but otherwise overrated.

Why did he lose interest as soon as he had had a woman? Some had been lovely. Recently, even the promise of newness did not excite him the way it had at first. Margot this afternoon. A new, extreme body type. Very slender in the ribs and broad and heavy in the hips. Was he only collecting bodies now? Like Simon. Suddenly he did not like himself.

He was acting like Simon. Simon had always claimed that no one else meant anything to him, and not having experienced this, he had not understood or believed it. But that was exactly how he felt regarding Ellen. He must not let Ellen find out. He could not stand Margot up, but he ought to make it for lunch only.

His desk clear, he picked up the big box of its contents and carried it down the hall to Brampton's office. The room smelled of paint. Larger desk, more book space. Even if it were small and dank he would be grateful for the opportunity to escape Randall. Lucy would be happier now too and not always weeping on his shoulder. When she was not upset she showed a dry, spare self-deprecating wit that put the world in perspective as nothing else could.

After transferring the contents of the box to the new desk he locked up and returned to pack his books. He had left his office open, and when he came back found Dan sitting crosslegged on his desk. "Hi, Hawk, need any help?" Dan's hair was cut shorter than usual. He was wearing slacks instead of jeans.

"No, thanks. If I pack the books myself, I'll know where they are, and the janitor's coming later with a hand-truck to move them."

"OK." Dan threw his cigarette butt out the open window. "Hey, what's happened to you anyway? Sounds like you've gotten into every woman on campus."

If Dan had heard that, it must really be getting around. He put the books he was holding into the box and asked, "Who told you that?"

"That Virginia Lee bitch with the creepy Southern drawl. Randall pays for her apartment, but she sells pussy on the side. I didn't like her. She's too lazy even to fake. What'd you think of her?"

"That if you paid for her you got gypped."

"Boy, aren't you coming on hard! But you're sure as hell right

218

about getting gypped. You got into her free, huh? A tightwad like her. You're really something!"

He didn't know why, but suddenly he was angry. He looked at Dan. "She'll come if you stick your finger up her ass," he said flatly.

"Honest? I never would've thought of that." Dan mulled this over for a while, then said, "But when you're paying, well . . ." He shrugged. "At least I didn't get a dose."

"I'm sorry, Dan."

"Why?"

"For being angry."

"That's OK. Look, Hawk, there's something I've gotta tell you. Why I came looking for you today. Randall and Virginia Lee had a big fight and broke up. She told him she'd screwed you, and rubbed it in real good that you're better hung and a better lay."

"She told you that?"

"Yeah. Randall'd told her all about us too, you can bet. She knows I know you. She'd had the fight with Randall a couple hours before I saw her and she was still replaying it. Madder'n hell because she wouldn't get any more free rent. Telling me what a bastard Randall is, especially lately. After all the listening I did, she should have cut her price. She really bent my ear. Sounded to me as if she'd screwed you to get back at him."

"Shit!"

"You didn't know you were being exploited, huh?" Dan was amused.

But he had been exploiting women. He had no legitimate complaint. And Virginia Lee had not appealed to him much. "I knew she was Randall's," he said. "I don't have a kick coming."

"Oh, yeah. But what I wanted to tell you was, Randall's out to get you now like he never was before. Cut out your liver with a dull knife."

"Yes, and thank you for warning me. Would you shove that box over?"

"This one?"

"Yes, thanks."

"Hey, what did happen? I mean, you and me—all that. You kept telling me you were a hopeless fairy. And now look at you. What in hell happened?"

"All I needed was a good woman to put me straight."

Dan laughed and said, "OK, now tell me. Ellen O'Connor, huh?"

"Yes." To change the subject he asked, "Tell me what you're doing now."

"I'm doing fine. I'll be working full time at the store all summer.

Air-conditioned! Now I'm selling menswear if you can picture that! But I'll be moving upstairs into furniture in a week or so. I've got me a new girl. Tess. Little and blond with big gray eyes. Stacked. She doesn't talk much, but she's real sharp, and she's sweet. I think she likes me."

"Dan? Could you tell me how in hell I'm going to stop? I don't chase women, they just keep turning up like flies around hamburger. I can't seem to turn a new one down."

"Shit! That's a different kind of problem. Sure as hell wish I had it."

"It's not that great. I feel guilty because of Ellen. I'm always worried she'll find out. She might leave me if she does, and I need her. I think I'm in love with her. I don't want to hurt her. I'm not getting on with my book, and I'm perpetually tired. I'm too old to act like this, but I can't seem to stop."

"Yeah, you are thinner." Dan looked at him critically, then sighed. "That's the damnedest problem I ever heard of. Too many women. Well, since you asked me, it's how you look at them. I saw you in operation once on the library steps. You didn't *see* me, all you could see was that Evvie. You look at them like there was nothing in the world half as wonderful. What do you see in Evvie anyway? She's fat."

"Fat women feel great. Soft, no bones. And most of them have lovely skin."

"A switch from Simon, huh? OK, OK, don't look at me like that. Hell, you damn near convinced me to try out a fat one myself. Might be fun at that. You really go hog wild, don't you? Anyway, does that answer your question?"

"Yes, but I don't know how I do it."

Dan lit another cigarette and reached over the edge of the desk to drop the match in the wastebasket. After a silence he said, "Hawk? I know you pretty well. Do you think that maybe after feeling guilty all your life you don't feel right if you're not guilty about something? Could that be why you're fucking yourself silly? So you'll have something to feel sinful about?"

He selected a slender volume to finish out the box and eased it into place. "Could be," he agreed, then, thinking more, decided Dan was probably at least partially right. "Yes, maybe. But how about making up for lost time?"

"Oh, sure, that too. But that isn't all. You just told me you thought you loved Ellen."

"Yes."

220

"Then which would you rather do? Try every pussy in New York, or make it with her? It's that simple."

It was not that simple, but there was truth in what Dan had said. "Do you think Ellen knows?"

"Wouldn't be surprised. Damn near everybody does. She's not like most women, though. Maybe she's waiting for you to get over the shock of being straight. But she won't wait forever."

"Yes, I see." But he was not straight. He still wanted Simon. He looked at Dan, sitting there watching him. The fuzz on Dan's upper lip was thicker now; he would be shaving soon. Green eyes watching him, those broad shoulders stretching the white T-shirt. He longed to hold him and kiss him again.

"Now you're looking at me like that. Hawk?"

He looked away. "I'm sorry."

"What's the matter?"

"I don't know. It's as if I don't know who I am any more. As if I can only be straight as long as I'm fucking myself silly."

"Identity crisis," Dan said wisely, obviously quoting someone or something.

"I suppose so."

"Shit! Why worry it? What kind of hole you stick your dick into doesn't make you who you are. Just because I used to make love to you doesn't make me a fairy." He jumped down off the desk and came over to him, took hold of his shoulders with a strong, firm grip and looked in his eyes. "Look, you can have me if you want me," Dan said earnestly. "Would that solve your problems?"

"No, it wouldn't."

"So, OK, you stupid cocksucker, straighten out and fly right." Dan gave him an affectionate squeeze, let go and went back to sit on the desk.

"You didn't mean that offer just now, did you?"

Dan paused to think. "Well, I was pretty damn sure you wouldn't take me up on it. But, hell, yeah, if you needed me. Yeah, I'd have gone through with it." That smile that seemed to light up the world. "Got to admit, I'm glad you didn't. But even if I had, that wouldn't make me queer, 'cause I know I'm not. And you helped me with that. Hear?"

"Yes."

Dan got off the desk and went to look out the window. Then, turning back from it, "I've got to go in a minute, but I was thinking, if I was you, I'd come clean with Ellen now. Before Randall gets to her."

He stopped packing books and squatted back on his heels. "Would Randall do that?" Then immediately answered himself. "He sure as hell would." He took the last half-dozen volumes out of the bookcase and dropped them loose into the last box. That was good enough. The janitor could put that one on top. "Dan, thanks. I'm going over to her place now."

All the way over to Ellen's apartment he tried to think of how to tell her. There was no good way, and he could not even think of how to broach the subject. He was going to have to do it though—no way out.

He knocked on her door. No answer. He knocked again, then let himself in with his key. He followed the sound of running water to the bathroom, then knocked on the closed door. "Ellen?"

"Hawk?"

"May I come in?"

"Come ahead." The room was steamy, smelling of French soap and bath salts. Ellen was lying in a brimming tub, her skin bright pink below the water line. As he pushed the door open, she reached with her foot and turned off the hot-water tap with her toes. She liked to bathe in water so hot he could not put his hand in it, and add more after she was in. Her hair was pinned on top of her head, showing off the line of her neck, the smooth curve down to her shoulder.

"I didn't expect you so early. Through moving?"

"Almost." He sat on the toilet lid. He didn't know what to say. He had been ready to confess to her, but he had not anticipated finding her naked in the bathtub. He could not think clearly while he was watching her. He looked away, but that was no help. He could hear the soft splashes as she washed herself. The room was suffocating and his pants felt tight.

"I'll be out in a minute." He heard her sit up and pull the plug. He took down a towel and held it out, ready to dry her as he always did. She came to stand in front of him.

Fragrant pink skin, so damned sweet and special. He wanted her more than ever before. He should not make love to her just before telling her. But perhaps he had better do it while she would still let him. She might send him away. He kissed the small of her back, then impulsively licked the valley between her buttocks. She looked over her shoulder, a little startled, then smiled.

He stood and hugged her to him, kissed her. He was sure he was not behaving wisely, but could not help himself. He observed wryly to himself that making love was a new way to procrastinate.

222

She went to sleep immediately afterwards. He wanted to think, to sort out his thoughts. He closed his eyes to rest them.

He woke with a start. What was the time? He fumbled for his watch on the bedside table. One-thirty. Too late to see Margot, too late even to call her and tell her he could not make it. He sat up and buckled on the watch.

He was alone in bed. He remembered that he had come here to tell Ellen what he had been doing before Randall did. No more Margots, Evvies or anybodies. Bodies. That was what he had been doing, he realized again, collecting bodies the way Simon did. Time he stopped in any case.

Where was Ellen? He had not heard a sound since awakening. He dressed and went down the hall to the living room, then on into the kitchen. There was a note on the yellow and green tablecloth weighted by a loaf of his favorite black pumpernickel bread.

"You'll find butter, lettuce, cold cuts and ham in the refrigerator. Mustard on the first shelf. I'll be back around two. Out shopping. Love, Ellen."

He ate three sandwiches and would have had a fourth, but he had used up all the mustard. He made coffee and was well into his second cup when he heard Ellen's key in the door. He went to let her in and tried to take the brown bag of groceries she was carrying. She would not let him. She went around him and out to the kitchen.

He followed. "May I help?"

"No," she said shortly, then added, "thanks."

She was angry with him. He should have spoken to her when he first came over. Randall must have gotten to her. He said, "Ellen, I'm sorry. I won't do it any more. I meant to tell you this morning, that's why I dropped everything and came over. Because I decided I had to be honest with you. None of them meant anything to me. I love you." He stopped, appalled. He sounded just like Simon. Had Simon been telling the truth all those years?

Ellen set down a jar of jam she had been about to store in the cupboard and turned to looked at him. "What are you talking about?"

"What Randall said to you."

"Randall? I haven't seen him in weeks."

"But you were so angry, I thought . . ."

She pushed back her bright hair. "Oh, Hawk! You know I don't like help with groceries. I felt as if you were crowding me. And I was in a bad mood because I just had a go-around with the butcher. I'm going to have to change butchers. He's been cheating me."

She poured herself a cup of coffee and sat down opposite him at the round table. Her hair was tied back with a turquoise ribbon that matched her full-skirted sleeveless cotton dress. She looked cool and lovely. She drank some coffee, then said gently, "But from what you just said, I can only assume you're apologizing for sleeping around."

"I'm sorry," he said inadequately.

"It's not news. You've been the talk of the campus for some time now. I was beginning to wonder if I ought to say something. You're getting so thin, and you're not doing your reputation any good."

"You're not angry?" he asked, astonished.

"No. I haven't any right to be. We're both free agents. I was even feeling guilty for starting you on your career as a Don Juan. I won't pretend I like it, but I'm not angry."

"Oh."

"Would you be angry if I did the same thing?"

"I don't think so. I'd be hurt though. I didn't want to hurt you. I kept telling myself you wouldn't find out."

She nodded. "I suppose I am, a little, but not as much as you imagine. You remind me of a kid that just discovered candy and wants to try all the flavors. Some of my brothers went through phases like that when they were in high school."

"I won't do it any more."

"Please don't make me a promise you can't keep."

"I want to stop. I don't like myself. Women aren't just objects to satisfy my curiosity, they're people." Too stiff. Why did he always sound like that when he felt uneasy?

"All right. But promise yourself, not me." She finished her coffee and got up to put away the rest of the groceries. She moved economically and gracefully, and the line of her body when she reached for a high shelf caught his attention. He wanted to remember her exactly that way, hair very red by contrast to the turquoise dress. He had not expected her to understand and was still surprised. "I love you."

She came over and stroked his head. "I love you too." He put his arm around her and she leaned against his shoulder, still petting him.

Impulsively he asked, "Ellen, please marry me?"

Her silence was too long. He looked up. She had her face turned away, apparently staring out the window. Finally she said thoughtfully, "I don't know what to say. I've got to say, not now."

"Please . . ."

224

"Shh." Her fingers were light on his mouth. "I haven't said I won't. Just not now."

August 22, 1947

Back from his nine o'clock class, Haakon dropped his briefcase on the couch and got out of his clothes. The heat was beginning to get to him. Standing in front of the electric fan, he reread the last paragraph of Ellen's letter.

> . . . then Uncle Brian (he looks exactly like Colonel Blimp, remember those cartoons?), said, 'Harrumpf, harrumpf, of course Ellen will stay.' And I said, 'No, Ellen won't.' There was an uproar, to put it mildly. You'd have thought I'd said I was planning to spit on a Bishop. Three of my brothers backed me up. I'd expected Joe and Peter to, but Mark was a surprise.

It had taken a lot of courage for her to defy her family. He imagined her standing there with that stubborn look on her face, and wished she were here so he could kiss her.

> I've already engaged a girl. My mother is well enough now so she doesn't need a nurse, but she should have someone staying with her, and of course she can't do housework. And, thank God for small favors, my mother took to her right away. I'll stay until Tuesday to settle her in, then I'll be back. You've no idea how much I've missed you.

He remembered seeing her off to Boston three weeks ago. Only three weeks? It seemed like much longer. After her train pulled out of Grand Central Station he stood on the gritty platform staring down the track until a squat, officious man in a dark uniform told him to please move on, that the platform was closed. The air smelled of electricity and dust. In the vaulted station everyone was hurrying somewhere and he felt as if he were the only person in New York who had nowhere he wanted to go.

Yes, he had missed her too. If she was coming back this soon, he had better get to work on the page proofs of *A Study of Persecution*. He wished he could think of a better title than that, something on the order of Tom's *Accents and Attitudes*. He wanted his time free when she got back. Double-checking footnotes was slow, dull work.

He put a folded towel on his desk chair so he would not stick to the seat and got to work, taking time at noon for a glass of milk, and at three for a cold shower. His fingers stuck to the paper, and he had to be careful not to rest his arm on any handwriting, because the sweat made the ink run.

He worked until nine, when the failing light reminded him he ought to eat something. Now he estimated that he would be finished by the time Ellen got back. Perhaps they could go off for a weekend to the coast.

He walked through the evening heat to Gino's. As he passed a store window he caught sight of a tall, thin, militarily erect figure in chinos and tan sports shirt. With a sense of shock he realized he was looking at his own reflection. He turned his head away, wondering why he looked sad.

He had wanted Ellen to come back. He should be happy that there were only a few more days before her return. Their relationship was comfortable. The roller-coaster excitement was gone, but what did he expect? He certainly enjoyed her. He no longer expected the kind of excitement he had experienced with Jim and Simon, but . . .

He dropped his letter to Ellen into a mailbox that was hot to the touch. Everything seemed almost alive with animal heat. Mica glittered from stone facings like tiny eyes.

Gino's was hot and empty. Gino himself seated him at the table best cooled by the ceiling fan and brought him a menu. He was the only one there, but it was near closing time.

He told Gino, "Give me what's good today." He had no appetite, and did not want to bother deciding what to eat. Gino brought him chicken cacciatore, a salad and a basket of fresh crusty bread, then hovered, lonely, with nothing to do.

A fat little man, black-haired, with twirls of hair growing out of his nostrils. Hair grew down his arms onto his hands and fingers. What would it be like to go to bed with so hairy a man? The thought was without interest, merely a query to himself.

He ordered a fiasco of Chianti and when Gino brought it invited him to share it. Beaming, Gino fetched another glass and sat down across the table from him. Gino talked about the difficulty of getting good lettuce and described how he revived the heads that arrived wilted from the market by putting cracked ice on them.

Gino cleared the empty dinner dishes and refilled the raffia-covered fiasco. The new wine was distinctly better than before, obviously something special.

"This is excellent," he told Gino after a taste.

"My brother makes it. He has a vineyard near Buffalo." Gino

began talking about his brother, then, indicating the empty room with expressive hands, said he would have an air conditioner next summer. He was losing too much business. It would pay for itself. But he had to save five hundred dollars more.

Ridiculous that Gino should be prevented from buying something he needed for lack of five hundred dollars. Haakon felt his pocket. He had his checkbook with him. He began writing a check, then had to ask, "What's your last name?"

"Pasinetti. Hey, what are you doing?"

"For your air conditioner, so I can eat in a cool place." Gino looked doubtful. He asked, "We're friends, aren't we?"

Gino nodded vigorously, "Si, si—yes," and accepted the check, saying, "But I pay you back right away." Gino began talking about his family, showed him pictures of fat, lively, smiling children. Miniature editions of Gino. "Good children I've had," Gino said. Then, "The beautiful red-haired lady, I thought you'd be married by now."

"I thought so too."

"Wait. Don't expect too much too fast. Women, they're strange people. Not like us. One day they say this, another day they say that. Give her time."

A fly landed on the spotless white tablecloth. Gino caught it in his fist. "Pretty quick, huh, for an old man?" He wiped it on his thigh, then burst into a spate of Italian invective at the idea of a fly daring to invade his domain. "Americans," he confided, "think flies make things dirty. Yes?"

"This is the cleanest restaurant I've seen." He realized that both he and Gino were no longer quite sober. He felt pleasant, and was thoroughly enjoying Gino's company.

"Yes, Maria, she keeps it so. A roach comes out of the food, she squashes it." He slapped the table in demonstration. "Understand! They come from the market, you can't keep them out."

Gino launched into a long description of how he and his wife tried to keep down insects. He pointed to the woven wicker basket of bread that was still on the table. "Like those. Before I put bread in I have to give them a good bang to knock the little weevils out. Customers don't like to see them."

There was a piece of bread left. He buttered it and ate it with a glass of wine, realizing, because Gino was watching him, that he did not share the exaggerated horror of bugs demonstrated by most Americans.

At a quarter of ten, fifteen minutes after closing time, he and Gino finished the second bottle of wine. He took his leave, shook Gino's square hairy hand and wished him a boy in his soon-to-be-born sixth grandchild. A good man. He was grateful for his friendliness.

Away from Gino's enthusiasm, he felt empty inside. He walked uptown along the sidewalk above the park. Tree branches cast long swinging shadows in the intermittent breeze.

It would be pleasant to have children, to have grandchildren. Be approved of by everyone. Would Ellen marry him if he asked now? He had stopped sleeping around, had stopped that day when he first asked her. He was ready to settle down.

He had lost Simon and could not have Dan. What would his life be like in five years, in ten? Walking on the same streets, going to the same places, doing the same things. Old and alone.

He was happy she was coming back. Why did he keep telling himself that?

He hesitated at the top of the stone steps he always took down into the park. The light at the bottom was out, the shadows black. He could not see past the turn in the stairs. He went slowly, giving his eyes time to adjust.

It was cooler away from the heated pavement. Leaves rustled. The air smelled of newly mowed grass and river water.

At the foot of the steps a hunched figure sat in the shadows. Male? Female? He could not tell. A dark piece of the darkness, barely recognizable as human, crouched over. A glimmer of white oval face as he passed.

He walked on. The harbor smell of the Hudson River brought back a memory of the troopship leaving Le Havre. Of Dan chewing on a candy bar, broad-shouldered in faded fatigues, hair bright in the sunshine. A lifetime ago.

He had not seen Dan for several weeks. No, he should stay away from him. He was too at odds with himself, too restless and lonely. Thank God Ellen would be back soon. He would have someone to go home to.

He became aware that footsteps were following him. Who? The figure in the shadows? Yes, it had stood and followed him. He had the impression that the person was not large. No reason to be nervous. But why would anyone follow him?

Perhaps he was mistaken. The other person could simply be going the same way. He turned down the next side path. The footsteps followed. A man's walk, he thought. A man wearing hard-soled shoes with leather heels. Not sneaking up. Making no effort to be quiet. He did not look back.

There was still a possibility that the follower was randomly going the same direction. He took another right-angle turn. Not a coincidence now. Could the person on the steps perhaps be a student who had recognized him as he passed—wanted to talk with him and then perhaps lacked the nerve to call out and stop him? Somehow, the cadence of the walk seemed familiar.

But it could be a man with a gun. People did get robbed here occasionally. The steps no longer sounded familiar. He was tense and uncomfortable. He was going to have to deal with this.

He rounded a turn in the path and stopped just on the other side of the circle of yellow light cast by a lamp, facing back the way he had come.

Simon came around the corner and continued walking toward him, not altering his stride when he saw him waiting. He was wearing an expertly tailored gray silk suit, a tie, and was, as always, bareheaded. He stopped several feet away, his face calm and emotionless.

"Simon?" Haakon said, not knowing what to make of his being there, following him in this manner.

"Hello, Haakon."

"What are you doing here?" Simon usually avoided parks. Simon's face was pale; his eyes looked large. The overhead light accentuated the chiseled bone structure of his face, the sensual curve of his mouth. He looked like a marble statue of a faun, somehow brought to life.

"Following you. Before that, waiting for you to take your nightly constitutional. You were late tonight. I was beginning to think I had missed you, or that you weren't going to be here."

"Why?" What could have compelled Simon to wait on hard stone stairs for what must have been at the very least an hour. And Simon was not pretending he had just happened to be there. He was admitting he had waited. A change in Simon? Or just a new act?

"Because I wanted to talk to you."

"You know where I live. You know my phone number."

Simon shook his head. "It's not that easy."

"What is it? Are you in trouble?"

"No, nothing like that."

"What, then?"

"You, me, what happened." Simon made a small faggish gesture with his hand, caught himself and stuck his hand in his pocket. That was not like him. He did not do things that might spoil the press of his suit.

Simon was too uncomfortable. Hoping to put him a little more at ease, he suggested, "Shall we walk on?" He read agreement in Simon's expression, waited for him, then continued along the path, shortening his stride to accommodate to his pace. "I don't understand," he said.

Simon took his hand out of his pocket. "I thought of phoning."

Their footsteps sounded together on the hard path. The breeze was stronger now, less steady. Leaves rustled all around them. "But . . . no. I wanted to see you face to face. I know I've no right to complain that you found someone else. But a woman? Haakon, I've been in and out of New York since New Year's. I've been trying to think of a way to talk to you for weeks."

"You've been watching me?"

"Yes, I have," Simon said flatly, making no attempt to embellish or to excuse himself. "On and off."

He had suspected for years that Simon kept track of him, perhaps even watched him, but this was the first time Simon had admitted it. He didn't know what to say.

"Not that I had to," Simon said. "You've been the talk of the campus. I do have contacts."

"I'm sure you do."

"I'll tell you what happened. I came back one morning, the way I did after Dan left. I know it didn't work that time, but I hoped it might. It was good other times. I checked the bedroom before undressing, and there you were with Ellen O'Connor, sleeping. I could see very well because it was beginning to get light out. So I left."

"And then?"

"I went home. I was so stunned, I was all the way back to the studio before it really hit me. Then I was furious. I actually smashed a camera I was so angry."

"Why?"

"A woman! There with *you*. Outrageous! And all those years you couldn't screw *me!*"

"Oh." He could see what a blow that could have been to Simon's vanity. They were walking along near the West Side Highway. A brief whiff of urine from a corner of the wall, the smell of exhaust, the whoosh of passing cars and, overriding all, the sound of leaves and the smell of the Hudson River.

In a different tone, almost pleading, Simon said, "Do you love her?"

"Yes."

"You've changed again," Simon said. "I feel the difference, I hear it in your voice. Every time you change, you're more of a man."

He stopped walking and turned to look at Simon. That had been a strange thing for Simon to have said, and the tone had not only been sincere, it had been admiring. With an odd blend of emotions in it too: sad and glad, pleased and afraid. "Simon?" It was dark by the retaining wall and he could not make out Simon's expression.

His face was a pale oval, his eyes enormous and dark. Pale. Yes, he had noticed earlier but had not thought about it. Simon should have a tan at this time of the summer.

"I . . ." Simon hesitated, cleared his throat, then said, "Am I too late, Haakon?"

"I don't know."

"I don't feel you there. You're talking to me as if I were a student. You're not there." He sounded afraid.

His concern crystallized, "Simon, have you been sick?"

"Just some cosmetic surgery." Simon laughed brittlely. "Bad case of grapes—hemorrhoids to you. Occupational hazard, you know."

"Simon, don't."

"Yes." Sadly. Then irritably, "If you don't want to know, don't ask, damn it! All right! I got involved with another sadist and got myself damaged. Had to check in for repairs, so had everything attended to at the same time. All right?"

"There's something you're not telling me."

"You want to know the details? I'll tell you if you insist, but you've always claimed you don't want to know."

"No, but there's more. What?" He was sure of it.

"No more. Only that the details are a bit sordid. If I try to tell you any of it, I'll end up making a story out of it so I won't have to feel it—trying to frost it over the way I always used to. I don't want to do that any more. Please don't ask me again." Simon sounded almost frightened.

Yes, of course that was why Simon had always had to embellish. Why hadn't he seen that before? It was wrong of him to push his inquiry. "I'm sorry."

"It is too late, isn't it?" Simon said, then with an attempt at lightheartedness, "I wasn't good for you anyway."

"The way things were, we weren't good for each other. Neither of us could grow, we just kept replaying the same scenes. Going around in circles."

"I know."

This was not another act. Simon was being straightforward, as if he had given up, decided that nothing he did would make any difference anyway. He held his hand out toward him and Simon took a step closer, then stopped. He wanted to comfort him and thought of putting his arm around him, but he hesitated.

With tears in his voice, Simon said, "Better if you don't touch me. I still want you as much as ever, I still love you." He swayed slightly, as if wanting to move away but unable to, wanting to move closer, but afraid of risking rejection.

"Simon?"

"Yes?" Was there a quaver in his voice?

"I don't know . . ." Feeling unsure of himself, uncertain what to do. He was worried about Simon, concerned about him because he seemed so defenseless.

Simon did not move or speak for a long time. Nearby a truck rumbled past. Then Simon said, "I'll be all right," and began to turn away.

"Wait." He had not been aware of reaching out, but his hand was on Simon's shoulder. He could feel that Simon was trembling.

"What for?" Simon stood, as if turned to stone by his touch.

He was about to take his hand away, release Simon, allow him to go, when, as if a switch had been thrown, he became intensely aware of his physical presence. Simon's warmth, the amount of space he took up, the sound of his breathing and the rhythm of it under his hand. The slightly nubby texture of the silk suit under his fingertips, the hardness of bone and muscle under his palm. He thought he could almost feel his heartbeat. Simon was more human and vulnerable than he had ever been before. No mythical demi-god, but mortal, even fragile—beautiful.

Fiercely, not caring who might happen by, he pulled Simon close and hugged him, kissed him hungrily, lust and love so mixed he could not tell where one left off and the other started. Wanting him so much he felt like taking him there, on the dew-drenched grass, Simon's way, his way, any way at all. How did not matter because what he wanted was to be closer than was possible, a timeless drowning, unseeing and unhearing. Simon's mouth tasted of bourbon, his body was wiry and yielding in his arms.

He broke the embrace, shaking, frightened by the strength of his emotions. He had never before felt like this.

Simon drew back slightly, then touched his cheek to get his attention. "Rape?" he said with quiet, affectionate humor.

He laughed aloud, partly out of nervousness, gave Simon a hug and released him. Suddenly all around was the rustling of leaves, the stridulation of summer insects. Beyond the wall the sporadic whir of passing vehicles. Far off, on the ink-black river, a ship's bell rang three brassy strokes. The loops of the Palisades Park roller coaster were strings of fireflies high on the cliffs. The smell of river water again, a whiff of exhaust, and the smell of leaves, dust, and half-dry cut grass. The park was a chiaroscuro complexity of moving shadows and pools of yellow light. Above, the city glow blotted out most of the stars. He could see the moon, thin as a surgical needle. Was the moon waxing or waning? He didn't know. And Simon was waiting. Small, slender as a boy. Patient.

"Haakon?"

"Yes, of course," he agreed, and they both turned at the same time and walked side by side, not touching or looking at each other, back along the winding path.

August 23, 1947

Haakon woke slowly. He could hear the sounds of city traffic, children's voices from the park, jazz on a radio in a nearby apartment. A warm breeze, smelling of river water, brushed across his skin.

Years ago, as a child, he had dreamed he was a winged horse. He had jumped through the moon, which was a silver hoop. Halley's Comet had the face of a benign tiger and miles of flashing tail made up of veils of cold gold fire. Together they had galloped recklessly across the black plush night, scattering the stars that lay on it like enormous diamonds, rearranging the constellations, cheered on by the crystal fish that lived in the Milky Way.

When he had awakened that long-ago morning, his asthma had been gone for the first time in months. To have his lungs work the way they were supposed to, to have the air just go in and out without a struggle, had been a state of grace. He must have been ten at the time, for Halley's Comet to have been in the dream. So long ago, and years since he had thought of that dream, years since he had remembered to be grateful for normal breathing.

Why was he remembering that now? The same sense of utter well-being, both physical and mental?

Simon was asleep beside him. He had awakened breathing in rhythm with him. He searched for a description of how he felt. Peaceful, yes. Not energetic, but there was a knowledge that he had more energy available. A feeling of being complete, whole, not divided against himself. None of those was accurate, but together the sum approximated truth.

He opened his eyes. Trapezoids of light fled across the ceiling. Reflections off the windshields of passing cars. Saturday. He could do what he wanted and get up when he pleased.

He turned his head to look at Simon. Simon was sleeping curled up, facing him. Young and beautiful. The mouth relaxed, lips slightly parted, was more sensual than usual. Eyelashes so long they did not look quite real. Simon had aged little. There was no gray at all in his dark curly hair. But fine lines radiated from the corners of his eyes, and the lines by his mouth, accentuated now by the shading of beard, were deeper.

Simon's body had not aged. It was as lean and muscular as it had been the day they had met. He was still wearing his ID bracelet.

Lovemaking last night had been unlike anything in his experience. Was it that he had finally been able to satisfy Simon? No—though there was enormous satisfaction in that success, in being able to please.

Simon had become different, had not used his skill to play on his responses the way a musician might play an instrument to demonstrate his virtuosity. If anything, they had both been clumsy, kissing, and clinging, slippery wet with sweat in the hot night.

Not too clumsy though, for communication had been easy and effective. A sense of reading each other's mind, of knowing each other's wants and needs almost instinctively. Not that there had been no hesitancy or doubt—for there had been—but they knew it didn't matter.

Simon had said in a quiet tone he had never before used, "I love you, my beautiful Dane."

So he was queer after all! No woman had ever satisfied him so thoroughly. Strange that he had not realized that much of his excitement had been artificial, the result of novelty and anxiety. With Ellen there had been the added ingredient of love, for he did love her. And he was grateful to her.

But even with her there was too much missing. Because he had never been quite whole before, he had not known that women only engaged part of his interest, not all of it as Simon did. He had had no immediate basis of comparison until now.

He rolled onto his side so he could see Simon better. Simon sighed, opened his eyes and smiled. "Good morning."

"Good morning." How pleasant it must be to awaken instantly like that, fully aware and geared to go. He envied him.

"How long have you been awake?"

"A few minutes." He stuffed the corner of his pillow under his head so he could relax and see Simon better at the same time.

"Shall I apologize now or later?" Simon asked.

He thought he knew what Simon meant. "It occurred to me that you couldn't have gotten in and seen me with Ellen if you hadn't kept a key."

"Thank you for not bringing it up last night."

"Why? I wonder now if perhaps I didn't expect you to keep a duplicate. What surprised me was that you'd left that inlaid box of your stuff."

234

"My douche? Well, knowing you, I was sure you'd never find it on that shelf. You're not much of a housekeeper. And I hoped you'd let me come back—wanted it here in case you did." Simon smiled. "You have to admit it came in handy."

"I don't understand you. I never could do that before. I'd gotten so I wouldn't even try."

"Yes, but I always hoped. And just to have you in me—even if that was all, even if it wasn't for long—was important to me. I don't think I can explain it to you. You're not at all like me that way."

"No, I suppose I'm not."

"I was wondering, did you like it?"

"Don't you know I did?"

Simon reached out and stroked his cheek. "Yes, I guess I just wanted to hear you say so."

He took hold of Simon's hand and kissed the palm. "I liked it, and I love you."

"I want to kiss you, but my mouth tastes like the bottom of a bird cage." Simon sat up. "May I use your toothbrush?"

"After all these years, you need to ask permission?"

"The new me."

"What's mine is yours."

Simon smiled, got off the bed and started toward the door. Then he paused. "Let me get breakfast?"

"There's hardly anything to eat in the place. Unless you want cream of celery soup or baked beans."

Simon made a face. "I'll go and look. Maybe I can whip something up."

Maybe Simon could; he was ingenious. Haakon stretched and lay there a little longer, enjoying his own weight against the mattress, the movement of air across him.

By the time he got up and went to the bathroom, Simon was through with it. Simon came to the door. "You weren't exaggerating. Weevils in the flour and a petrified pastry in the cupboard. In the *cupboard?* Haakon!"

"So that's what happened to it! I was going to eat it. I guess that was about a week ago. I went to jot down an idea for the book, and when I got back the damn thing had disappeared. I'd completely forgotten about it."

"How hungry are you? I could get groceries, or we could go to my place."

"I'd like to eat here." He was hungrier than he had been in weeks. He and Simon could not be seen eating breakfast together this near campus though, so they could not go to a coffee shop.

"Anything in particular you'd like?"

"Not that I can think of. Orange juice?"

"I'll get some." After Simon was dressed he said, "It's almost ten. Shall I pick up your mail?"

"Thank you." He gave him the mailbox key.

While he was shaving he realized that the tune of "You Are My Sunshine" was running through his head. He remembered lying on an Army cot, hearing somebody's radio, thinking about Simon. "You'll never know, dear, how much I love you." And being aware that if the other men in the outfit were listening to the words at all, they were dreaming about women.

He had liked being straight, liked being able to hold hands in public, liked the tacit approval of the world. Queer. Gay. The word "gay" did not seem quite as offensive now, but he still did not like it. How about bisexual? After all, he was able to make it with women too.

It was possible to love two people at the same time. He had not stopped loving Simon even when he had been in love with Dan. A different kind of love, fulfilling a different part of himself. And Ellen? Yes.

He could not doubt Simon's change. What could have happened to him? "The details are uglier than usual," he had said. No, he did not want to know. He could take on faith that whatever had happened had been horrible enough to shake Simon profoundly. And perhaps Simon had been ready to change anyway. He had tried to before.

Simon came back with a brown paper bag of groceries. He set it down on the table and took out four letters. "Your mail."

He took them, glanced through them and went to put them on his desk to be attended to later. Nothing important. Then Simon came over and handed him a manila envelope.

He took it. It was addressed to him in Simon's square black handwriting and had a canceled stamp. It felt as if it contained a periodical. "What's this?"

"The rest of your mail, and something I have to apologize for. I was tempted to hide it, take a chance that you'd never see it. You don't read magazines much. But I knew I'd have to tell you about it. You see, I seem to have developed a conscience." Simon shrugged, made a faggish gesture of negation. "At least I had last night with you." Then impatiently, obviously upset, "Open it. Look at it while I make breakfast."

"All right." He picked up his paper knife.

"Wait."

He looked up. "What is it?"

"I meant to tell you last night. That was one reason I wanted to talk to you, but then . . . I just couldn't. Do you understand?"

"Yes." No matter what the envelope contained, he could only be glad that Simon had said nothing to spoil the night before.

He slit the envelope and slid out the copy of *U.S. Photographers.* Diagonally across the top corner was printed, "Simon Foster Issue." The cover picture was a color closeup of Simon's profile, obviously a self-portrait.

Simon had done nothing to disguise the lines by his eyes. Strange. No, not really. Simon-the-fairy was inordinately vain, but Simon-the-photographer was unsparingly honest. And if it came down to it, the photographer always won.

A sheet of paper slid out of the magazine. It read:

Darling, This is my proof copy. The issue will be on the stands soon, and I didn't want you to stumble on one and be taken by surprise. At the time I submitted these photos I was furious with you. Otherwise I never would have done it.

I've wanted to publish "Ex-GI" ever since I first developed the print. I know it's one of the best things I've done, but I held back—and I did take the picture for myself. "Seascape" was plain spite. I'm sorry. Haakon, I love you and I wish I hadn't done it. I'd undo it if I could.   S.

Done what? He put the note aside and paged slowly through the magazine. First a section of war pictures. He had seen most of those. A section of prizewinning pictures: the old monk Simon had photographed that first summer they were together, the mountain lion at the Bronx Zoo. None of these was new to him. Then the last one in the section, the picture that had won Simon his most recent award, that had gotten him on the cover of the magazine.

"Ex-GI." Himself, naked, in color. It had been taken from behind and somewhat above. He was sleeping on his side, arm crooked over his face. GI haircut, Army watch, his Eisenhower jacket with its rows of ribbons on the bedpost. Simon must have put it there and removed it later. He was in his own bed, here in this apartment. When? Apparently the room had been warm, for he was completely uncovered, a twist of sheets and blanket at his feet.

"When you were home on leave." Simon answered his thought from the kitchen doorway. "You know, when you sleep after sex, sometimes I think Armageddon wouldn't wake you."

"The lighting?"

"Afternoon sun and fill-in flash. With your arm over your eyes like that, you never even twitched."

Looking at the picture, he said slowly, "You must have been very angry to compromise me like this."

"You're not compromised!" Simon sounded shocked. "I wouldn't do that to you."

"Anyone who's ever seen me without a shirt will know it's me." Not only from the shrapnel scar which was the center of the composition, but from the row of round scars down his backbone where he had skinned the knobs in college, the vaccination mark on his upper arm.

"No, they won't. I flopped it."

"I did immediately, and I've seen less of my own back than anyone else."

"In the mirror, Haakon. It's flopped. Didn't you hear me? A mirror image. Of course you recognized it. Others won't." Then pleading, "I wouldn't do anything to harm you, no matter how angry I was."

"Ellen will recognize me—the bed, the room."

Simon looked uncomfortable, made a gesture with his chin, another with his hands, wrists somewhat limp. "I did think of that. That's one reason I'm so sorry." Another gesture.

"Stop flapping your hands around like a faggot," he snapped, annoyed by the mannerisms, even though he knew Simon was doing it out of nervousness. Simon immediately clasped his hands together in front of him, as though he didn't know what else to do with them. The look of anxiety on his face intensified. "Simon? Are you afraid of me?"

"Not of you, but of losing you again. Maybe forever."

He looked back at the picture. Long lean body, prominent bones, countable ribs. Not much difference there, but the scar was far uglier since he had reinjured it, and the haircut was different. With any luck, Ellen would never see this, and if she did, it dated itself. She would know it had been taken before they met. The only thing she could learn from it that she did not already know was the name of his lover. He asked, "And 'Seascape'?"

"A few pages further on."

There was a series of landscapes and city views. Then "Seascape." The scene was hauntingly familiar, but for a moment he was not sure why. Two men, one tall and thin, the other shorter and broad-shouldered, walking side by side along the line of surf on a wide sandy beach. Footprints stretched out behind, gulls wheeled in the sky. The figures were small, punctuation to the tracks in the sand

and the emptiness of the shoreline. Innocent enough. And he could only be sure it was himself and Dan because of Simon's lead-in.

"You followed us," he said, understanding that Simon had printed the picture to tell him this. Would he have recognized it without pushing? Not necessarily, but again he might have. The scene drew him, and he would probably have kept going back to it, looking at it and puzzling over it.

Simon nodded.

"Why?"

"I couldn't help myself. I had to see. I . . . didn't interfere. You'd never have known if I hadn't let you."

"I wish you hadn't."

"Done it, or told the truth?"

"Both," he admitted unhappily.

Simon was silent for some time, then he said, "Yes, I see that being truthful can be selfish too sometimes. Oh, dear!"

"Never mind, it's all right."

Abruptly Simon turned and went back into the kitchen, apparently in response to the timer he seemed to have in his head, for there was the sound of pans being moved.

He stared sadly at the picture. What Simon had done had tainted the memory of that summer by changing the context. He could not be angry with Simon now because it was too late, and Simon was changed. The old Simon never would have considered telling the truth, but would have come up with one story after another.

The pictures had been submitted to the magazine months ago. That too was ancient history. But suddenly some of the things Simon had said in the past coalesced into a suspicion. He went into the kitchen.

Simon was setting the table.

"Simon, are there more pictures? Of me and Dan?"

"Yes, several rolls."

"Tell me all of it."

"Some with a telephoto lens, others too—close up, infra-red film. I'll give you the negatives, all the prints."

"No, I don't want to see them, and if I can trust you to give me all of them I can trust you to destroy them yourself, can't I?"

"All right, if that's what you want."

He couldn't help being appalled. "Do you blackmail people?" he asked. "Take pictures of them and blackmail them?"

"No, never! I've never used any of my pictures that way."

"Then why take them?"

"I don't know." Simon thought about it, then added, "Old-age insurance? No, I don't think so. Just to have, I think. 'I know something you don't know.' Yes, that's part of it. My own personal pornography collection, and some were taken with permission. Some of them are damned good too." As he talked, Simon was dishing up eggs and bacon. He set them on the table. "Eat while it's hot?" he said tentatively.

"All right." He was not feeling hungry any more. "You've never used any of them, ever?"

"Once. A member of Parliament with a young boy. I told him I'd send them to the police if he did it again. As far as I know he's behaved himself since."

"Would you have sent them?"

"Yes," Simon said with quiet fierceness. "The child was under ten and didn't like it. You're bloody right I would have. To the press as well."

"But you just took photographs? You didn't try to stop him?"

Simon flinched, then said, "I don't blame you for thinking that. I've never let you know me." He paused, looked away. "I don't want to make a story out of it. I tried to interfere, and got run off the grounds for my pains. Sneaked back and took the pictures through a window. At least that way I could prevent it happening again."

"I'm sorry." Simon was too complicated, he had too many secrets, and his life had been even messier than Haakon had thought. Ellen was an opposite, so straightforward that she could not imagine acting as Simon had. He wished her back, so he could go to her, go away from Simon's complexity.

He looked up from his untouched breakfast. "I love Ellen," he said, "and she'll be coming back soon. I think I want to marry her." He almost wished Simon had not come back, had not changed. He did not want to love him. "I liked being straight," he said. "I liked the approval, the freedom to show affection on the street—all of that. I don't want to have to give it up now I've had it. Even aside from how I feel about Ellen."

"Do you want me to go away? I will if that's what you want."

Simon meant it. God, what was he to do? Simon was here and Ellen was not. Lovemaking last night had been a fulfillment past anything he had imagined before. "No," he said almost in a whisper. "I love you."

"You'd have freedom if you came out of the closet," Simon offered after a moment.

"Freedom to do what?" he demanded angrily, thinking how inappropriate and ill-timed the remark was. "Associate with a bunch of queens? I don't like most homosexuals. You know that. I hate the rivalry, the passes, the promiscuity, the private jokes and endless innuendo. I don't like any of it. I've nothing in common with any of them."

"Not quite nothing."

"All right, but very damn little. You don't expect people to be friends simply because they're straight, do you? Why in hell should you expect me to like someone simply because he's queer? It's ridiculous."

"Put that way, I suppose it is."

"And furthermore, if I came out, it would make problems for my straight friends. A new kind of constraint. They might be afraid to be seen with me. You know about that."

"Yes, I do," Simon agreed soberly.

"And I don't want Ellen hurt. I care about her." Simon nodded agreement, watching him intently, seeming anxious. He had not touched his food either, the eggs and bacon were congealing on the plates. "She thinks she saved me," he said.

"Yes, that's important to women," Simon agreed.

But he couldn't give Simon up either. He didn't know what to do, how to decide.

"I'll stay out of the way," Simon said. "We can meet at my place. She'll never know about me."

He didn't like the solution. It fell substantially short of his standards of behavior, but he knew that it was what he was going to do.

November 8, 1947

Instead of spending Saturday afternoon with Ellen as he had originally planned, he told her he had an appointment. He took a cab downtown and, with automatic caution, gave the address of a restaurant around the corner from the street where Simon's house was.

As he settled back for the ride he realized that he had fled from Ellen in such haste that he had not thought to phone ahead to see if Simon were home. He asked himself why. Certainly he wanted to see Simon, who had only been back for two weeks after being gone most of October. Was he running away from Ellen, or was he going to Simon?

Lunch had been pleasant enough, they had not quarreled. Gino was delighted to see him with Ellen and gave them the special wine his brother made instead of the *vin ordinaire* he served everyone else. There was a fat family at a nearby table: fat mother, fatter father, three obese children and a chubby baby. A happy baby. Every time it laughed Ellen smiled, and he thought comfortably and fondly what a good mother she would make.

But the hat business, that was something else again. Absurd to let it bother him so much. He had met Ellen immediately after swimming and his hair was wet.

"It's freezing outside!" Ellen said. "You'll catch your death."

"I've never caught cold from wet hair," he replied, expecting her to drop the subject.

"You should wear a hat."

"I don't like them. Besides, I always lose them."

"You've got to get a hat," she persisted.

He found himself becoming irritated. He did not reply.

"Promise me you will."

To shut her up, he said, "I'll see." But the annoyance had lingered, and though he was sure he had not let it show, he had become more and more uncomfortable throughout lunch. He knew she expected to go to bed with him later and he had not wanted to. He had even felt a mild revulsion at the thought.

That was the trouble. He did not want to be owned by her any more than he had wanted to be owned by Simon. Simon did not try to possess him any more. He could be comfortable with him.

But Ellen—ever since she had been home—they were not even engaged and she was trying to extract promises about what he would wear. The hat thing was only the most recent of a long list of demands, most of them couched as concern for his well-being, so he was not even able to object without looking and feeling like a boor.

He paid the cab driver, waited until the taxi was out of sight, then turned the corner and hurried down the narrow side street past the almost identical brownstones, each with concrete or stone steps and closed doors. He let himself into Simon's house with his key and paused just inside the door to blow his nose, which was running from the cold.

He looked around the studio. Simon had removed most of the partitions, so he could see all the way to the back wall. The tree in the small garden behind the house was tapping at a window as if it wanted to be let in.

Steel beams held up the upper stories, and a wide curved metal stairway led up to Simon's living quarters on the second floor. He went to the foot of the stairs and listened. No sound from above. But Simon was certainly home. Lights were turned on.

He should have phoned first. His stomach suddenly twisted into a knot. What if Simon were upstairs with someone else? But recently Simon had been so different. Not like that.

He heard a hum and turned his head from side to side to locate its source. Of course, the darkroom exhaust fan. He realized he was smiling. Simon had proved over and over that he had changed. Why couldn't he get used to trusting him?

The huge room was cluttered with bits of props and clusters of photographic lamps. The arrangement and furniture kept changing, so it was never entirely familiar. Today the most striking objects in the room were an enormous potted palm with an ornately carved orange plush chair beside it on a low platform. He made his way around a plate camera on a tripod, detoured a white backdrop and a bank of reflectors, watching his feet so he would not trip over the cables that snaked across the floor. He turned the metal cylinder that was the darkroom door so the opening was toward him, stepped over the high sill, and turned it back, so the opening gave him access to the darkroom. He stepped out into warm redness.

Simon, in shirtsleeves, was bending over a tray watching an image come up on a print. Without moving, he said, "Hello, Haakon. I wasn't expecting you. What a nice surprise."

"How did you know it was me?"

"I never gave my key to anyone else."

"Oh."

Simon reached into the solution with tongs and removed the print, put it in fixative before turning. "I'll be done soon, then we can go upstairs if you like. Can you stay awhile?"

"All night."

"Good." Then, "Is your schedule improving any?"

"Not much. I wish to god I'd never accepted that damn promotion. I've had to drop another seminar, and I hate the paperwork." The room was hot and smelled of acetic acid. He took off his overcoat and folded it over his arm. He considered going outside to wait, but he wanted to be near Simon. He could never get enough of watching him. Simon's shirt, red in the light, was unbuttoned almost to the waist, his skin darker, the hair on his chest darker yet. He needed a haircut and the shagginess enhanced his beauty, increased his resemblance to Pan, made him even more desirable than usual.

He went to look at the print. It was a picture of an old man, face so deeply scored with lines that it looked almost like cracked stone. A face of rage.

"Johannesburg," Simon said. "I caught him as he passed me on the street, then got this one when he stopped to shake his cane at me. Isn't he magnificent?"

"Johannesburg?"

"I guess I didn't mention that. I was only there a week."

"You said Zurich and London." Then becoming aware of his own possessiveness, "But it's none of my business." He had missed Simon painfully during the month he had been gone, and still felt the remnants of resentment at having been left alone.

"I had to go," Simon said. "Really."

"Don't apologize. I'm being unreasonable."

"Actually, I rather like it." Simon smiled up at him. He finished with the print. "There now." He made a mock bow by the cylinder. "After you." There was only room for one person at a time in it.

He stepped in. A moment of total blackness, then the glare of ordinary light. He stepped out, blinking, waiting for his eyes to adjust. The door turned and Simon stepped out, stood a moment with his eyes closed.

God, Simon looked thin. It had not showed in the dimness inside, but the ceiling light in the studio was unsparing. The flesh around his eyes seemed dark, his cheeks hollow. During the month he had been gone he had lost weight. Simon had admitted to having been ill, but he did not seem to be improving. "Have you been to a doctor yet?"

"Of course," Simon said indignantly. "You know I take care of myself. I've been to several."

"What did they say?"

"Not much. Intestinal problem. It'll take care of itself in time. It's just that I haven't much appetite. Now come along." Simon took his arm and escorted him across the studio and up the stairs. The sitting room curtains were drawn, making it dark, and the bedroom door was open.

The room was lighted by the small amount of daylight that came through the damask curtains plus a small lamp by the oversized bed, and the lights over the paintings. Simon went in first and he followed, wondering if he would ever become used to this museum of a room. Mirrors, velvets, plush and satin, tawny and gold. Mirrored ceiling. Period French furniture, a glass-fronted case of homoerotic bronzes.

Simon took his overcoat and hung it in the closet, then disappeared into the bathroom. He looked at the paintings. One was an eighteenth-century rococo after the style of Fragonard, depicting Zeus and Ganymede. Though it was an excellent example of the

244

period, he did not care for the style. The other was a priceless school-of-Rubens as beautiful as any he had ever seen on exhibit. The subject was Caeser and Nicomedes—Caeser recognizable, though shown as a youth. He never could get enough of looking at it. The intricacies of the composition, the gemlike colors, the profusion of textures, and the beauty of the young man admiring himself in a mirror, trying on a string of pearls that looked real enough to pick off the canvas.

Long ago, when he had first seen the paintings, he had been shocked to discover that works of art depicting homosexual love existed, and he had found them exciting. Yet they were no more pornographic than most pictures in a museum, no more sensual.

Simon was back, helping him out of his jacket, hanging it away, asking, "Tea or bed?"

"I just had lunch. You?"

"You need to ask?" Simon came over and began to unknot his tie.

"I can undress myself."

"Let me? I like to."

"All right."

After they were in bed Simon said, "Your way?"

"Whatever you want." He had no preference. He wanted the closeness and emotional satisfaction of loving Simon. How was unimportant as long as Simon was pleased.

Why had Simon changed preferences since his trip? Strange. Had all that insistence on needing to be screwed been a way to badger him? Or had Simon used that as justification for his promiscuity?

"What is it?" Simon asked.

"Nothing." He kissed him tenderly and stopped thinking.

Afterwards he lay dozing, holding Simon, feeding on his closeness, enjoying the weight of his head on his shoulder.

After some time Simon asked, "Something go wrong between you and Ellen?"

"Why do you ask?"

"Because you're here instead of with her."

That was logical; he generally did spend Saturday afternoon with her. "I worry about mentioning her to you."

"I'm not jealous, truly."

That seemed to be the truth. Why was it that he kept thinking that Simon was pushing him to marry Ellen? That Simon had some sort of secret blueprint he was not privy to?

When Ellen had come back in September, and he caught sight

of her bright hair across the station, he felt light and happy. He wanted her as much as he had at first. But now . . .

He said, "I'd planned to spend the day with her, but I pleaded an appointment and came away. It's going sour, Simon. I don't quite know why. On my part—not hers. Sex for one thing."

"How?"

"You said once, 'A bore and a chore.' Not that bad yet, but getting there. At first it was as thrilling as being on a roller coaster, but I'm not afraid any more. Without that, there isn't much interest. Though she does feel good."

"Yes, women do," Simon agreed. "Soft. It kept me going back and trying them for years."

"She's not the way she was before this summer. She used to be willing to let me go my own way, be myself, but now she does things like nagging me to wear a hat. No, 'nag' isn't fair, but that's how I felt."

"But if you were married, you'd have a home. Probably children too. You've always wanted a child. Couldn't you get along with her? Learn to ignore what you don't like? Apparently she loves you."

"I suppose so."

"Why not make the effort then? Everyone would approve."

"Even you?"

"Myself most of all."

"Simon? Do you really mean that?"

"Yes, I do," Simon said definitely. "I want you safe, and I want you happy. You told me you were tired of living along the edges of life, always playing a part."

"That would be playing a part, can't you see that? And I can't give you up," he said. "I need you too much."

"You don't have to."

"But it wouldn't be right to marry her and keep on with you. What if she found out?"

"She knows you're gay. You said you'd told her so."

"That's not at all the same as her finding out I have a current lover, and you know it."

"I suppose you're right," Simon agreed. He was quiet for a long time, then he said, "But if I weren't around? For example, Christmastime. Wouldn't you be glad to have her?"

"I do miss you dreadfully, but you always come back."

"Supposing I didn't?"

"Then . . . but I don't want to suppose that." The idea was frightening.

"*Just* supposing. Go ahead."

"It's pleasant to have her when you aren't here, but it's still just a stopgap. Better than nothing. Though I'm very fond of her."

"You didn't answer my question."

"You know? The other day I suddenly saw the future, all laid out like a map. I was alone at my desk about to start some paperwork. I don't remember now what I was thinking that led up to it. Anyway, I knew that if I made an effort Ellen would marry me."

"My question," Simon insisted.

"I can't imagine wanting anyone but you, but I suppose eventually I'd find another man."

"Oh." Simon sounded disappointed.

"What?"

"I'd hoped you might have gone further in the other direction than that."

"I thought I had for a while, but it's too late for me now. Perhaps if I'd met someone like her when I was twenty . . ." The wind was blustering around the building. Simon was warm and solid in his arms. There was nowhere else in the world he would rather be. No one he would rather be with. He turned his head enough so he could see their reflections in the ceiling. Simon's olive skin contrasted with his own paleness. His profile showed clearly against his shoulder, Simon's hair dark and curly. He saw that his eyes were closed. Simon's shape under the fawn blanket was small next to his own length. "Why are you after me to marry?" he asked, puzzled.

"Because you'd be safer married. And I don't think you'd be unhappy. You'd have children and someone to take care of you."

"Safer?"

"You risk everything every time you see me. And I'm especially concerned now that that damned *Fairystory* book of yours is about to be published."

"*A Study of Persecution.*" he corrected. "It's not *Fairystory* any more. It deals with many persecuted minorities."

"I know," Simon said. "And it could just as easily have been written by a hetero. You *told* me."

"Well, it could."

"Perhaps. But people will wonder why you were that interested in faggots. No way around it."

"It's all explained in the book. Damn it, Simon! You read the galleys."

Simon turned his head and looked at him in the mirror. Smiling, he teased gently, "You and Hans Christian Andersen."

For supper Simon made smørrebrød—open-faced Danish sandwiches heaped with salmon roe, shrimps, herring—all his favorite delicacies. Each sandwich different, and all of them arranged in a design that was so artistic he found himself hesitating to destroy it by taking the first one.

"Where did you find smoked reindeer meat?"

"That's my secret," Simon said, delighted with himself because he had succeeded in offering a surprise and a treat.

But Simon ate little. They had fruit and cheese for dessert, then Simon poured brandy and lay back in his chair as if exhausted. His energy level had been down since his return. Formerly he had had more energy than most people. Now there were times when he seemed to have none at all.

"I'm worried about you," he said. "You keep telling me you're all right, but you're not getting any better."

"Some things take time. Not everything can be cured with a shot of penicillin, you know." Simon sat up straight, and with a burst of energy, gathered up the dishes and took them to the kitchen. He refused help washing up, acting as if drying a dish were a difficult art requiring a long apprenticeship.

"By the way," Simon said, putting away the plates, "next weekend I'll be going to Minnesota, just for a few days."

"Where, for god's sake?"

"Oh, East Jesus." Simon made a gesture that dismissed the entire state and everything in it.

"What for?"

"Pictures. A dairy company wants a portrait of a cow. I'll be leaving around noon on Saturday." Then, "If you've no other plans, I could spend Friday night with you and leave from your place."

"I was about to suggest that. Yes. But are you sure you'll be well enough to travel? Couldn't you put off the assignment?"

"Don't be absurd! Of course I'll be better by then. You'll see."

November 15, 1947

The small coffee shop, smelling of fresh bread and cinnamon, was bright and empty. Haakon took a table near the window where he could watch for Higgins and ordered coffee from a barrel-shaped waitress dressed in starchy white.

He was a few minutes early. He wished again that he had not been so insistent about needing Higgins's opinion on his new text. But when he had called earlier in the week he was frustrated to the point of anger by the book's organizational problems. And he had not anticipated having to leave Simon, or that Simon would be going out of town today.

Simon had not waked when the alarm went off, which was unlike him. He had been sleeping curled up, and though he seemed heavily asleep, he was restless—twitching, moaning softly from time to time.

A yellow cab drew up at the curb. The fat pigeon that had been marching back and forth like a sentry eyed it suspiciously and instead of making its turn at the end of its beat, continued walking uptown.

Higgins came across the sidewalk, saw Haakon behind the glass and raised his hand in greeting. He got out of his overcoat while they exchanged greetings and Haakon apologized for taking his time on a weekend.

"No, no, I eat breakfast here anyway," Higgins reassured him, and proceeded to order a full breakfast from the rustling waitress.

Higgins quickly read the sheets of outline he was given. "This won't do," he said, handing one back. "Too much like 'meanwhile, back at the ranch,' if you know what I mean."

"Yes." He had almost thrown that plan away himself.

"I like this, with a brief listing of what was probably going on in the rest of the world at the beginning, then getting on with China and Europe."

"But I can't do that in later centuries."

"No, I suppose not. But is there any reason why you have to organize every century in the same way?" Higgins buttered his pecan roll.

That was the answer of course. He should have seen it. But that was why he had wanted to talk with Higgins; Higgins was good at finding solutions to these sorts of problems. "You're right, as usual."

Higgins nodded and continued eating. He was neat as a wren in his well-cut brown suit. His gestures bird-quick and precise. "You've never had a problem organizing material before," he observed.

"I've always taken the easy way—following generals around. That even gives one a sort of plot. There's usually a climactic defeat or victory at the end of the story."

"True."

They discussed details of the projected text further. Then Higgins said, "I rather hope this will be more than a text. There's interest in the Far East, South America, Australia and so forth now that so many men have seen those places—and the people at home have read about them in the papers."

Then just before finishing his last cup of coffee, Higgins said,

249

"I did tell you that *A Study of Persecution* is all set for publication next week, didn't I? Copies in bookstores and so forth. We're expecting major attention from the reviewers. Did I mention that we're taking a full-page ad in the Sunday *Times Book Review?*"

"No, you didn't." A full page for a scholarly book? That didn't make sense to him. "It was not intended as a popular book," he protested. "Why so large an ad?"

"Would you like to see it? I believe I have a proof copy." Higgins set his briefcase on his knees and began looking through it. He went through everything twice. "I'm sorry, apparently I left it at the office. But you'll see it tomorrow."

"You didn't answer my question."

Higgins looked at him a moment before speaking. His eyes were an unusual reddish-gold color, lighter than those of most brown-eyed people, and seemed penetrating. "Anything to do with sex, sadism, or religion sells well," he explained. "And though this is not at all a popular treatment, it is clearly written. You do have a nice clean style—to the point, easy to follow. You'll see, it will be a *succès fou.*"

"I have a feeling I'm not going to like the publicity."

"Now, now, there's not a thing for you to worry about. I assure you, no one will call it anything but scholarly." Then suddenly becoming confidential, "Frankly, we need a book that will really sell just now. And some of your illustrations are extraordinary—those Spanish woodcuts from the time of the Inquisition showing homosexuals being castrated and buried alive. Where did you get them?"

"The source didn't want to be mentioned."

"I can see why! Now, don't look so disapproving! And do tell me, what made you research this area?"

"It hasn't been done before." Then, half truthfully, "As you know I was profoundly affected by the German concentration camps. I found that witchcraft, heresy and sodomy were all more or less considered the same thing by the Church. One thing led to another."

"I see, I see. Yes, of course."

"Now, about the publicity. I don't want anything lurid."

"Has Meadows ever printed any but the most sober ads?" Higgins asked. "Don't let your imagination run away with you."

But after he had left Higgins, he wondered if he had been given a runaround. He paused on the sidewalk, but then checked his watch. He would be late meeting Ellen if he didn't hurry. What was he worrying about? Meadows's advertising was always in such good taste it was downright stodgy.

When he got to the restaurant he saw that Ellen was already

there, seated at a table. He paused in the archway to the red-carpeted dining room. She was looking into the Manhattan in front of her and did not see him.

Her dress was new, a soft pale green wool with a slightly fuzzy finish as if it might have angora in it. Her hair was shiny, bright as sunshine. Lovely, lovely woman—physically, certainly. Mentally attractive too, especially all this last week, for she had not shown that possessiveness that made him want to run away.

To be married would be comfortable. To have a home to return to, someone always waiting. Children. He had always wanted children. Was it really unfair of him to want to marry her when he knew he could not give up seeing Simon? He would not be taking anything away from Ellen. She fulfilled different needs. He did not love her in the same way.

It was not a contest between Ellen and Simon. He had no doubt he would choose Simon if it came to a choice. The needs she met were peripheral, more to do with ease in living in a straight world. And he was grateful to her. Would he be cheating her because the affection he felt was shallow? Most of his guilt was over not living up to his own standards.

He crossed to her. "Hello, am I late?"

"Hi!" She smiled up at him. "No, I'm early." Soft smile, clear skin. "My feet are killing me—I was shopping all morning long. You're never late."

"Hardly ever," he corrected, seating himself. "Your dress is lovely."

Pleased, she glanced down and smoothed the skirt. "I got it this morning. I knew you'd like it."

He touched the fabric. "Soft." The waiter came over and he ordered an old-fashioned.

"I've never seen you drink that before," Ellen commented.

It was one of Simon's favorite drinks. He usually did not care for it, but today . . . "I was in the mood," he said, shoving the pick into the maraschino cherry and eating it.

After they had eaten they took a taxi uptown to his apartment. It was well after one o'clock. Simon was on a plane by now, on his way to "East Jesus," Minnesota. Simon would have cleared away all evidences of his stay; the apartment would be neat and the bed made.

In the past Simon had always been jealous. Why was he so intent now on marrying him off to Ellen? But Simon had changed so much that there was little use in trying to understand him as he was now by reference to him as he had been before.

251

In the elevator on the way up he leaned close to Ellen, inhaling the clean scent of her hair. He stroked it just as the car stopped. They stepped out into the empty green-carpeted corridor. Unable to wait, heart already speeding in anticipation, he kissed her. The metal doors snicked shut behind him. He remembered and looked forward to the silky weight of her long hair across his bare chest.

Yes, he loved her in a way. Quite a good deal, really. He would not be cheating her. Perhaps it was better not to love too intensely. It was far easier to be kind when one was not deeply involved.

With his arm around her, he walked her to his door, unlocked it, and stepped back for her to enter first.

She gasped and stopped so suddenly that his shoe grazed her ankle. Looking over her head, he saw Simon, still in pajamas, lying in the bedroom doorway. He ran to him, only half aware that he had brushed against Ellen so quickly and roughly that she almost fell.

"Simon!" He touched his face. Not dead, unconscious. He could see the flutter of pulse in the space below his jaw. At this time on Saturday Ben should be home. He hurried to the phone and dialed. Three rings. Four. Ben had to be home. If he was not, then . . . The phone was picked up.

"Dr. Solomon."

"Ben, Haakon here. Come up right away. Simon's ill."

"As soon as possible," Ben said crisply and hung up.

He went back to Simon and knelt beside him. How long had he been there? Simon's arm was bent under him. He moved it, eased him into a more comfortable-looking position. Dared he move him? Why not? He wasn't an accident victim, he had apparently fainted. "Simon, oh Simon," he whispered, gathering him into his arms.

A movement on the other side of the room distracted him. He had forgotten about Ellen. Holding Simon, still on his knees, he looked at her and wondered what to say.

She came slowly over and knelt down. "Simon Foster," she said wonderingly. "The photographer. I kept thinking 'Ex-GI' looked like you, and I wondered about the background. But the scar was on the wrong side, and the vaccination."

"He reversed the negative," he said automatically, feeling numb and at the same time intensely conscious of Simon in his arms. He wanted to care how she felt, but he had no room in his mind for anything but worry over Simon.

"I see," she said quietly, without rancor.

"Yes." She had not mentioned the picture before. She had said nothing about it, so he simply assumed that she hadn't seen the magazine. Simon was too still. When would Ben get here? He had phoned an eternity ago.

A rap on the door and Ellen went to let the doctor in. He was grateful to her for that. He watched Ben limp across the room, and demanded, "What's the matter with Simon?" A stupid question. How would Ben know? He had not yet examined him.

Surprisingly, Ben said, "I can't tell you. Confidence. Go ahead and put him in bed."

Simon was weightless, easy to carry. When St. Louis was ill and a prisoner of the Saracens, William of St. Patheus wrote, he "was so thin that the bones of his back were wonderfully sharp. Isambert had to carry the king . . ." Where was his mind wandering? What in hell was the matter with Simon?

He laid him down carefully and stepped away to give Ben room. He became aware that he was sweating in his overcoat, took it off and dropped it on a chair. "Ben, what's the matter with him?"

Ben gave Simon a shot, then looked up. "I can't tell you." Then he held out his hand. "Please help me up? I had my leg off, about to take a shower when you called. It's not adjusted right, and I've simply got to do something about it. You stay with him, he should come around in a few minutes. I'll be right back."

He sat down on the edge of the bed and, not knowing what else to do, picked up Simon's hand. It was cool, dry, bony as a bird's foot. Fragile. How was it possible that he had not noticed Simon's emaciated condition last night?

Simon moaned and turned his head back and forth on the pillow. The sound of his hair rubbing against the cloth was dry as autumn leaves, as the rustle of Death's garments. Death? A panorama of medieval danse macabre skeletons filled his mind. He winced away from the black and white grins, from the worms like skeins of yarn falling from the ripped abdomens, from the mouth of hell depicted literally as the jaws of a monster.

Simon opened his eyes. "Haakon? I'm afraid I've missed my plane."

"What's the matter with you?"

"I must have fainted."

"What's the matter with you?" he insisted.

"I'm dying of cancer," Simon said flatly, then managed a wavering smile. "Oh, well, I never wanted to grow old anyway."

"Cancer?"

"Yes. And to make the picture complete, of the rectum. Considering who I am, I consider *that* little joke of God's to be in distinctly poor taste."

"Oh, Simon." And thought, "As flies to wanton boys, are we to the gods. They kill us for their sport." Then was annoyed with himself for going off again into literary references. "Isn't there something that can be done? X rays, an operation? Something?"

"Nothing."

"Are you certain it's cancer?" Simon had to be wrong about that. Had to be.

"I've been to London, Zurich, Boston, Paris, Johannesburg, even Houston, Texas. They all said exactly the same thing. Radio-resistant, six months at best. At first a few of them promised me a few extra months if I'd allow myself to be mutilated, but no cure. I turned them down, of course." Simon sighed and looked past him to the door. "Hello, Ben."

"How do you feel?"

"Better. Yes . . . better."

"Now will you let me put you in a hospital?" Ben said.

"Absolutely not! I've engaged two nurses to take care of me at home. I will not allow myself to be humiliated in any more hospitals." Simon looked away from Ben, back to him. "Haakon, I know this sounds ridiculous, but I kept hoping I'd find a doctor who'd tell me it had all been a terrible mistake, that I wasn't dying after all, that it wasn't hopeless, that something new had been discovered— a cure. But today . . . Just as I was getting up to get ready to leave, I saw myself running from hospital to hospital, from doctor to doctor, like a frightened child searching a crowd for its mother. There's no hope. I'd get the same diagnosis at the Mayo Clinic that I have everywhere else."

Simon smiled with real amusement. "Do you know? I even made a trip to Lourdes. I knew better, but I did it anyway. It's a fantastic place. Church and carnival all mixed together. And faces! Faces of hope, of despair—and all the major sins too, particularly avarice. I took some magnificent pictures. I even got shots of a miracle!

"A young woman got up off a litter and walked after having been paralyzed from the waist down for six months. You could feel the hope like a deep note on an organ, all the way through your bones. I felt it myself, and got it on film too. You'll see.

"But then later, when I was walking through the town, I heard a doctor say that Lourdes is the treatment of choice for hysterical paralysis. So of course that's all there was to it."

Ben had waited, not interrupting, but now he repeated doggedly, "You belong in a hospital."

Simon stared at Ben for a long moment. "No. I won't spend what's left of my life being poked, prodded, bothered, dictated to, forced to eat slop, and being referred to as 'the carcinoma.' I promised myself that several months ago. At the time I was lying in a pool of blood, shit and barium, strapped down on a cart in a drafty hallway. I will die with dignity at home. Now, I would appreciate it if you don't bring the matter up again."

"You'll need hospital care," Ben insisted, then appealed to him. "Hawk, tell him."

"Tell him what? He's right. I'll take care of him. I can do it."

Simon's hand tightened almost painfully on his. He said fiercely, "No, you bloody well won't, you bloody idiot! You've already done enough of that sort of thing to last anyone several lifetimes. I'm not saying I don't want you around, I do. But you are bloody well *not* going to take care of me."

Then his hand relaxed and he said quietly, explaining, "While I was in London I engaged two male nurses. I gave them money for the plane fare, and arranged for them to come when I cabled. Which I did this morning. They'll be here tomorrow." He looked at Ben. "All right?" Then back to him. "You'll like them, Haakon. It happens they're both straight. The older one, Jack, is forty-five and has wanted to come to New York to visit his daughter and grandchildren for some time. He's a most dedicated and gentle man. The other, Colin, looks like a schoolboy. He'd wanted to be a doctor but lacked funds. I'll leave him enough for medical school in my will. He's still young enough to go. And he'll be a good doctor. He knows about pain. Nurses do. They have to clean up after, and listen to the moans in the night after the surgeons are all happily tucked in their beds."

He had to ask, "Simon, how long have you known?"

"It depends on what you mean by 'know.' In a sense I didn't know until this morning, because I refused to believe it. But I got the first diagnosis a couple of weeks before I followed you in the park."

"Oh." He remembered the feeling he'd had that more was wrong than Simon had let on. Now he could understand Simon's behavior. On the one hand hoping against hope, on the other planning for his death. Alone and afraid. He had felt the fear from time to time, and had not understood it. "Is that why you were in the hospital? For the diagnosis?"

"No, I told you the truth. I'd gotten mixed up with a sadist, and one day he tried to pull my wings off. But I'd been having intestinal problems on and off for several months, so as long as I was there, I got X rays. The discomfort was ruining my sex life."

Simon's openness in front of Ben made him uncomfortable. Then he realized why Simon had changed to oral sex. "You should have told me sooner," he said.

He knew by Simon's smile that he understood him. "No, I wanted to enjoy you as long as I was able." Then to Ben, "I need something stronger now, for pain."

"Yes, I know," Ben agreed. "I've given you a shot of morphine, and I'll be back this evening to give you another. When will your nurses be here?"

"I *told* you. Tomorrow. I even checked the weather. The prediction is fine and fair all the way from London to here for the next three days. With a bomber's moon."

When Ben left a few minutes later, he walked him to the door. He felt detached from himself, as if he were watching himself go through the motions. He could not bring himself to believe that Simon was dying, even though he did believe it too. "Is it as bad as he says?" he asked.

"A good deal worse. He doesn't have long at all."

"How much time?" he asked numbly.

"I don't know. I can't even make an educated guess. I wouldn't have believed he could have kept on his feet this long if I hadn't seen it for myself. Maybe a month, maybe more, maybe less. I just don't know."

"And there's nothing that can be done?"

"Nothing." Dark Jewish eyes, full of sympathy. "Haakon, I'm sorry. But that's the way it is. Back in July several surgeons thought a colostomy might prolong his life, but Simon turned them down flat. He said he'd just as soon have his nose cut off, or be castrated. I felt he made the right decision at the time, and I still do. The surgeon in the case is one of the best, but unfortunately, psychologically naïve. He showed Simon a colostomy bag. Simon laughed, called it a condom for an elephant, then was hysterical the rest of the afternoon. I had to sedate him."

If Simon could call an invisible scar a mutilation, how horrified he must have been by that. He said, "Even if that would have cured his cancer, it would have killed him."

Ben nodded. "Yes, that's what I thought. And it wouldn't have cured him. He already had metastases to the liver."

How could Ben talk about it so calmly? Simon was dying. The fact keep sinking deeper and deeper into him. He became aware that his stomach hurt, and had been hurting since he had seen Simon lying on the floor. Feeling distant, he said, "Yes, well . . . thank you for coming up on such short notice." He began to walk away, then realized he was being rude and turned back. He tried to think of some polite formula with which to get rid of Ben.

Ben said, "I know. He's my friend too." Watching him with concern. Then Ben put his hand on his shoulder. "I wish I could say something, but there's never anything . . . because, ultimately, lying is no kindness." He could see Ben's pain, though he could not yet quite feel his own. Ben gave him a pat. "Take it easy, and take care of yourself too. He needs you. I'll let myself out."

He nodded, wordless. When Ben was gone he blundered blindly across the room and found himself staring at his littered desk. File cards and papers, all the things that went into the genesis of a new book. The world history he had just begun. It was utterly unimportant. He could have watched it burn without caring. He turned away and closed his eyes. His face felt stiff and his nose was running. The cold tension in his stomach was almost nauseating and his throat hurt. Where was Ellen?

Simon was dying just as he had become the sort of person he should have been. If only . . . Oh, God! If only. He wanted to weep for both Simon and himself, but instead he pulled himself together and went back to the bedroom. Simon was lying curled up, his eyes shadowed and enormous.

He asked, "Is there something I can get you?"

"No, and don't *start* that with me. I won't have it."

"I want to."

"I don't! And that's final. I'll stay here until my nurses arrive, but you're *not* to take care of me. I can still walk."

"Please, Simon? There's nothing else I can do for you."

"Nonsense. And it would be bad for you. Now pay attention! I love you, and I believe you love me too. I don't want that turned into something horrible. Can't you see that taking care of me physically would do that?"

"Not bringing you a cup of soup or a glass of water."

"No, not even that. I know you. I won't let you get started."

"You're being unreasonable."

"Put it down to vanity then." Before he could protest again Simon said, "Stop shaking your head at me and come and listen." He patted the bed beside him. "Please."

He did as requested, sat down beside him and took his hand. "I love you," he told him. "That's why I want to take care of you."

"I'll need some help, but not that kind. I want to die with dignity if possible. God knows I've lived pretty much without it." Simon stared thoughtfully into space for a moment. He looked sad, regretful. Then briskly, sounding businesslike, "There are thousands and thousands of photographs that have to be sorted out. I want the good ones saved, but I don't want to leave the others behind. And there are the other ones too, the ones that could be used for blackmail. They have to be destroyed, and I can't trust anyone but you

257

to help me do it. Many of the men would be instantly recognized by anyone who reads a newspaper. I ought to have done it months ago, when I was better, but—"

"It's all right," he reassured him.

"No, it isn't. But I can at least partially excuse myself. I kept thinking I'd feel more up to it in a day or so." A quick indrawn breath, almost a gasp. "But now I know I won't . . . ever." A slight break in his voice. "Oh, Haakon, I don't want to die."

He put his arms around him and cradled him, holding him like a child, stroking his back, soothing him. "I know," he whispered, "I know."

Few people had Simon's gift of wholehearted enjoyment of the world and everything in it. He had never met anyone who loved life with Simon's intensity and concentration. It was this fierce greediness to capture as much of life as possible that made Simon the genius he was, that enabled him to photograph a crumb of bread so that it seemed entirely new, never seen before, though at the same time familiar.

When had Ellen left? He had no idea. Had she said goodbye? He did not know. So she was gone. He told himself that that was too bad, a meaningless phrase, because he did not care at all. Better for her anyway. She could go and marry a straight who could love her as much as she deserved, live happily ever after. In Boston. Fairies had no business marrying anyway. Better all around.

Simon lifted his face. "Kiss me?"

He did so, tenderly, lovingly, but without desire. Something had shifted in both of them. With an odd sense of reading minds, he knew that Simon felt as he did. They were no longer lovers. He did not think there was a word for it though.

Without the complication of physical hunger and lust, he began to be aware of the extent of his mental and emotional involvement.

That stupid song. "You are my sunshine, my only sunshine . . ." but without Simon there would be grayness, very little left to live for. Ashes and dust. He might as well die too.

Simon was holding his face, his hands caressing him gently. "Listen," Simon said, and waited until he was certain of his attention. "I don't want you to curl up and die when I do. I remember what you were like when we met, and I don't want you to be like that again."

He became aware he was trying to shake his head when Simon held it still. "But—"

"No, pay attention. We're the same in a way. And maybe not so different from everybody else at that. We don't want to hurt. I

258

managed it by plunging into the world and swimming fast enough so nothing caught up with me. You tried to manage it by keeping your feet dry. Neither way is much good. But I think your way's a little worse. I'd rather see you cruising in a park than turning into a mummy in a bloody library. At least that way there's some sort of human contact. We've both learned something about living these last months, and you've got to promise me not to forget. To keep trying, and go ahead and risk hurt. It's the only way to be human."

"Perhaps."

"Promise you'll try, anyway."

"I'll try. But it's not that easy—"

"Whoever said it was?"

V

When he awoke Sunday morning, he discovered that Simon had been up long enough to pack his suitcase and make breakfast. Simon seemed stronger, and was indignant and annoyed when he remonstrated with him for overexerting himself.

But for the first time Simon allowed him to carry his cameras and equipment bag for him, along with the suitcases, when they went down to the taxi, and in the cab he leaned back in the corner of the seat as if exhausted.

Simon got slowly out of the taxi and crossed to the foot of the steps up to his front door. He paused there, looking around. The day was bright and windy. "Wedgwood blue," Simon said, waving a hand to indicate the sky.

"Yes." He took the suitcases up the steps and set them down just inside the front door, then came back to help Simon.

Simon was watching the taxi, which still idled by the curb, a cloud of exhaust streaming behind it. There was a noisy lifter in the engine. "The driver's a fairyhawk," Simon said. "He recognized me too. Leave me here and get back in. Say something to him to convince him you're all right."

"Why?" He glanced at the cab driver. He was a big man, blue-jowled, with crew-cut hair. Big, but soft, out of condition. Beer belly. "He won't bother us here. Too many people around. And if it came to that, I could probably take him."

"I'm not concerned about *now*. His kind never do anything in the light of day, or alone either. They're only brave after midnight, in the company of at least three like-minded cretins."

"I don't go to gay bars. I've got nothing to worry about."

"If he thinks you're gay he's perfectly capable of attacking you on the street, and he knows where you live—he picked us up there."

Simon was probably right. It would be easy to convince the driver he was straight. All he had to do was get back into the cab and make a slighting remark about Simon. He knew all the ways of convincing people he was not queer. He had resorted to most of them at one time or another.

That time in London, the night he had met Jenny Hanover, he had been ready to go fairyhawking himself. "Sheep in wolf's clothing." Weak excuses to himself that he would give the fairies advance warning by making some loud remark or other. He could still be ashamed of his weakness.

Simon had instructed him to deny him, expected him to. But if he denied Simon he would be denying himself.

The wind ruffled Simon's curls. Simon was watching him, waiting for him to go back to the taxi. What was safety worth? It was not worth making a cruel joke about the man he loved.

Angrily and defiantly, not stopping to think any more, he scooped Simon up in his arms and carried him up the steps.

"You bloody idiot!" Simon said.

The driver was still watching. He had moved across the seat and was peering up through the side window.

Feeling an incongruous blend of rage and tenderness, he kissed Simon on the mouth before carrying him across the threshold into the studio and putting him down. Simon was looking at him intently, as if trying to understand. He said, "I had to."

After a moment, Simon nodded. "All right," he agreed.

He closed the front door on the world, placed Simon's cameras on a table, and picked Simon up again. He could not allow him to walk up that long flight of stairs to the second floor. The steps were so familiar that the muscles of his legs knew the exact height of the risers and depth of the treads.

The morning sun shone into the austere masculine sitting room. He carried him across to the bedroom, pushed the door wide with his shoulder and took him over to the huge bed, where he laid him down on the brownish velvet coverlet. The room was dark, curtains drawn. He snapped on the bedside lamp and was besieged by the many reflections of both of them. "Here?" he asked, glancing around and up at the ceiling. "Here, Simon?"

"Where else?" Simon was looking at himself in the ceiling mirror.

How could Simon contemplate dying here, having to watch himself deteriorate? He himself was far less vain than Simon, and he could not imagine being willing to die in this mirrored museum.

Still contemplating his reflection, Simon said, "You do have a point. This is one hell of a place to die."

"There's the other bedroom on this floor and three on the one above. Use one of the others."

"No, I think not."

"Why not!"

"Call it penance." Simon smiled at himself ruefully. "I got myself into this." Turning his head to look at him, he gestured indicating the whole room. "My fairy castle. I thought it up, put it together. There's a part of me here that I don't much like, but it *is* me too. I want to die whole, not in different places."

"I wish you'd reconsider."

"Not now. Perhaps later."

The doorbell chimed. Simon glanced at the antique clock on the dresser. "That must be Jack and Colin." He reached over and pressed the button releasing the front door lock, then lay back again.

"I'll go get them and show them up."

"Thank you."

He wondered what the nurses would think of Simon's room. It had so obviously been designed for orgies, with that bed big enough to hold five or six people, the mirrors. A fairy's room. He paused a moment by the glass-fronted cabinet full of bronze statuettes of men. A Greek Priapus, an early Roman Apollo, a Pan. A set of six groups of homosexuals making love. French, exquisite in their own way, but they certainly would shock.

He turned away and went to the head of the stairs, wondering if he were ashamed of Simon. He had to admit he was, much as he did not want to be. Embarrassed for him.

Two men were standing by the front door, both holding luggage. Colin would be the tall thin one who looked about nineteen, though he was twenty-six according to Simon. His hair disarranged by the wind, was fine and fair, almost colorless. His ears stuck out. He looked up on hearing him and smiled in greeting. Bad English teeth.

Jack was shorter and blocky, built like a wrestler. His crinkly hair was black, going gray, with a bald circle like a monk's tonsure on top. He had bushy eyebrows, and the backs of his hands were heavily veined, as if he had done a lot of work with them.

He started down the stairs and they started up. They met halfway, and after some awkwardness with the luggage, which had to be set down, shook hands. Colin became faintly pink. He introduced himself and took them to Simon's room, stepped back for them to enter. They both stopped in their tracks on getting a look at the room. Colin promptly turned scarlet.

Jack advanced toward Simon after his initial hesitation, his face showing nothing. "I'm glad to see you again, sir, though sorry of the reason," he said, taking Simon's hand.

"Good to see you, Jack. You too, Colin." Simon was holding out his other hand to him.

Colin advanced slowly, took it, dropped it quickly. "Hullo."

Simon smiled, "Don't be such a bloody Presbyterian!"

"I'm not, sir. I'm Church of England."

"I don't care what you *call* yourself, you've a Presbyterian soul. There, there, I shouldn't tease you. You've a right to be shocked. My bedroom *is* rather startling—too much like a bordello, wouldn't you say?"

Colin's flush deepened, then he said, "Everyone to his own taste," and began to fade back to normal.

Jack had been looking around. Now he said soberly, "That bed won't do, sir. It's half the size of a cricket field. We can't possibly care for you properly."

"I suppose it would be difficult. All right, we'll get a hospital bed for later, put it in the studio for now. But I'm not bedridden yet, you know." Simon was using a faggot accent and gesturing too much. "Haakon, darling, would you please show Jack and Colin their rooms?"

"Yes," he said tightly, heard himself, and wished he had not sounded so disapproving. To them he said, "This way, please."

He left them on the third floor, which was a self-contained apartment, to pick out their bedrooms and settle in. He went back down to Simon.

"Shall I take the other bedroom on this floor?"

"Yes, of course." Simon said abstractedly, then, "Why do I act like that? I was watching myself, and I didn't like what I saw. And calling you darling in front of them. Why do I do things like that?"

Up until now he had not understood it either, but suddenly it was clear. "To point out that you're queer."

Simon thought for a moment, then nodded. "Yes, I suppose so. But they already knew about me from when I met them in England. They took care of me when I was in hospital in London. I made passes at both of them."

Simon smiled. "Colin, as you can imagine, turned purple. He's a real innocent, and shy, but knows who he is for all that. The

264

man's an encyclopedia of mottos and proverbs, and resorts to them whenever he's at all shaken. He said, 'One's man's meat is another man's poison,' and was uncomprehending when I laughed at the pun. But he liked me anyway, and forgave me."

"And Jack?"

"He doesn't show anything in his face. He started when I gave him a feel, then calmly took my pulse, which was what he had come to do. And after he'd noted it down, he said, really very kindly, 'I'm not that sort, sir. I don't hold it against you, but I'd rather you didn't do that again.'"

"I see."

"So I hired them because they're good nurses, and because they can both handle me and I don't upset them too much."

"Now that you've proved to yourself again that you don't upset them too much, I hope you'll be able to stop acting like that."

"Don't be pious."

"Yes, I was being . . . I'm sorry."

"I embarrassed you."

"This whole damn room embarrasses me. And yes, you did. I don't like to stand by and watch you act like a fruit." Why was he reproaching Simon for doing exactly the same thing he had done when he had carried Simon up the steps? He knelt by the bed and took Simon in his arms. "I'm sorry."

"It's all right." Simon's hand smoothed back his hair. "You've spent a lifetime denying. Of course you're upset."

Haakon got ready for bed at ten. His bedroom was connected to Simon's by way of the bathroom, which was as extreme as the bedroom. The pale green marble tub was almost big enough to swim in, and the faucets were gilded panthers; the water came out of a lion's mouth. Since the mirrors promptly steamed, he did not find himself troubled by them.

He brushed his teeth and began to shave before remembering that there was no reason to tonight. He finished because he had started, then, in pajamas, went to say good night to Simon.

Simon had been looking at his reflection. "Haakon? Do you think I'm still beautiful?"

"Of course," he said truthfully.

"No, really."

"Really. Entirely beautiful."

There was a discreet tap on the door. "Come in."

It was Jack with a syringe. "Time for your shot."

"I'd noticed," Simon said wryly. He was lying curled up.

Looking back, he realized what this position meant. He understood how long Simon had been in pain, and was appalled. Simon had never hinted at it, never showed it in any other way.

"Can I get you anything?" Jack asked Simon, wiping his arm with a dab of cotton. A sudden sharp whiff of alcohol made the room smell like a hospital.

"No, thank you. If there's anything later, I'll use the intercom."

"Right-o."

After Jack had left, he sat down on the edge of the bed. Simon rested his hand on his thigh and lay quietly watching him. "Will you sleep here with me?"

"Won't I disturb you?"

"No, of course not. Quite the opposite. I need you close. Or would it be too hard on you?"

"No, that part of it's over for me too."

"I rather thought so, but I wasn't sure. Please, come and hold me."

Simon moved over to give him room and he got in beside him. Lying on his side he held him, feeling the softness of Simon's curls against his throat, his weight on his arm, his breath against his chest.

He loved him with a deep, despairing tenderness, sexless, but at the same time passionate. He would have found it easy to weep, but could not allow himself the luxury. Holding Simon was both one of the easiest and most difficult things he had ever done.

November 17, 1947

When Haakon wakened Monday morning, he found that his left arm was numb up to the elbow from Simon's weight. Gently he worked it out from under him and lay trying to flex his fingers until they began to work, and he could feel the prickle of renewed circulation.

He got out of bed carefully so as not to wake Simon, tucked the blankets around him and went to dress. When he got to the kitchen he found Colin making coffee.

"Would you like a cuppa?" Colin asked.

It would probably be terrible, but he wanted something hot. "Yes, thank you."

The coffee was not good, but not as Britishly bad as he had feared. While he was drinking it, Colin put toast and two soft-boiled eggs

266

in front of him, then sat down opposite with an identical breakfast for himself.

"You're supposed to be taking care of Simon, not me," he protested.

"D'you mind? I was noticing how thin you are, and got to thinking that you probably don't eat a proper breakfast."

Colin had not blushed, so he obviously considered himself on firm ground. Haakon felt somewhat pushed around, but the sensation was not unpleasant. "Just don't go to any trouble on my account."

"No, sir, but what's the bother in dropping two more eggs in the water?"

He ate the toast and eggs, and when he was finished, unaccustomed as he was to eating much this early, felt too full. He looked in on Simon but he was still sleeping heavily. He returned to the kitchen. "Colin? Will you tell Simon I'll be at the university? I don't know how long I'll be gone."

"Yes, sir."

"Why's he sleeping so much?" he had to ask. It worried him.

" 'Tis the drug. It's named after Morpheus, the god of sleep, y'know."

"Yes, of course."

"Better for him, sir. I've cared for many intestinal cancer patients. Was on the cancer ward five years. For some the pain is fierce. Though you'd never guess it to hear him, I believe Mr. Foster has it worse than most."

"You like him, don't you?"

"Yes, sir. Jack and myself both. Brave little man he is. Fortitude. That's the word."

"Yes." Abruptly, almost on the edge of tears, Haakon said stiffly, "I must run along now."

The metal stairway seemed to echo under his feet. Never before had it sounded so resonant. On the table by the front door was a box of Simon's business cards. He pocketed a half-dozen. There was no handier way of giving people his address.

The street glared in the sun. A thin layer of sparkling snow, not yet dirtied, covered the pavement. His footprints followed him to the corner, where they became lost in the many prints on the more heavily traveled avenue. He caught a cab and went to the university.

Lucy was not at her desk, but her coat was in the closet. He went into his office, leaving the door open. He had picked up the phone and begun to dial Grimes when the Dean came charging in looking even more like a rhinoceros than usual. "Have you seen this?" he demanded, waving the book review section of the *Times*.

"No, I didn't look at the papers yesterday." He took the section and looked at the full-page advertisement the Dean had it open to. A Meadows Press ad for his new book. A woodcut in the center, one of the more appalling torture scenes. Some lurid statistics on sodomy laws. The scope, the scholarly nature, the intent of the book were buried in a description set in much smaller type. "Damn!" Higgins had been giving him a fast shuffle. He should have gone back.

"Why didn't you clear this book with the university?"

"Clear it?" He was surprised. "Why?"

"Obviously it's sensational."

"Wait a minute!" he interrupted. "The book is not sensational. It's a straightforward, carefully documented study of persecution. Anti-Semitism, persecution of all minorities—heresies. It's no more titillating than a textbook. This ad gives a totally false impression and I'm as upset by it as you are."

"Heretics and homosexuals! Such a subject. What on earth possessed you?"

"It's not been done before."

Grimes sighed. "You scholars will be the death of me. You'll write on anything that hasn't been done before, won't you? Did it ever cross your mind that this could be compromising? What will people think?"

His mother had always been asking what people would think. "Whatever they damn please!" he snapped. "This book could just as well have been written by—" He had almost said heterosexual. He must be careful not to betray himself out of annoyance. He had promised Simon he would do nothing to jeopardize his job. "Anybody," he finished. Dismayed anew by the ad, he said, "But I agree with you that this ad is appalling. I can't understand Meadows. They've always been quite stodgy, so there was no reason for me to ask for approval of their ads."

"We can prevent their running another like that, but there's no help for this one," Grimes said. "The damage is done, we'll just have to ride it out. I'm afraid we can anticipate some unpleasant publicity."

"I suppose there might be." He had a set of galley proofs in his bottom drawer. He got out the thick rubber-banded bundle. "These are the galleys," he said, handing them to Grimes. "Read them and see for yourself."

"Thank you, that will be a help. If there are reporters I'll be in a position to answer them intelligently. I'd better get right on it." The Dean turned to go.

"Wait! I was just phoning you to tell you that I must have a month or so leave of absence."

"What?"

"I have to take some time off."

"With this breaking? You can't be serious."

"I'll take the time whether you agree or not. It's important."

Grimes sat down abruptly in the nearest chair. "I don't know what to make of you. Don't you think you owe me an explanation?"

"My best friend is dying and I want to be with him." The Dean was looking at him thoughtfully. A lot of thinking was going on behind that wide bumpy forehead. Even if Grimes suspected him, he would convince himself Haakon was straight if left alone. He heard himself say, "Or lover, if you prefer."

"I don't believe you. I won't."

He had not expected this response. Irritably, he said, "Come off it. You've wondered about me for years."

"And always decided you were all right. Damn it, you don't act like a pansy! Especially since the war. And what about Miss O'Connor? All the talk about you last semester." Grimes laid the galley proofs on his knees, got out a handkerchief, took off his bifocals and began to polish them.

He could still back out, pretend he had been joking. Grimes would be happy to leave it alone, he could see that clearly enough. Instead he said recklessly, "I've been homosexual all my life. Sure, I gave women a try, but it didn't work."

"And this book?" Tapping the proofs with his glasses.

"Could just as easily have been written by a heterosexual. I honestly believe that you'll find little, if any, bias, and nothing to embarrass the university."

Grimes put his glasses back on and looked intently at him. "Damn it!" he burst out. "I like you! And you're one of our best teachers, and aren't you starting a new textbook? Now what do I do?"

He shouldn't have given in to impulse; he should have remembered his promise to Simon. Too late now. There seemed only one solution. "I'll get my resignation to you this afternoon." All these years of playing a part, of fear of exposure, and he had thrown it away in less than five minutes. Unnecessarily. No more students— no possibility of being hired to teach elsewhere. A scandal. What would he do after Simon died?

"No, I won't accept it. I won't let you throw your career away."

"I can if I want to," he snapped, annoyed to have the conversation continue just as he had thought it finished.

"Think of the good of the university then. You've been here for over twenty years, and you just got promoted. Please don't tell anyone else, and just let me forget this visit."

He was going to have to try to explain. "I'm sick of pretending. I'm getting old, I want some time to be myself."

"What's yourself?" Grimes said. "I don't imagine that you want to wear a dress or hang about in Greenwich Village giggling at passersby. Honestly now, what would you do that would be any different from what you do now?"

All these years he had considered Grimes an intolerant dolt. He had thoroughly misjudged him. Obviously a man did not become Dean—and do the smooth job Grimes did—without having brains and wisdom. Grimes had certainly made a good point, one he had not considered, even though he could now see that it had been bothering him. "Nothing much, I guess," he admitted. "Probably nothing at all."

"We can forget it then?"

He considered this. It would be stupid to throw away his career. And teaching, seeing students learn and blossom, would be a help in getting over Simon. Nor should he forget that as a known homosexual he would face different restrictions, might compromise some of his straight friends.

Apparently he had nodded, for Grimes, nodding, said, "Good." Then asked, "Why, Haakon? Why now? Because your friend is dying and you're depressed?"

"I don't know." The question was serious and deserved a thought-out reply. "In a way, I started making the decision when I undertook publishing *A Study of Persecution*. I'd had a taste of freedom. Going out with women, and being out in the open is a kind of freedom. And, somehow or other, I've stopped being ashamed of who I am. I always was before. Partly it's that I have to be proud of Simon, and I can't be ashamed of myself without being ashamed of him. That sounds wrong. I don't know how to say it."

"I think I know what you mean," Grimes said after some thought.

"I'm going to stay with Simon now, I won't alter those plans."

"I wouldn't ask you to. Does your staying with him necessarily compromise you?"

"Probably. I'm afraid Simon's too well known, too notorious. Simon Foster, the photographer."

"Yes, I've admired his work. I used to be quite a shutterbug,

270

you know. And yes, he is notorious." Grimes was silent, staring into space. Then he said briskly, "Yes, you'll doubtless be suspect, but we can ride it out. Don't worry about it."

"Thank you." He was grateful for Grimes's understanding, and sorry he had not thought better of him in the past. He took one of Simon's cards out of his jacket pocket. "I'll be here if you need to contact me for anything."

Grimes stood up, took the card and tucked it away, then held out his hand. They shook hands, and he understood that he had agreed to keep quiet and pretend nothing had happened. He didn't know whether he was sorry or not. Grimes said, "Take it easy."

"Thank you."

Two hours later, his desk organized and dozens of memos dictated to fill in whoever took over his duties for him, he went to look for Dan. He had to make a trip to the executive offices to get his schedule, and then waited to catch Dan as he came out of an English class.

"Hi, Hawk!" The beautiful smile, broad shoulders and strong face. "What'cha doing here? I never expected to run into you here."

"I was looking for you."

"Oh?" Dan stopped walking, then nodded and said, "I'll cut German."

"No, no need to cut a class. This won't take long."

"What's the matter?"

"Simon's dying." Each time he repeated it he believed it a fraction more. "I'm taking a leave and will be at his place. I just wanted you to know."

"Oh, shit!" Sympathetic, reminding him of the Army.

"Yes."

"How about Ellen?"

"That's off."

"Shit!"

"I'm afraid so. She was there when I found Simon . . . but I'd rather not go into that."

"I'm sorry, Hawk. About Simon." Dan gestured, "All of it." Then, "You look kinda rocky. Can I help? Do anything?"

"I appreciate your offer, but no." He gave Dan one of Simon's cards. "You can reach me here if you want to." Dan read the card and put it in his pocket. Dan seemed to want to say more, but before he could, Haakon said abruptly, "See you later," and wheeled and walked off. He felt ragged and raw.

He should have said goodbye properly, but Dan understood.

Ellen had a period free now and he had to see her. He went to her office in the Arts Building and knocked on the door.

"Come in."

He closed it behind him. "Hello." She looked tired and upset. There were dark circles under her eyes. How could he have forgotten how much he cared about her? He wondered what he could say, if there was any way to make what had happened easier for her.

"Hello, Hawk." She sounded distant, or perhaps only overcontrolled.

"Ellen, I'm sorry." But that wouldn't help. He began again. "I'd like to explain—"

"Hawk, please."

"But—"

"Hawk, don't explain. Please don't." He could see her pain. Her eyes were too bright, tears just about to start, but she blew her nose and said, "I've been thinking, and I guess I understand."

The distance between them, only a few feet, was uncrossable. He felt large and awkward, did not know what to do with his hands, did not dare move them, as if he might find himself making one of Simon's faggoty gestures. He loved her more than ever, but could not say so, because what he felt for her was too much less than she deserved.

She had been talking, and he had not heard her. She was saying, ". . . but I could see . . . well . . . I was pretty sure you didn't hear me."

"Hear you?"

"At your apartment, when I said goodbye."

"Yes." Realizing that she had said goodbye, though he had not heard her, had not known when she left. She was grieving over the lost relationship right now. He almost felt like weeping. He wanted to say he was sorry, but could not. She was asking him about Simon. He had to clear his throat before he could speak. "He's dying," he answered her. "Cancer." He still could not believe that, though he could not avoid believing it either.

"If only . . ." he said, then did not know how to go on.

"If only?" she queried.

"Yes. I've thought . . ." He should be quiet, should not try to tell her how important she was. This was the wrong place and the wrong day. But he heard himself blundering on. "I've thought, if only I'd met you—someone like you—when I was younger. Before . . . years ago, maybe." He did not think he was making sense, took a breath and finished, "But of course I didn't and now it's too late."

She was watching him. Clear eyes seeing him. Hair like sunshine. She nodded and looked away. "Hawk, I do understand. But please go away."

Clumsy, he turned and fumbled for the doorknob.

"Hawk?"

"Yes?"

"Give me time. We can be friends." Her voice caught. A breathless, mirthless laugh. "God, how trite!"

Wanting to comfort her and knowing he could not, he did not turn. The knob turned in his grip. He felt the latch click out of the striker plate. His knuckles were white.

"Goodbye, Haakon." Her voice was steady.

And the only thing he could do for her right now was to leave.

He walked out into the glittering morning. Just enough new snow to make everything clean. It was becoming colder and, though the sun was out, a few flakes were falling. Christmas-card sparrows were pecking at a bread crust beside the walk.

He felt as if he were dying.

A young girl hurried past, her long green muffler flapping over her shoulder. "Hi, Mr. Hvitfelt!"

"Hi." Automatic. But who was she? My god, of course, Binky. He looked after her. How strange to find the world going right along just as if nothing were wrong. He went toward Broadway to find a cab.

December 5, 1947

Haakon paid the cab driver and paused on the sidewalk in front of Simon's house. Though he did not like to leave Simon, he found himself hesitant to return. Time with him sometimes seemed to have a dense claustrophobic quality that approached nightmare.

Last week's snow had retreated to the gutters, where it formed rock-hard black ridges on each side of the salt-whitened street. The day was overcast, the wind light. He looked up at the narrow strip of sky between the buildings. Somewhere, muffled by walls, a dog barked insistently. Several blocks away an air drill stammered. He went up the steps and let himself in with his key.

Simon was lying on a low round heavily padded platform that he had used extensively for studio shots. Today the cover was olive green. Simon spent most of his waking time there now, using his bedroom only to sleep. He was half reclining, propped up on a heap of multicolored pillows of all sizes and shapes and textures. Around him were a dozen piles of photographic prints.

"Hello."

"Hello, I'm glad you're back," Simon said.

At the other end of the room, near one of the windows that overlooked the back garden, was a bone-white hospital bed. It had been there for a week. He ought to be used to it. But it was like a gallows outside a condemned man's cell. It could not be ignored. Even when he didn't look at it he was aware of its presence.

"I'm sorry I took so long." He took off his overcoat and left it on the table by the door. "But I got caught by some reporters—about my book. If I'd known I'd have to deal with the press, I'd have worn a suit." He had on old Army clothes, because he had thought he would be alone in his office attending to paperwork.

"It's probably better you didn't. It won't do any harm to point up your masculinity and remind them you were in the war. Besides, you look so sexy."

That last remark was a needle. He did not reply.

"There's another excellent review of *Persecution* in today's paper," Simon went on. "Looks like it's headed for the best-seller list."

"Higgins said it would be a *succès fou.* He seems to have been right. But it's not a success I can enjoy, and I don't like the sniggery tone of some of the reviews either."

Did Simon's face have a little more color in it, or was it only the reflection of the dusty rose pillow he had under his head? He was wearing a kaftan with narrow bands of gold and black embroidery edging the neck and sleeves. He looked biblical, like an apostle or a prophet. He had begun to dress in loose Arabic garments when his abdomen started to swell. Ascites, Ben had said.

He thought it safe to ask, "How are you feeling?" Simon got angry if he was feeling bad.

"Ben left about an hour ago. He took out more fluid, and that relieves the pressure." Simon moved several piles of photographs so there was room for him to sit beside him. "Bobby Lee was here earlier. I can't stand that little Chinese faggot, though I have to admit—to you only—that his color work is superb."

"What did he want?"

"Damned if I know. We've never been friends. He'll dance on my grave. Perhaps he came to gloat, though he was excruciatingly polite."

Simon had apparently been looking at some of his favorite pictures. On top of a pile was a color candid of Ellen. Her hair was bright in the sun, and Simon had caught the essence of her smile, the clarity of her skin. Haakon became aware of a dull gnawing pain in his chest.

"Please don't make any decisions about her now," Simon said. "You may find you'll want her later, even if only as a friend. Don't paint yourself into a corner."

"Please, let's not talk about it."

"You mustn't cut any ties with anyone now. You're likely to need them all."

"For god's sake, you sound like Horatio. The role doesn't suit you." He could not maintain his calm when Simon talked about being dead. He put down the picture of Ellen and picked up another print.

A portrait of a gypsy in orange and rose-madder satin. Spread out in front of her was a pattern of Tarot cards. A large brindle dog sat beside her, head on her knees, and a toddler in deep purple satin with gold bands on it sat at her feet playing with a spoon. Her black hair was done up in braids around her head, and her only jewelry was a pair of small gold earrings. He allowed himself to become absorbed in the picture, deliberately fleeing the present, imagining that this woman with her old-young face, austere and ageless, looked like an ancestor who had lived in the Middle Ages. A battered aluminum coffeepot in the background made the picture modern and prevented it from being unreal, too much like a stage set.

"My fortune," Simon said.

"What?"

"The cards—see. The Moon, and the Chariot reversed. Death and the Tower of Destruction. She let me take her picture finally because the hand was so bad that she felt sorry for me."

"You went to a gypsy to have your fortune told?"

"No, I saw her in a storefront in East Harlem. She wouldn't pose at first, so I asked her to read the cards hoping to soften her up. That was the day before I followed you in the park. Really, a very strange experience. She had me shuffle and cut the cards, and we tried three times, but each time they added up to death. I'm sure it was a coincidence. I *don't* believe that stuff. But, see there? The Lovers. That kept coming up, and I thought that if the rest of the fortune was true, and I knew it was, that maybe that was also. At any rate, it gave me the courage to try."

"Simon, will I ever understand you?"

275

"Do you need to?"

"Sometimes I think I do. I don't know. Perhaps not."

Simon patted the coverlet, and knowing what he wanted, Haakon lay down with his head against Simon's hip, his body at an angle. Simon began to stroke his hair. He wondered how many hours they had spent in this same position in the past weeks. It was as if time had coagulated. It seemed to drag endlessly while he was going through it, but each night he felt as if he had barely glimpsed the day as it flashed past. Another day gone. Too many minutes and not enough hours. Outside a cat yowled, a truck passed, the tree in the garden tapped on the glass. Watery sunlight began to shine through the front windows.

"You've seen my life," Simon said contemplatively. "All my work. In some ways that's what I am."

"I've thought at times that you wanted to capture the world and store it in your files."

"Yes, that's not far from the mark. Cats and rats, cheeses and sneezes. Old and bold, weak and sleek. The Seven Deadly Sins and all the deadly virtues."

"Yes." He remembered a portrait of Simon's grandfather in cope and mitre. The clean bone structure and straight nose were almost identical. And Simon had said, "The thing he couldn't forgive was that even though he could disinherit me on paper, there was no way to hide the bloodlines." But Simon was beautiful. The Bishop was not because his expression was cold, bitter and grim, his mouth tight and lipless.

"War and peace," Simon went on happily. "Blood, sweat and tears."

"Yes." An Army chaplain with the wind snatching at his stole, standing in front of a row of muddy men—blessing guns. A pattern of tracers and star shells in a nighttime barrage. A dead German boy in a uniform several sizes too large and civilian shoes. The burnt homes of Dresden like broken teeth.

"Churches and birches. Bread and bed."

"Yes." White trees weighted by diamond ice. Stained-glass windows. A bird-pecked pear with bright striped wasps clustered around the wound. Pictures of men making love. They had spent hours dropping them into bleaching agent, watching the images fade and vanish. A garbage can full of wet blank paper and film at the end of the day.

"Haakon? Those compromising photos—was seeing them very hard on you?"

"After a little while I just felt numb. And by the time we were done I'd begun to feel guilty. I'm a historian, and there I was destroying priceless documents, covering up facts."

"I never would have thought of it that way. But of course you're right. I don't know what else we could have done though."

"Neither do I."

Simon put a black-and-white print in his hand. "Remember?"

A thin stooped fair-haired man in a crumpled suit. Himself over a dozen years ago, the Acropolis behind him baking in the sun. He said, "When I look at this, I can't imagine what you saw in me. I look like a constipated prude."

Taking it back, Simon looked at it and said, "The first minute of the first hour of our first day."

"Yes." His mind veered away. He remembered the many portraits Simon had shown him of himself. He had seen the change, watched that aloof withdrawn man become alive, seen sadness shift to worry, and worry to tentative happiness. That first summer with Simon he had learned to smile again. "I never did learn to laugh, though," he said.

"A little—just a little," Simon contradicted. "You were my sleeping beauty," he said after a moment. He put down that first photo and picked up another. Looking at it, he said, "I kissed you and woke you. I watched the thorn hedges dissolve so you could rejoin the world, start to live again. You have become so very beautiful, Haakon. Not that I take all the credit. You did most of it yourself. The Army helped, and Dan and Ellen too. But I *was* the one who woke you up, and otherwise you might have remained asleep the rest of your life."

"I might well have."

"Even though there's pain in this, it's my favorite," Simon said, handing him the picture he had been looking at.

Himself, naked and asleep. His hands were over his head, his knee drawn up, his face in profile. "Why?"

"Because you sleep like that so often."

"Pain?"

"I took that after you told me about Dan, and developed it the night he phoned you. I'll never forget watching the image come up and wanting to cry. I didn't cry. But I felt as if I had an iron burr in my throat. A bit later I drank a pint of bourbon as if it were medicine and went to meet Narcisio. Laughing."

" 'For I am the Cat That Walks by Himself, and all things are alike to me,' " Haakon quoted.

"Precisely. I wish now that I could have been different. Not had to keep running away. God, how I used to miss you!"

"And I you. And because you were the one who went away, I never could believe that you were lonely too. I used to torture myself imagining you the center of attention in some exotic place. I used to think I meant no more to you than the others you told me about."

"And I'd be there at a party, acting the professional happy butterfly and envying you your honest solitude. Lonely as the last of a species. Why the hell couldn't I have changed sooner?"

"It's all right."

"No it isn't!" Simon said angrily. "I wasted *both* our lives being admired and playing queen of the May. We could have been happy, if only I could have let us be."

"Really, it's all right."

"But it's not!" Simon said furiously. "It's not! Why couldn't I have changed sooner? Why did I have to wait so long, until I was under sentence of death?" Then suddenly calm again, "But of course I couldn't change—not *until* I was going to die. I was so afraid of love. Haakon, forgive me."

"I did a long time ago, but you don't need to be forgiven. You did the best you could. We are our pasts."

Simon giggled. "Colin's catching."

"Huh?"

"Those platitudes. You know what he'd say about what we were just talking about? 'Each man thinks his sack the heaviest,' or something of the sort. It must be nice to have a head completely stocked with a saying for every occasion. I've never seen him at a loss."

"He's at a loss until he thinks of one, though, hadn't you noticed?"

"You're right! No, I hadn't."

Simon's hand lay lightly on the back of his neck. Sun flooded the room with light now, lay warm across his feet and legs. He stretched and kicked off his shoes, pulled one leg up. There was a prolonged silence. One of the nurses was moving about upstairs. A pan dropped. "Under sentence of death," Simon had said. Simon was going to die. He could not imagine a world without Simon and did not want to. The steel beams holding up the second floor made strong right-angled patterns. He looked at his watch. The hands seemed stuck, slowed past any reason.

"Are you awake?" Simon asked after some time.

"Yes."

"I've been thinking. I've had enough of watching myself decay. I'll sleep down here from now on. I'm not going to go upstairs again. This studio is more myself than that fairy hideaway anyhow."

278

He was overcome by anguish and could not respond. After a moment he said with difficulty, "I love you."

Simon stroked his cheek, replied, "I don't want to leave you either, but there's not a bloody thing I can do about it."

"I know."

Then Simon smiled and said brightly, "Did I tell you about my funeral? No? I had it all planned. I made up a list of five hundred names, and I was going to send out engraved invitations. Can you imagine it, darling? Men from every corner of the earth—and I've been in the corners.

"Indians, Turks, Japanese, Moors, Bengalis, Peruvians—Simon Foster's UN, diplomats, businessmen, legislators from both the houses, American and British. More big wheels than you can imagine.

"I had a simple, tasteful announcement worked out for people who are real friends—not many of those. And a slightly sinister one for the bulk of them, just to add incentive. And a third category of people I was grateful to. For example a pair of male hustlers in Antwerp who were kind to me once. I was going to enclose plane tickets. Of course they'd promptly cash them, but at least they'd think of me while they drank the proceeds. That last group—I sent them all money orders instead. Or rather they will be sent out by a secretarial service as soon as my death is announced."

Simon was talking in a casual, even playful tone. He was enjoying recounting this, and mentioned his death with no sadness or regret. His face was cheerful and serene. Haakon yearned to be able to enter into his mood, but could not. He felt immobilized with grief. He turned his head away so Simon would not see his face and perhaps read his expression.

Oblivious, Simon chuckled. "What a field day for the press! Imagine them with their cameras and notebooks. Can't you hear them asking each other if all my mourners are gay? Or half, or exactly how many? Gossiping about what so-and-so said once about someone.

"The graveyard at Foster Point is so small they'd overflow all over the beach. There are a few dunes there, and that hard-edged grass that blows in the wind and makes a sad, dry, lonely kind of sound. They'd all get sand in their shiny shoes."

"Where?" he asked. The subject of where Simon was to be buried had not come up before.

"In Maine. The town of Foster was founded by some ancestor or other. You've seen pictures of it. That small-town series. Quiet streets shaded by enormous trees. Long green tunnels, neat houses.

The garage used to be a livery stable, and there are bits of tack and horse collars still hanging on nails in the back. Sidewalks of Vermont slate."

"Yes."

"When I was small I visited my grandmother for part of several summers. I was happy there. Anyway, there's space for me in the family plot, and that's where my parents are buried."

He could neither swallow nor speak. He groped for Simon's hand and felt it placed in his.

"I haven't told you about my scandalous gravestone. I commissioned it years ago, spent several months posing for it in deacon drag. Carrara marble, and the artist is a genius. You've never heard of him because he forges stuff and then cooks it or corrodes it or whatever, then has a farmer plow it up or chucks it into the sea and then goes skin-diving with a fat cat. The pity of it is, he's a genius in his own right. He doesn't have to go through all that. But perhaps that's the part he enjoys most, who knows?

"When I wrote him I didn't want the statue after all—it's life-size—he wrote back that he would call it St. Simon in honor of me. He plans to pass it off as early Christian, along with some other odds and ends he's made."

"Why did you change your mind?"

"If I'm going to spend eternity in the Foster graveyard, I think it behooves me not to get all the relatives spinning in their graves. Wouldn't be restful. Besides, the amusing part was the idea. Planning the details came to be a bore.

"Oh! Over by the door in that wooden crate. He sent me a small bronze of it. It came this noon. Please open it for me?"

He found a hammer and pried open the box, removed a quantity of bright golden straw and lifted out a bronze statuette about eight inches high. Simon had not exaggerated the artist's skill.

He carried it over to Simon and set it down on a low pedestal next to the platform. There was a resemblance to St. Francis. The face was pensive, and one hand was held out as if in entreaty or for a bird to light on it. The folds of the alb, the cincture, the diagonal stole, were carefully and expertly modeled.

But . . . "Scandalous?" he asked.

Simon grinned. "Turn it around."

"Oh, I see." One hip was thrown out just enough, the tilt of the shoulders and the modeling of the cloth all added up. From the back it was a statue of a drag queen. "I see," he repeated. Marvelously impious mischief. Simon thumbing his nose at the entire straight world. Simon's eyes were sparkling with amusement. They both began to laugh, and then were unable to stop.

Simon suddenly curled up and held on to his belly, wincing with agony, but still giggling.

Haakon's concern stopped his laughter. "Does it hurt a lot?"

"Only when I laugh," Simon gasped, then reached out to him and pulled him close. They clung together a long time, until Simon at last relaxed.

Later that evening, newly ensconced in the hospital bed, Simon wanted to look at the statuette again. He turned it back and forth admiring it, set it on the bed tray and contemplated it. Smiling, he said, "The two sides of Simon Foster. The frontside and the backside. Heads and tails. Which is better, my beautiful Danish cocksucker?"

"Neither. Both."

"Ah, so true." Then very soberly, "When we used to make love, I'd feel I couldn't get close enough. I suppose as long as we both have skins, are separate people, there isn't any way to."

"I know, I've felt the same way."

"May I give you this? And the others upstairs too. Do you want it?"

"Yes, very much."

"That should solve part of your problem, maybe all of it."

"Which problem?"

"About who you are. Who but a fairy would own such things? Who else would want them? I want you to have the school-of-Rubens too. I know you love it."

"Where would I put it?"

"In your living room. Or bedroom. Or squirrel it away in a bank vault if you like. I don't care. But you should have it. It's in my will, by the way, that you're to have anything you want. I left it a carte blanche so you'd have a free hand."

"Oh, Simon."

"There, there now, don't get sentimental."

"I guess . . . thank you. Yes, thank you."

"Haakon, I want to see a priest."

"Huh?" The turn in the conversation was totally unexpected, but Simon was serious.

"Yes, I've been thinking. I'm what you might call a superstitious Christian. Surely you've heard that the lost sheep is worth more than the hundred good and respectable ones. It's all in the Bible. I think the time has come for me to repent, return to the fold, and all that rot. After all, I'm hardly in a position to sin any more, am I?"

Not knowing what to say, he concentrated on practical details. "Any priest in particular?"

"Definitely. Episcopal. And this joke is too good to pass up—I want Father Hal Queensbury." Simon began to giggle. Then he gasped and said in a businesslike tone, "He's young, has a slum parish, St. Leonard's, here in Manhattan. He'll do anything to get a few bucks for his winos and crooks. Besides, I got the impression that he rather liked me."

"You're serious."

"Of course I am, though I more than half wish I weren't. Death's breathing down my neck, Haakon. I'm beginning to be afraid. I mean, what if they're right? They *could* be."

"I suppose so."

"On the other hand, it *has* occurred to me what a huge joke it would be if the only way to get to heaven were to burn chicken feathers under the nose of some obscure African idol. And on the other hand, since nearly all my friends will be in hell, what do I want to go to heaven for? And on the other hand— But that's too many hands. So I go round and round like the ragged rascal around the rough and rugged rock. In the final analysis, I want a priest."

"We can call him in the morning."

"Yes, let's. And Father Queensbury can bury a queen. Isn't that appropriate? Kiss me now. I'll do my repenting tomorrow."

"And say you're sorry for your life?"

"For my *sins*. 'Bless me, Father, for I have sinned . . .' Nice tinned formula. Tidy. I doubt that it fools God, but if God isn't a sadistic idiot or an insane child, then he's so far beyond *our* understanding that any attempt to second-guess him is meaningless anyway. Mercy is a possibility. I think it behooves me to ask, since the worst that can happen is that I'll be turned down." Simon smiled. "And if *that* happens, I can always have a go at seducing St. Pete."

"You just might succeed," he said, trying to match Simon's playfulness.

"Now kiss me."

He bent over him and felt Simon's arms around his neck, pulling him close. He had not intended a French kiss, but Simon's lips parted under his and he drowned in a kiss as sensual as any he had ever experienced. It contained all the unspoken love between them as well as the finality of goodbye.

This was goodbye, even if that had to be said again and again, as it surely would. Unable to prevent himself, he began to weep, and Simon held him and comforted him until he was able to stop.

December 9, 1947

After Simon decided not to go upstairs again, he had some of his living-room furniture brought down: chairs, a sofa, a small bookcase, tables, and lamps created a cluster of comfort around the austere white bed. Haakon could never approach it without being reminded of a stage setting, but once he was seated in the big leather armchair by the bed, he could ignore the size of the studio, the photographic lamps and islands of staging.

From the chair he could see out into the walled garden. He had paced it once, and found it to have the same dimensions as his mother's garden. No surprise, that. All the brownstones of this vintage seemed to have been built from the same blueprint.

The Japanese maple Simon had planted so close to the building was bare now. In summer its deeply cut leaves cast ragged shadows into the room all morning. The brick patio and carefully kept grass were covered by a carpet of grayish snow. Exotically twisted pines postured by the back wall. The noon sun glistened on their long needles.

"Now go on," Simon said.

"Yes, 'Sailing to Byzantium.' " He found it in the index and turned to the page, began to read:

> "That is no country for old men. The young
> In one another's arms, birds in trees
> —Those dying generations—at their song,
> The salmon-falls, the mackerel-crowded seas,
> Fish, flesh, or fowl, commend all summer long
> Whatever is begotten, born, and dies.
> Caught in that sensual music all neglect
> Monuments of unageing intellect."

He paused. "All those years, and I never knew you liked poetry."

"I don't in general. Just a few poems of a few poets. I love listening to you read. It's odd, I hadn't noticed in years, but you still have a funny foreign way of saying o."

"I've been told so. Tom Enfield said I'd retained it because I can't hear it. He tried to show me once, but— Funny though, I only spoke Danish before I was seven, and I've forgotten most of it."

Simon said, "I know. To a Britisher I sound American, and to Americans I sound British. I'm not native anywhere. Don't want to be. I hate both countries—and love them both too. During the war I was grateful they were allies. It would have been dreadful if they'd not been. I don't know what I'd have done. . . . Read some more."

> "An aged man is but a paltry thing,
> A tattered coat upon a stick, unless
> Soul clap its hands and sing, and louder sing
> For every tatter in its mortal dress."

Simon held up a hand to stop him, saying, "I like that. The defiance. The 'unless.' More than making a virtue of necessity, actually praising one's faults because error is human. Skip the next bit, I don't care for it."

He had read on silently, "What does 'perne' mean?" he said, with that flicker of surprise he always felt when he came across a word he did not know.

"I looked it up once. Spool."

"Spool? In a gyre? That doesn't make sense."

Simon shrugged. "That's what it said in the dictionary. But that's why I don't care for that part. The images are jumbled, and I've wondered if Yeats was being lazy. Gyre isn't right there, though it's beautiful in that other poem, 'turning and turning in a widening gyre, the falcon cannot hear the falconer.' Turn the page and start at the top."

> "Consume my heart away; sick with desire
> And fastened to a dying animal
> It knows not what it is; and gather me
> Into the artifice of eternity.
>
> Once out of nature I shall never take
> My bodily form from any natural thing
> But such a form as Grecian goldsmiths make
> Of hammered gold and gold enameling
> To keep a drowsy Emperor awake;
> Or set upon a golden bough to sing
> To lords and ladies of Byzantium
> Of what is past, or passing, or to come."

284

"'Set upon a golden bough to sing,'" Simon repeated. "At one time I would have wanted that. To be an *objet d'art,* unique, beautiful, mechanical. But not any more, even though the idea still has some appeal."

"Yes." He could easily understand how that idea might delight Simon. "But it makes me think of an expensive wind-up toy."

Simon chuckled, "I hadn't thought of that."

The doorbell sounded, startling him. He prepared to get up to answer it, but Simon gestured to him not to, so he sat back again. He heard Jack coming down the stairs and crossing to the door.

After a moment, Jack crossed to them and said to Simon, "Three reporters, sir."

"For me? I haven't done anything interesting recently."

"They know you're ill, sir. But they came to interview Mr. Hvitfelt about his book."

"Tell them he's not here. And that I am not at home."

"They know he's here." To Haakon: "One of them followed you, sir."

Suddenly Simon said angrily, "Damn Bobby Lee! I wonder how many pieces of silver he got for selling us out? Now I think back, he got here about ten minutes after you'd left the other day. He must have seen you."

Jack said, "Shall I send them away, or do you wish to speak to them?"

"Send them away," Simon said. "Talking to them won't be the slightest use. Tell them I'm dying. If they know that, it might possibly inspire them to show a little decency, though I doubt it." Then to Haakon crossly, "I *told* you that bloody book would get you into trouble."

He could not interest himself in any of that nonsense. "I don't care," he said.

"You've *got* to! You've got a future and I insist that you plan for it." Simon stopped talking and he realized he was shaking his head. Simon went on, "Haakon, listen, I keep thinking that as long as one of us is alive, the other won't entirely die. Wasn't there a tribe of Indians—or was it the Chinese—that believed that?"

At seven-thirty that evening George arrived, face pink with cold, looking worried. As they crossed the studio, George apologized. "I wasn't sure if I ought to descend on you like this, but that card you gave me has no phone number. The number's unlisted. And I have to talk to you."

He had intended to write the number on the business cards

he had given friends at the university, but apparently he had forgotten. He introduced George and Simon. The quickly controlled look of shock and pity on George's face reminded him again of how little Simon resembled his self-portrait taken less than a year ago, the one on the magazine cover.

George unbuttoned his overcoat but would not take it off. "No, there isn't time." He took a newspaper, folded to an inside page, from his pocket and handed it over. "You've probably not seen this."

There was a reproduction of the woodcut in Meadows's advertisement, a picture of himself and one of Simon. The article was a half-page long, nonspecific, full of innuendo. Simon was characterized as notorious and several of the scandals he had been involved in were rehashed. *A Study of Persecution* was described as lurid and referred to as a best seller. There was no mention of Simon's illness. The reporter had written, "We are not calling this a love nest."

He handed the paper to Simon. "I can't see that we'd have a case," he observed. "He stays this side of libel."

"That's not why I'm here, Hawk. Bill Grimes called me and said that Clem Grey invited him over for what he called 'an informal, preliminary meeting.' Grey's trying to gather as many trustees and so forth as he can. He wants your job."

Teaching had always been important to him, but he could not make himself care. "What do you want me to do?"

His indifference must have showed. Simon threw down the newspaper and said fiercely, "Don't be dense! You must defend yourself."

"What could I say?"

"You'll think of something. Poor old Wilde did so well that his first trial ended in a hung jury."

"But not the second." Why was he angry? "And I damn well am not going to stand up in front of my colleagues and make an ass of myself bleating about a 'love that dare not say its name,' or whatever that idiotic phrase was."

"Hawk, be sensible," George said. "This article implies that you're engaged in some sort of round-the-clock orgy. All you have to do is explain that Simon is ill." George fidgeted, fingering the buttons of his overcoat. "Hawk, we really must hurry, the meeting starts at eight." Looking at his watch.

"Go on!" Simon insisted.

"The cab's waiting," George said.

He still could not interest himself in the problem, but it was

286

easier to go along. In the cab, trying to do what George and Simon wanted of him, he said, "Can you fill me in a bit more?"

"I don't know much beyond what I've already said. Bill and I feel that Grey is carrying on a personal vendetta, probably egged on by Randall. I know Grey's been down on you ever since you slapped Betsy's wrist over that paper."

"And I've been number one on Randall's shit list for years," he agreed. It all seemed so petty. He wondered what he could say, what sort of strategy he could use. Before he could work out anything they were in front of Grey's mansion and going up the stone steps.

The marble-faced foyer was too bright. An obsequious servant, dressed in black like an undertaker, took their overcoats and led them into a room through double white doors, mumbling something about "the library." A library? Too few books, and those there were looked unread. Matched gold-stamped leather bindings in rows, as if they had been purchased for decorative purposes.

Heavy mahogany furniture. An impressive oval table. Clem Grey sat at one end, his square, meaty, pink-scrubbed face almost amusingly solemn. To his right was Llewellyn Teasdale, tiny, old and dried up. Teasdale had a reputation for being prejudiced and irascible, but he also had a reputation for fairness. It was rumored that he was the most powerful man on the board of trustees.

Randall was looking pleased with himself. Innocuously bland round face—but somehow sinister. Like a teddy bear with a rat inside it.

Bill Grimes was planted solidly in an armchair looking like a monument of himself. Motionless. The light reflecting off his bumpy forehead. The servant seated George next to him. Henry Campbell was by the fireplace, the most openly hostile. His black hair seemed to bristle with outrage, and his heavy eyebrows almost met, he was scowling so hard. "As I was saying," he said, "the university does not need this sort of publicity."

"One moment please," Teasdale said in his light old-man's voice. "Has Mr. Hvitfelt seen the article in the *Mirror?*"

"Yes," he told them.

"Very well." Teasdale nodded to Campbell to continue.

He realized that he had not been offered a chair. He rested his hands on the back of the chair in front of him. Teasdale was inspecting him with eyes so pale they looked as if they had been bleached.

"That book of yours," Grey was saying accusingly. "We—the university deserves an explanation."

287

"Have you read it?" Grey shook his head. Haakon looked around at the others. "Any of you?" Obviously only Grimes and George had.

"I've seen several reviews, however," Grey said.

"Unless you have read it and seen for yourself what I wrote, you've no right to object to it," he said firmly, then realized he was scolding them as if they were students who had failed to do their homework. Not at all the way he ought to treat trustees.

Oddly, instead of being indignant, they looked uncomfortable.

Campbell cut short the silence. "We demand an explanation of this." Shaking the newspaper at him. "Why are you . . . um . . . residing with this Foster?"

The tone was intolerable. No one should speak of Simon like that. "He's a friend, and he's dying. Of course I'm staying with him. I intend to remain there as long as he's alive."

"Simon Foster is a notorious homosexual," Randall contributed smugly.

"Suppose he is? What in hell has that got to do with his worth? He's also an Anglican deacon and the best damn photographer in the country."

"Peter told me . . ." Grey began, inclining his head toward Randall.

"Randall! Aren't you beginning to get just a little tired of playing Othello to his Iago?"

Randall scowled, now looking anything but innocuous, and seemed about to speak. But unexpectedly Teasdale chuckled. "Othello! Iago! That's very accurate."

"How is it that you know Foster?" Campbell persisted.

"It's none of your business," he snapped. George and Grimes both looked alarmed. He ought to be more diplomatic, but he could not control his irritation. "Are you proposing that I should bring you a list of everyone I know and get your permission to be friends with each of them? I consider your questions both tasteless and ridiculous."

Grey said, "The very fact you know Foster puts you in a bad light. Makes one wonder."

"Wonder what? I'm not a mind reader. Be specific." Haakon stared at Grey until he looked away.

"I'm not being unreasonable," Grey said. "You not only know him, you admit you're living with him."

Grimes said, "Foster knows Haakon, Haakon knows me. Therefore I'm strange?"

288

"Of course not, Bill. You aren't living with him."

Teasdale said, "Clem, you've a mind like a sewer. Or weren't you paying attention when Mr. Hvitfelt told us that his friend is dying."

"People like that are capable of anything," Campbell stated, as positive as if he had read it in the Bible.

He told himself that he must not lose his temper, but the room began to look pink, and though he heard every sound, every rustle, rub of fabric and throat clearing, he began to feel slightly deaf. "God, you're disgusting!" he said between his teeth, beginning to tremble with rage.

Abruptly Teasdale pushed back his chair, fumbled for his cane and stood up. Into the silence he said coldly, "It is clear to me that we have made a mistake. Clem, I suggest you cease hounding Mr. Hvitfelt and allow him to go about his business." He glanced around with an almost impish smile. "You apparently believe that I stay in my ivory tower, but I am fully aware of the personal nature of both Mr. Randall's and your grievances."

Did he know about Virginia Lee? Haakon found himself shaking the dry, warm bony hand. Teasdale said, "Haakon, I apologize for being a party to this."

Campbell said loudly, "I'm not satisfied—"

Teasdale glared at him. "I assure you that no man who felt in the least guilty would behave as Mr. Hvitfelt has. A man who doesn't feel guilty cannot be guilty, unless he is a psychopath. We have known Mr. Hvitfelt for a quarter of a century. He is not a psychopath." Teasdale scowled at Grey and Campbell. Grey looked down at his hands, Campbell shifted restlessly. "I am going home, and suggest you do likewise." He started for the door, punctuating his progress with thumps of his cane.

There was a sudden buzz of conversation and scraping of chairs, muttered apologies to Haakon.

He was confused. George and Dean Grimes had stood up. Grimes came over and shook his hand in a congratulatory way, said something he did not catch and left. Grey was sitting at the head of the table staring at the newspaper and shaking his head slightly. Randall looked angry and disappointed.

George took Haakon's arm and steered him out of the room. He went along feeling bewildered. What had happened? He had not defended himself. He had stupidly lost his temper, been nearly suicidally rude.

As they went down the steps, George said, "I'd always heard that old Teasdale was the real power."

He nodded, then said apologetically, "I didn't mean to lose my temper."

"I never would have advised it," George said as they turned east toward Broadway. "But since it worked, apparently that was the right thing to do."

He still felt a residue of indignation. "They had no right talking about Simon and me like that."

"My God!" George said. "If they'd guessed what it was that made you so mad! I'd like to invite you over for a drink. How about it?"

"I've been gone too long. I must get back. Thank you though." Then looking at George's friendly round face, "Thank you."

"Yes, well . . ." They were standing at the foot of the library steps. He glanced up at the seated Alma Mater remembering the day he had come back from the Army and almost knocked George down. George said, "Will you be all right, Hawk?"

"Yes." He knew George was asking a broader question than it seemed. George knew him better than anyone but Simon, had known him longer than Simon. "Don't worry about me. I'll miss Simon—more than I've ever missed anyone. But I'll live through it, and eventually get over it. One gets over anything eventually." He hoped that was true.

December 14, 1947

Cold blue-gray predawn light paled the sky outside the windows. Unlit photographic lamps brooded in a cluster near the head of Simon's hospital bed like surrealistic birds.

Throughout the night Colin and Jack, patient as hounds, alert, efficient and knowing, had stood watch. Now Colin was upstairs making coffee. Jack, reassuringly official in his starched white uniform, had posted himself at the foot of the bed.

In a large armchair off to one side, Hal Queensbury slept in an untidy heap, looking like a college boy with his spiky orange hair, turtleneck sweater and moccasined feet. Even asleep he was an intrusion, a potential rival for Simon's attention.

The huge room was more than half dark, all the light concentrated near Simon. The emaciated body in the immaculately white bed was the center of the world.

Shadows shrouded the corners of the room like cobwebs, all the black cables snaking across the floor pointed his way, the cameras on their tripods meditated, and the tall lights stood guard.

Simon's skin was a tight yellow membrane stretched over the bones of his face—a face of old ivory, a carving from a dream. The lustrous curls of his hair, the thick eyelashes were out of place, too alive and too rich. Like a wig on a skull. Simon seemed asleep now, though it was hard to tell. His breathing was slow and regular; his chest rising and falling under the white sheet was the only sign that he still lived.

Simon had seemed so much better this past week that this night's precipitous decline was doubly shocking. Ben Solomon had come early in the evening and sat with him until ten. Then he had gone to bed, explaining that he had been too short of sleep for days. Ben was upstairs in one of the bedrooms. He had left instructions to be called if there was any change.

Haakon had asked Ben to tell him Simon's condition, hoping perhaps for a lie. Ben had said bleakly, "I'll be surprised if he lasts the night."

Now Simon was looking at him, pupils dilated, eyes big as a small child's. "Haakon?"

"I'm here."

"When I was very young my father took me on his ship. It was gray and all buttoned together with rivets big enough to trip over. I wandered off down a ladder and a sailor found me, carried me laughing on his shoulder. He showed me the seagulls. He told me to look at the ocean and imagine the fish swimming down there all cold and silent. A million fish, and whales the size of houses calling to each other in the endless dark at the bottom of the sea."

"Do whales call?"

"The sailor said they did. Why not? They're animals like us, with enormous brains, as cunningly contrived as our own. Do you suppose they know when they are dying?"

"I don't know." He was numb with grief.

Simon looked at Jack standing stolidly at the foot of the bed. "My friend."

"Yes, sir."

"And Colin? Where is he?"

"Above, making a bit of coffee. Would you like a little?"

"No. Perhaps some water. My mouth is dry with fear." Simon waited for Jack to put the glass tube to his lips so he could drink. Then, glancing down at himself, he said, "Pregnant with death. It's in me like a huge maggot chewing away at my life. Ugly, ugly. I never wanted to be old, but I *did* want to die beautiful. Haakon, I'm sorry. I was wrong to come back to you just as you were about to forget me. I've spoiled things for you, and now I'm going to have to leave you alone. I love you, but I'm a selfish man. Oh, God! 'consume my heart away, sick with desire and fastened to a dying animal it knows not what it is.' "

"It wasn't wrong, Simon. I've always loved you. I've no regrets." But he wished desperately that Simon could have changed sooner.

"If only I could have changed sooner, when there was still time."

"No if-onlys. We had what we had. I'm grateful you finally let me know you." And that was true too.

"Where's Ben?" Simon asked.

"Upstairs asleep," Jack replied patiently. Simon had asked this question at least two dozen times over the course of the night. "Do you want me to get him?"

"There's nothing he can do for me. Let him sleep." Simon shivered. "It's getting cold."

Jack quietly picked up Simon's hand and took his pulse. Colin had come back with a tray of cups and a pot of coffee. Jack signaled to him with a quick nod, and Colin unobtrusively set down the tray and went back up the stairs to get the doctor.

"Where's my confessor?" Simon asked, and Jack went to wake the priest. As soon as the nurse touched his shoulder, Queensbury unfolded himself from the chair and came to stand by the bed.

Simon smiled. "Good morning, Father. Tell me, I've not forgotten anything have I? I've gone through all the formulas. I'm shriven, am I not?"

"You've been given absolution."

"I prefer 'shriven,' it has such a fine medieval ring to it. 'And we have erred and strayed from thy ways like lost sheep . . .' Haakon, I explained to you about the sheep, didn't I? What do you suppose a lost deacon is worth? But the more thoroughly lost you are, the more rejoicing when you're found. No one makes a fuss over you if you've behaved yourself all your life. That doesn't seem fair, does it?" He looked at the priest. " 'And we have left undone those things that we ought to have done . . .' Not much fun there, I must say. 'And done those things we ought not to have done.' And that part unfortunately was quite hard to regret. If there is a God, I suppose he knows I have reservations." He closed his eyes. "Haakon?"

"I'm here." It was almost full light. The artificial lights paled as the sky burned blue beyond the windows. The first rays of sun tipped the branches of the trees in the garden with gold. Sparrows swarmed outside, twittering uncaringly, and then were gone. "I'm here," he repeated, sick with wanting to offer comfort, with his helplessness to do so. Simon's hand was cold in his, a bird's foot without substance.

"I don't want to die," Simon said quietly. "I don't want to be dead. It isn't fair. Why should rats and roaches scuttle about begetting babies and stuffing themselves with food when I'm gone? I . . ." He turned his head from side to side, sighed, seemed to relax. "The pain's lessening," he said with wonder. "Going away, getting smaller and smaller.

"When I was a child I met a horse, and he had the secret of the universe in his eyes. The answer to everything, to life and death, and how many angels can dance on the head of a pin. He was a hunter, and he'd impaled himself on a broken branch. He died screaming, poor beast. I watched his eyes get dull, saw specks of dust settling on them. Will you close my eyes for me?"

"Yes."

"My love, Haakon, my beautiful Dane . . . my darling. Do you remember Rome? We made love in the heat of the afternoon while birds chirped and squabbled in the vines outside the window. And everything was in one piece. Whole. The world was ours—the blue sky and the cold vermouth. The scent of Turkish tobacco, black tobacco. Do you remember? It's strong and right in the dry sunshine of Rome, but rank and dead in the fogs of Scotland. We threw the cigarettes away and bought Players. Pale Virginia tobacco. And drank warm brown stout. Strange how things become different according to climate. Do you remember? Mary, Queen of Scots. I made a joke, and you were angry because the guard at the castle overheard me. So prim and proper then, but you outgrew that. Haakon?"

"Yes, I'm here."

"Don't leave me."

"I won't." He remembered all of it vividly, and the knot of grief in his gut became a knife of pain. "I love you."

"Do you remember?"

"I never forgot."

"We were young then. Strong and beautiful. Ah, how I used to tease you. I'm sorry for that, but you looked so funny when you were upset. You were so predictable. In Glasgow, do you remember? I made a joke about kneeling at the altar and sucked you off in the cathedral—and how upset you were later because I'd come on your shoes! Do you remember?"

"Yes, I remember."

"And do you forgive me?"

"I forgave you a long time ago. I think it was something you had to do, though I never understood why."

"I didn't either. Don't yet. But that day I fell in love for the first time—the only time in my life. It makes no sense, but there it is. When I was away from you I could hear your name in train wheels, in the sound of the sea. Birds called it to me at dusk, and leaves whispered it to me in the morning. I wish I'd treated you better. But I wanted to be free of human emotion. Free. So I hated you and kept running away. Fled you 'down the labyrinthine ways of my own heart.' In the end you prevailed. Kissed me and made me human. Oh, God, how I love you! Haakon?"

"Yes." He was not really weeping, but his face and neck were wet with uncontrollable tears. "Simon, I love you." He felt Simon's hand contract on his.

The silence lengthened, then Simon said softly, "We were beautiful. God forgive me, I can't regret that."

Simon took a deep breath and it was a long moment before he took another. A pause, then another. Then silence. Simon's hand quivered briefly in his and went limp. His eyes were huge, luminous and blind. Haakon reached out and carefully closed them.

He became aware of the sound of liquid dripping and looked down. A widening pool of blood was spreading over the hardwood floor under the bed. Bright arterial red, not quite real-looking. Blotches were wicking up into the sheet too, irregular splotches. Why wasn't the mattress soaking it up? Of course, there was a rubber sheet.

He was startled by a movement. When had Ben gotten here? And the priest and the nurses were standing there too. He had forgotten about them. His throat and mouth were stiff but he said, "He died."

No one contradicted him.

A scream of anguish and outrage was building inside him and his throat went into spasm repressing it. He wanted to howl and tear his hair, but he could not. He was too bound by civilized restrictions, by the need to consider the feelings of others.

All he could think, over and over, was Simon, Simon. He put his face against Simon's dead hand. The tears would not stop. They kept running easily, wetting Simon's fingers, running between them to soak into the sheet. He closed his eyes, wishing he were dead too. Time had ticked itself into meaninglessness. No clock had any importance. He could have stayed there forever, turned to stone, nothing real but the agony of loss.

A hand touched his shoulder. He clenched his teeth against his sudden rage at the intrusion. Instead of striking out, he forced himself to lift his head. He hoped Hal Queensbury had not touched him, for he was revolted by the idea of professional priestly sympathy.

"Come along, sir." It was Jack. Quiet, reliable Jack. Sadness in his voice. Jack cared too. "Come along, sir, there are things we must do now. And you've not slept for two days. Come along."

"You care, don't you?"

"More than I'd expected to," Jack replied with his spare, unswerving honesty. "In my own way, I think I came to love him. Colin too. Not your way, sir, but . . . He was a man, sir, for all his fairy ways. There aren't many of them."

"Yes."

"Come along now. Let me put you to bed. He'd want it."

"Want it! Don't you ever say that to me again. Simon is dead. He'll never want anything again. Ever, ever, ever."

"I know," Jack said, "but come along."

Simon was a waxen effigy, his dark-lashed eyes closed, his sensual mouth and clever brain becoming cold. The priest was reading something out of a little black book. In case Simon was right, he hoped it would help. Queensbury came to a pause and both Colin and Jack automatically murmured, "Amen."

He remembered the sound of Simon's pure voice singing hymns and Gregorian chants in the shower. Simon standing by his fireplace, naked and beautiful. Like the Cellini Perseus.

"Not here," he said. He could not bear to wake up again in this house. He had to keep his word to Simon and himself to pick up his life again. "I'm going home," he said, and started toward the front door.

He felt himself stopped. Colin, wanting him to put on his overcoat. Of course, it was winter outside. Cold. Kindly and efficiently Colin arranged his scarf and buttoned his coat. "There now."

Overcome with gratitude, he managed to say, "Thank you." What had he been going to do? He squeezed his eyes shut and shook his head to clear it. Where did he want to go? Home, yes. But his feet were in his shoes and his shoes were not moving. He looked at them. Someone took his arm. Ben.

"Let me take you home. I'm through here," Ben said.

His body seemed to be functioning again, but nothing else was. The world was in splinters, all mixed up with memory and time. Like a puzzle. But the purpose of making a puzzle in pieces was so they could be put together.

He became aware that the shrapnel scar was aching fiercely,

and straightened. He didn't want to remember Simon dead, but he had to go back once more.

He had known the bed could not be seen from here, but it was not until he began to cross the room that he realized how many screens and backdrops there were. He made his way around to the right of a bank of reflectors and stopped.

Hal Queensbury, in a pea jacket and earmuffs, was on his way out. His appearance of concern had not been an act. Haakon began to be ashamed of his jealousy. Perhaps sometime he might want to talk to this priest who did not condemn men like himself and Simon. But not now. He was relieved when the priest went to the left of the reflectors and passed without seeing him.

One more step and he saw the bed. Red and white sheet. Sunlight reflected off the pool on the floor. Jack and Colin, in white, stood beside it. They had covered Simon's face.

"We should get to work before he stiffens," Colin said.

"In a bit."

"A lot of cleaning."

"Yes, blood's bad. It sticks so." But Jack did not move, and neither did Colin.

"I didn't expect to care so much," Colin said after a moment.

"Some of them get to you. I don't suppose one ever gets used to it. And in a man's home, you see so much more of his life."

"Those jars of caviar, the books," Colin agreed. Then, "Do you really think Mr. Hvitfelt will come back?"

Jack nodded and, looking around, saw him standing there. He went to the bed, intending to take a last look at Simon's face. He touched the sheet and knew he did not have to look again after all. He slowly traced the shape of Simon's head and cheek, his neck and shoulder, through the cloth. The body was still warm, though cooler than life. He turned away. And wanting to do something, not able to speak, he held out his hand. Jack took it, then Colin.

He left them to get on with what they had to do and went back to the door. Ben was waiting.

He stepped out of warmth and quiet into coldness and noise. Traffic, the rumble of a subway, the bustle of people on their way to work, taxis honking, the quick impatient pulsebeat of the city. He found himself walking faster.

But Ben was with him, and having difficulty keeping up. He slowed his pace.

296